"A luminous portrait of a woman with remarkable artistic talent, courage, and wisdom. Agnes Pelton grapples with the devastating consequences of a family scandal and her own secret passions during the tumultuous early twentieth century in America, when women had not yet won the right to vote. Beautifully written, the book is not only a feast for the senses but also a profound meditation on the creative process and the regenerative power of art."

—**HELEN FREMONT**, author of *The Escape Artist* and *After Long Silence*

"In her remarkable debut, Mari Coates recreates the life of Agnes Pelton, an important, overlooked figure in twentieth-century American art. At once meticulous and sweeping, *The Pelton Papers* offers not just a highly readable novel about one woman's fascinating life but also a kind of manual for how to live as an artist while staying true to the self."

—**NAOMI WILLIAMS**, author of *Landfalls*

"Ahead of her time and driven by a spiritual gift, Agnes Pelton speaks powerfully in Mari Coates's lovingly dramatized novel. Secret desires, family scandals, brushes with Djuna Barnes and other luminaries—interesting subplots abound. This is an inspiring account of a born artist who followed her calling from New York to the desert and continually discovered the transcendent through her art."

—**RACHEL HOWARD**, author of *The Risk of Us* and *The Lost Night*

"A beautifully written imagining of the intimate world of artist Agnes Pelton, whose spirit and underappreciated work Mari Coates brings back to life."

—**PEG ALFORD PURSELL**, author of *A Girl Goes into the Forest*

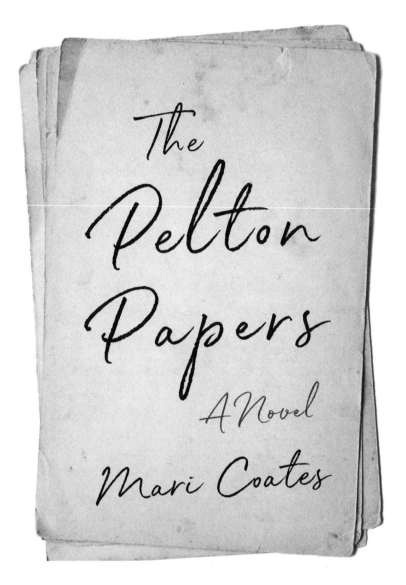

The Pelton Papers

A Novel

Mari Coates

SHE WRITES PRESS

Published 2020
Printed in the United States of America
ISBN: 978-1-63152-687-9
ISBN: 978-1-63152-688-6
Library of Congress Control Number: 2019917600

For information, address:
She Writes Press
1569 Solano Ave #546
Berkeley, CA 94707

Interior design by Tabitha Lahr

She Writes Press is a division of SparkPoint Studio, LLC.

This is a work of fiction based on the life of American painter Agnes Pelton (1881–1961). While conforming closely to the facts of Pelton's life, the author has invented some characters and imagined certain events, relationships, and situations.

For Gloria

And to the memory of my sister Nancy

CATHEDRAL CITY, CALIFORNIA

JANUARY 3, 1961

DRAW A LINE FROM STUTTGART, where I was born—a child lured by beauty—circle the cities in Europe where my mother took me while my father traveled, and then in my seventh year, arc it over the ocean to Brooklyn, where we settled at last with my grandmother. My parents had met in Europe, a pair of expatriates, each temporarily liberated from a family tragedy. My father, from a fine Southern family, was orphaned early and decamped to the continent to find himself. My mother's circumstances were more complicated. She had intruded upon her mother and their family minister, found them in a compromising position, and frightened, had told her father about it. This unleashed a scandal that led to a very public trial in New York at which she was forced to testify. Afterward, my shattered mother was sent to Germany to resume her music studies, where she met and married my father, and where I was born in 1881.

Imagine my parents, groping their way around Europe with me in tow, a sickly, fussy child, my mother's imminent concert career halted before it began by overwork as a student—they called it frozen hands. Think of it: after all she'd been through, her life's dream destroyed by overzealous teaching at the conservatory! My father, sensitive and moody, undertook long, exhausting walking tours, leaving my mother with me in random hotels. Eventually he would limp back to us, and she then had both of us to try to nurse to health.

Picture me small and swathed in fur while my parents moved about restlessly: Stuttgart to Basel, then Rotterdam, Paris, and back to Stuttgart. I have such an impression of darkness in my past, as one would, compared to the brilliance of this desert light. Dark rooms in high-ceilinged apartments in Europe. My early life under a pallid sky crowded with heavy clouds, the weak sun making a brave front but retreating every time. And yet there was such beauty to it: streaming silver trolley wires over rain-washed streets; sharp shadows intersecting at perfect angles with the buildings; the sky racing by overhead while faces peered down at me in my protective bundle. My health from the beginning was dangerously precarious. My mother, whom I called *Maman* in the French way, was forever leaning in to touch my forehead with her cool fingers.

"She's feverish," I can hear her saying to Papa, whom I can see sitting across a marble-topped table, enjoying his newspaper and a cup of coffee. A small cigar burns in his fingers, and the smoke fascinates me, trailing in leisurely ribbons around his head and then disappearing. A sigh from Papa. He pulls a large watch from his vest, a beautiful thing with gold hands and a rising sun/setting moon, which I am permitted to hold when I am fretful.

"We've barely been here twenty minutes, Florence," he says. His lips are tight and his eyes distant. He glances at me, wrapped in blankets even though I'm at least three, maybe even four years old, and should be sitting prettily on a spindly chair between my parents. But I am always bundled, always defended against something. Cafés were a compromise. Maman would have kept me away from all dangerous crowds, and Papa would have plunged us into the markets, the museums, the fancy stores with the huge windows and high ceilings.

One day he did precisely that. We were striding down a boulevard, and he was carrying me. Maman was next to us, hurrying to keep up, and then he turned abruptly through a revolving glass door into a grand perfumery, a sudden smile on his face. When Papa smiled, his whole face would expand and open, and there was an impression of dazzling beauty. He inhaled deeply, and I followed his example. The air was tender with scent.

"Isn't that wonderful?" he whispered. We zigzagged through the strolling shoppers to the very center of the store.

"Look, Aggie, look up!" he crowed.

I did, leaning back so suddenly he had to grab the front of my coat with his free hand, and there, soaring overhead was a wondrous Tiffany glass ceiling.

"Flowers!" I cried, pointing.

"Yes!" Papa was delighted with me.

"Flowers!" I repeated, louder.

"Hush, darling." Maman was aware of people looking our way. Children were not welcome in a store with so much fragile and valuable stock. But I was in heaven. Light streamed through the Tiffany blooms, catching hundreds of perfect bottles, row upon row on shelves that seemed to climb endlessly, colors such as I had never seen glowing all around me.

On a counter nearby was a tall, ruby-red glass container. Papa threaded his way through the crowd while Maman held the tail of my little coat. There were so many people! I think I had never before been in a crowd.

"William," Maman said. "William, we should go."

Papa stopped and regarded my mother evenly. His eyes were close to me, much closer than usual. His hair, dark and brilliant, curled over his high, stiff collar, his beard smooth and trim. While he and Maman argued quietly about whether or not it was dangerous for me to be exposed to so many strangers, I reached with my hand and carefully, gently touched his beard with the tips of my fingers.

It is how I imagined a cat might feel. I was not allowed to pet cats or dogs or any animal, with the occasional exception of the milkman's horse, and then I was immediately whisked away to wash.

Papa batted my hand away as though shooing a fly. Mortified, I started to cry, and Papa thrust me into Maman's waiting arms.

"There now," she tried to soothe me, patting my back. I was quickly borne out of the perfumery and into the cold, where a light snow had begun to fall.

BROOKLYN, NEW YORK

EIGHT SKETCHES FROM CHILDHOOD

1888

1.

IT WAS BECAUSE I HAD suffered yet another life-threatening illness at age six that our little family decided to return to America. Again and again my parents had been told that their rootless European wanderings were endangering my health. These travels were also draining their resources, which was my father's dwindling inheritance. I imagine he refused to discuss it—beneath him, I suspect. Against his repeated objections, my mother wrote to her mother in Brooklyn. There must have been a little back and forth between them, but it was quickly decided that we would go there to live, in the shrouded house my grandmother had retreated to after ruination and scandal, bankruptcy and divorce. The plan was for Maman to open a music school to support us. While I helped her pack—I loved digging into boxes, finding forgotten treasures, making things with odd bits of discarded paper—Papa retreated into numb acceptance. His life as a gentleman of leisure was coming to a close. I was frail, afflicted with chronic bronchitis, and quite small for my age.

We took the train to Bremen and boarded a grand-looking ship. There were hundreds of people on hand for the departure. With the ship's rails jammed with waving passengers and the crowds waving from the docks, it all looked like a dance, and I could not understand why Papa was so morose.

We were at sea for many days, and then early one morning Maman roused me, helped me get dressed, and bundled me into my coat and hat. She grabbed my hand, and we hurried up the narrow stairs and out onto the crowded deck to watch our progress through the Narrows and into the great harbor of New York. The sky was grainy, and the mood of the people jammed up against the rail was reverent as the recently erected Statue of Liberty loomed. The crowds surged for a better view, and Maman lifted me up. Below us, on the steerage deck, a great cheer went up. Maman began to weep, and I twisted my head to regard her anxiously.

"It's all right, darling." She was smiling and crying at the same time.

"Look." She pointed at the crowned head and the massive torch as we slid past. "Isn't she beautiful?"

"Oh, look," she said again, clutching at the rail with her free hand. The harbor ahead was a tangle of ships' masts, the water around us thick with smoke-billowing ferries and stocky little tugboats bobbing and plunging through one another's wakes. I had never seen such a riot of activity. As the sun rose over the city, our ship bellowed its mournful signal, which was answered immediately by an approaching tug. Delighted, I looked at Maman. She hugged me hard, and I had never seen her so happy. The breeze was fresh and strong against our faces.

"Home," she murmured.

From the dock we took a carriage across lower Manhattan, over the Brooklyn Bridge, and through block after block of Brooklyn until we finally turned down Pacific Street and pulled up to number 1403. Papa helped me down, and I saw a curtain move in the window. The front door opened slowly, and a small white-haired woman peered out with a shy smile. Maman took my hand and led me up the front steps.

"Agnes, say how do you do to your grandmother." I complied, and Grandmama's face flushed with pleasure when I curtsied. Then to my astonishment her eyes filled, and she pulled my mother into her arms, murmuring, "Florence, Florence," over and over while my father and I stood to one side.

2.

I would discover that every room in the house on Pacific Street was dark and draped and heavy with thick, black velvet. The exception was the foyer where a glass transom over the front door permitted a shaft of light that fell, in turn, on the staircase, the walls, and a blue Chinese vase. Next to the stairs a tall-case clock ticked loudly and struck the hour with a surprisingly light bell—I had thought it would be deep, to match the imposing size of the clock. I liked touching its satiny surface, a dark mahogany that promised permanence. I traced my fingers over the lower part of the wall, which was covered in embossed leather. A flower pattern had been pressed into it over and over, every flower exactly the same as the one before, climbing up until it ended—some of the flowers losing their tops—in a strip of molding.

"Don't get the walls dirty now, dearie."

My grandmother moved slowly down the hall from the kitchen, where she'd just had her breakfast, a plain roll and coffee. Her black dress rustled, and she carried her Bible. I stopped touching the wall immediately and stood stiffly in place, my hands clasped behind me. She nodded in my direction as she passed, a brief vacant smile on her face, and settled in the front parlor by the veiled window. Completely ignoring me now, she opened her Bible, laid it carefully on her lap, bowed her head, and prayed silently.

3.

"Nothing goes away until it is confronted," my grandmother was fond of telling me. I always wanted to close my ears then, fearful of sinking into the thick morass of my own sins: not helping my mother, arguing with my mother, not practicing the piano enough, drawing when I should be conjugating Latin verbs, entertaining defiant and disrespectful thoughts.

The chill between my parents deepened. Their quarrels grew louder and seemed constant. I watched my father set out his tortoiseshell hairbrushes on the dresser he would share with my mother—in Europe they had always had separate bedrooms—and heard the word "backwater" over and over, spat out and laced with contempt. Maman did not respond. She continued to unpack her steamer trunk, hanging her dresses in the cramped Brooklyn closet, folding her undergarments and laying them in the backwater Brooklyn bureau drawer. The ceiling was lower than what we were used to, and it surprised me to realize that Maman was tall and physically imposing. She had become stocky in build, and her hair, combed into a wavy pompadour in front and gathered into a bun at the nape of her neck, added an inch or so of height.

I helped her unwrap the sachets of lavender from Provence that she had been given as a going-away present and watched as she tucked them among her silky underthings. She kept her back to Papa as if to keep what was hers, hers, and separate from him.

But backwater or not, I was settling into the hazy September days. For the first time in my life, I could survey them from my own room, which was on the street side of the second floor, small and square with two windows and a closet. My grandmother's bedroom was down the hall a bit, past the bathroom, and my parents shared the large attic room on the top floor.

I had a small dresser and chair with a table for drawing and practicing writing. I was proud of the way I could form letters and make flourishes at the end of certain words—my first name, for instance. I loved to write it: the big triangular "A," small "g" with a deep, round tail, tidy little "n" and "e," and then the "s," which swept up before it curved down gently, then swooped out and upward in a long, triumphal string, as though a kite were attached. I then folded it back over itself several times and finally let the entire glorious enterprise come to rest.

My mother allowed me to choose decorations for my walls. In the small attic storage room, I found a set of framed flower studies—Grandmama said that they had been Maman's when she was young—lovely watercolors, which I asked for and was given. Papa helped me choose places for them on my wall, and he hammered in the slender nails on which we hung them. I was impressed that we were able do this: no hotel or apartment building we'd lived in before had ever permitted it. The few pictures and paintings that traveled with us were always suspended on dark, braided ropes from the molding near the ceiling.

I knew that whatever kept my grandmother clothed in penitential black was also related to my mother's reserve and the sadness that veiled her face. The scandal itself, while never spoken of, seemed to reside in the house alongside us and kept us wary and watchful.

On Sunday mornings, the only day she left the house, my grandmother placed her prayer book and Bible in her reticule and pinned on her wide-brimmed black hat. She always invited my mother to come along. At Maman's polite, "No, thank you, Mother," she opened the front door and stepped onto the stoop, pausing for a moment to sniff the air. A hansom cab waited, and the driver stood by the curb ready to help her climb in. He vaulted easily back into his seat, and with a flick of his whip over the horse, they would be off. We would not see her again for hours. I was always disappointed that Maman declined to go along; I was wildly curious about "the Brethren" and the "meeting" my grandmother had told me she was attending.

"Is it like the meeting in our parlor on Wednesday evenings?"
I asked.

"No," she said, "that is a *prayer* meeting. On Sundays we have
a *worship* meeting."

My parents did not say why they declined to participate, but they
always retreated to the upstairs on Wednesday evenings, when a rather
severe group of Brethren filled our front room. As soon as my parents
had disappeared, I would creep back down and lurk near the parlor.
The heavy sliding doors would be closed, but I could peek through the
crack and watch. Sometimes the Brethren stood in a circle, clasped
hands, and prayed in unison; sometimes a single male voice spoke
for them all. I could only make out certain words, but there was no
mistaking the fervor with which the prayers were offered up.

4.

Our small piece of Brooklyn was placid and slow, and our house
was part of a new row of brownstones, all of which looked alike.
If you stood at our corner, you'd see an orderly line of front steps
with railings, one behind the other, in perfect symmetry. I didn't
tell Papa, but I thought our street was beautiful.

Outside my window the leaves of the sycamore were curling
and turning brown, and round burrs were forming. Down the street
a stand of maples had begun to change from deep green to the
beginnings of gold. In the back of the house, the sunroom—the
only room where the windows were not covered—led to a small
walled garden. On either side were neighbors who also had gardens,
and who in the slanted light of autumn were outside digging and
mulching and preparing the flowerbeds for winter.

My parents' struggle grew more consuming, and I began to
linger more boldly outside their door to listen.

"I don't know how you can consider such a thing, Florence,"
I heard my father say.

"We cannot continue to live off my mother, William," was her retort. I heard her footsteps, and she threw the door open and glared at me.

"Little girls should not be listening at grown-ups' doors, Agnes!"

"No, Maman."

5.

The "thing" that so appalled Papa was the music school Maman had resolved to open. She was fired with new purpose. In the morning she descended the narrow attic steps to the second floor, and then to the kitchen where soon the smell of coffee began to rise—so rich and inviting, and so disappointing the first time I was allowed to taste it. I climbed out of my bed, which was still a bit high for me, swung my legs down, pulled on stockings and shoes and smock, and hurried downstairs. Maman had made coffee for herself, Papa, and Grandmama and a cup of chocolate for me. She had sliced bread for us to eat, but it fell to Grandmama to butter my piece, to which she added a generous spoonful of jam before patting my head affectionately, excusing herself, and repairing to the front parlor and her prayers.

Maman finished her own bread quickly, left the table, and settled down to work at the desk she had moved into a corner of the dining room. She had opened a bank account with the money from the sale of her piano back in Europe and was arranging the purchase of a new instrument. This she had done against Papa's entreaties to turn this money over to him. He had decided to open an art gallery, which he felt was an appropriate way for a gentleman to earn money.

"I could demand it from you, Florence," he said abruptly one morning, while we were all still at the table. "As your husband."

Maman said nothing.

"You took a vow to love, honor, and obey," he continued.

"Hush, William," Maman said. Grandmama looked down at her plate. I knew I should do likewise, but I could not.

"Hush?" Papa's voice sounded as if he had swallowed marbles. Maman glanced out the window. No one said anything, and after a moment everyone resumed eating. The only sounds were the clink of silver against plate and cup, the ticking of the wall clock. I kept very still. Finally, Papa dabbed at his mouth with his napkin. He seemed to have all the time in the world. He brushed his beard lightly, making sure no stray crumbs lingered there, then folded his napkin, inserted it into the silver ring that bore his initials, and placed it on the table.

"Excuse me, ladies," he said, rising from his chair. "I have a busy day ahead." He clicked his heels for emphasis, inclined his head in a brief bow, and departed the kitchen. I noticed that the more upset Papa got, the more elegant his movements became. It gave him a terrible beauty, and my heart broke watching him. A few minutes later we heard the front door open and close, and a heavy blanket of quiet covered Maman, Grandmama, and me. The three of us sat together; Maman's face was impassive, but when I looked at Grandmama, I saw fear, guilt, and sorrow.

6.

Papa did not return that day, nor the next, or the next. His absence seemed to inspire Maman to drive herself—and me—harder. On the second day she pulled my schoolbooks out of the box they had traveled in, and my heart sank a bit. It appeared that the holiday was over. After breakfast on the third day, instead of working at her desk in the dining room, she set up our schoolroom in the adjacent corner. This consisted of a small table for writing and figuring and drawing, plus a slot in the nearest bookshelf for my texts. These, Maman knew, were sadly out of date and entirely inadequate, but that didn't seem to matter. She presided over the renewing of my education with steely ferocity, demanding that I read through the tattered primer yet again, beginning at the beginning.

"I *finished* this, Maman," I said.

"Never mind, it'll be good practice. A good reminder."

"But it's a *baby* book."

"It doesn't matter, Agnes. The point is to practice."

I knew better than to argue, so I opened the book and stared at the script: the alphabet in large letters, starting with a simpering "A," my own beloved first initial, plus the well-worn list of words beginning with "A." I lowered the book.

"Read," Maman commanded. I waited for Maman to realize her error and pick some other book. She stood over me stiffly.

"It's for *babies*," I finally blustered, afraid of her wrath but too deeply committed to withdraw.

"Read it." Her voice was tight and quiet and dangerous.

"No," I whispered, dropping the book and running from the room. Now I was truly terrified. I had committed three serious offenses in the space of a few seconds: I had dropped a book on the floor, and from the sickening sound it made when it hit, had likely caused the binding to break; I had turned and run in defiance; and worst, I had told my mother "no." I scurried up the stairs. In my room I threw myself onto my bed and wept. I heard Maman's footsteps as she pursued me, and I both feared her arrival and longed for it. But halfway up she stopped, and then I heard her go back downstairs.

A few minutes later my grandmother made her slow way up the stairs, peered into my room, and settled herself on the edge of my bed. Tentatively she touched my back and began to rub gently.

"There now, dearie," she said. "There now."

In a little while I quieted, and she took me by the hand to the bathroom, where she helped me wash my face.

"Would you like a little milk?"

I shook my head. My stomach, always subject to flutters, was upset and I felt queasy.

"Never mind," Grandmama said. "We'll just go sit quietly, shall we?"

Together we descended the stairs, one step at a time. In the front parlor she perused the titles on the bookshelf. She found a book of Bible stories, pulled it down, and settled herself in her armchair. She patted her lap for me to climb on, and I did so. While I wanted to protest that only babies sat in laps, I kept still and leaned back against her soft, talc-scented bosom and felt comforted. This was the beginning of my affection for my grandmother. She opened the book and leafed through the pages. Each story was accompanied by a full-color plate of a faraway place of diminutive trees, houses made of stone, and tidy earthen roads that wound prettily off into the distance, where everyone, even the men, wore long, flowing gowns.

"Now, Agnes, do you have a favorite?"

My face flushed. I had no favorite because I had never been exposed to these stories, and I suspected she knew that. I shook my head.

"Very well," she said. "Let's start with the one about Moses, shall we?"

I nodded my head even though I was quite sure she was not waiting for me to agree, and she began reading about the enslaved Children of Israel and their Egyptian masters. I could hear Maman's footsteps as she left the kitchen. I wiggled a bit, frightened of what might be coming next. My reader contained stories about children, usually boys, who defied their parents and whose fathers removed belts to strike them. Maman did not wear a belt, of course, and she wasn't my father. Perhaps because there was no clear model for where we found ourselves, I began to tremble. Grandmama pulled me closer and continued the story of the infant Moses, placed by his Hebrew mother and sister in a basket to save him from Egyptian slaughter, and Pharaoh's daughter finding him in the basket hidden in the bulrushes, and naming him "Moses, because she drew him from the water."

Maman's footsteps halted at the doorway. I turned my head and was surprised to see sadness in place of anger in her own tear-stained face. Abruptly she turned and crossed the hall to the studio, where she began to play the old upright piano that had been here when we arrived. She had chosen a simple Bach fugue with a pair of intertwining melodic lines, and now accompanying my grandmother's soft voice, the music swelled and seemed to set our house in order. By the time we sat down to supper, Maman seemed to have recovered, and it was as if nothing had ever happened between us. But in the morning the hated primer had disappeared from my desk. A few days later a new grammar school text was delivered, and we continued with our new life.

After Maman's death many years later, I would find the battered primer among her things and wonder why she had kept it, what it had signified for her. Perhaps it marked the end of my compliant childhood, warning her that soon I would begin to find ways to do as I pleased. When those days did in fact come about, I tried to make my own way quietly and without the hurtful defiance that had seemed to threaten us.

7.

Without Papa to disapprove, Maman redoubled her efforts to get the music school established. She pinned her hat on each morning and walked through the front door, closed it firmly behind her, and marched off to another grammar school or high school to meet the principal and possibly the music teacher and ask for help in informing promising students that the Pelton School of Music was open for lessons. She carried a large handbag, more of a carpet bag really, into which she had placed letters from her professors in Stuttgart, recommending her as a musician and a teacher of theory. Before donning her hat and coat, she always checked the bag to make sure these letters were there, even reading them once more to refresh her confidence.

"To whom it may concern," they all began, "Let it be known that the bearer, Florence Tilton Pelton, has successfully completed the Stuttgart Conservatory course in piano,"—or "theory," or "Solfège," or "the teaching of violin"—and "is fully qualified" to take on pupils. Each letter went on to praise my mother's devotion to music, her patience with children, and the writer's unshakable confidence in her integrity: "She is a person of high moral character."

I thought her impressive. She wore her hair parted in the middle and pulled back into a tidy bun and kept her collars high on her neck and her sleeves long. She would return late in the day, weary and hungry, sometimes with hopeful news and the names of prospective students, sometimes empty-handed. On those evenings she talked little, and Grandmama fixed our supper.

Finally came the day when the new grand piano, its legs having been removed, was unloaded from a freight wagon and hauled on skids and pulleys up the front steps by five burly men. Grunting and maneuvering with great difficulty, they pushed it through the double doors and dragged it on blankets down the hall. They reassembled it in the dining room, which, with the connecting front parlor, would soon become the Pelton School of Music. It was a magnificent beast, and we were admiring it when my father appeared in the doorway.

"Papa!" I ran to him and threw my arms around his waist. He touched my head absently and stared at the new piano.

"So," he said. "Here it is." I disengaged carefully.

"And here you are," Maman countered. "We were worried, William."

"I can see that," he said.

My grandmother took me by the hand and said, "Let's go to the park, shall we?"

The park? I shook my head, but my grandmother had me in my coat and both of us out the door before I could object. When we returned a bit later, Maman took me upstairs and told me Papa was gone. He had decided to return to Europe, she said. Just like

that: "Papa has decided . . ." As though he had calmly jotted down
the advantages and disadvantages to each option and the "Europe"
list was longer. I thought of him tucking his list into a pocket and
patting it, rising from his chair with a cheerful smile, and saying he
was off to Stuttgart.

"Did you tell him we needed him?" I cried.

"Oh, darling." Maman sank to her knees and reached for me,
wanting to fold me into her arms. But I pushed her back.

"Did you tell him?"

"I did, yes," she whispered. "I did tell him."

"What did he say?"

"He said to tell you he loves you. And not to worry, that he'd
be back."

This I knew immediately, viscerally, in the marrow of my bones
was not true. I knew my father would never return to live with
us in our new home, and I began the painful business of trying to
untangle the many threads of my new-world self that were mingled
with his. Every day I discovered another one—from the wonder of
watching the sun break out after a rain and turn wet pavement to
silver, to the pushcarts of Atlantic Avenue, to the thrill of riding on
a trolley car. In each case I deliberately snipped our connection, as I
imagined him doing, the better to recover my own sense of wonder.

8.

Maman opened her school later that fall. She started with only four
pupils, but she was a patient and encouraging teacher, and soon
those four became seven, and then twelve, and then twenty. And
then their younger brothers and sisters were sent to clomp up our
front steps, and their cousins, and their friends. Each hour of most
days they arrived in orderly intervals, and another lesson would
begin. I was not permitted to attend the new public school because
of lingering fears about my health, but to my great delight, Maman

found Miss Sunder (who joked about being a teacher called "Miss Understanding"), an energetic young woman who assumed charge of my education.

We hadn't needed the doctor since our arrival in Brooklyn, even though my fever still rose and fell like an unreliable tide. At those times I sat up in bed with my drawing board, paper, and pencils. Maman gave me flower pictures to copy, and Grandmama gave me the book of Bible stories for children with color plates, but I had no interest in either. My subject matter was Papa: Papa by himself, Papa with Maman, Papa and me in front of a house, Papa and me next to a tree, and on and on. The drawings were little more than stick figures, really, which disappointed me and frustrated my mother.

"You can do so much better if you work from a picture," she said, indicating the collection of images she had given me for copying.

To which I coolly replied, "Do you have a picture of Papa I can use?"

"Watch your tone, Missy." Maman drew herself up. Later she brought me the small framed daguerreotype of him that she kept on her dresser and left without a word. I studied it closely, searching for my father in the formal, suited figure, and worked carefully all morning on a drawing.

Papa wrote that he had left Germany and returned to the family home in Roseland, Louisiana, to be with his brother. I hadn't remembered hearing anything about this mysterious brother. Maman said that he and Papa were orphans, that it was just the two of them in this world. She showed me a photograph of a pillared white house in a fairy-tale landscape of huge trees with rough black trunks and tangled branches, and something called Spanish moss, which was lacy and white, hanging like ghosts in the branches.

I wrote Papa letter after letter, usually with a drawing inside. I drew all the time now. Maman, who replenished my supply of paper each week, could hardly keep up with me. I worried about what this was costing, but she seemed quite cheerful and rather proud.

"You're getting to be quite the artist."

I waited for a letter. The sound of the postman's heavy shoes on our front steps marked the center of my day, but his delivery never included an envelope addressed to me.

When the telegram came, it was such a surprise that my mother, who had answered the door in puzzlement—"Who could it be at this hour?"—gaped at the Western Union boy, standing on the stoop with his shoulder bag and cap. It was early and we were still at breakfast. The boy offered my mother the yellow envelope. She stared at it before taking it, as though she weren't quite sure why he was handing it to her, but she'd accept it to be polite. He waited, and she fumbled in her bag for a coin to give him, but still he waited. At last he said, "Will there be a reply, ma'am?" and she was forced to open it in front of him. The color drained out of her face. Finally, she noticed him still standing there and said, "No, no reply," at which he turned quickly and darted down the front walk to the street and out of sight.

"Florence, what is it?"

Maman couldn't speak but handed the telegram to my grand-mother, who read it and quickly clutched it to her chest in case I was trying to see what it said.

"Agnes, go upstairs," she said.

When I hesitated, she said it again more vehemently.

"Go upstairs!"

I ran, tears already running down my cheeks. I didn't know, but I knew. I was not surprised when Maman came into my room a few minutes later.

"Agnes," she started, sitting on my bed, where I had buried my face in the pillow. I raised my head, which was already pounding. She held the telegram in one hand and her face was a mask, her composure intact. Her features seemed frozen: her nose, which in the half-light of my room appeared angular and sharp, cast a slight shadow across her cheek. Her eyes, always soft and somber, pooled, and she swallowed many times. Her face was nearly gray with effort, and when at last she spoke, it was in a whisper.

"Agnes," she repeated, and her voice broke open. It was deep and ragged, and I was frightened by the sound she made. It was as though she had been ripped inside all the way to her heart.

"Agnes," she said again, but this time her inner door was closed. The barrier I had never known existed was back in place. Her voice came again, and it was not brittle or harsh but flat and seemed to have an impenetrable surface.

"Agnes, your papa has died." She dropped the telegram and covered her face with her hands, away from my probing eyes. When she rose to look at me, her face was dark but composed. "I must go to him."

She pulled herself up and left my room. I heard her climb the steps to her bedroom and close the door. The telegram still lay on my bed where it had fallen: "William taken from us. Come at once."

That day, as she packed a small valise, I sat in the corner of their attic room and thought, over and over, my father has died. I wondered if I would survive.

"His soul has taken flight." Grandmama was standing at the top of the attic stairs, slightly out of breath. Maman ignored her, which shocked me. After a moment, my grandmother turned and went back down the steps, taking them slowly, one at a time. I shrank into the wall, worried by the idea that, loosed from its mooring, his soul might be lost and alone.

Maman left that afternoon. She did not suggest I should accompany her, nor did it occur to me to ask. I pictured her on the train, sitting up in coach, pulling away from New York with its concrete angles and easing south, into the land of the photograph— broad spreading trees that were always green, with pale wisps of moss hanging from their branches. Miss Sunder had explained that these swatches of white were *in* the tree but not *of* the tree. Perhaps Papa's soul was somehow in the world while being no longer of the world. That brought a kind of relief; until that moment, my father had been utterly gone. Now it occurred to me that he could be everywhere. He could belong to me in a private, secret way, and no matter what happened, I would always have him.

When Maman returned from Louisiana, I overheard her tell my grandmother that Papa had died from taking too much morphine. I could hear that she was ashamed of this, so I never asked her about it, but instinctively I understood. He had been ill and weak and helpless and had tried to comfort his sadness; instead, he put himself to sleep permanently. We did not talk of him after that.

CATHEDRAL CITY, CALIFORNIA

FEBRUARY 6, 1961

INVENTORY:

THE LANDSCAPES SHOULD GO TO the gallery. Harriet can sell these eventually, and that will relieve the family of whatever burden I've been.

The abstracts. Maybe they will sell at last. So many admirers, so few buyers. Why does one sell and another remain? For the stupidest of reasons. Because it can only go in a particular room and the colors are wrong for the drapes, or the walls, or the room already has wallpaper, and the like. Or, worse, they admire the image, stand in front of it raptly, are clearly moved by it, and then they shake their heads and say, "It's a little startling, isn't it?" Or "What will so-and-so think of this?" Meaning, "What will so-and-so think of *me* for buying this?" (I send blessings to those who received the messages conveyed in these pictures; especially those who absorbed the messages and fell in love with the pictures and paid for them and took them home and hung them in prominent places. You who did this, you kept me going over the years, all of you, and I send you love as often as I think of you. And when I am not thinking of you, my heart still sends you love.)

BROOKLYN, NEW YORK

1896

I MUST HAVE BEEN FOURTEEN when I started telling every-one who would listen that I was going to be an artist. I spent every possible moment of the day drawing pictures, often furtively when I should have been doing my lessons. Sometimes when rain kept us indoors and prevented our afternoon "constitutional," Miss Sunder would bring out the watercolors, and she and I would sit at the big table in the kitchen with a bowl of water between us and share the little pots of paint. At night, when I went to bed, I carried my drawing pad and pencils up to my room with me. I was beginning to under-stand how the world changed when you rendered it for yourself. Out of the life-altering act of beginning to look deeply, I enjoyed a new kinship with everything around me. I felt I was journeying into the soul of each object I drew. I kept this wondrous new experience to myself: "That is blasphemy, Agnes," I could hear my grandmother say. "*Things* don't have souls." But I was alive with the knowledge that everything possessed a unique essence and therefore its own self and was, even if imperceptibly, different from everything else.

I knew that my family was different from other families, but I also carried a sense that I was different, even within our own small triad. Drawing gave me a territory of my own, a place from which to view the world in all its differentness, and without shame. In celebration I drew the newel post at the foot of the stairs, the Chinese vase in the foyer, the front door, the tree outside our house, the milkman's horse and wagon, the ragman and his cart—even the glorious ornate lamppost with its glowing globe that lit our street at night. I labeled everything in neat print across the bottom of the page. I thought Miss Sunder was beautiful, and I tried to draw her likeness, but I was not successful and erased my efforts quickly. I did not try to draw either my mother or my grandmother; the muffled stillness of our house seemed to forbid it.

I often ran out of paper, and when I did, I foraged around to find more. Maman's desk was usually a good resource, and if she was busy teaching, she never minded when I helped myself; she said I was blooming, which made her happy. One day I could find no paper anywhere, and it occurred to me to look in the storage room in the attic. This was off-limits to me, but I had begun to be rebellious and thought I'd go up there quickly and be back before anyone could object. The attic stairs were behind a door that needed oil—this was also how Maman got to her bedroom, and I always knew when she was going up or down.

I wasn't sure if it would be audible to her in the piano studio, but just in case, I turned the knob carefully and crept up the narrow wooden steps. It was dark in the stairwell, and I groped my way along until the turn, where the watery light from a small glass skylight revealed Maman's bedroom on the right. The storage room on the left was unlocked, and I opened the door into a long, stuffy room with a dormer window to the street and a small, square one at the back. I knew immediately that I had invaded Maman's private sanctuary; the force of her presence, usually so tenderly disposed toward me, felt like a wall and stopped me where I stood. A divan, covered with a beautiful paisley shawl, had been pushed against the wall where the roof slanted inward. Right next to it was a desk—an antique ladies' desk, its blackened varnish cracking. A tentative border of inlaid mother-of-pearl, broken here and there, wound around the desk lid. A fragile gingerbread lattice rose high from the back and held a worn oval mirror in its center. It was a presence, that desk. I studied its dozen tiny drawers, its half-empty inkwell, the tall stick pen, and the leather-trimmed writing surface made of moth-eaten felt.

I knew I should leave at once. My legs wanted to run, and my heart was rattling. Instead, I opened each of the small drawers, finding a pair of keys in one, an old button in another, nothing at all in the others. But in the large center drawer, where I thought I might find blank paper, was a thick packet of letters tied in a bundle. I picked these up carefully. The stamps were foreign, and the return address was in Paris. With a shock I realized that I was holding letters written by my grandfather to my mother.

I had asked her about him, of course. Every now and again I'd wonder where he was and why he never came to see us. Maman always responded rather vaguely that he was in Paris and that he was very busy. Her face, and the subject, would close abruptly, and that would be that. I knew my grandparents had ended their marriage and that divorce itself was nothing we were ever to speak about. I stood quaking for a moment, and then it struck me that here, in my hand, was evidence that she knew more than she had said. And that she had lied to me.

Not caring any longer if I was discovered, I came back downstairs with the bundle of letters in the pocket of my smock, intending to confront my mother and demand an explanation. I marched to the front parlor, which housed the Pelton School of Music. Through the sliding glass doors, I could see Maman seated on the piano bench next to an unhappy-looking student. She pointed to the music, explaining it note by note, and then at her insistence, he tried the passage again. It was only slightly improved, and I heard Maman's, "Again, please," before I gave up and turned into the small room across the hall where my grandmother sat on the love seat at this time of day with her crocheting. Without saying a word, I pulled the letters from my pocket and showed them to her.

I'm not sure what I expected—surprise? weeping? anger?—but after a moment in which she was clearly startled, she composed herself.

"Come and sit by me," she said.

She took the packet from my hand and tucked it into her embroidery bag and reached around to draw me close. I was restless and excited, and she chafed my bare arm gently to calm the energy racing through my limbs.

"Those letters are from your grandfather. As you can plainly see, they are addressed to your mother. I will return them to her."

I felt my face grow warm in the silence.

"You have survived," she said. "So many times we thought we might lose you. But you are fourteen years old and in tolerably good health. That is something to thank God for, Agnes, and I hope you do so every single day. You were very sickly as a baby. You were much too small and did not gain weight as you should have. We did not think you would live the first winter after you were born. Your mother was so frightened that she brought you here all the way from Rotterdam, where you and she were living, so that I could see you at least once."

I forgot the letters for a moment.

"I was here?"

"You were here."

I searched my memory, my thoughts darting all about, trying to recall having seen these walls, the stairs, the bay window. My grandmother.

"Where was Papa?"

"He was traveling. He had started taking long sojourns that he said were solitary, but he always seemed to end up with friends. Your mother didn't know these friends, had never been introduced to them. You and your mother stayed here for six months, and then she received a letter from your father, instructing her to come back at once. You were in tolerable health, and so she returned to Europe for the next five years.

"And now your health has improved so much, we can send you off on a new adventure. Are you pleased about that?"

I nodded. In point of fact, I was enormously pleased. Just days ago, we had received the official letter admitting me to the General Art Course at the Pratt Institute. I would start in the middle of September, afternoons only, because Maman worried that a full day would be too taxing. I accepted her terms and, in my mind, dismissed her fears. Instead, I daydreamed about what a real school would be like, how I would at last be away from Pacific Street and part of a place where I would learn to make art.

"I'm glad. It will be a new world for you, dearie. A place to develop your considerable gifts. But you may meet people there who will tell you things, terrible things, about us, about your family."

What these things were, I struggled to imagine. I knew we lived under a cloud, and now the idea of learning why made me cold with fear.

"Much of what these people say—" She drew her breath in sharply. She seemed on the verge of abandoning the conversation.

I would not have minded; I wanted to run and hide. She went on.

"Much of what they say will be true. But before you judge us, remember that everything your grandfather and mother and I did, we did with purity of intention."

She drew me closer, which was awkward. I had gotten bigger over the summer and my legs splayed out over the chair's edge. I thought about what a long time it had been since Maman and Papa and I had come to Brooklyn. How even Papa's death seemed a distant memory. And how, from our very first day in this house, my grandmother had been an immutable fact of my life. She never varied her wardrobe of black crepe dresses, and each morning precisely at nine o'clock she came to this room to read her Bible and to pray. But eight years had bent her back into a permanent curve, like a question mark, and her blue eyes were milky and opaque. Sometimes she stumbled when traversing the distance from bedroom to kitchen to parlor.

Her cheeks flushed and her breath came lightly and quickly. She hesitated again, staring into the space in front of her.

"Your mother was your age, just fourteen, when all of what happened began." She seemed surprised at the thought.

"It was all a very long time ago." She tucked a wavy strand of soft white hair back. "You may think that I'm a lonely old woman," she added.

It had never occurred to me that she was lonely. After all, she had me and Maman. And she had the Brethren, who arrived faithfully each Wednesday evening for a prayer service, and with whom she worshipped on Sundays in the drafty meetinghouse on Atlantic Avenue.

"I was redeemed, Agnes. That is what I want to tell you. That is what is important. I was broken, deserted, abandoned, and then the Lord lifted me to himself and forgave me. I was pulled out of darkness and into light. There is always welcome for the sinner, Agnes."

I had long puzzled over what my grandmother could possibly need forgiveness for. My own sins, I knew, were legion. I was selfish. I had disobeyed my mother as recently as the previous evening, flouting her strict bedtime rule in order to draw, knowing that she worried about my health. I had crushes on several of the older girls who came for lessons—girls who seemed so sure of themselves— and I ignored my schoolwork to gaze out the window and watch as they came and went. And now I had intruded into my mother's private sanctuary. My grandmother had said nothing to me about these failings; she never did. "Judgment is mine, sayeth the Lord," was the harshest pronouncement she ever made. I felt miserable and small and thought I should ask for her forgiveness. I longed for the moment of comfort that I knew would come—my head against her soft bosom, her hand stroking my hair, her murmured, "There, there." I was about to speak up when abruptly, a decision apparently having been made, she sat up straighter.

"We are all sinners, Agnes. Do you understand that?"

"Yes, Grandmama."

I sensed an enormous shadow falling over us, over me. I wanted her to stop. I wanted her to suggest that we walk to Atlantic Avenue and find some fresh peaches, come home, and have them with cream. I knew that something was ending for me and something else beginning, and I was sure that what was beginning was heavy and would be with me forever, like the mark of Cain. She drew a deep breath and started to speak.

"I sinned against the Lord, against my husband and my children, against the congregation of which I was a part, and against the man who trusted me with his griefs and needs." She paused. "And then I sinned again by denying my grievous wrongdoings." She sipped from the glass of water next to her.

"You know nothing of this," she went on. "We have tried to shield you from it, but I see that has not been possible. The sins of the fathers are indeed visited upon their children. Your mother will be angry at you for going where you've been told not to go, but she will also understand that we cannot shield those we love, no matter how much we want to. We shall all have to bow to God's will and accept his judgment."

She took her arm from my shoulder and clasped her hands.

"Do you know what an affair is?" she asked. Numbly I shook my head.

"It is when people indulge in marital relations outside of marriage."

I didn't understand this either, but somehow, I knew it concerned sex, which Miss Sunder had recently introduced via elaborate diagrams concerning flowers and bees and the carrying of seed, hastily adding that men carried human seed and women received it during marital intercourse. She had turned red at that point, and I had concluded that the topic was so dangerous as to cause one's eternal damnation merely by contemplating it.

Somewhat thrilled, I braced myself. Just then across the foyer, the parlor doors slid open. My grandmother, who had been about to speak, held her silence while the boy who had been struggling through his lesson dashed out as if escaping, nearly colliding with the girl scheduled for the next hour.

"Come in, Louise," Maman murmured, closing the doors behind them.

Once we heard the inevitable scales that Maman always insisted on at the start of every lesson—"I always know if they haven't been practicing"—my grandmother stirred.

"There was a man whom I believed was from God, the Reverend Henry Ward Beecher. It was at his Plymouth Church right here in Brooklyn that your grandfather and I met, fell in love, and were married. We both wanted with all our hearts to do God's work. Your grandfather was a journalist for a newspaper produced by some wealthy members of the parish called *The Independent*. It was intended to make Mr. Beecher's thoughts and writings against slavery, many of which were produced by your grandfather, available to a wider audience, which it did."

My grandmother's eyes grew teary as she began to tell me of her marriage to Theodore Tilton, her sense of being part of something important, her joy at the birth of their first child.

"That was your dear mother. She was baptized in Mr. Beecher's church, during the Sunday service in the presence of the entire congregation. It was a very large church, Agnes; people came from all around, even Manhattan, to hear the Reverend Mr. Beecher preach. He was very inspiring." A dryness came into her tone, almost a bitterness. This was so unlike her, I looked up into her face. Her eyes were fixed straight ahead, staring at what, I wondered. The opposite wall held family photographs in round, gilded frames: me as a baby, Maman as a young woman—an unhappy-looking young woman, I now saw—my aunt Alice, my uncles. So fierce was my grandmother's gaze, I felt she could have set the house ablaze.

"Your grandfather was a deeply committed person," she said. "He loved Mr. Beecher with the passionate fire of spiritual friendship. But Mr. Beecher's marriage was not a happy one, so he often took refuge in our home and basked in the love he found with us."

As my grandfather's own reputation grew, he began to travel widely to lecture, leaving my grandmother and their growing family at home in Brooklyn Heights for weeks and months at a time.

"During your grandfather's long absences," she went on, "he urged me to continue to welcome the pastor into our home, and I did. And I feel duty-bound to tell you, Agnes, that his company was not burdensome. Never had I felt so listened to by anyone, not even your grandfather, who could be harsh and angry. Sometimes he turned violent and acted as though he hated me, and I think perhaps he did."

She stopped and glanced down at me, concern on her face for how I was receiving all this. I sat numbly, frightened at the idea of anyone hating Grandmama.

My grandmother continued. "Your grandfather wanted me to agree to what his like-minded companions—none of whom I trusted—called 'new marriage,' which would have been nothing more than condoning his occasional infidelities."

She looked at me again quickly, and almost to herself added, "I could not. Would not. But in his sermons, Mr. Beecher affirmed that God permitted, even celebrated, all expressions of true love. When he and I were alone, he told me that what had sprung up between us was sacred. 'We did not go looking for it, Lib,' he said, but there it was. However, he said, not everyone would understand. And for that reason, we would practice what he called 'nest hiding.'"

"What is that, Grandmama?" I asked timidly.

"It's—keeping a secret. You'll understand when you're older. Mr. Beecher and I had a bond similar to the bond your grandfather and I had been blessed with at the outset of our marriage. We were close; do you understand?"

I nodded. I thought of my bond with Miss Sunder, and then quickly realized that was not what my grandmother meant.

She drew her breath in sharply. "I must tell you the truth, Agnes, and that is that I have never been so happy, before or since. Which is why you must never trust happiness. It is elusive at best, and of the devil at worst."

She continued in a low, hurried voice. I gathered that my mother began to see things that troubled her fourteen-year-old eyes—a hand where it didn't belong, tender white flesh that should have been covered, a face unusually flushed—and reported these to her father. He demanded that my grandmother make a full confession to him, which she did reluctantly. Months later, someone wrote about it in a newspaper, and to repair his dignity, my grandfather sued the pastor for "criminal intimacy." My grandfather was fired from *The Independent*. There was a trial that lasted six months. On the witness stand, my grandmother was unable to bring herself to publicly admit the nature of her friendship with Reverend Beecher. He was found not guilty, and our family was sent into what seemed an irreversible spiral of destruction.

She wept a little in telling me of how deeply upset my mother had been by all of this. "But," she said, daubing at her eyes with a lacy handkerchief, "your mother was always a gifted pianist. So, the great blessing was that she could take her refuge in music. Your grandfather and I decided to send your mother to Europe to study and to recover, and to have a new beginning for herself in life."

My grandmother's voice was full of weariness now, and I thought she would send me away so that she could read and pray. As if understanding what I was thinking, she took my hand and held it in both of hers where they rested on her lap. She experienced "true conversion," she said, and with the solace of the Holy Spirit, she also experienced a change of heart—assisted by the Brethren, who had allowed her into their small society and encouraged her.

"'En-courage,' Agnes; a wonderful word, full of meat and bone."

For one last time, she placed herself in the public eye. She wrote letters to the newspapers, recanting her testimony and admitting the affair. Mr. Beecher had been sending her monthly checks to help the family stay afloat, and now that money stopped. The Plymouth Church officially excommunicated her, and my grandfather exiled himself to Paris where he made a meager living writing romantic novels and occasional articles. My grandmother had saved most of the money Mr. Beecher had given her. She bought the house we were living in and repaired to this quiet piece of Brooklyn, where she swathed herself in black and became a penitent recluse.

"Those are the wages of sin, Agnes. You must never forget how easy it is to dance to the devil's tune."

When she had finished speaking, my grandmother picked up her Bible and began to read. Her hands trembled slightly with the effort of holding the book. Her face was drawn and pale; the subject was closed, and I knew she would not raise it again. I tiptoed away and upstairs and remained in my room until called for supper.

I lay on my bed, eyes closed, and worried about the devil and his tune. How did you know what was good and what was not? And if you had believed that what turned out to be sinful was good, was that your fault? Was it fair that you should be punished as my grandmother and grandfather had been? I thought not. If God was not going to be fair, I didn't see the point in trying to do his will. I had a small mirror over my dresser and took my own measure as best I could: I saw a gawky, awkward, homely wretch who was horribly shy.

That very day my mother forgave me for intruding in her world, but I remained troubled and kept to myself for the rest of the summer, counting the days until I would start at Pratt by marking them off on a calendar. There were twenty-four, then twenty-three, and I could see that time would truly pass and I would survive. Meanwhile, all I would do was draw, so my lessons became torture for both me and my beloved Miss Sunder, who left us at the end of August.

PRATT INSTITUTE

SCHOOL OF FINE AND APPLIED ARTS

1895

BECAUSE OF ANOTHER BOUT WITH bronchitis, I started Pratt two weeks late. Clutching the letter that instructed me when and where to report, I climbed the red brick steps and opened the door to a new land.

I was in a large, airy building: long halls and bare wooden floors, with a faint smell of polish over a mustiness I did not find unpleasant. At every angle were tall uncovered windows, and thick, creamy light poured everywhere, creating shadows in one place, vanquishing them in another. Apart from our professional art course, Pratt housed a high school. I flinched when a loud bell clanged and froze as doors opened and adolescent boys and girls rushed about with a confidence that took my breath away. My heart pounded, and I stood where I was, a solitary rock in the stream of students. At a second, shorter jangle of the bell, the hallway emptied; silence, punctuated only by the slam of a faraway door, returned.

I consulted the letter that had come to Maman only days before: "Dear Mrs. Pelton, We were sorry to hear of Agnes's illness.

Afternoon Program classes have begun, but she may report to the Registrar on Monday, October 22, at one o'clock in the afternoon." To my relief, the office was clearly labeled in black letters on cloudy bubbled glass, and I ventured forward. Inside, a brisk woman behind a desk inscribed my name in her book, and I was officially enrolled. She handed me a card with my schedule written on it, and with a brief smile pointed me toward the stairs and the art rooms on the top floor.

My first class was Composition with Mr. Arthur Wesley Dow, and at just a few minutes past one, I found the studio-classroom. Mr. Dow had not yet appeared, and the room was full of noise and chatter. I shrank into the doorjamb until another student waved at me and pointed to an empty place next to her.

"Are you Agnes?" she said. "I'm Jane. You're to sit here." She pointed to a pair of what looked like dinner party place cards. As her last name was Peterson, she was assigned the right side of our table, and I was on the left. I brimmed with sudden happiness: here was my place.

Jane and I were plainly the youngest of this group. Most of our classmates were in their late teens or were young women who intended to teach art. There were also a few young men, looking serious in their stiff collars and neckties. Promptly at one thirty, according to the large clock up front, one of the girls who had lingered in the hall flung herself into the classroom and hissed, "Here he comes! Here comes 'Pa' Dow!" Everyone giggled and then hushed and busied themselves with arranging things on their desks. I alone turned toward the door, which opened almost at once, so that when our teacher entered, he looked directly into my face.

"Ah! Miss Pelton, I presume?" There were titters, and I felt color flood my cheeks. I managed to nod before averting my eyes.

"We've been expecting you," he said, quelling the amusement around him with a pointed glance. "You've not missed much." My ears roared, and I squirmed a bit until the class quieted. Mr. Dow strolled to the front of the room carrying a stack of large-format books. These he placed on a podium next to what was clearly his desk. He was not especially imposing, but he was younger than I had imagined. His beard was well trimmed and came to a natural point, like one of my sable brushes, and he wore a tweed suit with a vest and a gold watch chain that looped from one small pocket in the vest to the other. What was so funny about him, I wondered, and why did they call him Pa? He picked up a thick piece of chalk and turned to write on the blackboard behind him: LINE, NOTAN, COLOR. When he was finished, he brushed his hands off lightly and pointed to the words.

"These, ladies and gentlemen—" Some of the students giggled, but at his steady gaze settled down.

"These," he repeated, "are the elements of form and design, the very foundations of art. Can anyone tell me what *notan* is?"

He paused.

"No? I'm not surprised. I didn't know what it was either, for many years. It is not a word we find in our Western art practices. *Notan* is a Japanese word, and it means dark-light. Light-dark."

He took a piece of heavy white paper that had been lying on the front desk and turned it so that we could see the image on the other side. It was a black-and-white block print of a cat sitting next to a vase that held two tulips. The details in the figures were minimal—a few angled lines giving shape to the vase, briefly suggested eyes and whiskers on the cat. The cat itself was round and stylized, its ears almost touching the top of the page. The tulips were nearly as tall as the cat, and the black was stark against the white background.

"*Notan*," he said again, tapping on the image. "A difficult word to translate. It means 'light-dark' as I said, but in point of fact it describes the weight of the dark against the light, and, crucially, the amount of light that can prevail alongside the dark." He looked about the room, willing each and every one of us to understand what he was saying.

"*Notan* beauty," he went on, "is the harmony that is achieved by correctly arranging dark and light spaces."

His smile turned his face bright against his soft dark beard, and I was transfixed. At home we knew all about the weight of the dark; now I had hope that the light in Mr. Dow's classroom might be strong enough to challenge it.

Mr. Dow was handsome and kind. He walked about the room, hands clasped behind him, and stopped to correct our work, bending forward a bit as if to soften the criticism, even though his words were never harsh. He addressed us as "Miss" and "Mister," which still made some of the girls titter behind their hands. He did this, he explained, because he was training us to be teachers, and it was important that we always be aware of our position and authority relative to our pupils. Of course, we had no pupils yet, he said, but formality had the effect of reminding us of the responsibilities that lay ahead.

He lectured at the beginning of each class, setting out again and again the principles of *notan*, of framing, of composition. Some of my classmates stared out the window, bored with the repetition. But once we began the exercise he had given us to demonstrate the lesson, it was apparent that they had not heard it enough. We settled in to work then; the room grew quiet, and the only sounds were the hush of charcoal sweeping across paper and Mr. Dow's footsteps as he passed among us, murmuring small encouragements all the while: "Very nice, Miss Welman" and "Bring the shape to the outer edge of the paper, Mr. Bennett."

Mr. Dow made me think of a dove. Maevis Akerman told me the reason they called him "Pa" and made fun of him was that he was too nice, too soft. I didn't care if he was. Especially when he stopped at my desk: "Let's see what you're up to today, Miss Pelton." He would study my work as carefully as if it were in a museum, which made some heads turn.

I wasn't sure if the others were angry or jealous or contemptu-ous, but I had become the teacher's pet, a label I heard whispered just loud enough for me to make it out. I pretended that I didn't care, and I didn't, not really. It would have been nice to make friends, as Maman had said I would, but nothing could compare with the gratification of Mr. Dow's admiration.

I heard that he had a family—a wife and three children—and I fell into daydreaming about him returning home each day from teaching. I pictured his house—not unlike ours—and imagined Mrs. Dow: beautiful, of course, with long golden hair. I imagined the children holding up their arms to be lifted into his embrace, one by one, and calling out, "Papa! Papa! Papa!"

I told my grandmother about being called the teacher's pet, and she said, "Don't boast, Agnes, and they'll come around in time."

"I don't boast, Grandmama," I protested.

"And don't boast about not boasting," which silenced me.

But she was right about time and its capacity for smoothing out conflict. One of the loudest "whisperers," as I thought of them, suddenly reversed herself and made it a point to admire one of my class exercises. Others followed suit, and I began to make friends. Jane Peterson was moved to another studio table, and I was paired with an Irish girl by the unlikely name of Molly Malone. During our midafternoon recess, we fell into the pleasant habit of taking short strolls around the perimeter of the campus, during which she hooked her arm casually through mine, giving the occasional squeeze for emphasis. This filled me with pleasure even as I won-dered about the propriety of such familiarity. Molly seemed unaware of my discomfort, and I understood that such gestures were entirely natural to her and the other girls. We talked about our work, and Molly talked about her life and her home with such ease it took my breath away.

"You're so good at this, Agnes," she'd sigh, the "r" rolling roughly off her tongue. "You're *talented*. I'm not really an artist," she continued, "but my mam is determined I'll be a teacher, and"—she released peals of laughter—"I can't keep facts in my head to save my life, so it better be art that I teach!"

"I don't want to teach," I said, realizing that it was true. I had never voiced a private thought to anyone outside my home, but Molly thought nothing of it.

"You don't have to teach," she sighed. "You'll be an artist." I felt a thrill like a shiver, and once again heard my grandmother's "Don't boast." I said nothing in reply to Molly, but she was already pointing at one of the older boys, a class ahead of ours, calling him handsome and wondering if he had someone special.

PRINCIPLES OF COMPOSITION

III.—WAYS OF CREATING HARMONY

Fine art, by its very name, implies fine relations. Art study is the attempt to perceive and to create fine relations of line, mass, and color. This is done by original effort stimulated by the influence of good examples.

As fine relations (that is, harmony, beauty) can be understood only through the appreciations, the whole fabric of art education should be based upon a training in appreciation. This power cannot be imparted like information. Artistic skill cannot be given by dictation or acquired by reading. It does not come by merely learning to draw, by imitating nature, or by any process of storing the mind with facts.

The power is within—the question is how to reach it and use it.

Arthur Wesley Dow, *Composition*

BROOKLYN, NEW YORK

1897

PRATT CONSUMED MY EVERY WAKING moment. When I wasn't actually at school, or hurrying to get there, or reliving another beautiful day as I strolled home, I was in our back sunroom, which Maman had given me to use as a studio. There I worked diligently, arranging lights and darks to form designs, learning the proper composition of any work of art. I barely made it to the table in time for meals, and as soon as I had eaten and been excused, I was back at it.

My grandmother, who was nearly blind by now, did not approve.

"You're spoiling her, Florence," she'd say as I scampered off.

To me she said sternly, "Are you saying your prayers?"

I pretended not to hear her and ducked out, but no matter how quietly I moved, she could tell I had left.

"You must be watchful and not fall into sin," she called to my back. "'For, I, the Lord thy God, am a jealous God. Thou shalt have no other Gods before me!'"

I was not reading my Bible. She had given me my own copy when I turned ten, and until starting Pratt, I had dutifully sat with her while together we read, in alternating verses, the stories of her dark and angry God, and the bloody anguish of her Savior. I wanted no more of it. I wanted light and inspiration, and Pratt was teaching me that I could have both.

One morning I did not hear my grandmother get up. I would never enter her room unbidden, so I called upstairs to Maman. When she came down, we opened the door to my grandmother's room and found her lying on the floor, her cloudy eyes open wide and fixed with fright, her mouth working but unable to speak. We put a pillow under her head and covered her with a blanket, and I was sent to get help. I ran as fast as I could go. Our doctor's office was on the ground level of his house, but it was too early for him to be there, so when I arrived, I did the unthinkable. I ran up the stairs to the residence and banged my fists hard against the glass door. It took a minute, but his wife came to the door and let me in.

"It's Grandmama," I panted. I burst into tears, and Dr. Day appeared, his breakfast napkin still tucked into his waistcoat.

"I'm coming," was all he said.

His handyman harnessed his horse to the light buggy and brought it around to the front, and we climbed in and flew back to 1403 Pacific Street.

Dr. Day was a large man, and his bulk filled our front door-way and then the door to Grandmama's bedroom. You could tell, then, how serious this really was, to have the doctor coming upstairs before finding out if my grandmother was properly covered. He towered over her as she lay on the floor, and then he dropped to one knee and took her wrist to take a pulse, pulling out his large, moonfaced gold watch. I could see the second hand as it made its jerky way around elegant Roman numerals once, twice, before the watch was slipped back into his waistcoat pocket. He pulled a stethoscope from his black bag and listened to her heart, her lungs, her back. I knew he would know what to do and how to make her better. I waited for him to stroke her forehead with his palm, as he had often done for me, certain that this would comfort her body into losing its terrible rigidity.

He put the stethoscope away and stood up stiffly. He seemed to be thinking intently, and we certainly did not wish to interrupt. The only sound in the room was our breathing—Maman's light and shallow like a bird's, the doctor's, with its little whistle through his large nose, Grandmama's almost panting. I could not hear my own. "She's had a stroke," he said finally. "Let's get her into her bed." I knew the word "stroke," and while I didn't know exactly what it meant, I could see that even Dr. Day was powerless in the face of its might. Had God cut her down with a stroke of his sword? If so, then there really was no hope for me, who had been selfish and who had also fibbed about reading my Bible. But Grandmama was never selfish, and she had read her Bible faithfully, every day of her life since her deliverance, until her eyesight abandoned her.

The doctor directed us how to place our hands, and at his signal we tucked them beneath her, lifted together, and barely managed to get her into bed. Her milky eyes closed and then opened again and seemed to peer about the room. Was she wondering what had happened? How she had come to this? I was trembling with fear and grief, overcome with remorse at how I had been neglecting her. She seemed to look directly at me. "Vanity," her sightless eyes seemed to accuse, and I poured out my deep remorse in a silent answer: Forgive me.

We could do nothing but wait. The doctor said that she might improve and that she might not. Maman asked me to make a notice to tack to the front door telling her students that the Pelton School of Music was temporarily closed due to illness. Relieved to finally have something to do to help, I dashed downstairs to my sunroom-studio and sorted through all my paper. When I was satisfied that I had found the whitest, I printed the message in black block letters—thick, so that the balance between dark and light would be correct. I used a thick pen nib and then a small brush to make the letters larger. It took me nearly an hour, but when I was through, I felt calmer. As I worked, I tried to think of how I could comfort my grandmother. I decided I would read to her from the Bible—softly, so she wouldn't be frightened or think there was any special import to it. I promised myself that if she recovered, I would read to her every day.

The image of her face as she looked up at me from the floor remained vivid after I closed my eyes and hovered like a shadow when I opened them. No amount of making art could dislodge it for long. I dreamed she and I were talking, and when I woke in the morning, I rushed to her side to see if she had recovered. My mother was in the chair by her side, as she had been all night. Grandmama was sleeping, her breath light and fitful. She woke then and saw me. Her face was impassive and stiff on the right side, but her eyes seemed to search out Maman and me. I felt she was trying to tell me something I needed to hear. Was she getting closer to heaven and able, like an angel, to see inside my heart and examine my soul? I wanted to ask her when she closed her eyes again.

Dr. Day came and explained that she was now in a coma, and he could do nothing more. He said he'd be back later but told us to summon him at once if she worsened. As she slipped further from us, Maman began to wilt. I ran downstairs to the kitchen to make her some tea and toast. She sipped the tea but left the toast on the plate, and I finally took it away. When I came back, Maman was kneeling beside the bed, weeping, grasping Grandmama's two hands in her two hands, and her head was bowed low. Softly she crooned, "Mama, Mama, Mama," which frightened me. I looked closely at my grandmother and realized she was not breathing. I instinctively jerked backward a step and started to cry. I thought of my father's death and the way my mother had wailed in grief before she managed to control it, for my sake I now knew, but here she was helpless.

———————

For a long time after my grandmother's death, we did nothing to change the house. She had been taken from us so abruptly that it felt as if she had simply gone to the shops or to her prayer meeting and would be terribly upset when she returned to see the black drapes pulled down and her things packed away. This wasn't by decision; Maman and I simply never talked about it. We continued to dwell in Grandmama's presence, aware of her aura infusing the house like the musky scent of talcum.

I dreamed about her often, waking with a troubling sense of her presence, while the dream itself would evaporate almost instantly. This happened over and over and made it seem as though we had been conversing intently over—what? The weather? The days were growing longer, and she and I had always marked the coming of spring, solemnly gazing out the front window, which faced west, and noting the angle of the sun, the trees growing supple and green, their leaves budding on the ends of branches. Or maybe I'd been telling her about my day at school. It had been our practice to have tea after I returned each afternoon, and while most days the conversation was of the most ordinary sort, in my dream state I felt we had talked intently about many things.

I longed for her. One dream stayed vividly alive: we were together in an empty white room, Grandmama seated on a plain chair, me opposite her on another one just like it, so close our knees practically touched. I leaned into her as she bent toward me. It was clear that I was visiting her in some kind of neutral setting, and I knew I could not reach for her nor could she touch me. Still, I was overjoyed to see her, and I said, "I miss you so," and she smiled.

———————————

We left her room intact: the worn Oriental rug next to the narrow bed, the dresser against the wall, her small armchair by the window, and on the wall behind her bed, a pair of lightly tinted etchings of two children, a boy and a girl, their eyes piously turned upward, their hands clasped in prayer. Grandmama's silver hairbrush and mirror rested at their usual angle on the scarf atop her bureau, along with a sewing box and small tortoiseshell case in which she kept thimbles and buttons—notions, she had called them. Her small bedside table held a Bible, a book of inspirational sayings, and a fresh handkerchief.

Occasionally Maman quietly removed the white lace doily and dresser scarf and washed them, and she polished the wood surfaces and wiped the dust from the framed photographs of me, herself, my aunt Alice, and my cousin Laura. In the closet, my grandmother's black dresses hung in a line like sentinels. The lavender sachets still tucked among the intimates in her drawers exuded traces of perfume that hung lightly in the air. I often came into her room and sat quietly, astonished that she could have vanished so completely while her possessions carried on.

In the days following her burial, the newspapers screeched like magpies about the "Beecher scandal" and we lay low. Then they found someone else to harass, and once again we were blessedly anonymous.

BROOKLYN, NEW YORK

1909

MY TIME AT PRATT ENDED in 1900 with a triumphal graduation, and the following year, Maman was thrilled when Mr. Dow invited me to teach in his Summer School of Art in Ipswich, just north of Boston. Aside from a few male art students, the classes were composed mostly of women whose families were escaping the heat of the city and who wanted a cultural activity to distract them. Mr. Dow's grand plan was to broadcast his gospel of modern composition far and wide to those who would teach art and those who would practice it—he saw me as belonging to both these groups—and to those whose practical talents fell short but who could be taught to appreciate it. To Mr. Dow, appreciation was far from a small thing: it was the essence of art.

"Now, ladies and gentlemen," he'd say as he paced around and around the classroom. "Fine art—the study of fine art—is found in the *appreciation* of fine relations between line, mass, and color. And what do I mean by 'fine relations'?" Invariably an eager young man would wave his hand to answer. Mr. Dow, also invariably, would ignore him and continue: "I mean harmony and beauty, which can only be grasped through appreciation."

I was as enthusiastic as he about this revolution in composition, but in Ipswich that summer I felt entirely out of place as a teacher. I was twenty and appeared no older than sixteen, and my students were middle-aged matrons who wanted neither my suggestions nor the information I could impart. One dowager actually laughed when I tried to instruct her. "My dear," she said, "you cannot possibly be old enough to be teaching!" I drew myself up, mustered as much dignity as possible, and told her firmly, "I will be twenty-one in two months' time," at which she chortled along with the others who were unabashedly listening. After that, I did what I could, supervised the classes to which I was assigned but firmly and finally abandoned the idea of supporting myself by teaching art. My pupils and I gritted our teeth and managed to be civil to one another, but as a group they sulked through classes, glowering at me and their own tentative efforts until Mr. Dow came by for his daily visit. Then their heads popped up, their faces lifted, and they basked in his presence, like flowers receiving the sun.

I returned to Brooklyn in September, disappointed and discouraged, and with the happy years at Pratt behind me, quickly sank into a deep melancholy. You could say that I retreated, becoming less and less able to make art. An inner voice, harsh and severe—a murderer with an axe—told me that all that was finished, and now I needed to attend to "real life." Where it came from, I will never know. It wasn't my mother's, and it wasn't my grandmother's. But it was powerful enough to make me put art aside—for years, I must admit—to stay close to home and put my time and efforts into helping my mother with the music school.

Perhaps coincidentally, I formed an attachment to one of her pupils, a young woman called Gertrude whom I barely knew. How could this happen, you might well ask. I can't say; it seemed to have nothing at all to do with me. I had been working in Grandmama's parlor, which we were using as an office, going through the ledger and writing notes to those who owed money. Maman was expecting Gertrude and came in to inquire if I'd had any word from her. I said I had not.

"That's not like her," Maman replied. She returned to the piano studio and closed the sliding doors. After a moment I heard her begin to play a Chopin étude. Her touch was light, tender, and precise, and bloomed with subtle passion, and I almost felt that I was intruding on a private moment. I was struck as never before by how each note seemed to evoke a different color: the lower tones pulsed deep violet in my mind's eye, while the quick notes at the top range skipped back and forth above the chord, making a brilliant array of yellow and white. I was so caught up by this display that I didn't hear the front door open.

"Oh, no, I'm too late!"

Gertrude stood in the open doorway, framed by a rich blue October sky. She seemed uncertain and then stepped inside and shut the door carefully.

"My mother was just looking for you," I said. Gertrude flushed.

"I'll tell her you're here." I moved to open the sliding doors, but she reached out to stop me.

"Wait," she said, and we both stood still until the final note sounded and the reverberations fell like dying sparks.

"Thank you," she said. She turned, her hand resting lightly on my arm, and released a smile from, it seemed, her innermost self. "You don't know how often I beg her to play that."

Maman peered out.

"Ah, there you are," she said.

"I'm sorry to be late, Madame," Gertrude murmured and darted into the music room behind my mother. The light caught her honey-brown hair, and a faint aroma of lilac lingered. Astonished, I stepped into the space where she had just been and breathed it in.

I looked forward to her weekly lessons, and my spirits rose, anticipating her presence. I'd keep an eye out until I saw her, walking up the steps to our door. I was always surprised by how ordinary she looked; I had, of course, described her to myself as a rare beauty. Which I suppose she was, in certain light. My rush of joy remained connected to the moment when she had seemed to look deeply into my eyes. It was a feeling of having been recognized, and it had never happened to me before.

My energy increased, and gradually I felt the glimmerings of inspiration, so that instead of reading in my leisure time, I pulled out my art supplies. Tentatively at first, fearful of the axe-voice and afraid that overexertion—overexcitement, really—might bring on illness, I began to make drawings. When all stayed quiet and disaster did not encroach, I allowed myself to do more—pastels and then even paintings. Maman noticed and said, "Darling, it's so good to see you happy and working on your art again."

Those pleasant days, which I felt I could ride forever, came to an abrupt end shortly after the New Year, when Maman followed Gertrude out after her lesson.

"Goodbye, my dear," she was saying, and kissed her on both cheeks.

"Goodbye, Madame," Gertrude replied. "And thank you for all you've taught me."

What was this, I thought.

"Agnes," Maman turned to me. "Say goodbye to Gertrude. Her family is moving to Boston."

I tried to keep the shock from my face.

"Goodbye, Agnes," Gertrude said, and extended her hand. She had never before said my name, and I was reminded that we were not, in fact, friends. I took her hand, she shook mine lightly, let it go, and walked out of our house and our lives.

"Such a sweet girl. I will truly miss her," Maman sighed. "Why don't we get a cup of tea?" Then she saw my face and said, "Are you all right?"

"I'm a little tired," I said, struggling for control. I followed Maman into the kitchen and took the teapot from its shelf while she put on the kettle. She talked about Gertrude, how sorry she was to lose her as a student, how much she hoped such a talented young woman would continue her studies. I could do nothing but nod gravely in agreement.

"She'll very likely marry, have children, and that will be that," Maman sighed.

"Maybe not; not everyone does."

I won't, I thought. I will never marry.

"She will."

And good for her, I thought. She will be normal; I will not. I knew this to my toes, but I tried to carry on with life as usual. I rose early each morning to have breakfast ready for Maman when she came downstairs. I brought in the milk from the back steps, brewed a pot of strong tea, and cut thick slices of bacon to fry and bread for toasting. While I worked, I took myself sternly to task: You didn't even know her, I told myself. It is unnatural—unnatural—to miss someone with whom you have never even carried on a conversation. Was I unnatural? I had seen these women in downtown cafés, many of them dressed like men, swaggering and proud of their effect on the pretty women they had with them. Impossible, I thought immediately, relief flooding my chest. I would never be like that.

But grief quickly returned. What was happening to me? It was like a death without the body and without the mourners. It was worse than a death: no one could know of my loss, and I prayed that no one would discern my shame. The surrounding streets that only recently had been charming and alive now turned gray and solid. The very light was different. It flattened the world instead of illuminating it. Objects—breakfast plates, silverware, teacups— took on more weight, and gravity seemed to exert a stronger pull. As an artist, I knew this should interest me. But I grew feeble and feverish; my cough returned, and Maman, who looked increasingly worried, sent me to bed. I retreated into this soft sanctuary and fell into an exhausted sleep.

For weeks I lingered in this state. I slept all the time and never felt rested. I could not seem to touch the bottom of my intense fatigue, and my dreams were full of frantic struggles: trying to run from something that was chasing me but being barely able to move my legs, or swimming in an agitated ocean, far from shore and completely alone, knowing my mother was looking for me. I'd come awake suddenly, out of breath and weeping. I will die of this, I thought, and I will never understand what has killed me. When awake, I felt I was made of lead and sinking through quicksand. I kept a book near my bed so as to be able to open it and appear to be reading should Maman check on me, but I took in nothing.

The art impulse vanished as well. I knew I was a terrible burden to Maman, who was doing everything she could. Between pupils she brought me tea and beef consommé. She stroked my forehead to see if I was feverish. She put mustard plasters on my chest and dosed me with honey. I thought, I must get up, this is too much for Maman. But even when I succeeded in getting out of bed, I could not muster the strength to do more than cross the room to sit in my chair and stare out the window. Each day I willed myself to be free of Gertrude. I thought perhaps some demon spirit had taken hold, and I cried because my grandmother, the saintliest person I had ever known, was not there to protect me or rid me of it.

I wept over everything, even the few leaves remaining on the oak tree outside my window, curled into a papery brown and clinging here and there to the odd branch. I took up my small sketchbook and made meticulous drawings of their shrunken twisted shapes. When snow came and pulled down the last of them, I began to feel some relief, and I came downstairs. Maman was delighted.

"Why, darling! You're better!"

"I'm bored," I said pointedly, and we both smiled.

"At last you're bored." She pulled me close and gave me a long hug. "That is very good news."

It is a cliché that travel refreshes the spirit. In 1909 my mother suggested a year of study in Italy, for even though I was fully restored to health, I suffered from lack of inspiration and could not find a way forward. One day Maman pulled out some of my old drawings and brought them to the front parlor where I had been reading.

"Look," she said. She held up a large pad, and barely able to see over it, began to slowly turn the pages. These were my contour drawings—page after page of intricate, detailed, and confident flower studies. Then she held up the bright, chalky pastels I had made in Ipswich during my disastrous summer of teaching there; then the charcoal figure drawings of Pratt's clothed model—young ladies being far too delicate to confront the human form in the nude—along with studies of the model's head and hands. I remembered that I had planned a painting from these.

"These are good," she said. This pronouncement in itself was surprising. We didn't boast in our house, nor did we lavish much praise. We assumed that we were gifted people and that the gifts we'd been blessed with were exactly that and not for us to claim. But looking at these drawings that had so long been out of sight and out of my thoughts was a kind of revelation in itself. I could regard them impersonally, as though someone else had made them, and I could recognize for myself that they *were* good. Very good, in fact.

"You have a talent," she said. "It must not be allowed to languish and die."

I had been aware that many artists and writers were flocking to Europe—Paris, for the most part, and also to Italy. Maman had seen in the newspaper that one of them was Hamilton Easter Field, a fellow Brooklynite who had taught me painting for a brief time at Pratt and was now teaching in Rome. She had quickly seized on this idea and at frightening speed arranged for me to study life drawing with him at the British Academy there. And so it was done. A year of my life claimed and spoken for. I didn't need to say it, but I worried how I would manage and if all this effort—and money; Rome did not come cheaply—would be in vain. The very phrase nettled me: it would be my charge, therefore, to wrest art from poisonous vanity.

———————

It was late autumn when I sailed. The ship's horn let go a sharp, plaintive blast, and with a shudder we pulled away from the pier. Dozens of wheeling gulls make a final shrieking pass, and I clutched the rail and watched as the crowds below got smaller. Here and there waving arms dropped, and the white handkerchiefs they had been holding disappeared. The effect was as if dozens of candles were being snuffed out, one by one.

The crowd on board also began to disperse, but I kept my feet planted where I was, reluctant to lose sight of my homeland. I had hoped to avoid this feeling by coming alone to board the ship and depart, and my mother had allowed me to persuade her that I was quite well now and there was no need for her to make the trip to see me off.

"Very well," she had said in an uncharacteristically small voice. We were in the foyer waiting for my cab. My trunks had been delivered to the pier several days before, and all I had with me now was an overnight bag and a hatbox. I put these down to embrace her, and she took hold of the lapels of my velvet jacket with both hands and drew me close, as she had done when I was a sulky, rebellious girl. I waited for an admonition to be good, whatever that could mean, but instead she whispered, "I do think it would be hard."

Her eyes had welled suddenly, and she let go of me to cover her mouth and stop the tears.

"Dearest." I put my hands on her shoulders. I was shocked to realize that she had lost some height and was no longer taller than me. "It's just for a year."

"Just a year," she repeated. "That's right. And you are fine now, all put together again."

I gave both her cheeks quick kisses and she smiled.

"What a time you've had," she said.

"Thank you, Maman." I threw my arms around her and held her tightly.

The ship slipped down the river, and a raw, wintry drizzle fell on the several of us who remained at the rail. An elderly couple was the first to turn back into the cabin, then a young couple I thought must be on their honeymoon—they were sweetly affectionate and yet reserved with one another—then the others like me, who were solitary. When we cleared the Narrows and began to encounter open sea and a cold, stiff wind, I followed suit.

For someone with as temperamental a constitution as mine is, I have always been a good traveler. The second-class dining room was only half full that first night, no doubt in response to the thrusts and dips of the ship as we pushed out into the North Atlantic. The only other people at my table were an English couple on their way home from visiting relatives in Tarrytown. Mr. and Mrs. Prentiss-Smythe, from the place card. We exchanged thin smiles and assessed one another warily, keeping a hopeful eye on the three still-empty chairs. When it was clear that no one would be joining us, Mr. Prentiss-Smythe cleared his throat reluctantly and introduced himself. He plainly did not approve when I said I was by myself—what is it about women traveling and dining alone that makes people so uncomfortable? They did not care for America, he said. Terribly noisy, he said. His wife was a pinched little thing with papery skin who was apparently content to let her husband speak for her. Oh, I replied. And then we three gave close attention to the soup sloshing in our bowls and said nothing for the remainder of the meal. The second-class saloon was equally sparse and discouraging, and I made my way back to my cabin.

In truth, I had never traveled like this on my own. The sea was gray, and the ship was gray, and I worried anew that I would find it all too daunting. And how would I manage in Rome? I thought I might be joining a class already in session, and the idea sent me into a panic. Too, I would have to get settled before I could even present myself at the academy. I did have the name of a respectable pensione, but even what Maman and I supposed to be careful planning seemed foolhardy and doomed to failure. I tucked myself into my bunk bed and tried to sleep.

The weather remained inclement all the way across the Atlantic, even as we dipped south into warmer currents. The ship was heavily fitted with dark wood paneling, which, rather than lending an impression of great luxury, merely added to the gloom. Nor did I meet anyone I wanted to talk to. The steward found some heavy blankets for me and brought out a deck chair that he placed in a sheltered niche. I wrapped up and settled in, and spent my days gazing out at the sea, gray and black and capped with white.

I wrote letters home, most of which I tore up and discarded over the rail, the paper fluttering and spinning before being lost to the waves. The letters were full of loneliness and a rising despair that the trip would prove useless, that it was wasting money best used for other things. My talent, in which Maman believed so fervently, seemed as remote as the horizon.

Even so, the ship soothed me. Its motion held me suspended in one place while it carried me—and my life—forward. Bundled up in my overcoat, scarf, and hat, I walked the deck and let the salt air startle me awake. I was keenly aware that I was twenty-eight years old, and while I knew I appeared much younger, certain life paths seemed to have been set. I had no husband, no prospects for a husband, and, I reminded myself, no desire for one. From what I had observed, marriage was at best an uneasy dance in which the partners negotiated a distance that would eventually become permanent. Whatever happiness they managed to create was as fragile as the midocean sunlight blinking through the mid-Atlantic clouds.

ROME, ITALY

1910

Pensione Bellini, Rome
January 18, 1910

Dearest Maman,

The crossing was fine, not too stormy. I enjoyed myself, as I always seem to on board a ship. It's like a small city, moving forward inexorably. There's something about its containment—and the reassurance that the arrangement is temporary—that makes it easier to talk to strangers. For the first two nights, meals were sparsely attended, as I had expected. I don't know why it is that I have no difficulty at all in getting my sea legs—a small compensation for being laid low so often on land—but at least this time around I knew better than to wear my best dress the first night.

The pensione is delightful, commanded by the redoubtable Signora Bellini. Several other British Academy students are boarding here, and we all struggle a bit to obey the Signora's boisterous exhortations to

"Mangia! Mangia!" the daily feasts of pastas that come in all shapes and sizes. Breads, meats, salads—apologies, Maman, but never have I seen such a spread. If I'm not careful, I'll be big as a house by the time I get home.

———————

At the pensione, ours was a talkative group of mostly younger students from all over Europe—English, German, an Italian from Milano, and a handsome Dutchman that all the girls seemed to like. It turned out we would all be starting the spring session together, which was a great relief. I even made a friend of sorts, a lively British girl named Maude, who made a point of attaching herself to me, for what reason, I could not tell. She was lighthearted and full of affection and good humor until she began to talk about the need to come to the continent in order to be taken seriously as an artist, and not "just another woman who thinks she can paint," she said.

———————

Pensione Bellini, Rome
February 6, 1910

Dearest Maman,

Italy is pale and earthy and ancient, and teeming, it seems, with garrulous Americans. You hear English in the trattorias and museums and on the streets, punctuated now and then with Italian—basso voices thrumming, and high voices racing up and down an unwritten scale. But here in the pensione I am the only American, which is a relief. Signora Bellini is everywhere all the time, her considerable bulk moving through the house with surprising grace for so large a woman. She is very strict with linens—one clean sheet and towel per week, no exceptions—and very generous with food. Breakfast is the sparest meal—no one in Italy seems the least interested in eating before midday—just thick, strong coffee and biscotti which is always set out on the sideboard no matter how early I come downstairs. Lunch is a grand affair that starts with pasta every day, followed by meat or fish and some kind of green vegetable. Sometimes there's risotto, which my fellow guests approach with skepticism. Rice, says Miss Hensley, the Scottish woman who has a room near mine, "should be dry and fluffy" (only when she says "dry" it sounds more like "dray") "and certainly not mixed with cheese." Having ignored the English couple on the way over, I am completely at ease ignoring Miss Hensley, which she does not like.

––––––––––

At the British Academy, I joined the life drawing class. At first it was shocking to be in a figure drawing class with women *and* men, all of us making charcoal drawings of the same nude model. It certainly made a change from Brooklyn. So odd to see women behind easels set right next to those of the men, all of us staring dispassionately at the woman posing in the center. There was no talking, which suited me fine. Soon, along with everyone else in the room, I became entirely absorbed in the marvelous intricacies of the human form. It seemed a revelation to me the subtle ways that the human spirit could make itself evident within that form. A smooth curve of the model's back became a graceful arc that seemed to me an expression of strength. A face that might appear impassive on the model as she posed revealed implications of sadness, joy, and intelligence.

In a scene that uncannily recalled to me my first day at Pratt, the big studio doors broke open, and in strode Hamilton Easter Field, as handsome in his Bohemian way as I remembered—dark, mustachioed, and fired with passion. He did not lecture but began making his way around the cavernous room, greeting students he knew, introducing himself to those he hadn't yet met. All activity came to a stop, and even the model relaxed and pulled a robe around herself. Mr. Field was in no hurry; he paused to discuss each student's work in low tones, breaking into laughter here and there as he encountered an old friend.

I stood a bit stiffly. I might not have been the oldest student— one of the men had thinning gray hair—but I was likely the oldest of the women. Suddenly I felt exposed, thrust into view. From being one of the youngest at Pratt to this; I wondered how I could have permitted illness and despair to gain the upper hand such that years could go by without my really noticing.

I knew I was out of practice. I had a short, impromptu speech prepared about how hard I would work to catch up, but when Field found his way to where I was working, he held a hand up to silence me. He put all his attention on my drawing. I had laid my paper on a table rather than up on an easel—it is easier to control the line when it's flat—and he loomed over it. I was shocked at his size. I had not remembered that about him. From a distance he had not appeared imposing, but standing next to me he seemed to fill his space and my space and the space around us as well. Finally he raised his head— large, square, almost leonine—and pointed to the line of leg, which I had extended in one gesture from the ankle, past the knee, around the thigh and the buttock, letting it thicken slightly as it described the model's back. I felt certain he was about to criticize my effort as not refining the figure carefully enough and tried once more to explain that I was relearning drawing and trying to rediscover my line. Again, he waved my explanation away, and his face broke into a beatific smile.

"This—" he pointed to the line that worried me. "—is *lovely*."

I was flustered and surprised and could not help but return his smile.

"You look familiar. Have we met?"

"Years ago, Mr. Field. You taught me painting at Pratt."

"Ah, yes! A fellow Brooklynite! How is that sweet old place?"

"Just as you left it," I replied.

"And you are—?"

"Agnes Pelton."

"Now I remember. I believe that Arthur Dow wrote to me about you."

"Yes, I believe he very kindly did."

"Well, I am not disappointed, Miss Pelton, no indeed. I am not disappointed." He scanned the drawing once again, touched my arm briefly, and moved on to my neighbor.

Of course, I understood that my years of training had not been completely forgotten. In my heart, though, I feared that the listless efforts of the recent years along with my obsession for Gertrude (for that, I realized at last, was what it was) had consumed me so completely that nothing remained with which to make art. But my hands remembered. My hands remembered what they could do and what they were intended for. My life had a purpose beyond mere survival, and this purpose had been inscribed in my body. I rushed to the studio every day, where I filled sheet after sheet of plain newsprint. Several of us adjourned to a café after class with blank books, where we continued to draw, using each other as models and when possible, using the other patrons, too.

The blank book I had brought from home was quickly filled, and I set out for the art supply store near the Academy. In Rome, even shopping for a simple sketchbook can feel like an indulgence. Never had I seen so much beautiful paper in one place! There were pads of all sizes too, and I decided on one with a rougher-than-average texture. I chose four new pencils as well. To make sure I could see the texture of the paper, I walked to the front of the store where light streamed through a pair of large windows. This caused the clerk to watch me carefully. He was a small man with well-oiled and carefully sculpted black hair, but his forehead began to gleam with perspiration. His collar was too tight and caused his neck to bulge over it. He wore a bow tie and vest and jacket and clasped his hands, waiting for me to choose a sketchpad or try to run from the store without paying. Artists had an unsavory reputation here, it seemed.

I held up the open pad and tilted it so the light brushed the surface. There were tiny shadows all across the page, which made it look like a miniature desert landscape. I turned to the waiting clerk and smiled.

"This one," I said, and carefully counted out the heavy coins into his hand.

Back at the pensione I opened the book, and with one of my soft new pencils drew a quick line. The graphite brushed across the white page much as the sun had done in the shop. Immediately I took it downstairs and, seeing how bright the dining room was, drew everything on the table: the cut glass salt boat, the oil lamp in the center, the flowers in their porcelain vase, even the silverware, laid out and ready for our next meal.

I felt such a surge of happiness that I began to scribble. The lines seemed to come alive; they became threads I used to wrap around objects, creating little cocoons on the page. Soon nothing was just itself, everything was a series of curves and angles that my fingers, through my pencil, were able to touch and explore. The tiniest shoot on a flower stem was a proclamation of triumph, a celebration of the life force, which I also rejoiced to feel pulsing in me. My hands, which had always had a remarkable capacity to reproduce on paper what my eyes were seeing, now offered me a way to connect to the world.

———————

Pensione Bellini
February 22, 1910

Dearest Maman,

Thank you for the packet, which arrived yesterday, you will be happy to know. No one but you would think to mark one's half-birthday, and it made me laugh. But I did need handkerchiefs, and the sachets are lovely. I didn't open the parcel in front of any of the other boarders or even Signora Bellini as I do feel self-conscious. At age twenty-nine and a half I am sure that I am the oldest among the students here. Stuff and nonsense, you will say, I can hear you now, but I am not able to shake it.

Several of the boys from the Academy have moved out, preferring to rent their own flat. It changes the atmosphere here a great deal. I thought I would not mind their leaving at all, but it's left me feeling a bit bereft. Maybe I'm just feeling blue today, missing you and home. But never fear, darling Maman, it will pass, and I shall be right as rain in no time.

————————

As Rome began to warm up, Field seemed to conjure a heat of his own. He was a force of nature when it came to teaching art, striding about the studio delivering ad hoc lectures on everything from Renaissance flower paintings to sculpture and Italian marble. One day it was the state of art education: "Art schools are anathema to the making of art!" he shouted. "Every child has in him a naturally occurring artistic bent. Some of you, those of a practical nature, are realists." He glanced at Friedrich, one of the Germans, who always named a problem straight on and then enumerated the steps to solving it. "Some of you"—he smiled at Guinevere,

from London—"who are devoted to order above all else, are clas-
sicists. And some of you—" To my embarrassment and not a little
pleasure, he looked directly at me. He continued. "Some of you,
who are of a poetic temperament and seek beauty above all else,
are romanticists. But then—" He paused dramatically. His face
began to glow, and I could see tiny beads of perspiration beginning
to form on his forehead. "Then," he went on, his voice more of a
growl, "the art school steps in and *trains* you. Like a vintner who
takes a branch of a vine that wants to go one way and bends it
until it goes another. But we are not branches! And when we are
trained against the design of our own natures, we lose not only
our joy, we lose our unique way of seeing. We lose our spark. We
lose our gift."

By now everyone had stopped painting to listen. Mr. Field was
in the center of the room, the burning sun to our orbiting planets.
He held himself motionless, and his voice dropped to nearly a whisper. "Moreover, dear friends, in countries where practical people
are in the majority—in America, for example; in Germany to a
lesser degree—they dominate the others, and the damage to art is
devastating. Students come out of school as imitators and realists."
He drew in a deep breath, his chest swelled, and he extended his
arms in a sort of appeal.

"You can see how wrong this is," his voice gathering strength.
"The art teacher ought to be like a gardener who tends each plant
and helps it produce that which it was created to produce. You can
appreciate the subtlety here, the difficulty of this." He resumed his
stroll about the studio.

"It is, I'm afraid, Utopian to expect a professor of art to pos-
sess the skills of a horticulturist. We are more like butchers, and
the schools in which we teach more like sausage machines: many
different elements go in"—he pointed to each of us in turn—"but
what comes out is—sausage." At that, apparently discouraged to
the point of exhaustion, he turned and left the studio.

No one moved for several minutes. Then Aalbert, the handsome Dutch boy I'd met at the pensione, began packing up his paints. He loosely draped his canvas-in-progress, put on his jacket, and announced, "The mention of sausage makes me hungry. Who wants to find some to eat?" Everyone laughed then, and several of the others put their paints away and followed him out the door. Maude and I looked at each other. "When in Rome." She shrugged and grabbed her wrap. "Come along, Agnes." Her giggle was merry, and I finally followed suit.

We found Aalbert at a trattoria near the Academy, holding forth at a large table and surrounded by the students, all of them male, who had followed him from the studio. Maude and I peeked in and watched him declaiming and gesturing broadly.

"Full of himself, that one is," Maude said. We were about to leave when he caught sight of us.

"Ah! There you are!" he shouted. Next to me Maude had brightened and was waving. I turned to go, and she grabbed my arm. "No!" she hissed. "You're not leaving me here." Reluctantly I let her pull me into the crowded café. Someone, the Italian boy, I think, found two small rickety chairs and pulled them up to the table. The others—Friedrich, Gunther, Alonzo, Jacob, Pieter, and Zachary—made room somehow, and there we were. Our arrival had obviously interrupted a lively debate, and all eyes were on us. A waiter scooted over.

"Caffe?" he said.

"No, grazie," I started to say, but Maude inserted herself and smiled at him. "Si!" she beamed. "Du-ay caffes," she said in her deliberate Italian, her British accent ringing through it like a bell. I wondered how soon I'd be able to break away.

"Well," Pieter, one of the Germans, said, "let's ask them: what do you think of the nonsense Field was spouting?" Maude, suddenly shy, mutely turned to me and waited.

"If you're asking me," I said finally, fixing my gaze on Maude with all the disapproval I could muster. Her eyes registered not the slightest trace of concern; instead they fluttered with earnest and helpless ignorance. I gave up and looked at the faces trained my way. Some were open and interested—like Aalbert, for instance—and others seemed to be waiting for me to demonstrate my womanly inferiority.

"If you're asking me," I repeated, "I would not call it nonsense at all. Perhaps you who think of Mr. Field's philosophy as nonsense were not so fortunate, as I was, to attend a truly progressive school of art. That is not your fault, but I should point out that your contempt actually proves him right."

There was a stunned silence. Maude's jaw had dropped. I had to check to see if mine had not dropped as well: I was as shocked by the boldness of my words as they. It was Aalbert who broke the spell.

"Brava, Agnes!" His voice seemed to boom out over the café. He looked delighted with me. "There, you see?" he said to the other men. "You have been positioned in your places." I had to smile at his twisting of an English phrase, and Maude laughed outright. Aalbert, of course, assumed that we were happy to have been so staunchly—and idiomatically—defended. In fact, we *were* pleased. Maude chattered away about it all the way back to the pensione. She linked her arm with mine, as if it was the most natural thing possible. I suffered a twinge of panic but steadied myself and did not pull away. Instead I took stock of this new self, wondering if life could really be so simple.

––––––––

Pensione Bellini, Rome
March 6, 1910

Dearest Maman,

You will be glad to know I have now eaten every type of pastry Rome has to offer. My friends Maude and Aalbert and I went in search of a delicious bit called Bigne di S. Giuseppe, or cake for St. Joseph's day. It's usually only available on the actual day, but we found it fairly near the Academy and stuffed ourselves to the point of unseemliness before staggering back to the pensione for supper. Maude I've mentioned, but Aalbert is Dutch and very handsome. All the girls flutter about him and maybe because I don't, he seeks me out and we have lovely walks and talks. Hamilton Field is astonishing. He has more energy than anyone I've ever known, and his generosity as a teacher seems boundless. I am learning a great, great deal and will bring home much work to show you.

Early one foggy morning, as we three were huddled over steaming cups of caffe con latte, Aalbert said that he had been invited to Florence. Did we want to go? Maude said we certainly did, but I, ever the responsible adult, asked had we been invited, meaning all three of us, and if so, by whom, and if we were to accept, when would we go and where would we stay? I expected his face to fall at, for me, the unusual barrage of questions, and that, blushing, he'd admit he had no idea. Aalbert was like that. Two of the things Maude and I had privately agreed we loved about him were, he leapt into the unknown with an open and full heart, and he blushed at the slightest jab. But this time he did neither. It was already arranged, he said.

"Field is going, and Sterne and Laurent." Maurice Sterne was a painter friend of Mr. Field's, and Robert Laurent was Field's protégé. Robert Laurent was about twenty. Mr. Field had encountered him as a young boy in a Breton coastal town, now an art colony, where he was living with his parents and helping his father on their small fishing boat. He had apparently observed Field painting there and had rather furtively, Field thought, brought some drawings to show him. They indicated an impressive and precocious talent, and Field went at once to his parents to inquire what plans they had made for their gifted son's proper training. The Laurents were dumbfounded, first at what their son had produced, unbeknownst to them, in the way of art, and then at what this exotic stranger said: Robert had a gift, Field said, and should be permitted to study art—not, as he put it, to risk life and limb out on the water. "Anyone," he had told them, "can catch fish. But very few can capture the attitude of the fishermen mending their nets, or the sea when it's angry."

From that day, Laurent accompanied Field on his painting excursions. When autumn arrived and he returned to Brooklyn, Field persuaded the Laurents to let the boy accompany him.

By now Robert was a sunny and happy young man, who, for all practical purposes, was Mr. Field's adopted son. There was talk of impropriety between them, but I saw no hint of it.

"Oh, do come," Aalbert said. "It will be the chance of a lifetime."

I did badly want to go. We had all been reading about the Renaissance painters, and to see these pictures and altarpieces in their sacred settings, where they had moved and inspired people for hundreds of years, was a necessity at this point. Why come to Italy and not see Florence? I started thinking of how I could afford this. Aalbert seemed to read my mind.

"It's the Dodge villa," he explained.

Everyone in the Roman art world knew (or knew of) the Dodges. Edwin Dodge was said to be wealthy and idle. Some years ago, with his wife Mabel, he had joined the ever-growing wave of American artists, writers, and aficionados, and come to Italy to escape the rigid provincialism at home and to breathe the air of the Renaissance.

"She was a widow," Maude said, "with a child, and they say that Edwin Dodge courted her relentlessly. *Relentlessly*," she repeated, jabbing her finger into the café table. "She refused him over and over. Can you imagine?" She turned to me. "If I had a rich man begging me to marry him like that, even if he was ugly as a toad, I'd say yes. Wouldn't you, Agnes?"

Before I could say anything, she answered her own question.

"Well, perhaps not you. But I'm nowhere near as high-minded as you. You know how he got her to agree?"

I glanced at Aalbert and we both demurred. I was about to suggest that she didn't know either, not really, that gossip didn't count as information, but she was too eager. "Why, he *seduced* her. She fainted in his private railway car, and he seduced her then and there. And later, I heard, he promised he would buy her a villa and let her furnish and decorate it as she wished, and she finally gave in. And he was as good as his word." At that she sat back, flushed with triumph.

"There are so many rooms," Aalbert went on, "they'll never even notice."

I was by no means sure of that, but I bought my second-class ticket all the same, and two days later the three of us boarded the train.

VILLA CURONIA

APRIL 1910

ITALY EXUDES A GENEROSITY THAT is entirely foreign to New York. It seemed to me that everywhere I went in Italy was suffused with the rich and ancient bouquet of vineyards, at once pungent and sweet, and the yeasty smell of rising bread. The air was always soft on my skin and the cobblestone streets difficult to negotiate, but even hauling a travel case over the uneven surfaces we marveled at the boxes of flowers at every window, stuccoed walls where the occasional mosaic (undoubtedly put there by the ancient Romans) was still bright and colorful.

The Dodges' Villa Curonia was in Arcetri, which was south of Florence. This, Aalbert told us, was where Galileo had worked and died and was buried. We hired a pony cart at the Florence railroad station and enjoyed the quiet clomp of hooves against the ancient stones as we made our way into the hills. We left the grassy plain and began to wind through the jagged tufa, clumps of olive trees, and brush, until we came upon a stand of magnificent cypress trees, standing tall like sentinels and ringed by May roses, which, despite the name, we would learn, bloomed all year long—as if by order of la Grande Signora of the house we could now see in the distance.

The three of us were uncharacteristically subdued as we pulled up in front. All was utterly quiet, with no signs of life or the reputedly generous hosts.

"I'll see about this," Aalbert said. He jumped down and strode up to the front door with a swagger I knew was covering his discomfort. He lifted the huge brass doorknocker—the head of a lion—and it banged sharply against its plate. After a minute or two a servant opened the door. Aalbert spoke to him, pointing to Maude and me in the cart. The servant said something and closed the door firmly in his face. Crestfallen, Aalbert returned to the cart.

"Well, I said we were with Hamilton Field, and he said, 'Non a casa.' I can't imagine what could have happened."

"You mean Field isn't here? What about Laurent or Sterne? Maybe the footman doesn't know Field's name," Maude said. It was hot sitting in the full sun. Reluctantly Aalbert went back to the house. The servant opened more quickly this time, listened attentively, and, a bit more gently, closed the door again.

"It's no use, I'm afraid," Aalbert said. "The fellow just keeps saying, 'Non a casa.'"

"What shall we do?" Maude asked.

Aalbert affected an air of nonchalance. "We are in Florence, after all. Let's look around and come back later."

"What, and be humiliated again?" Maude said. "How on earth did this happen? What made you think Field was here?"

Aalbert, his face nearly purple, looked miserable. "Well, he said . . ." His voice faltered. Actually, it was very like Mr. Field to burst out with an idea and then let it evaporate while he chased the next one. I tried to remember how many of Italy's beautiful lira I had tucked into my bag and whether I could afford a hotel for the night. For the first time since arriving in Europe, I felt a cold knot of fear and wished I were back home in the sleepy safety of Brooklyn and 1403 Pacific Street.

"We should get something to eat," I heard myself say. I was

about to tell the driver to take us back to the city when the villa's great front door swung open again. A small woman with dark hair twirled in buns over her ears, one on each side, and dressed in a flowing, lightly brocaded gown called out, "Halloo?" Her American accent was unmistakable, even though it was clear she was trying to sound anything but American. Maude and Aalbert sat uncharacteristically frozen. Apparently, my taking the initiative to suggest a meal had put me in charge for the moment. Before I could panic, I called out my own hello.

"We don't mean to disturb you. We were looking for our teacher. We thought he was a guest here. Hamilton Field?"

"Oh, yes! But he's not here right now. Why don't you come in and we'll find you some refreshment."

Hot and grimy from the trip, we followed her meekly into the house. It was clear to me, at least, that she had not expected us and was entirely unprepared for an additional three guests. I tried to think what we should do—go to a hotel? Go back to the station and return to Rome on the first train? But if I was preoccupied with this quandary, neither Aalbert nor Maude seemed to think anything of it at all. We were left in the main drawing room while our hostess went in search of a servant who could bring us something cold to drink. Evening was coming on hard now, and the other house guests began to emerge from their rooms, or the cool dark library, or the shady parts of the garden. My anxiety grew nearly unbearable as, faced with the sight of beautiful women in beautiful gowns, I became distinctly aware that I had not brought the right clothing. I was also fairly certain that my two companions had not either.

"We are art students, Agnes." Aalbert shrugged. Art students or not, the enormous social gap between us and the other guests was indisputable. Mrs. Dodge reappeared in the doorway.

"We are a little crowded this week," she said. "I hope you two don't mind sharing a room." This to me and Maude as our hostess waved at us to follow and set off down the long gallery. We hurried past an astonishing collection of portraits, landscapes, and tapestries before being ushered into a lavishly appointed room with a bed and a sleeping couch and French doors that opened onto the garden. I drew my breath in sharply, which seemed to please Mrs. Dodge. It was the most beautiful room I'd ever seen. The walls were a creamy white, the better to show off the paintings hanging on them. A portrait of a young woman looking out coyly while holding a book stopped me in my tracks. The depth of the blue in her dress, the delicacy of her features, the exquisite detail of her sleeve were mesmerizing; I felt I could be with that painting and never want for anything else ever again. A sculpted relief of horses and charioteers cast in polished brass caught the later afternoon light and sent it across the room to an enormous porcelain vase standing by the door like a sentry. Maude seemed to have shrunk a little, but she straightened her shoulders and said, "This is all so beautiful."

"Yes," our hostess agreed. I noticed that I was already thinking of her as "Mabel," that I had already claimed her as a friend, which, in that moment, struck me as unlikely to the point of absurdity. I put it down to the atmosphere of the place: extravagantly elegant, like one of the Florentine palaces, and yet alive in a way that was impossible for any of those fixed-in-time museums. Of course, I told myself, people actually lived here. But it was more than that; the Dodges were driven, it seemed, by a frank curiosity and an eagerness to know something beyond themselves, and this broadness of outlook took pride of place over all the treasures that had been so carefully collected in this house.

"This is my work of art," she said.

"It is magnificent," I said simply. Our hostess stood in a band of light that fell equidistant between the enormous porcelain vase and the window. She had picked up a slender velvet ribbon and was tying it around her head. Her gown was cut low in front and was high-waisted, and she wore a large jeweled medallion at her throat. In that instant, she *was* a Renaissance woman—the subject of a portrait, perhaps, by Filippo Lippi or Agnolo Bronzino. The room shimmered slightly, and we were all part of the painting, part of that other age.

Mabel, the first of us three to move, turned to Aalbert. "We'll find you somewhere to sleep," she said cheerfully, and beckoned him to follow her out the door. He looked at us helplessly, and Maude mouthed, "Go!" Somewhat dazed, he did.

An elderly maid appeared next with a fresh pitcher of water and poured it out into the porcelain bowl on the dry sink. She smiled shyly and immediately ducked out.

"We," Maude whispered deliberately, "are in another world." This sent us both into fits of laughter, and we clapped our hands over our mouths lest we be heard. The laughter was nervousness, to be sure, but also unbridled joy at having been delivered into this place. We each did our best to wash off the day's journey before changing into what we hoped would pass as evening clothes. Maman had tucked one of my grandmother's broad lace collars into my trunk—I'd not discovered it until unpacking in Rome—and I placed it around my neck. The exquisite pattern of flowers and star-like points stood out against my dark silk dress. As I fastened the collar's tiny pearl buttons, I could almost feel Grandmama's hands fall lightly on my shoulders, as though I had summoned her to this dreamlike other world and she were standing behind me. My heart was beating quickly but strongly, and I was—what? I was happy. Grandmother leaned on my shoulders, and I could hear her voice close to my ear: "There's no harm in joy as long as you remain watchful and alert and be careful as you go forward."

Maude and I had no idea where Mabel had taken Aalbert, so we found our way back to the vast drawing room where nearly a dozen other guests were milling about sipping sherry from tiny crystal glasses. Even Mr. Field, who towered above everyone but Edwin Dodge, was wearing dinner clothes when he spotted us hesitating at the door and made his way over.

"Ah! You are here!" He turned his large, leonine head and called out, "Mabel! Have you met these three?" Our hostess, her arm snuggly through Aalbert's, emerged from an intense-looking conversation and waved.

And so began a week that made me feel I had entered not just a fantastical world, but a novel, or perhaps a play, where all the characters remain out of sight all day not to emerge until night. The other guests laughed a great deal and were full of energy, and they seemed to love nothing more than a good argument among themselves, which, of course, was resolved before the evening's end. I had never known such people.

Villa Curonia,
Arcetri, Tuscany
April 19, 1911

Dear Maman,

I'm writing from a villa near Florence, where several of us, including Mr. Field, are the guests of Mr. and Mrs. Edwin Dodge. She is originally from Buffalo, and we are to call her Mabel. She met Edwin on the trip she made to Europe to recover from the death of her first husband. Imagine, Maman, there she was, the mother of a baby son, and her husband dies in a hunting accident. She is a remarkable person, more fiery and passionate than anyone I've ever met. I cannot fathom where she gets her energy.

The house itself transports one back to the sixteenth century. Mabel told us she wanted to erase from her consciousness "the emptiness of American culture" so as to immerse herself in a world of classical beauty—to celebrate, as she put it, the creative impulse in man. Oh, Maman, I wish you could feel the excitement here. The spirit of the Renaissance is palpable, infusing our days and inspiring us to greatness. Does that sound foolish? It would not, I promise you, if you were here. All my love to you, dearest Maman. I am ever grateful for your wisdom and generosity in sending me into such beauty. I promise you, it will not be in vain. I shall make you proud.

———————

If the nights bordered on raucous at Villa Curonia, the days were quiet. That first morning, the house seemed not to wake up at all. I rose quietly so as not to disturb Maude, who had insisted on taking the sleeping couch and giving me the bed. I dressed quickly in a light skirt and blouse and threw my smock around my shoulders. As an afterthought, I put my vellum pad and box of pastels in my carry-bag, and, silently as I could, opened the door and shut it behind me.

Aside from a pair of servants standing attentively on either end of the sideboard, I was the only guest in the dining room. I thought to make some foolish excuse and turn around, but I was hungry, so I kept going, one foot in front of the other. I helped myself to fruit and a thick slice of ham, conscious of the clank of the heavy meat fork against my fine china plate, and sat down at the big table. Almost at once a bowl of caffe latte appeared at my right, and I turned to thank the server, but whoever had brought it was already standing stone-faced against the wall. Silence roared through the enormous room. I forced myself to eat what was on my plate, thanked the waitstaff, and fled as soon as possible.

Outside, I crossed the stone piazza and nearly broke into a run to get clear of the house, suddenly terrified of being seen, waylaid, and spoken to—a childish panic, to be sure, but I had no say in the matter. I crashed through a bushy copse, scratching my arms and my face before coming out to find myself on the side of a hill. Feeling completely alone at last, I stopped to catch my breath. The morning dew still sparkled, and patches of fog lay like wool in the valley below. The world stretched out in front of me: the city of Florence— Firenze—as it must have been hundreds of years ago. To the north I could see its towers—the Duomo, San Marco, Palazzo Vecchio's needlelike turret; spires of lesser churches, the domed chapel of San Lorenzo, the capacious Piazza della Signoria. In the expansive stillness of the early Italian morning, I found it easy to imagine Medici horsemen galloping across the plain, holding their bright standards. I drew in a full breath, inhaling aromas I couldn't identify—pungent, sweet, and musky. My relief at being alone was palpable.

There was a road about one hundred feet below me, and I made my way down the hill to inspect it. It curved around a promontory made of rock so sharp and dark it was almost black with an undercoat of bronze. The valley was out of sight where the road changed from a rutted earthen path to deeply set stones—not as uniform as the cobblestones I was used to in Brooklyn, but unquestionably laid there by someone. The Romans? The Etruscans? There were so many civilizations in this part of Tuscany, layered one on top of another. We had learned that the marvelous Renaissance churches all around us had been built atop Roman temples, which in turn had overlaid Etruscan sacred sites. It gave one the feeling of an eternal presence.

A few steps later, the towers of Florence were once again visible. I found a flat piece of rock to sit on and settled there. The air had a strand of sharpness from the mist still rising from the valley, and I teased myself that fauns were darting through the trees, and the gods and goddesses were all near. As much as I tried to dismiss it, I felt a visceral connection to these beings and the unquenchable creative force that was as fresh and alive on this day as it had been thousands of years ago. I took out my vellum pad and pastels and, using the flat side of the yellow stick, spread a thick band of color across the empty white page. This I covered with a swath of light green, and then with another darker green on top of that. Together the colors took on a vibrant depth, and I was startled by their liveliness. Here was music, a harmonious triad right on the page, resonating as if in one of the cathedrals, each brilliant tone lingering to overlap the next.

As the noon hour approached, I heard heavy footsteps trudging up the hill. I turned, and Aalbert, shaggy blond hair blown over his eyes, waved and grinned cheerfully. He had a canteen slung across his chest and carried a bag in one hand and his box of watercolor paints in the other.

"Did you bring those from Rome?" I called out.

"I did," he hollered back. Traces of his faint Dutch accent mingled with his Oxford brand of English made his voice solid and square, like wood—warm and durable and comforting.

"I don't remember seeing them."

"Agnes," he said, flopping down next to me. "You are teasing, I think, but I would not go anywhere without my box of magic colors. It was in my portmanteau. Just in case."

"Ah, your portmanteau." Maude had teased him about toting such a large bag onto the train.

He pulled out a large cotton handkerchief and wiped his gleaming forehead. "Hot," he said. He gestured at the distant city. "I am going to paint it today." From his knapsack he pulled a pad of thick paper. He opened his paint box and poured a small bit of water from his canteen into the tray.

"Ahh," he sighed. "This is nice. I hope you don't mind," he said, suddenly aware that he might be intruding on me. "I had to get away from the house. The others were all getting up, and one of the women—Miss Talbert?—told me she had *plans* for me. That's what she said: 'I have *plans* to spirit you away, Aalbert.' She's American, I think, like you."

"That sounds intriguing," I said.

"Oh, Agnes." He pronounced my name "Ahh-gnes," which I found endearing. "You know I don't want to be spirited away by a strange woman, or by any woman, for that matter."

I felt a shock go through me. Aalbert swiveled around to stare at me. "You did not know this? Oh, dear. Perhaps I make a mistake. You were thinking that I like the women?"

I tried to find a rejoinder even as I sought to grasp how he—how anyone—could treat the topic with such casual ease. He put his arm around my shoulders. "Except you and Maude, of course. You and Maude I am liking a great deal. Because you care for your art and my art. Well, *you* care. Maude, she makes me laugh."

He got very quiet. "I shock you. This is very awkward." He looked unhappy and then his face grew even darker. "I did think, Agnes, that you would understand—"

"Yes, I see, because I'm older than the rest of you. You're right, Aalbert, I should have understood—"

"No," he said brusquely. "No, because I thought—" His usual easy self-confidence vanished for a moment, and then I saw him reassert it. "I think you do not like the men, isn't that true?"

My face burned, and I struggled to keep myself steady.

"Of course I like men," I said. I was shocked by the force behind my retort, by the urgency of my desire to extinguish his words. Apparently, without meaning to and without the slightest exertion, he had pried open a part of my soul that I thought was so well concealed it no longer even existed.

"Do you mind about me?"

"I don't mind, Aalbert," I said. "This won't change things between us."

He squeezed me lightly, dropped his arm, and reached into his knapsack again. Out came a hunk of cheese wrapped in a napkin and half a loaf of bread.

"You are hungry?"

"I am," I said gratefully.

"You never remember about food, I think," he said, cutting me a piece of cheese with his pocketknife and tearing off a hunk of fresh crusty bread.

"I do remember about food," I protested. "I didn't expect to be out this long."

"It is so beautiful, Agnes. We will eat and then we will work, yes? You will let me paint next to you? We will not talk."

His food disappeared in two or three huge bites, and true to his word, he said nothing as he squeezed colors into the paint tray, swirled his brush in a small pot of water, and began spreading a warm green wash across the heavy paper. I finished my bread and cheese and resumed my pastel landscape. Picking up each sharply squared stick of color, I marveled at its purity and how each embodied the essence of its color. Then I tried without success to identify even one interaction with Aalbert that might have caused him to think of me as a lesbian. Did green understand that it was green? Did yellow? Did blue ever reflect on how it showed itself forth in the world?

I think it must be that only in that languid setting, in the warm bath of an Italian midday, could I have reflected on myself in that manner. If it was true that some essential part of me could be recognized and identified, not by me, but by others, then I felt fortunate that its existence was being announced by Aalbert—a sweet man more a like boy in temperament, who had trusted me with his secret and intended only good for me, his friend.

But underneath this sanguine acceptance roiled memories of Gertrude—a girl with whom I'd had only the most casual acquaintance and who had done nothing to instigate the feelings I suffered. As they tore through me again on that Florentine hillside, I didn't know what to think or say or do, or what it might mean.

Villa Curonia,
Arcetri, Tuscany
April 24, 1910

Dearest Maman,

I'm becoming sinfully indolent here. Most days the house stays utterly quiet. Heaven, really, for me, as you might imagine. But all that changes in the evening, for once the sun has sunk low in the sky, guests come trailing out of their rooms, women dressed in gorgeous gowns, the men in black tie and tails, all of them ready for sherry in the drawing room or on the piazza. After an hour or so of pleasant conversation, as faces have begun to grow red from the wine, Mabel rings a gong and we all file in obediently for dinner. She is quite a sight with that gong. It's large and brass, and she holds it up with a purple velvet ribbon, pausing for a moment, and then solemnly striking it with a rounded stick covered in beautiful cotton padding. She then holds it even higher, letting the ring reach where it will. Everyone must stop what they are doing—and they do!—which is remarkable for such a boisterous crowd. A hush falls until the sound has faded entirely, and then Mabel lowers it, hands it to a servant, and turns solemnly to lead us all inside for a magnificent dinner.

Mr. Field, who had been at a museum the day we arrived, herds us his students about like little sheep. It's very sweet really. He held out his arm for me to accompany him into the dining room last night. Very kind of him but he needn't have worried. My shyness presents no problems here at all: everyone is so eager to talk, they don't notice that I am not, so they eagerly pour

out their hearts to me. What they are thinking, when
they might go home, what they hope to do when they
get there, how they plan to keep this thrilling energy
alive. I am basking in the attention, Maman. My head
is getting quite swelled, but don't worry. I'm sure it will
be down to size in no time.

––––––––––––––

We went sightseeing. Mabel arranged a touring car for us—me, Mr.
Field, Aalbert, Maude, and Maurice Sterne—and off we went, early
in the morning to Florence. The huge vehicle held us all, jostling
as we bumped and swayed down the hill. The car was open, and
thick chunks of cloud scudded across the endlessly blue sky. The
light was watery and pale and seemed to bend, and everything
was illuminated. Mr. Field, as usual, took charge. He was seated
up front with the driver and turned to yell over the noise of the
engine, "The Duomo! Right there, straight ahead. Just to its left
and a bit behind it, the cathedral campanile. There, to the right,
the Foundling Hospital: we are all foundlings today, rescued by the
divine Mrs. Dodge. Notice how 'Dodge' sounds almost like 'Doge'?
And over to the left, the spire of the Palazzo Vecchio!"

Sterne and Aalbert had been chattering as we descended the hill,
and now, like the rest of us fell into silence as first the distant towers
and then the city's ancient wall came into view. Field rattled off his
list of the sights we'd visit before taking in the great Uffizi Gallery. It
sounded exhausting, and I nearly said so. He must have seen my face.
Looking directly at me, he added, "Then it's across the river for lunch.
And then a special treat for Agnes: the friary cells of San Marco."

"Why a treat for me?" I asked.

Field's smile glinted with mischief. "Because, I think in another
life you were a monk or a nun or some sort of hermit. You will feel
right at home there."

"What about me?" Maude called out.

"You? We will find the great statue of David for you. Very large," he said, winking at her. Everyone laughed, especially Maude.

Field had named what I had identified as my greatest fear in coming on this trip: intense closeness with others and little opportunity for the solitude I always counted on to refresh me. And so much activity: I knew I had to husband my strength, and I began by taking slow, deliberate breaths, which helped calm me.

As we entered the city, the sudden noise of the engine caroming back at us from the stone buildings and streets made talk impossible. Before long we entered the broad open space of the Piazza della Signoria, the car halted, and Field jumped out.

"Change of plan," he called out. "The driver cannot chauffeur us about. He will meet us back at the portal gate this afternoon. That does not mean we cannot start with the Duomo, so shall we?" We clambered out and scurried to catch up with Field as he strode toward a narrow notch between buildings. Coming out onto a piazza, a flock of pigeons—a small sea of gray waves bobbing in front of us—rose up as one and began to wheel about. The white on their wings caught the bright sun, and they flung themselves out in two complete circles before settling back down where we had disturbed them. Little islands of tourists were clumped here and there in front of the cathedral entrance, and in every case all eyes were fixed on either the docents or the guidebooks they had opened to the proper page and were now inspecting carefully. Behind them the great cathedral of Santa Maria della Fiori stood indifferently, its stones timeless and stolid, Brunelleschi's magnificent dome sheltering all that the tourists were reading about. On our way inside, the Baptistery, with its geometric patterns of black and white bricks shimmered in the morning light.

We saw the Duomo, the Baptistery, the Or San Michele, the Logia dei Lanzi, the Medici Palace, the Pitti Palace, and the Foundling Hospital. At some point we stopped to eat lunch—all of Italy seems to shut down for the noon meal and siesta; we would partake of one but not the other—and then went on to the monastery of

San Marco where Fra Angelico had set out to create a vision of heaven meeting earth.

Inside, the church was all hushed darkness and quiet. Our group seemed to respond by scattering, first one then another, turning to solitary study of a window or picture. I was pulled to the front where the extraordinary altarpiece of the Virgin Mary seated on a wooden throne and holding the child Jesus, both of them surrounded by saints and friars, loomed at least ten feet above. Fra Angelico had painted this on wood and had used bright red robes and capes to pull our eye to Mary in the center and then the important saints around her. He had used gold, of course, to indicate halos and fine trim on some of the robes. Interspersed were monks in humble black robes, and the effect of this light-dark—his own version of Mr. Dow's *notan*—made the entire expanse of picture come alive. There were no chairs or pews, so I let myself sink down against a supporting pillar and gaze up and into it. Immediately the gold began to vibrate against the reds and blacks, and I felt the picture grow larger as I became smaller.

I must have fallen asleep. When I woke and looked around, I saw none of our group. Instead of being frightened, I felt elated. Cautiously I ventured out of the church and into the cloister itself, where some of the cells that Fra Angelico had decorated with frescoes were open. Other tourists were present, but the reverence of the place seemed to cast a spell on all of us. I stepped into cell after cell, feeling a slight change in each of them. When I came to the cell in which Fra Angelico had painted the Annunciation, I felt strangely at home. The angel visiting the Virgin Mary to tell her that she would give birth to the Christ child stood at a remove. Mary prayed across from him. Their heads inclined toward one another, and the space between them—simple and unadorned—was awash with natural light. Here was the artist connecting earth to heaven, while I experienced my own frisson: imagining Angelico, living in this place hundreds of years before and painting what now moved me. I removed my shoes. I wanted to feel the floor that was connecting us and touch the walls that he had touched. After a minute I put my shoes back on and made my way outside. I had no idea where my companions were. Unruffled, I decided to wait where I was, knowing that they would come for me and I had no reason to worry.

———————

A week later we took the evening train back to Rome so as to avoid traveling in the worst of the heat. Maude and Aalbert, exhausted from one last day of sketching out of doors, soon fell asleep. The train carriage's dirty window was open from the top, and I stood and swayed and leaned out to watch the light dwindle and land grow dark. Inhaling deeply, I took in the fragrance of earth and the green corn that was rising from fields that spread like carpet all the way to the black Umbrian hills beyond. The softness of the Italian twilight soothed me, and as I listened, the train wheels clacked gently, all is lovely, all is lovely. It was then that I received my own vision of heaven: as the sky deepened to its darkest blue, traces of gold remained—like a persistent memory—and illuminated the horizon from end to end, even as the sun itself dropped out of sight. Immediately I recognized the transformative element of the Renaissance altar pieces and paintings I had been studying so greedily all day; it was the presence of gold, of light, beneath the dark, persisting through the dark. It was not there, and it was unmistakably there. I knew at once that this was what I had come to Italy to find—the light infusing the dark—and I began then to think about how I might paint my own illuminated world.

———————

At the end of my year in Rome, our little group of friends dispersed—me back to Brooklyn, and Aalbert back to his home in Amsterdam. Maude surprised us by announcing she would stay on in Rome, having met a wealthy Italian she had decided to marry.

"He proposed?" I had asked, ready to be indignant at not having been in her confidence.

"Oh," she laughed. "He doesn't know yet."

We all promised to write, and we did for a while, but quickly our friendship receded into the nostalgic past, where for me it has remained enshrined. Later I would learn of Aalbert's death in the Great War, which hits me hard to this day. I wondered if he had his watercolor box with him.

OGUNQUIT, MAINE

1911

I CAME TO THE DESERT for its light and its silence, but thinking back to 1911 and the first of several happy summers in Maine, I must say that there is no silence quite like that of fog. Field and Laurent had also returned to America in the spring of 1911, and after time at home with my mother, I followed them to Field's newest venture, his Summer School of Art in Ogunquit. I had been reluctant to leave Maman again so soon, but my very first morning in Maine, I stepped out and breathed the fog in deeply, savoring the tang of salt and pine. My mother and I had often retreated to the outer end of Long Island to escape Brooklyn's heat, but Maine's version of the sea breeze had more heft somehow. Everything was different. I had worried about feeling homesick, but in Ogunquit I wanted to dig my bare feet into the Maine sand and imagine roots reaching down and taking hold. The air was sharp and grainy enough to be visible. I walked out on a driveway of smashed quahog shells that curved out in a thick line of white. Down by the creek, where Field and Laurent had built a pier, a dory rose into view in tiny increments as the tide pushed in from the bay.

The sparsely situated trees around our cluster of buildings had been twisted and bent by the wind to follow the contours of the rough land. I spent many hours admiring the fierce beauty wrought by their struggle to survive, and scribbled them in my sketchbook, studying the intelligence of nature's line in the face of adversity. Clearly there was nothing shameful about survival even if one had to bend.

Field's Summer School of Art was perched on the bluff above the inlet; we had space and open air, and a sky whose reach was limited only by the clouds that crowded the horizon. I spent my first week tramping about the beaches and the rocky meadows. No one asked me where I was going—indeed, no one was in evidence at all most mornings when I emerged from my room carrying my box of pastels and pencils, an oversized pad tucked under my arm—and I explored the landscape trying to divine its secrets. The others also found pleasing views, and I'd often encounter Robert Laurent, his straw hat set back on his head, painting. The first such morning he smiled—a bit sheepishly, I thought, probably at the sheer pleasure of being by himself. He lowered his brush, apparently to talk, but I waved and kept walking. His relief was evident.

"We are all hermits," I called out, and Laurent nodded and resumed working. I found my own favorite places to work, and sep-arately we all painted or sketched until we were hungry, at which point we made our way back to the house—"chickens returning to the coop," Field said fondly—where we lingered in the kitchen while Mrs. Smith from the village cooked our dinner. The rustic rhythms of Ogunquit—the blessed solitude that was possible even in company, the light and space and air—were to set my life as an artist in motion.

BROOKLYN, NEW YORK

SEPTEMBER 1911

AT THE CLOSE OF THAT first season, after we returned to New York, Field gave me a small showing at Ardsley House, his new Brooklyn residence and gallery—or, as his descriptive pamphlet put it, his "headquarters for the incubation and birthing of a distinctly American modern art."

Maman came with me to the reception and was gallantly treated by Field, who offered his arm and escorted her slowly through the exhibit. When he returned her to me, she exclaimed over my sequence of pastels: I had tried to capture the feeling of a full day on the seacoast, from the dove-breast dawn, to the brilliant blue apex of early afternoon, and into the plangent violets of evening. There were a dozen works, and somehow on the wall of Field's gallery, they ceased to belong to me even as they afforded me pleasure, which I had not thought artists were entitled to. We send the work into the world, and others receive it. Now I was receiving what I had also made.

If I had assumed that I'd merely settle back into life at home, my show at Ardsley House shifted the landscape. I received a lovely congratulatory note from a couple I had met in Ogunquit, Jerome and Kitty Myers. He was a painter known for prowling the Lower

East Side to paint neighborhoods no one else would venture into. I greatly admired his skill and his sensitivity to the tenement dwellers, and Kitty was such a warm and nurturing presence, I quite forgot to be shy with them. Their note invited me to come along to a salon given by their friend Mrs. Charles Thursby, who, Kitty said, was very interested in helping artists. Especially women artists. I wrote back to accept before I changed my mind.

"I don't know why you go to those things," Maman said at supper that night.

"They're interesting," I replied. Which was an understatement, to be sure. I had been to a salon only once before, and from what I could tell, they were calculated gatherings of the most unlikely combinations of people: newly arrived immigrants, communists, socialists, artists, writers, and the leading lights of New York society, all packed into an elegant parlor. That a meal was promised after the discussion meant that everybody—especially those who were more poorly dressed—stayed until the end, even if they were more inter-ested in the moment when the dining room doors would open than they were in Marx or Sigmund Freud or whatever Alfred Stieglitz was showing in his new gallery. But as evenings designed to provoke, inspire, and even outrage, the salons were unqualified successes.

"'Interesting.' These people are trying to persuade you to aban-don your principles and compromise yourself."

"I will be fine, Maman," I said. To some degree, she was right. What in our family we called "principles," the radical crowd scoffed at as convention and bourgeois bondage. I regretted having told her about another evening at a Village café, which I had found disturbing, both for the overt sexuality I'd seen and for all the shouting and arguing and insistence on smashing convention in the salons.

"You won't even know what hit you," she said. "First thing you know, you'll be saying or doing something shameful. And once something's been said, it can never be taken back, you know that."

"I really don't say or do anything, Maman." I was impatient to be on my way. "I'm sorry to disappoint you, but all I do is sit and listen."

"That can be very dangerous."

"They want to be dangerous," I said recklessly. "*We* want to be dangerous. We want to upend the art world and disturb the social order."

"Where did you hear that? That isn't you, Agnes. It sounds like someone else talking now."

"I have to go, Maman," I said and pulled on my coat. "I'm meeting Jerome and Kitty Myers."

Her eyes widened. "Are you saying they are part of all this?"

Immediately I regretted involving my new friends. Maman had met them at Ardsley House and had been favorably impressed.

"Well, then, I suppose you'll be all right," she said, conveying with every fiber of her being that she supposed no such thing.

The Myerses were waiting for me outside the Thursby residence on Fifth Avenue. I apologized for being late, but they gaily waved my concerns away, and together we spent a few moments watching an odd mixture of people converge on the house. Men dressed like peasants in Russian felt coats and boots were escorted by perfectly coifed, fur-encased women who flaunted their wealth along with their delight in "slumming." Mrs. Thursby was at the front door, warmly greeting us all as we entered. She embraced Jerome, lightly kissing both of Kitty's cheeks. When Jerome brought me forward to introduce me, she stopped him.

"Miss Pelton and I have met, haven't we, Miss Pelton?"

I was surprised that she remembered our brief acquaintance of the previous year. It had been at the home of another wealthy socialite, and I had taken away an impression of Alice Thursby as diamond hard and a good deal older than the woman before me now.

"But perhaps you do not recall?"

"Of course, I do," I said hastily. "How nice to see you again."

"Do come in, all of you." She was dressed in velvet even though the air was almost sultry—a deep, wine-red velvet, with tiny white rosebuds sewn along the neckline. Her skin was pale and her eyes dark. They peered out from beneath eyelids like hoods, and I was stricken with shyness. But then we were inside, Jerome and Kitty on either side of me, gently guiding me forward.

I had expected the house to be grand, but I was not prepared for the art that lined the walls all the way to the high ceilings. I spotted a still life by Cézanne and a small seascape by Homer. Off to the right was a gallery, and I resolved to slip away as soon as possible and inspect the collection.

"Alice was a painter herself," Jerome said quietly as we made our way into the enormous salon room. "She studied in Paris and was quite ambitious, I believe, until her marriage. She's a Brisbane, you know."

I did know. Her brother, Arthur Brisbane, a good-natured and generous soul who would commission a wall mural from me a few years later, sat on the board of *The New York Times*. Another black mark against Alice, I thought, imagining Maman's disdain at hearing I was mingling with "newspaper mongers."

Upstairs, the main parlor—a ballroom, really—was full of men and women smoking and talking. The noise was deafening, and when someone called Jerome and Kitty away, I stood to one side— decoratively, I hoped—while a gramophone played a jazzy piece and a couple started dancing.

I edged around the room toward the gallery, which was empty of people. Living ones, at any rate: here, I deduced, were several generations of Thursbys and Brisbanes on huge canvases that lined the walls. In the center was a magnificent full-size portrait of our hostess, painted with extraordinary verve and signed by John Singer Sargent.

Dubbed "The New Woman," I could see immediately that it differed from his other classic portraits of high society women, which he posed standing regally, haughtily even, wearing formal gowns in an elegant setting. Here Sargent had seated Mrs. Thursby, her elbows akimbo, on the edge of a plush, white satin chair. In the painting her eyes smile, and her lips are parted as if she is speaking, perhaps scolding the artist for keeping her fixed in this chair when, really, she should be out changing the world. Instead of evening clothes, she wears a dark skirt (tones of lavender under brown) and a fitted black jacket over a high-necked white blouse. Her left leg crosses the right, and her right foot rests on a footstool. On the floor is an Oriental rug, and the drapes behind her are a subdued green-gray brocade. In my own painting, I had given little thought to background and concentrated on subject. But in Sargent's witty treatment, a simple setting had become context: an intelligent, inquisitive woman, impatient at being held back but too well bred to disobey the painter, was clearly determined to depart the Victorian setting—and all it implied—as soon as possible. Background had become subject.

"Are you lost or hiding?"

I whirled around and there she was—older than the woman in the painting, of course, but full of the same unmistakable verve. My face colored and she laughed, but her eyes were warm, and I had to smile.

"Hiding, I suppose."

"I don't blame you," she said. "I wasn't really expecting such a large crowd. They're all chattering away in there." She gestured toward the salon from which we could hear the low roar of voices.

"Then you are hiding too," I ventured.

"I suppose I am."

That struck me at once as uncommonly generous. It was clear that she hadn't felt the need to hide in a long time.

"That was painted in London," she said, indicating her portrait. "A lifetime ago."

"He seems to have caught you very well," I said.

"He's a good painter." She shrugged. "Jerome says that you're talented."

"That is generous of him."

"Nonsense. You must know he's not inclined to empty compliments. Especially if the person he's talking about is not within earshot."

"I hardly know what to say."

"I'd like to see your work," she said. "Where is your studio?"

"At the moment," I said, too flustered to think of a clever reply, "it's in the back room of the house I share with my mother."

From an invisible pocket in the skirt of her dress, she pulled a tiny pad and matching gold pencil and thrust them at me. "Would you write the address here?"

"We live in Brooklyn," I said.

"As long as you don't live in Timbuktu, I expect I'll be able to manage."

Alice appeared the next day in a long automobile driven by a chauffeur, who waited in the car when she knocked at the front door. I was in the back garden, reading, and heard nothing, so it was left to Maman, who was in the middle of a lesson, to answer. She poked her head out the back door and called to me.

"Do you know a Mrs. Thursby?"

"Why?"

"She's just arrived."

And then, as if on cue, the regal Alice Thursby appeared behind her.

"Good afternoon, Miss Pelton. I hope I'm not interrupting your work."

Maman was visibly affronted and appeared ready to escort Alice right back out the front door. I stood, trying to put my book down unobtrusively.

"That's all right, Mother," I said. She glared at me then and muttered. "Well, I never," but she had a pupil waiting and turned on her heel.

"Do show me your work." My guest beamed. "May I call you Agnes? You must call me Alice."

———————

That was in April of 1912, and in May, Alice organized a tea party at her house to show my pastels: "I get so tired of men having all the attention, don't you?"

We used an intimate ground floor drawing room and together arranged the order of the pictures, eliminating one and adding another, thinking about how to price them. I had to admit that I had no idea of their value, so she consulted with Field, who made appropriate suggestions for someone just beginning a career. She then added between ten and twenty dollars to each.

"We have to be aggressive," she insisted.

About a dozen society women came on the appointed day. Alice quietly suggested that the pictures would be worth a great deal one day, and, astoundingly, her guests bought everything.

"Now, save that money," Alice said, pressing it into my hand. "You'll need it to move into a real studio."

She waved away my thanks. "This is the happiest I've been in years, since my dear Charles died. I intend to continue." She placed her hands on my shoulders: "I feel sure we shall make something of you."

———————

A few weeks later I departed for another season in Ogunquit. With Field's encouragement I began to paint in earnest. In spite of worries about stamina and health, I produced a dozen works in quick succession. Most were of the Maine seacoast, but more and more I was letting my imagination shape the mood and tone of my pictures. Field was pleased with the shift in direction they signaled—on a rocky shore, primitive human figures rose out of the stony landscape—but the canvas that received his undivided attention was a remembered landscape of the woods at my aunt's farm in Connecticut, where my mother and I often visited in the summer. I had wanted to paint something for my mother, a scene she would recognize and take pleasure in looking at, and one that would evoke the happy times we'd known there together. Instead, the woods at the edge of the meadow thickened into a dense copse of trees tangled with heavy vines. The scene was forbidding and sinister. Even as I tried to turn it into something pastoral and serene, the wall of black-green remained so thick that should one venture in, one might never emerge from its density. In the foreground and precariously close to this woodland, I painted the figure of a woman facing front, arms open to the viewer, flowers scattering in her path. Was that a smile she wore or a grimace? I left it unclear. I also gave the female figure the same color value as the trees to further obscure where they stopped and she began. This was not suitable for Maman, but it excited me. I could not deny that I was present in every stroke of the brush—my *self*, my fears and emotions.

As I was finishing the painting, Field simply appeared as he was wont to do and stared over my shoulder. I felt my grandmother's presence hovering there as well. "My goodness," I imagined her saying, "let us hope that no one understands what *this* means." I could hear the rustle of her black dress as she turned away. It is bad, I thought; it is a bad painting. Look at it, it is gross and clumsy and vulgar.

"What's the title?" Field asked.

"It doesn't have one yet," I whispered. He nodded—rather curtly, I thought—and walked off. My despair took hold and settled in. I grabbed canvas, easel, and paints and rushed back to the house. Field kept a room where each of us had an area for storage. I covered the new painting loosely and leaned it up against my other finished pictures on the floor. Running to my small attic room, I wept my grief into my pillow.

At suppertime, after everyone had gathered at the big table, I crept down the stairs and out the door and fled to my favorite refuge, a rock nestled behind other rocks at the water's edge. Other strollers were enjoying the late daylight and surf, but they could not see me tucked away, unable to stop the tears. What made me think I could paint, I wondered. I had made a fool of myself. I should leave, I thought. I should leave, go home, forget all this. I stood up and brushed bits of rock and sand from my skirt and wiped my face as best I could with my handkerchief. My weariness, at once familiar and overwhelming, settled in, and I made my slow way back to the house. On my way upstairs, I forced myself to smile at the diners, who were now enjoying peaches and cream.

"Agnes! There you are!" Field called out. "Come and meet someone." I tried to wave him off. "No, no, you must." I tentatively ventured into the dining room, but no one seemed to notice anything amiss.

"Agnes," Field said, "may I present Walt Kuhn, secretary of the newly formed Association of American Painters and Sculptors. Kuhn, this is Miss Agnes Pelton, who painted the pair of landscapes you so admired. She's even coined a new term for them: Imaginative paintings."

I tried to keep my face clear of the shock that went through me, but I was not successful.

"I knew you'd be surprised!" Field exulted.

Kuhn reached past him to extend his hand. "I'm very impressed," he said. Before I could respond, he went on: "A few of us are putting a show together—we've called ourselves, rather grandly we hope, the Association of American Painters and Sculptors—and I'd like these two pieces to be in it." He nodded at Field, who held up the same woodland painting I'd thought worthless—I would title it *Vine Wood*—and a picture of figures on the beach I'd titled *Stone Age*. I don't know which was more shocking, seeing the canvases I'd left in the storage area or the idea that someone liked them. Robert Laurent pulled me toward a chair.

"It's not bad news, Agnes," he said.

"No," I agreed. I desperately wanted to get to my room to be alone and sort through the last few hours, and to try and grasp what was being offered to me. I listened intently for what Grandmama might say.

"May I think about it?" I asked. Field sighed and shook his head. Kuhn seemed unfazed and replied cheerfully, "I'd like to say 'of course,' but the reality is, we are going to do all this in a great hurry, and I need to know your decision before I leave."

"Tomorrow," Field tacked on. Kuhn held up a copy of a catalog from an exhibition in Germany. "I've only just received this," he said, I thought a bit sheepishly. "I was painting in Nova Scotia, and another of our new Association—do you know Arthur Davies?"

"*Everyone* knows Arthur Davies," Field interjected.

"Quite so. He's in Europe at the moment—saw this show and thinks we can put one like it together here. He's booked passage for me for day after tomorrow, so I have to get to New York immediately. We'll be signing up a lot of these Europeans, but we'll be using as many American artists as is appropriate, and you, Miss Pelton, fill the bill very nicely. I am very taken by the strength of your vision in these and would like to put them up on a wall—still to be located," he added genially. "We hope to get it all done by this winter."

At that, other jaws besides my own dropped.

"Sounds impossible, I know," Kuhn went on, "but we want to overturn the art world with as little notice as possible. Take them by surprise. What do you think?"

"I think it would be very exciting."

"Good! Then it's settled. For pity sakes, Hamilton, haven't you got anything to drink in this place?"

That night, I half expected Grandmama to visit and berate me, or at least warn me of something dire. She did not, and I opened a new journal. Across the top of the first page I wrote, **Calm, Aspiration, Tranquility, Abstraction, Folded Wings, Sleep, Vision.**

BROOKLYN

DECEMBER 1912

EVERY TIME I STOPPED BY Ardsley House, it seemed that Field was immersed in plans for the big winter exhibition. Walt Kuhn and Arthur Davies had returned from Europe in the late fall, and both were full of excitement about what they had seen. From the Cologne Sonderbund Show, they had dashed to Paris, signing up painters and sculptors as fast as they found them.

"Forbes's Gallery won't be big enough," Field reported. "Kuhn is looking for a bigger space. Much bigger." At this he rolled his eyes. "I fear that they are courting disaster. Is America ready for the Cubists? I doubt it. Better to ease the public into the new art rather than risk setting back our cause."

He had taken to treating me as a confidante, which both flattered me and made me uneasy. I did not want to become embroiled in the arguments that had begun to fly between my several mentors. "Mentors," plural, was an idea I was still adjusting to. Field was already planning a solo showing of my work to follow the Association's exhibition, and he kept trying to persuade Kuhn to take more than just two of my pieces.

"Maybe the next one," Kuhn replied when Field brought it up to him in my presence. They had quietly entered the studio where

I and several others were doing figure studies. I could hear the low rumble of their voices with only the occasional word, but from his eager glances in my direction, it was apparent that Field hoped I would smile or in some way engage Kuhn to make it impossible for him to refuse. I found this deeply embarrassing and pretended to be engrossed in my drawing. Laurent, working just across, shot me an encouraging glance, which I did not acknowledge. (Yes, I did know how fortunate I was—imagine being in exactly the right place at exactly the right time, in the company of powerful advocates who could position one at the forefront of American art! Is the female sex doomed or blessed with a certain demure reticence?) To calm myself, I focused on the comforting hush of charcoal against paper, which has always felt monastic to me, sacramental. Abruptly the studio door swung open, and I heard Field and Kuhn depart. I kept my eyes on my paper, redoubling my efforts to capture the torque of the model's back as she twisted away from me.

My other mentor was Alice Thursby, who had attached herself to my cause and whose motorcar frequently crossed the Brooklyn Bridge and pulled up at Pacific Street without any warning. My new life, as I had begun to think of it, would expand to include such friends with whom I could discuss art. I would not shy away from arguments, nor would I shrink back when challenged. It would be like Italy: I would be part of the pulse and flow of New York and not think it unusual to have a friend, even one who took a keen interest in me and my work.

I wondered if my new attitude had made an impression on my mother, because she began to warm to Alice as well. If not busy with a piano student, she would escort our guest to where I was working. Eventually even that small formality fell away, and one day I glanced up from my drawing to see Alice.

"I was thinking," she said, trying, I could tell, for a deliberately offhanded tone, "that you should be exhibiting in Manhattan."

"Yes, well, the show that's planned will accomplish that."

"That is but one exhibition in which you'll have two pieces."
She waved my words away.

"And Hamilton Field wants to do a solo show at Ardsley
House."

"That's in Brooklyn. No, we need you to be showing in Manhattan. Let us follow right up with a very exclusive private showing
in the gallery at my house," she said. "We'll invite Mr. John Quinn."

I knew little of Quinn. I had heard his name in connection
with the Association and knew that, as a lawyer, he was counsel to
the upcoming show. More to the point among artists, Quinn was
also a passionate lover of modern art and bought it in quantity.
It was said that dealers and collectors kept their eyes on Quinn,
and when he bought an artist's work, that artist's career—perhaps
immortality—was made. I was skeptical, but Alice's excitement was
contagious. It became more and more of a struggle to maintain a
level head and not fly off into fears of failure and fantasies of success,
either of them powerful enough to raise a fever and send me to bed.

To that end, I sternly kept myself in check, but I did ask around
a bit more about Quinn. I learned that he kept a large apartment
on Central Park West, which was more of a storage facility than a
domicile. Paintings and sculptures, many of them still in their crates,
were stacked in every room; many people doubted he even knew
the extent of his own collection. (They were wrong.) Quinn spent
as much time in Europe as New York, sailing back and forth buying
pieces from the French and English.

Just imagining Alice's exhibition made it difficult to keep myself
grounded. And then, a few days later, passing a newsstand on my
way to the grocer's, my eye was caught by a boxed announcement
on the front page of one of the evening papers: "The Association
of American Painters and Sculptors . . . pleased to announce the
International Exhibition of Modern Art" at the 69th Regiment
Armory on Lexington Avenue from February 17 to March 13. Of
the Europeans to be shown for the first time in the United States,

the list included Odile Redon, Francis Picabia, Vincent van Gogh, Paul Gauguin, Marcel Duchamp, Paul Cézanne, Wassily Kandinsky, and Henri Matisse. The American contingent would be led by Albert Pinkham Ryder, Marsden Hartley, William Glackens, John Sloan, and George Bellows, as well as "a wide selection of additional local artists"—which included me.

Now it was real. I bought the paper, nearly forgot the groceries, and rushed home to show Maman. We were still unaccustomed to newspapers in the house, but Maman was thrilled to see this one. She immediately cut the notice out and from a high shelf in the kitchen pulled down a scrapbook I had never seen.

"What is that, Maman?"

She looked embarrassed and opened it to the first page, where I read, "Agnes Lawrence Pelton, works and achievements."

"Why, Mother! I am shocked!"

She drew herself up and with great dignity said, "It may be the sin of pride, but at least it is not on my own behalf."

The President and Members of the

Association of American Painters and Sculptors

Invite you to be present

At the formal opening of the

International Exhibition of Modern Art

Sunday, February sixteenth, 1913

From two to five o'clock

at the Armory

69th Regiment of Infantry: N.G.N.Y.

Lexington Avenue, 25th and 26th Streets

PLEASE PRESENT THIS CARD AT THE DOOR

NEW YORK CITY

FEBRUARY 1913

I FILLED OUT THE OFFICIAL stickers with the title of each painting, my name, and the year it was painted. I pasted them on the back
of Kuhn's two selections—*Vine Wood* and *Stone Age*—and crated
them up. The Railway Express wagon collected them, and off they
went to the armory, to be hung along with more than 1,200 other
pieces. It was the first time I had felt my "children" were leaving
home. The truck pulled away, leaving a black cloud of exhaust
to hover over Pacific Street. My feelings were a confused mixture
of pride and worry, and concern for how they would be received,
understanding in the marrow of my bones that there was nothing
further I could do to help them on their way. They were going out
into the world.

On the afternoon of February 16, which I recall as a particularly blustery Sunday, my mother and I entered the vast Armory to
attend the preview for the artists and the press. The Association
had completely transformed the hollow cavernous space and had
done so in only two days. On either side of the great brass entry
doors stood a pair of tall fir trees, welcoming visitors into what was
clearly intended as a place apart. We stopped and, not wanting to

impede the stream of eager attendees, stood to one side. Arm in arm we lingered, inhaling the trees' fragrance, so evocative of Ogunquit, where this particular journey had begun.

"Thank you," I whispered to Maman, for it was true that without Italy none of this would be happening. Without saying a word, she squeezed my arm and together we entered the great hall. Gallery A was devoted to American sculpture and decorative art and was dominated by George Grey Barnard's monumental piece of statuary, *The Prodigal Son and His Father.* It seemed that we artists were all prodigals, now in the embrace of a generous and forgiving parent, one who welcomed the new and daring.

The hall had been strung with streamers from the center of the ceiling to the outer walls, a device that lent intimacy to the hollow Armory. Small hexagonal exhibition "rooms," created with burlap, wood, and bamboo, were festooned with garlands of spruce and cedar, and small fir trees stood like sentinels all around the hall. We began our tour with the Americans—after all, this was the Association of American Painters and Sculptors.

"Where are your paintings?" Maman asked, sotto voce.

"I don't know," I whispered back, but my heart was pounding in anticipation of coming across them in this great hall. It was clear to me that the assembled exhibition was of monumental importance, a feeling that was confirmed when we came to the ground-shifting work of the Europeans. To provide the viewing audience with the source of this modernism, the organizers began with Impressionist and Post-Impressionists, including van Gogh, Cézanne, Gauguin, and Duchamp.

We came to the Fauvists, named for their "wild beast" freedom with color, and entered Matisse's room, where Maman fell silent when she saw my expression of delight.

"You like this?" she said, a bit timidly.

I rooted myself to the floor and breathed in slowly. "Yes. Yes! One could plunge directly into those colors and never wish to leave."

On the other side of the hall, the American rooms resumed.

We found drawings and pastels as well as oils—the work of men and women hung together, side by side, in the spirit of democracy that was flourishing in this environment. Finally, in one of the last small rooms, we found my two modest contributions. Walt Kuhn and Jerome Myers also happened to be there, inspecting my pictures with the propriety usually reserved for new fathers, and were full of extravagant praise. Their flushed faces and unconstricted elation indicated to me and Maman, whose eyes widened as they talked of my "genius," that their judgment should be taken with a substantial grain of salt. It was a relief when Kitty Myers stepped forward to greet us warmly and to congratulate me.

Even now I see that first day as a cascade of images, small moments fixed in time and shuffled like cards: the pictures, oh, the pictures! Cézanne's landscapes where blocks of muted greens and browns were interrupted by bare canvas, showing us that everything matters in composition, including the surface onto which we are setting the image; Duchamp's scandalous *Nude Descending a Staircase*, which at first was impenetrable, but once it began to reveal itself, never stopped doing so; the powerful dreams of Odile Redon, who is not so well known now but who had an entire room to himself, and for good reason—anything less would have destroyed the very world he was transporting us to; Maurice Vlaminck, who seemed to be applying paint with his hands, so thickly did it lie; and Matisse! His astonishing use of color—a face painted green, a pair of goldfish in the milky blue water of their bowl, a blue nude—and his joyous impulse to adorn everything with decorative crisscrosses and flowers. I was glad the Matisse room had a bench because I did need to sit down, so powerfully did the color and euphoria affect me.

By the time Maman and I departed that day, I was aware of having received a sense of permission. From whom or what, I could not say with certainty, but I thought it might have been from Matisse himself, whose exuberant pictures had broken me open.

My frequent excursions into Manhattan to revisit the Armory Show and attend the salons had seemed like little escapes from home and Mother and were a delight. The longish trip required from Brooklyn, the feeling of entering another world once over the bridge, all of it was wonderful. But the truth of it was that at the end of those days or evenings, I was inexorably drawn home, like a spider to her web. I could venture out all I wanted, but I was always bound to return to its center. And now that the initial excitement of the Armory had receded, Maman had become fretful. Even as she collected newspapers and clipped any mention of my name, her boasts about my achievements were laced with anxiety about "abandoning" her for my "new friends."

Alice had announced her intention to find me a studio in Manhattan, and I was still formulating how I could call off the search when daily notes began to arrive. "I have started exploring Greenwich Village," she wrote. Thinking silence would discourage her, I didn't reply at first and then decided I had better. After each day's progress report, I sent my objections: one location was too far from the river, one was too close, another was too noisy, another in too dense a neighborhood. I needed the inspiration of nature, I told her, and this, I came to realize, was true. Our small garden on Pacific Street was an overgrown wonder, and I found myself retreating into its dense green quiet more and more. It seemed I was meant to stay in Brooklyn, so when Alice swooped down one afternoon, I was completely unprepared.

"Eureka!" she cried, finding me in the sunroom. "I have found it! You must come at once!"

I protested, and then we were in her automobile, riding across the bridge into Manhattan. She refused to tell me anything but kept her face fixed with an intriguing but somewhat irritating smile. To my surprise—which clearly registered on my face and which made

Alice giggle—the car turned north at Broadway and then north again at Fifth Avenue. Not Greenwich Village, then, I thought. I watched as the downtown flew by, and I gaped like a tourist at the great library on 42nd Street. Just as I had decided that she must have simply been taking me for a change-of-scene ride, the car turned east on 59th Street and stopped at number 19, a rickety old building with garrets visible at the top. Alice was irrepressible. She told Milton, her driver, to wait.

"Come along," she said to me, and in we went. It was as if we were children, climbing the stairs to an attic we had long wanted to explore. At the end of the staircase, Alice produced a key from her pocket and with a flourish opened the door in front of us. The room itself was filthy, but on the north side directly opposite the door were huge, floor-to-ceiling slanted windows. They were filthy too, but Alice had cleaned one of the panes, to show me what it would be like, and light poured in. It washed the room and made it shimmer. I turned to Alice, who was watching me.

"How is this?" she whispered. I realized she was nervous. I saw that I held sway in these matters and took note of the subtle shift implied in our relations.

"Perfect," I managed.

"Central Park is right over there." She pointed to the green treetops half a block away. "So, nature is nearby."

"Oh!"

"But it can only be for a few months," she went on, now all business. "These buildings are all coming down to make way for hotels, and the rent here is much lower than it should be. You'll not have long, but you'll be able to get something started, won't you, dear?"

"I will, yes." I took in both the place and her term of affection.

"Well. Good." She held out the old-fashioned key. "Here."

I took it and held it. It was heavy in my hand, and its contours were still warm from Alice's hand. I thought about how that warmth carried her kindness and generosity, and how the key was opening this new door for me.

"I'm off," she said. "I'll send Milton back for you," she murmured and ducked back down the stairs. Left alone, I took stock. The place was filthy, there were mouse droppings, and the windows were so caked with grime I thought it possible I'd never be able to get them clean. I crossed the room tentatively.

"My studio," I whispered. "My studio." I repeated it over and over like a drum roll to keep me marching. The parts of the window that could be opened were on the side, casements that moved with the turn of a handle. The one I tried was horribly stiff. I decided to take it as a sign: if I could not open the window, I would not move into this space. But finally, the crank began to loosen, and then the window itself, stiffly and jerkily, moved. The sky was a shocking blue after the gloom of the dingy studio, and I could just get my shoulders through to lean out over the ledge. There were dozens of cooing pigeons jostling one another, and the filth made me recoil.

I jerked back to close the window and go home when something stopped me. It was a tiny glint on the floor. I leaned down to pick it up. An earring. A small gold coin attached to a wire. Possibly it had belonged to a model, someone who had sat here for hours, who had pulled it from her ear, impatiently, anxious to pack up and go. The coin was Greek and looked very old—impossible to tell with so much dirt—but I drew my handkerchief from my pocket and polished it, and soon its patina glowed. This, I knew, was the sign, a gift from the gods themselves. I held it tightly and looked out the open window. Busy and oblivious, Fifth Avenue was full of automobiles, horse-drawn omnibuses, and the occasional pushcart. Life in all its vivid splendor, I thought. Central Park formed a block of green to the left, its trees rising close and gentle.

I told Alice I wanted to make the space my own with my own two hands—something I had always been too sickly and delicate to do. She wanted to send her household staff, but I said I needed to do the work of preparation—the cleaning—that would enable me to do the work of making art. What I didn't say was that I wanted to be alone there. That first day the murky windows, their single sparkling pane a porthole to the outside, loomed over the room, and the sky, barely visible beyond, seemed a great vaulted ceiling—my own cathedral. Suddenly I understood why Vincent van Gogh had painted his room in Arles so many times: to know one's space was to touch it with one's whole being. On the planked wooden floor, surrounded with wainscoting, was a pair of broken chairs, as well as an old easel and ladder. I loved the simplicity of the space, loved the sense of silence while the great city below went about its fractious business.

Alice appeared on the second day and confronted me, exhausted by then and covered in filth. "You will have not a shred of energy left for painting," she said. I had to admit she was right. We had set a date in early April for a private showing at her house—this, she said, to corral the social set before they all disappeared for the summer—and I was already worried about producing enough for that. We had decided that I would add two new paintings to the three that were finished, and that we would feature my pastels. I had easily fallen into thinking about "us" and what "we" were planning and enjoyed the sense of companionship this provided.

Alice sent Willis, her man-of-all-work, who with his nephew scraped and scrubbed the place from stem to stern. I was thrilled to see how limpid and translucent the light was when the job was finished. She dispatched Milton with a davenport from her own sitting room, which he and the building custodian hefted and maneuvered into the small elevator and then up the final flight to the garret. It was velvet, the color of claret, and its mahogany legs were carved in twists that ended in elaborate swirls. One end swept upward like

a surging red wave so that one could recline on it and rest, which I
needed to do fairly often.

Alice thought I might want to stay there some nights rather
than travel home to Brooklyn, and she brought me a gas ring for
making tea or for heating the occasional meal. She arranged for a
telephone to be installed. I felt it was an unnecessary extravagance,
but she convinced me it was the most efficient way to make our
vision a reality. "Collectors will want to visit your studio and will
want to be able to arrange visits," she said. (Maman's eyebrows went
up when I handed her the new number.) Alice dropped in so often
with things I might need that I became accustomed to hearing her
call out from the garret's landing and looked forward to her arrival.

I was diligent. I left home each morning at around eight o'clock,
boarded the subway in Brooklyn, and got off at 59th Street. I loved
climbing the subway steps and emerging in the wholly other world
of Manhattan. It felt like entering a theater. Sometimes I lingered
to draw the pleasure out and bought roast chestnuts at the corner.
The man who sold them was small and wore a hat that was also
small, and his hands were blackened by the roasted nuts. I felt we
were conspirators, two watchers in a world that hummed around
us, busily oblivious. It made me laugh to realize that he also felt a
guardianship of this small corner. That we both looked each day
with satisfaction as the streetcars came and went, and automobiles
tooted their horns, and people rushed.

I walked toward Fifth Avenue at a leisurely pace, preparing
for a day of work and thinking through that day's objectives. These
included two new paintings that I had begun, one inspired by a
symphony depicting nymphs and sprites in a woodland. I saw an
imaginative landscape in which vertical lines suggested the bars
that divide musical scores into beats. The symphony's pulsing tempo
became for me the heartbeat of the cosmos. I used muted, earthen
colors out of which lively, barely visible spirit-creatures emerged
and were caught up in a dance.

The other piece was more realistic in style—a young girl holding vines of blooming morning glories stands on a hill against a deep French ultramarine sky, with suggestions of clouds below and in the distance. I worried again about making "women's art" and tried imposing a more abstract style, which I abandoned. I was finding it more and more difficult to create abstract pictures. I wanted not stylistic triumphs like Cubism but works that would use a realistic image to plumb the essence of human experience. If I could but ride the miraculous energy that had carried me to Ogunquit and the Armory and Ardsley House and given me this friendship with Alice—if I could simply follow the path before me—I would break through to a new art, a spiritual art, an art that provided its viewers with a portal to the sacred.

Maman warned me about stretching myself to the point of exhaustion.

"You do not work for Mrs. Thursby," she said. "It is good of her to put on an exhibit, but you do not need to sacrifice your health in return."

It wasn't that I felt I owed it to Alice, I told her; it was that I was fired by inspiration as never before.

"Be careful you don't burn up," she said.

Sure enough, within days I was ill with the bronchitis that had so plagued me as a child. It crossed my mind that this might be some sort of biblical judgment on me and my ambitions. "Vanity," my grandmother often said—just one word that she felt needed no elaboration. Perhaps it was vanity. Did it matter? Would I do anything differently? I decided I would not, that in fact I was helpless to take a different course. That meant I needed to reject this notion once and for all. I picked up a sketchbook and tried sketching out the idea of "judgment." At the end of a feverish hour, I had nothing but a confusion of black and blacker clouds, something like a whirl-wind, which I dismissed as clichéd and literal. I felt I was up against an indistinct barrier but one that seemed to grow larger with each effort, and I worried that Alice would feel she had made a mistake.

The private showing at Alice's house took place on an evening in early April, even though I had no other new paintings to offer. We hung *Vine Wood*, *Young Woman at her Mirror*, and *West Wind*, with *French Music* and *Morning Glory* included as works in progress. We also hung twenty-five pastels, which Alice said the people she was inviting would likely prefer anyway. Many of her friends attended and were generous with their praise. Some were escorted by husbands in dinner clothes who quickly repaired to a smaller parlor set aside for smoking.

John Quinn did not appear.

Alice had attached "sold" cards to the pastels that she intended to buy anyway, hoping it might encourage more purchasing. Several of the women expressed interest, a few bought outright; one lady apologized for her husband's absence and asked if she could take her choice home for him to inspect. It was one of my Imaginative pictures. She sent it back the following week, apologizing profusely, and said he had found it "too gloomy" for his taste. "I am sure you'll be able to sell it very quickly," she wrote in her note. "I do find it profound and evocative and am very sorry not to be able to keep it."

Alice was so pleased at the success of this first showing that she said we should hold another one right away—this time at my studio, because, she said, "that is where the real dealing takes place anyway." I knew she had John Quinn in mind. She pressed two hundred dollars into my hand for additional furnishings. I tried to refuse the money, but she insisted.

At home that evening I told Maman, certain she would insist that I return the money, that she would find a way as she had so many times before. Instead she said, "That is very generous of her." She rose heavily from the supper table and carried her plate to the sink.

My surprise was quickly displaced by shame. I saw how childish my assumption was and how thoughtless. Maman was growing older.

The slight bend of her back, thickness around her hips, attitude of her head, and lines in her face showed how weary she was.

"Maman," I said, "I am sorry. I did not think."

She said, simply, "I believe in you," and turned on the faucet and began washing. "Now, come and help me."

The afternoon mail brought a note from Alice: "Have you met Mabel Dodge?" she wrote. "I think you said you had crossed paths in Italy. Mabel is a childhood friend of mine, very interested in the modern art—she gave the Armory Show a sizable sum of money—and she might be very helpful to you. She is holding one of her salons tomorrow evening, and I think we should attend. Will you meet me there? She lives at 92 Fifth Avenue. I will arrive by nine o'clock."

One couldn't go anywhere without hearing about Mabel Dodge. Having abandoned Italy and the Renaissance, she had made a grand entrance into the Greenwich Village world of radical politics and art, and quickly made a name for herself with the Armory Show and her "white" salons. These gatherings were said to surpass all the others in the city in terms of the number of guests, vaguely scandalous goings-on, and lavish spreads of food. Maman and I were preparing supper when I told her I'd been invited to another salon.

"That doesn't sound very wise, Agnes. You were so sick just two weeks ago."

"I am fine, Maman. Please don't worry."

"That is easier said than done, I'm afraid. I do worry. Nor am I any too sure you should be seen at those places."

"Darling Maman. Alice will be there. I'm very likely to see others I know. Maybe even the Myerses."

"You don't know that," she said.

I set dishes at our places and tried another tack.

"Imagine, Maman. At Mabel Dodge's apartment, everything is white: the walls are covered in white silk, the rugs are white, the furniture—"

"Awfully hard to keep clean," she said. She set down a bowl of beef stew and began ladling it out.

"They say it's a metaphor," I went on. "The salon is like a blank canvas, and all the people coming together create the art. It is intended to provoke and stimulate."

"It has certainly accomplished that," she said.

"You have to admit it is new."

"Just because a thing is new doesn't mean the whole world has to come to a halt to admire it."

"I will be fine," I repeated.

"I don't trust that woman."

"Who, Mabel Dodge?"

"No."

"Alice? You don't trust Alice?"

"I think you should be careful."

I agreed. My surging affection for Alice should be kept hidden, even from—or especially from—my mother. I pushed it down and drew myself up.

"So far, Maman," I said, "it would appear that Alice should be careful. She has done nothing but encourage me, and she has stood behind her words with material support. All of which I have told you about, and all of which, up until this moment, you have condoned."

"You are an adult. You don't require permission from me."

It was true. I was thirty-three years old. I pressed on.

"I do not understand your tone or your sudden reversal. I thought you were happy and excited about the shows, the sales, and the possibility of a major collector being interested in my work. A great deal of this comes directly from Alice, and I do not understand what you are objecting to."

Even as I said this, I regretted it; I didn't want to hear what my mother might say by way of explanation.

"She treats you like some sort of pet, Agnes. You are a diversion for her, an entertainment. I am extremely concerned about how you'll feel when she tires of it all and drops you for another distraction. Or goes away. You are very sensitive."

I sat rigidly and hoped I appeared calm. I knew she was referring to Gertrude. For the first time I knew she understood: the illness that had leveled me all those years ago had come out of that loss, however inappropriate and imaginary it might have been.

"Please don't worry," I said. I folded my napkin, left the table, and went upstairs to my room. I had draped several items of clothing over the bed and chair, hoping to decide on what I would wear the following evening. Earlier, I had enjoyed pondering the nature of white and how it encompasses the entire spectrum and had thought I might wear several different colors together to symbolize it. Now all these clothes looked more like the makings of a costume for a gypsy carnival than an artistic statement. I put them away, shut off the overhead light, and got into bed. My thoughts raced and refused to come into focus. Alice was not Gertrude, and I was not obsessed with her. I was simply happy in her presence and grateful for all her efforts on my behalf. Not only had I recovered from my attachment to Gertrude, I had changed in Rome and even more so since my return. I had acquired the confidence that can only arise from sincere recognition of one's talents, and I did not intend to fall victim to emotional yearnings again.

The streetlamp outside my window sent its light in a watery pattern against the ceiling and the walls, and I waited for sleep. When nothing seemed to calm or quiet my heart, I resorted to a game I have often played, reviewing for myself the visual details of my room. I saw that the wallpaper was faded, and I decided that once the showing in my studio was over, I would strip it off in favor of paint. I noticed a subtle crack in the east wall that had spread into the ceiling and nearly reached the plaster rosette in which the overhead light was mounted. In the corner was a small armchair, and I noted that it was soft and plush, faded and worn, and that it had belonged to my grandmother but now was mine. The Oriental rug by my bed had also been hers, as had the mahogany bureau. Even though I did not use them, her silver hairbrushes were arrayed on a dresser scarf on the bureau's top. I was startled to realize that she seemed more present in the room than I.

I got out of bed, and in the ghostly half-light pulled from the closet a sheaf of old drawings. The largest was of our garden in spring—the locust tree in bloom, nodding its head with thick clumps of white blossoms cascading down from the branches. I tacked it to the wall, but it did little to dispel my grandmother's aura, nor did it overcome the heaviness of our common past. I sat on the bed again and let its weight settle over me. It came to me that as long as I lived in this house, there was little I could do but surrender; the history of who my grandmother was, and by extension who my mother and I were, would permeate every corner of my life. I took a certain comfort from this understanding, as though our past was grounding me and without it I might blow away. That was simply that. I felt at peace as I settled back into bed.

THE WHITE SALON

92 FIFTH AVENUE

1913

THE FOLLOWING EVENING, I CHOSE a pale green dress to symbolize the rebirth that comes with the spring and gave myself a long look in the mirror. I had pulled my hair back to convey maturity—I have always looked younger than my age—and now I took a powder puff to my face. I toyed with the idea of adding black lines to my eyes and decided against it as something that might cause irritation as the evening proceeded. Feeling satisfied then, I wrapped myself in a light cloak and went downstairs. Maman was reading a book in the small parlor and did not look up.

"I won't be terribly late," I said.

"Yes, you will," she said.

I left the house, closing the door with deliberate care but a certain emphasis to let her know that I was undeterred. Outside, the evening had gathered and the air was fresh. An earlier shower had rinsed the slate sidewalks, and a pleasant metallic aroma infused the air. I walked briskly to the subway and dropped my nickel into the slot.

At Union Square I exited the train and the station and turned north at Fifth Avenue. Number 92 was quickly spotted by the steady stream of people entering the building and crowding into the elevator. I hung back to see if Alice might be waiting for me in the lobby, but she was not. My courage flagged for a minute, and I pushed myself into the next car going up.

The doors opened directly onto the foyer of the apartment and into a cacophony of voices. As prepared as I was for a crowd, my breath grew rapid and shallow, as though there could not possibly be enough air for all of us. Everything was indeed white, and it seemed to reflect sound as sharply as light. I did not see Alice right away, but I did see Mabel Dodge clinging to the arm of a handsome young man. This was John Reed, better known as Jack, who had embraced Communism and was now holding forth to an attentive circle of listeners. He seemed entirely unaware of Mabel except for covering her hand with his own as it rested on his arm.

And then Alice was at my elbow—from where she had come, I had no idea.

"Isn't it grand?" she said. "Over there—don't let him catch you looking—see? John Quinn." Right next to Quinn and talking animatedly was Walt Kuhn, and I found that his presence reassured me a great deal.

"We will go talk to him, but first you must greet Mabel."

"I doubt that she'll remember me," I said, suddenly nervous again. Although it had been only a few years, Italy and Florence and the villa seemed long ago and far away.

"Then we shall introduce you again. She certainly knows your name from the Armory." Alice looped her arm through mine and steered me forward.

"Isn't this fun?" she murmured. "The man next to Jack Reed is his writer friend Gene O'Neill. I understand that O'Neill is helping Jack write about the labor strikes they've all been so taken up with. That grim-looking woman is Emma Goldman."

"I fear I am overdressed," I said.

"Nonsense," Alice replied, maneuvering us skillfully to our hostess. "Mabel, may we borrow you for a minute?"

Mrs. Dodge dropped Reed's arm, and he moved off at once with O'Neill as though he had been released from a harness.

"Why, it's Miss Pelton, isn't it? I recall your visit to the villa with so much pleasure."

"How kind of you to remember," I said.

"Your study of art with Hamilton Field, has that continued as a fruitful association?"

"It has," I said. "Mr. Field recently mounted an exhibition of my work at his new Ardsley House gallery."

"You should have come, Mabel," Alice said.

"I should indeed! I did see and so admire the work you showed at the Armory. Unfortunately, as soon as that show closed, Jack and I became embroiled in the terrible labor problems in New Jersey. We were practically living there." She took my hand into both of hers.

"I recall with such affection how sympathetic a companion you were, Miss Pelton. How you grasped immediately what I was trying to create at the villa. I felt that you and I were a pair of old souls, perhaps from a past life."

I was flattered, and I am sure I blushed. "I enjoyed seeing it all. It was one of the highlights of my year in Italy."

"We must get together another time, just the two of us. It would be a delight to talk with you about everything that's happened since." She glanced over to where Reed was talking to another roughly dressed man, turned back to me, squeezed, and released my hand. "I must go and greet some new arrivals, but I promise you will hear from me and soon." And then without any apparent haste, she floated off in the direction of the foyer.

"I think you've done yourself some good," Alice said. She circled my waist with her arm and moved forward. "Let us carry that spirit over to Mr. Quinn."

The room was dense with warm air, but I had promised myself I would not flag or try to escape when it all felt like too much. Looking back on it, I see that I was in a state of intoxication—not from what I had imbibed, but from the open and free atmosphere of Mabel's salon. And the ease with which both Mabel and Alice displayed their affection for me. Maman had called me Alice's pet. I thought it likely that she was right, but I was beyond caring what that might mean. I wanted to be part of what I'd just heard someone call "this essential moment." Head high, I marched across the room with Alice.

Quinn and Kuhn were still locked in what appeared to be an intense discussion, and I was gratified when Walt looked up as we approached and favored me with a warm smile.

"Ah, one of our brilliant American moderns. Hello, Agnes, how nice to see you here. Do you know John Quinn?"

Quinn glanced my way and looked slightly puzzled. I thrust my hand out.

"How do you do, Mr. Quinn. I believe we met at the Armory."

"Ah, yes, nice to see you." He turned back to Walt, and I could feel my face flushing. I had seen society women deliver such icy pleasantries even as they erased from their consciousness the victim standing in front of them.

"We must leave this for another day, Kuhn," he said. Walt smiled at me cheerfully, oblivious to my discomfort.

"I was just saying that we have painters in this country as brilliant as any that Europe has produced, and that Quinn here should be buying them up before the prices are too high even for him."

"Yes," Alice chirped. I'd never seen her so obviously discomfited. She tried again. "John, you really must see Miss Pelton's work. We are planning a studio showing . . ."

Something seemed to catch his eye. "Excuse me, ladies." He nodded briefly at Alice and me and moved away toward the buffet doors, which were now opening.

"He'll come around," Alice said.

"He will indeed," Kuhn agreed. "Feeling hungry yet?"

We joined a long line, and I selected carefully from the feast in front of us, hoping not to distress my always delicate stomach. I found the cacophony of the salon oddly stabilizing; Alice and I could barely hear one another, so we abandoned conversation altogether. She spotted Quinn with a plate, forking food into his mouth—something that would presumably keep him from escaping—and shouted that she would see me later. I watched her home in on him, aware that she was doing it for me and my work, which sent a thrill through my body. Fear or excitement? To this day I couldn't tell you. I looked at my own half-full plate and knew I could not swallow a single thing, and so—repenting the waste—handed it to a maid and fought my way out of the dining room.

It was long past midnight by the time Alice had had her fill of the salon. Many people had already left, but the core group of radicals and writers led by Jack Reed were still in their corner, shouting at one another, their shadows playing against Mabel's white silk-covered walls. The room was hot and smoky. I fought to keep my pasted-on smile intact, but I had begun to feel faint and thought I might topple over. I spotted an empty chair and sat, the crushing fatigue finally asserting itself. Mabel's lovely white carpet was stained with some kind of food that had been spilled and then ground into it by careless feet. Across the room she leaned up against Reed as though the hour was still early and she was captivated by his every word.

"How long do you think that will last?" Alice was behind me. Instinctively I rose and turned. At the sight of my face, which was most likely ashen, Alice's changed abruptly. "Oh my, we must get you home. Come along."

I tried to reassure her with a smile and concentrated on the task at hand, which was to find the maid who knew where my cloak was, collect it, and walk to the elevator.

"No, wait," Alice said. "I will get our wraps." She strode off in the direction of the foyer, where I gathered the guest closet was to be found. She quickly returned with her arms full and draped mine around my shoulders. A liveried butler stepped out of the shadow and helped Alice with her coat. I was puzzling about the extreme luxury of Mabel's apartment and why it would attract so many politically radical Greenwich Village denizens when Alice offered to help me to the elevator. I declined and willed myself to walk steadily and briskly.

Outside, a line of automobiles waited. Alice looked up and then down the street until she spotted Milton and waved him over. We climbed into the rear seat and settled ourselves, me needing to rest my head. Milton pulled away and turned the car south on Fifth Avenue. I felt I should sit up and behave like someone who has been given a lovely time, at least until Ninth Street when I assumed Alice would get out at her house and let Milton drive me home. We passed Ninth. Alice took my hand and held it.

"Poor lamb," she said. "Poor, poor lamb."

"Alice," I started to apologize.

"Hush," she said. We rode in silence, the tires thrumming through quiet streets that would soon be alive with commerce. I was too tired to feel the mortification I knew would be mine in the morning light. I should have simply waved goodbye to Alice at a reasonable hour, thanked my hostess, and gone home on my own. I would have kept my promise to my mother not to stay out too late. I would have been able to sleep and would have awakened refreshed and ready to return to the studio.

When we pulled up at Pacific Street, Alice wanted to help me in, but I said I was able to manage. I tried again to apologize and thank her for seeing me home like this. She shushed me again and put her arms around me. She carried the faint odor of smoke from the salon with a trace remaining of her perfume.

"You should have told me," she murmured. "I would never have let the evening go on so long."

"I should have," I agreed. "I didn't want to disappoint you."

"My dear girl, the only way you could disappoint me would be if you didn't trust me, if you felt you couldn't confide in me." She released me then, and her eyes brimmed with emotion.

"I do trust you," I said, and heard my own words take root in my body. I thought and did not say, *I love you.*

"I hope so. Milton will see you inside."

I opened the front door cautiously, not wanting to disturb Maman if she'd been able to go to bed and sleep. She was reclining in Grandmama's parlor chair, her head back and her mouth slightly open. I felt a wave of remorse. Kneeling next to her, I shook her gently.

"I'm home, Maman." She opened her eyes with a start.

"Thank God," she said and lifted herself heavily to her feet.

"I'm so sorry."

"Never mind, you're safe and you're home. Let's get to bed."

She was groggy, so I helped her up the stairs and to Grandmama's room, into which she had moved over the summer. In my own bed at last, I tried to sleep. I expected the exhaustion and the embarrassment of my near collapse to overwhelm me. I was unprepared for a buoyant sense of excitement that kept my heart racing and my mind alert. I kept exclaiming to myself that I had been at my worst. Alice had witnessed the physical weakness I feared would cause her (and Field and Mabel Dodge, for that matter) to withdraw her patronage and her friendship. Not only had she been kind and loving, she had apologized and reassured me that I could trust her. I was euphoric.

When sleep finally came, my dreams were raucous and vivid, and I was with Alice somewhere I couldn't identify. We were holding each other, and her cheek caressed mine. In my dream I said, "What a surprise!" She laughed, and then I laughed too. When I awoke, I felt as though I were slipping through the membrane of the dream, like a character stepping from the pages of a book. I listened for activity in the kitchen, heard nothing, and was glad that Maman was still sleeping, happy to have a few more minutes to savor this extraordinary lightness.

Quietly I crept downstairs to make tea and slice the bread. Maman had still not come down by the time I finished my own breakfast, so I returned to my room to dress. I studied my image in the mirror. I felt I had a new self, and I wanted to meet her. I heard my mother stirring and hurriedly donned my usual studio work clothes. By the time Maman appeared at my door, I was packing up a few things and ready to go to the studio.

"Today?" she said. "Are you sure?"

"Yes, I'm sure. I've made tea." I peered at her closely. "Are you all right?"

"Yes, I am," she replied. "As, I see, are you." She touched my cheek briefly. "I am glad."

My heart soared again, this time in response to my mother's knowing kindness. I had groped for some word of explanation in anticipation of her questions, but seeing that there was no need, let the happiness brim inside me.

My elation faded as I walked to Fulton Street. The fatigue I thought I'd escaped now took hold. I might have turned around and gone home, but I simply did not have the strength.

The train pulled in and the doors opened, spilling out dozens of people in a hurry. Waiting, I admonished myself: You know better, I thought. *You know better.* My chest was leaden with the bone weariness it was my duty to avoid. A young man stood and offered me his seat. I nodded my thanks, sank down, and let my glance drop to shut out the crowd around me.

By the time I reached 59th Street, I was able to make my way to the studio. Up in that blessed space, I lay back on my velvet chaise and closed my eyes. "Never trust happiness," I heard my grandmother say. To calm myself, I took up a drawing pad and opened to a blank page.

I thought that if I could find a way to see Alice clearly and describe her for myself, I might find grounding. I took up a soft pencil. Slowly I traced what I recalled of her contours, her body shape and proportion, the way her head was set above her shoulders, that distinctive curve of her arm that Sargent's "new woman" portrait addressed. The first results were pallid, cartoonish. I had a silly head with silly hair over a body that did not really curve but rather looked like pieces stacked up one on the other. I put down my pencil and took up a piece of charcoal.

All right, I told myself, let's try again.

Charcoal drawings had always been anathema to me. Where I saw myself as tidy and poetic, charcoal demanded that I get dirty. The dust from a piece of vine charcoal falls off the stick relentlessly and covers everything—smock, hands, face, hair. And because it never really blackens the paper, you must dig and press and push hard to get the gesture you're looking for.

I put aside the pleasant, silly sketches and took up a large sheet of newsprint. I started in the center this time, looking for the center of Alice. I swooshed the charcoal stick on its side, fast, back and forth, shimmying up the page until I had a torso. Then, before I lost my courage, I took up pressed charcoal for its deep, velvety black, and darkened around the outside to find her contours. I always feel a certain agitation when making quick charcoal drawings, but my excitement on that day was of a different sort: I could have been touching Alice. My fingers and the charcoal they held were forming the roundness of her thigh, her waist, the drape of her blouse upon her breast, her throat. I stopped to look at what I had done. The figure in front of me was, in a word, beautiful.

My heart beat rapidly, and I took up the charcoal pencil to finish. Drawing quickly around the body shapes, this, I knew at once, in order to own them—I was a mother tucking and patting her child before sending her out into the world—tucking an excess smudge back into a line, lightly smoothing the collar that now appeared. I let the line extend upward, up the neck and throat and around the shadow that was Alice's hand and face. Here I began to slow down. I traced what I remembered of her eyes, her mouth, her nose, her chin. The suggestion of contour below her cheekbones, the narrow line of jaw, the slightly trembling intelligence that informed her face. Then her hair, lush and lovely, with a playful strand escaping here and there. I lowered my pad.

Shocked, I saw that my friend had become my beloved. I sat for a long time with the drawing in front of me. The light moved across the studio and marked the passing of the day. I removed my smock and washed my hands, all the while experiencing a calm I had not known before. I would never tell her, but I would find a way to contain happiness, along with sadness, grief, exhaustion, and despair. The day was fading, so I made my way home.

———————

Alice didn't seem to realize that something had changed for me, and I felt it imperative to maintain the stability of our connection without allowing these new feelings to intrude. Did this urgency arise out of simple ambition? My grandmother's words of warning echoed in my ears: ambition is folly, she had told me once: "That which the Lord intends for you will make itself known, and you will clearly see the way, for the Lord thy God will provide the light."

In the weeks before I was to vacate the atelier, Alice's arrangement with the landlord nearly at an end, I traveled there daily to bask in its atmosphere of quiet and detachment. I set the half dozen unfinished canvases against the wall to see if a solution would make itself known in any of them. Clutched in my hand, my finger marking the page, was Kandinsky's brilliant The Art of Spiritual Harmony. It had just been translated from the German, and Field had sent it to me with a scribbled note tucked inside: "I thought of you when I saw this in the window at Scribner's. I hope you find it inspiring. With my best wishes for your continued success."

I had showed it to Maman that morning, who was most impressed, and then I had tucked it into my bag to look at on the subway. As the train rocked toward Manhattan, I opened it. Every page was filled with inspiration, to be sure, but more importantly, Kandinsky had laid out a clear system for the expression of the spiritual experience, which he affirmed as one's inner life, inner truth, and inner radiance. "To harmonize the whole is the goal of art," he said, and abstraction was the means. I felt this keenly and deeply and yearned with my whole heart to find access to my own essential core. Kandinsky's aim was to help the artist achieve that and, through art, to open an inner door for the viewer.

At 59th Street, I nearly missed the stop and jumped up just in time. Climbing the stairs to the sun-filled street, my heart sang, "I have the key, I have the key" even as I cautioned myself against expectations that this small and precious book would lead immediately to the making of meaningful pictures.

The sun filled the studio in a way I found deeply inspirational, and with my works in progress surrounding me, I resumed my reading. Every chapter—"General Aesthetic," "The Movement of the Triangle," "Spiritual Revolution," "The Language of Form and Color"—laid out the system and strategy formulated by the master himself, if I could take it in and make it my own. I reclined on my chaise, reading the book and studying my own efforts until the light passed over the paintings and left them in shadow. By day's end, euphoria had been displaced by discouragement, and I was enormously tired as I departed for home.

The subway was slow, and it was well over an hour before I unlocked the front door. Maman was sitting in the parlor, a strange expression on her face.

"Are you all right?" I asked. Her face colored with embarrassment.

"I had a little spell," she said.

"What do you mean. A 'little spell'?" I dropped my bag on the hall table and rushed to kneel by her chair. Her eyes, sharp and blue as always, now filled with tears.

"I'm sorry," she said.

"Dear heart, don't be silly." I squeezed next to her on the chair and put my arm around her.

"I'm sure I'm fine," she said timidly.

"We'll call the doctor."

"No!"

"I think we should."

"No," she said again. "I am sure that I'm fine. Just a dizzy spell."

We sat leaning into each other for a long moment. It was clear that neither of us wanted me to get the doctor. Not just because of the expense—our bank account was shrinking faster than the music school could make it up. No, I think it was that neither of us wanted someone to tell us officially what we already knew: Maman was getting on in years, and we needed to accept that her strength and energy were on the wane. I grieved that I could not simply tell her to close the school and sit in her chair all day, if she wanted to, with her sewing or a book or whatever might please her, and that I would take care of everything.

"You must be hungry," she said. "Let's get some supper."

Reluctantly I shifted away from her and watched warily lest she lose her balance trying to get up, but she seemed entirely herself once more.

"See?" she said brightly. "Just a spell."

———————

When by morning it seemed clear that Maman was fully restored, I returned to the studio. The half-finished paintings were still lined up against the wall like a mocking chorus. I ignored them and set to work on a new canvas, this time using Kandinsky's system. A strategically placed dot meant one thing, a line another, a triangle something else. Color, too, carried deep significance and caused a specific and predictable response in the viewer. I began to set these symbols into patterns of my own design and was ecstatic at my progress.

The weather grew warmer and the garret stifling, but I was diligent and filled with a new fire. I had seen Kandinsky's work at the Armory and again at Stieglitz's gallery, and I was thrilled at how my own efforts seemed congruent with what I recalled of his. Alice came by often to admire and exclaim. One morning she brought with her the author and suffragette Zona Gale, whose books aimed to give women a sense of their own independence and worth. I might have been taken aback at Alice's boldness, but Miss Gale was satisfyingly direct. She shook my hand firmly and looked closely at my new work, which I had tacked up on the walls.

"Miss Gale is writing a new book for children," Alice murmured.

"Not new," the writer said. "A new edition of an older book."

"Yes," Alice said, eager to get on with the good news. "And she's looking for an artist of note to illustrate it."

"Yes." Miss Gale continued to peer at my pictures.

And so it was arranged. When I got home that evening and told Maman, she was thrilled. When I told her what the publisher would pay—$175 per illustration for seven pieces—we were both giddy. Maman said she would have to be especially nice to me if I kept bringing in money like this.

The pace of life quickened and I found it harder than ever to sleep. My pulse thrummed loudly in my ears and animated my dreams. When jolted awake in the morning, I knew that I had dreamt but was unable to remember the dream. My waking, then, was infused with a vague sense of distress as I tried to recover what my unconscious self had so recently been immersed in.

Maman began to take note of this. One particularly difficult morning, when my mirror told me how haggard I looked—my eyes were puffy, and a line had begun to etch itself into my forehead—she inquired in a neutral tone about my plans for the day.

"I think I'll go to the studio," I said, as if this idea had only just occurred to me.

"There is no need to take that tone, Agnes."

"No, I don't suppose there is, although really, Maman, I don't understand why you are asking."

"I don't understand why you don't understand. I am concerned. Your color is not good, and you are pushing yourself too hard."

In spite of myself, tears welled up and spilled over. It was true that I was exhausted but not from the work itself.

"I must finish these illustrations. Macmillan has given me a due date." I tried to sound patient, as if this were the first time the explanation had been offered.

"I know," Maman said quietly. She reached for the teapot to pour herself another cup and forgot to use the tea strainer. The pot was nearly empty, and sludge filled her cup. She said nothing, just returned the teapot to its trivet. I was immediately filled with remorse for my attitude, my frequent—and long—absences, the flurry of busyness that was taking my time and draining me of energy. I stood.

"Let me make a fresh pot."

"No," she said. "I don't really want more tea. I don't know why I did that." She said this sadly. Later I would wonder if this was when her decline began. But for the moment, I gritted my teeth and pressed on.

"Artists should never have families," one of my colleagues had said after his second wife left him. "We must be selfish. We must protect our work and pour everything we have into it. People cannot be allowed to distract us from that great charge." I had not agreed when he said this but was forced to concede that it might be true. I stood behind my mother and leaned down to embrace her, my arms around her arms, my cheek against hers.

"I must go," I said.

"I know," she replied. She kept her eyes fixed on her plate where a piece of toast lay half finished.

"This will be over soon," I said. "The Fifth Avenue building is coming down, so I won't have the studio anymore. Then you will wish I was not home all the time, cluttering up the sunroom with all my materials."

"I will never wish that."

I looked around our drab kitchen, its walls dark from cooking. I hoped that at the very least I could pay to brighten it up.

I pulled myself together and kissed the top of her head quickly, which made her smile.

"There," I said. "That should hold you for a while." We both laughed then. Those were the very words she had used with me when I was small and she was occupied with the music school.

For all my anguish about leaving my mother, the minute I was out of the house and walking down Pacific Street, my thoughts turned to the painting I had begun. I was determined to use Kandinsky's principles, applying specific colors in an attempt to create visual music. I have always loved systems—most likely the result of the musical training my mother had given me in childhood—and I was eager to apply a musical logic to the task of painting. In music, each note has a value and lasts precisely as long as that value: one beat, or one and a half, or two, or longer. Kandinsky had written that each note also related to a color, something I had sensed years earlier, and here it was, set out in a usable system. I had started this picture with great enthusiasm and high hopes before Miss Gale came along, but now I was finding it difficult. Alice had stopped by for one last visit and was studying it.

"What is wrong, do you think?" I finally asked. She did not speak for several minutes.

"There's nothing wrong," she finally said. "It's absolutely correct. But it isn't you." I knew she was right.

"Put it down for now," Alice suggested. "Wait until you've moved into the new studio."

She had surprised me yet again by finding another studio, this time in Greenwich Village—"Not your first choice, I know," she had said, "but it will supplant a need to return to the sunroom." I had blushed a bit at that, and when she noticed, she quickly added that likely it would be temporary. The new space was grittier and dingier than my sweet aerie, but it would put me among other artists again, which idea lent a buoyant energy as I held out hope for an artistic breakthrough.

But truly, my days were filled with Alice. It was her verve, her vivacity, the light scent of lilac, and her optimism. I felt no need of the companionship I might have found in that building, so it was a severe shock when, on the last day of June, she announced that she was sailing for Europe.

"Well!" I said brightly. "I don't know how I will manage without you." She laughed as though I were making a joke.

"You, dear girl, will be so busy with your painting, you won't think about me at all. But I will be thinking about you."

I forced a smile.

"And guess who else is sailing for Europe? On the same ship."

I shrugged, my voice having retreated.

"John Quinn! And I will make him promise to buy at least one of your paintings, that you can count on."

Battery Park was green and subdued, with not even a whisper of a breeze to stir the foliage when I set up my easel. I placed it so I faced north, up the river toward the ever-growing city. I opened the large vellum pad I'd brought, unpacked my drawing materials, and unfolded the lightweight stool I'd nearly forgotten I owned. It had been a long time since I had done this—not since Ogunquit, in fact—gone outside to be in the open air and draw such scenes as I found. Even as I felt myself settle into the pleasurable rhythms that come with drawing *en plein air*, I tried not to feel that I was falling backward. I was not abandoning abstraction as an ideal, a philosophy, and a method; I was simply putting it aside.

Taking a long, slow breath in, I noted the heavy scent of water behind the aroma of something spicy—geranium perhaps—and the freshly mowed carpet of grass. I took up my soft, flat carpenter's pencil and let my hand skip about the page to draw the broad outline of river, narrowing as it flowed north; the old stone Castle Garden that had once been an entertainment pavilion, then the immigration entry point, and then the Aquarium, but which now sat hollow and empty; the harbor fire station with its red and white boat docked at the end. All of that I kept to the right side of the page, letting the river take pride of place down the center. I sketched in where I might place a few of the smaller working craft and the passenger ferries that moved sluggishly like beasts of burden from New York to New Jersey and back, at least a hundred times over a day.

I lowered the pencil and sat completely still, watching. I had truly forgotten the joy of interacting with the landscape in this fashion, of being the observer and also being part of the scene itself: passersby were glancing over to where I worked, trying to get a look at my paper, murmuring to themselves, I thought, about the presence of an artist down here where the boats came in. A noisy cabal of robins chattered and called to one another while they poked their beaks into the soft grass, occasionally coming up with a worm. This is wonderful, I remember thinking.

Then a huge black hull came around the imperceptible bend to the north and immediately filled the river. I stood as if a lady had just entered the room and quickly sketched the ship into my drawing. It was this I had come to see—Alice's ship departing for Europe—it was this I was determined to draw.

On deck staring back toward the city were crowds of passengers, Alice likely among them; perhaps she was even standing next to John Quinn and badgering him to buy my work. She better hurry, I thought; my days as a fresh new face on the art scene were numbered.

The ship slid past the shore quickly and silently, pointed its prow outward, and began to thread its way past the Statue of Liberty. I watched until it entered the Narrows; then, remembering my purpose here, I flipped to a new page on my pad and quickly drew it as it receded, the name on its stern no longer readable. The wake frothed and caught the currents and played itself out in meandering briny lines through the harbor. When the liner began to disappear into the ocean mist, I packed up my things. All my supposed "progress" was swallowed by loneliness, and one thought—She's gone—echoed repeatedly through my head.

I started walking. I had intended to leave my paint box, easel, and pad at my new studio, but my feet picked up speed on their own, and I nearly ran to the Brooklyn ferry. She's gone, she's gone, she's gone. I trudged onto the boat, stumbling over my easel, and found my way to the rail. Bells clanged, chains dropped, and the oily river swirled as we pushed away from the dock.

By morning a dull ache had lodged itself like a burrowing animal just beneath my chest. In spite of myself, I found the sensation familiar and comforting. It had never been our family custom to inquire about obvious signs of one another's distress, so if my mother had taken notice of my pained expression, she gave no sign. Instead, her breakfast conversation was full of ideas about how I might find another commission.

"Books are such a good place for your work. Books last, Agnes. And books will be seen by so many more people than those who can afford to buy a piece of art!" She thrust a sheet of paper at me and looked pleased.

"What is this?"

"I had some time yesterday, so I went to the library and looked in the Manhattan telephone directory and wrote down the names and addresses of all the major publishers. Look," she said, pointing to her neatly prepared paper. "I've listed them geographically."

I stared at her, baffled, and she continued.

"You can start on Fourth Avenue and work your way uptown, or better, maybe, start on Fifth and work your way down. Then you'd be closer to the ferry and home."

"Maybe tomorrow, Maman," I said. "I'm a little tired." I pushed the list to one side and poured myself a cup of tea.

"Well, then," she said. Her face was crestfallen but not defeated. I recalled that very expression from my childhood on the rare occasions when I had defied or disobeyed her.

"Take it a few at a time," she went on patiently. "You don't need to make new drawings. You can carry the illustrations Zona Gale didn't want in your portfolio. It won't be too heavy."

She had touched a sore spot and I didn't reply. I still burned at the recollection, a week ago now, of Miss Gale quickly and briefly reviewing what I had brought her: a series of the fanciful pictures she had asked for, representing herself as a child in various settings.

"This one is good, and this one, but I don't like this." She handed back the offending drawing, which was exactly in tune with the others she had approved. I must have looked puzzled.

"That expression," she said. "Much too defiant."

"Oh," I said. "I could soften it."

"No," Miss Gale said, distracted. "Let's try something else." And with that she rose from her chair, and I was dismissed.

Maman seemed to realize she'd said the wrong thing. She had no interest in coddling a mood she considered detrimental to my health or productivity, but neither did she wish to be cruel.

"Never mind," she tried. "Maybe tomorrow when you feel better."

"I have to go to the studio tomorrow. I haven't yet finished the commission I have." I could hear the truculent self-pity in my voice.

"Of course, dear," she said. She picked up her list and put it back on her desk.

"I'm doing the best I can," I said.

"I know you are, darling."

That I was finding it difficult to earn a living at my art should not have been a surprise, but I had come to rely on Alice more than I had known. Without her reassurance, waving away my fears and inadequacies with brisk imperial gestures, I didn't see how it would even be possible.

Maman patted my shoulder and left the kitchen. Noting her upright carriage, which throughout my childhood had made her seem remote and disapproving, I managed to set my own misery aside: here was my mother, whose dreams of a concert career in Europe were replaced by a sickly child; whose strength had carried my father and me to Brooklyn and had established the school of music, which was still supporting us after all these years. Embarrassed, I resolved to take strength from her example.

Upstairs I washed my face and dressed in my most businesslike clothes, a dark blue dress with a subdued floral pattern. I tucked Maman's list into my portfolio with the rejected illustration and several other studies I had made for an Imaginative work and set out for Manhattan.

On a whim, I decided against using the list and instead presented myself at Macmillan and Company. As boldly as possible, I asked to speak to the art director. The receptionist managed to look down her nose at me even while peering up.

"Is he expecting you?"

"I believe so," I said, shocking myself. I could imagine Alice laughing behind her hand.

"Your name, please?"

"Agnes Pelton."

The woman scribbled a few words on a piece of paper and folded it into a cylinder, which she then tucked into a pneumatic tube, the thwack of the vacuum sending it on its way. We waited. Finally, she invited me to sit down. We both stared at the tall, highly polished case clock in the corner, its spidery hands moving the hour along in tiny increments. When it struck four, we looked at each other as if by prearrangement. Feeling that this obvious charade must end, I rose to take my leave.

"Miss Pelton?" A short, bald man was peering out of a door behind me. "Please do come in. My apologies for keeping you waiting." I couldn't resist glancing at the receptionist, who was as surprised as I. This was Mr. Hightower, and he kept up a running commentary as he led me back through a warren of offices, each with a secretary at a desk just outside. Hurrying to keep up, I couldn't make out a word of what he said. At last he turned into a spacious office in the building's corner, where enormous windows pulled the city in close.

"I don't know how I managed to overlook your appointment," he said riffling through a mess of papers on his desk. "Please do sit down."

"Mr. Hightower," I started, "it's very kind of you to see me."

"Nonsense," he fluttered his hands. "You had an appointment."

"Well, no, sir, I hadn't."

"Ha ha!" He beamed at me. "You artists are intent on upsetting all the rules, aren't you? I believe I saw your work at the Armory, did I not?"

Flattered, I nodded.

"I don't recall the pieces specifically, but I did so admire the show. Thrilling, really. All that modern energy sweeping us up. What a ruckus you all caused! Well!"

He clapped his hands quickly. "I believe you are working with Zona Gale, are you not? We are so very pleased she has joined our list."

I nodded. "Yes, I am."

"Are you enjoying it?"

"I must say that I am," I said, hoping he wouldn't notice the trick of language. "I would like to continue with book illustration. I believe it suits me very well."

I was shocked at my own boldness. If he was aware of my discomfort, Mr. Hightower gave no sign.

"Well, then. Let me see what you've brought."

I unfastened the clasp of my portfolio and pulled out several pastels, including the one that Zona Gale had rejected.

"Oh, my," he said. He picked each one up carefully and carried it to a work table, where he leaned over to study them.

"These are exceptional, Miss Pelton, just exceptional."

I was flooded with relief that I could go home and tell my mother I had landed another commission and would be regularly illustrating books for Macmillan. I was on the verge of pouring out my thanks—out loud to Mr. Hightower, and silently to whatever deity had supplied me with just enough courage to try this.

"But," he added, "I do think that what you do is far beyond what we ordinarily need here. You are that rarity, Miss Pelton, a real artist. You should not squander your gifts." He carefully gathered the pictures and gently returned them. "Thank you for coming by. It has been a real pleasure."

———

I was a bit disoriented when the elevator man pulled the doors wide to let me out on the ground floor. I noted the time on the big clock in the lobby—just after five. As I walked back into the day, the throngs of people on their way home from work jostled me so often that I stood to one side and leaned against a building. What had just happened? Had Mr. Hightower been mocking me? I felt a surge of panic and was immediately overcome with missing Alice. She would know exactly what to do next; she would laugh away what had become a constant fear, low grade and lodged in my body like a fever, that my success to date was an accident and had now come to a proper halt. I imagined my grandmother, her black dress rustling, nodding sagely. "Everything has a beginning and an end, Agnes," she might say. "Bad times will end, but so will good times. It is best to understand that when you're young."

The deep weariness I had awakened with that morning reasserted itself. I stumbled to the subway, dragging my portfolio and half wanting to discard it in the street along with my ambition. My throat was sore, and I felt the beginnings of a head cold, which I knew would be enough to keep me away from the studio for the rest of the week. This was all so familiar, the pull of it, the ease of it. Maman would put everything aside to bring me tea and make me toast and hot broth. I could feel entitled to her ministrations having tried, really tried, to find work for myself.

At the Brooklyn ferry stop, I stepped off the train with the crowd and struggled to the street, wondering if I would make it another step, never mind the three blocks to the boat. Rounding a corner and coming toward me, I saw a familiar face—or, rather, a figure held at a familiar angle—and thought for a second it was someone who had been a kind friend all those years ago at Pratt. But it couldn't be she, because Jane, her name was, was my age, and this girl looked to be about sixteen. Then I had a sense of vertigo, as if I were tumbling headlong into the rabbit hole past, where I'd be myself at thirty-four and everyone else would be sixteen.

"Agnes?"

"Jane?" I stopped abruptly, causing more than one commuter to trip as they navigated around me. Dear God, it was she. I tried to appear pleased to see her, which I would have been except, except . . .

"How are you, Agnes? I saw your pieces at the Armory! What a thrill."

I waved away her praise and started to ask about her work, but it was too hectic. "Oh dear," I said, looking at the watch on my wrist, "I must catch this ferry, but so nice to see you again!"

"You, too!" She smiled and turned, and I hastened to rejoin the flow toward the river. My misery deepened. I knew I was running home to my mother, acting as though what was ailing me was the same as the illness I had suffered with all my life. I knew that it was not. I was in the grip of a discouragement so unremitting that every aspect of life was bleak, black, bottomless. It would not be cured with soup and tea and tender care, and it frightened me as never before. I could not, could *not* permit heartache and grief of this magnitude to pull me down so low. I did not have the emotional or physical stamina for it, and it was time to admit that.

There was no question about the source of my agony. Borne along by the stream of ferry-bound humanity, I was convinced of the absolute necessity of quenching, extinguishing, banishing, expelling from my heart and mind this need for Alice, this attachment to Alice.

By the time I reached Pacific Street, the promised head cold had begun to blossom, and I could do nothing but succumb to Maman's orders that I get right to bed. Two days later I was still there when she climbed the stairs clutching the morning mail, which included a note from Alice. Beaming and out of breath, she handed it to me.

"This will perk you up," she said. I took the envelope and opened it and caught a faint whiff of Alice's perfume in the beautifully embossed note paper. She was writing from the ship, she said, and hurrying to catch the final mail before the pilot boat returned to port. The card was indeed rushed but full of Alice's buoyant spirits. She clearly had no sense, not the slightest, of the nature of my feelings for her, and the chatty tone of the note confirmed that she didn't share them in the least. In fact, it was clear that she was entirely oblivious to the drama that had been raging in my heart. She briefly described her cabin, its porthole, and a few of the other passengers, particularly one of her socialite friends sailing with her husband for "six months of *rest*," having "completely *exhausted* herself over the winter season." I laughed at Alice's mischievousness: this generous lady had been to our uptown studio showing and had enthusiastically purchased three pastels.

The note had indeed given me a lift even as it had broken my heart. Suddenly I understood that the heart must be broken before the spirit can be liberated. That I must think of the heart as a vessel, a container of infinite love: until it has been broken open, love cannot be free. I knew that I loved my friend. I knew there was no shame to loving her, and I accepted it as fact. That in itself was a liberty. I also knew that in her own way, she loved me, just not in the way I loved her. I knew I must accept that and accept her, and that I must release the sadness, which I began to do, to let it flow through me and out. It was a relief finally, after years of struggle, to come to terms with my limitations, both physical and emotional—to put aside that which was keeping me from the work at hand, the making of art.

GREENWICH VILLAGE

JUNE 1916

FIELD HAD TOLD ME ABOUT available space in the famous Jefferson Market building, and I had signed a rental agreement and arranged for my things to be moved in. On a hot June day, I emerged from the subway at Sheridan Square to acquaint myself with the new studio and begin sorting materials. The trees sheltering Christopher Street nodded, drowsy with early summer heat. On Sixth Avenue they came to an abrupt end, and I was out in the bright glare of Bohemian New York. A left turn from Twelfth Street, and I was at the Jefferson Market Building. The brownstone entrance and dark wooden door were a bit forbidding, but I found that simply entering the building was to feel immersed in art-making.

I stood in the cool shadow of the foyer and listened. Behind the first-floor doors I could detect movement, and above I heard someone's shoes scrape as they climbed, presumably, to the ateliers on the top floor. Those studios were occupied, so the second floor had been the nearest I could be to the light. The staircase itself sagged alarmingly but held firm as I climbed upward. Steps, floors, and walls—everything, it seemed—was dark and dank, and the building smelled of mildew. I turned the key in my new door, and to my delight the room itself was airy and open to the afternoon light. I had seen it before, of course, but only in the morning and I'd not adequately taken it in.

Now I inspected the ceiling, the single light bulb hanging from a twisted wire in the center, the deep brown walls of high wainscoting, and the bare wooden floor. I swept carefully so as not to raise dust—or make noise, I realized—and wiped down the windowsills and the walls. Down the hall I found the water closet and a bucket that I filled and toted back without letting too much slop over, and I got down on my hands and knees to scrub the floor of the flecks that were not dried paint.

I set my easel up to catch the light from the window opposite the door and, next to the shelf, hung my chart of colors—a carefully detailed sampling of all the hues and their gradations for which I had pastels. On the stool next to my work chair, I placed the wooden case in which I kept my oils and unpacked each box, setting out the jugs and pitchers that Maman and I had decided could be put to use in that way. The remnants I put aside for still lifes or even to take the occasional meal.

The walls were studded with nails where someone must have hung tools and pictures, and, feeling the companionship of this unknown predecessor, I hooked my cooking pot onto one of those. I uncrated my half-finished canvases and pulled out the sketches I had made at Battery Park and the earlier charcoal drawing of Alice. I strained to see them as others might, to imagine what someone else would make of them. Probably, I decided, they would see just a set of competent sketches and one quite good drawing. What did it matter anyway if someone saw that I was fixated on a ship traveling down the Hudson on a summer morning? What did it matter if they studied a woman rendered in charcoal? I tacked them up on the wall.

I was tired then, and with everything more or less unpacked, I slumped down onto one of the hard chairs and looked around. I could hear the hollowness of the room itself, matching my own hollowness. Even with the homey touches I'd added—the shawl covering the cedar chest, the mismatched chinaware—the studio felt barren, spare to the point of sterility. I wanted to cry but did not. If this was the world of art, I was part of it now, like my neighbors in this building. They were still unknown to me, but here we all were, listening for the same muse, struggling together toward the same goals, hoping to create something that would last.

The studio grew dark as the day faded. I washed my hands and face, hung up my smock, picked up the paisley shawl I'd draped over the daybed, and left the building. My exhaustion was bone deep, and I still had the walk to the ferry. To distract myself, I had made a habit of creating letters to Alice. "You should see this," I would say: "Night is upon us, and here come the Village denizens—artists and models, writers and musicians, all manner of creative people, it would appear—emerging from the shabby buildings and gathering at the cafés." I began to study faces, narrating the different shapes and aspects. I approached Patchin Place. "Oh, my," I continued addressing Alice, "I do believe that's Djuna Barnes."

I was sure it was she, swathed in clothing that was thick and black and much too heavy for a warm evening. She seemed encased by all that fabric, but her eyes burned out, daring whomever she encountered to meet them. She was candid about her romantic attachment to both sexes—she flaunted it, actually. If you happened to be in one of the tearooms that were all the rage and you merely glanced her way, she would train those dark, electric eyes at you, a little smile playing about her mouth. It wasn't warm or friendly; it was a challenge. She seemed to relish the idea that one would be outraged.

Still, I often read the brief sketches of other Villagers that she wrote for newspapers, and I admired them. They were fresh and somehow subversive and revealed surprising aspects of her subjects that took the reader behind each well-constructed public persona. Even so, despite her authoritative tone, I thought I detected a need for approval as palpable as my own.

Directly behind me a man's voice called out, "Djuna!" Startled, I whirled about. "Why, Agnes!" he said. It was Jerome Myers, and in spite of my fatigue I was happy to see him. He pulled me in, his arm encircling my shoulder affectionately as he propelled me forward to meet up with Djuna, now almost upon us.

"Where are you off to?" he asked. I told him the Brooklyn ferry, and he laughed. "Oh, dear. You really should come along with us."

"I saw your gallery showing," I said. "I thought it exhilarating."

"Well, now, that is very nice of you." Of all our small Armory coterie, he seemed best poised for fame and possibly fortune. His solo exhibition at the Macbeth galleries had been a huge success. Many of the newspapers ran admiring reviews, and recently a reporter had followed him around on one of his typical Lower East Side days, drawing and painting the immigrants there.

"Djuna," he said, reaching for her with his other arm, "here's someone you really ought to meet. Maybe you can write about her."

She squirmed away and peered closely at me as Jerome introduced us. I was surprised at how young she was. Her face was beautiful, but there was a sadness to those fierce eyes, and my impulse was to comfort her.

"You're a painter?" she asked. "I must see your work."

I told her where my studio was, and she said she knew most of the other artists in the building. The way she said it, I felt foolish and shy and out of place, and more than ever I wanted to get home to Brooklyn.

Jerome said, "We're off to get a coffee and then go to Mabel Dodge's. You've been to her salons?"

I was relieved that my near-collapse at one of these evenings had apparently not become fodder for the gossip mill, and then I wondered if that were true.

"I have," I said demurely.

"Ah, yes," Djuna Barnes said. "I believe I recall seeing you there with Mrs. Thursby. Isn't that right?"

"It is," I replied. Ever the reporter, Barnes fixed her eyes on me, sensing a story and willing me to reveal it. I pointedly stared back as steadily as I could, but she made me feel that she could bore right into me, see into my heart and read my thoughts and my secrets.

"Well, then," Jerome said. "You really must come along."

"Not tonight," I said lightly, "but thank you for inviting me."

I tried to affect nonchalance as I resumed walking to the ferry. At last I turned the corner, wilting with the relief of being securely out of view. On the Brooklyn side of the river, I splurged and took a taxi home, having been completely depleted of strength.

I unlocked the front door, heard a crash, dropped everything, and called out for Maman. In the kitchen I found her on her knees, gathering up coins; in jagged pieces on the floor was the old Mason jar where we kept our "mad money."

"Maman! Be careful!" I took her hand and helped her up. "What on earth?" She burst into tears.

"I didn't want to worry you."

"Why? What is happening?"

"I must pay the egg man." She covered her face with her hands and wept. It emerged that he had been by that afternoon to collect his money, and she had put him off, pretending she was occupied with a pupil.

"I was so ashamed, Agnes. Imagine lying to that man."

"We don't have money for the egg man?" And here I'd just indulged in a taxi. My shame at having done so was quickly supplanted by anger.

"We don't have money for the egg man?" I repeated. Then I remembered that of my illustration earnings, a large portion had gone to fix a plumbing problem. Still, we should have had enough in the bank from the music school.

"We do have money," she said. "We have quite a lot in the jar, but I had forgotten to get it. I could not bring myself to take it from the jar right in front of him. What would he think? What would he say? Soon it would be all over the neighborhood."

I sank into the other chair. "You've needed to take money from the jar?"

"Not every week."

"You shouldn't need to take it *any* week," I blustered. "Maybe on a Saturday or Sunday when the bank is closed. But really, Maman, you must keep enough cash in the house so that these emergencies don't arise."

She said nothing, but her tears continued.

"Now, now, it's all right," I said. I leaned down to pick up the large pieces of glass on the floor and swept up the remaining shards with the broom and discarded them. I then swept up the scattered coins and poured them onto the table where we could carefully remove any remaining splinters.

"Come along," I tried, slipping back into what my grandmother might say to comfort me when I had broken something as a child. "It's not the end of the world." Still she was silent, and I began to comprehend.

"Are you saying that we are without sufficient funds?"

"Temporarily," she managed.

I took the black-bound ledgers from their shelf and spread them out on the kitchen table. I had not looked at them for weeks. Where figures indicating income should have been, the columns were full of blank spaces.

"So many pupils owe you money," I said.

"I know," she said, her voice small and tight.

"Really, Maman," I said, exasperated, "we must speak to them. *You* must speak to them."

"Oh, Agnes," she said, dabbing at her face with a handkerchief. "I have tried, and I cannot, I really cannot." She rose heavily and made her way toward the front parlor. When had she become so timid and tentative in her movements?

I shut the ledgers and returned them to the desk in the corner—the same desk she had sat at all those years ago, working out how to start the Pelton School of Music. I was filled with shame and panic: she had indeed created a school, a very good one at that; she had taught dozens of pupils of various levels of skill and talent, including myself. I had done what? Survived a parade of childhood illnesses, under her careful ministrations; attended art school, thanks to her encouragement; tried to begin a teaching career and failed; found the help and teaching I needed to begin a career as an artist. Taken a taxi.

In the days that hurried forward, I arrived at the studio early and left late. I seemed to have been jolted by Djuna Barnes and her electric energy. I teetered between nervous excitement and exhaustion, the combination of which kept me from sleeping for more than an hour at a time. Maman commented on the deepening circles under my eyes.

"I see what you're doing to yourself," she said. "You'll make yourself sick."

I blamed my fevered pace on two exhibitions to which I had been invited to contribute: a show at St. Mark's Church curated by Jerome Myers, and a gallery showing with the newly formed group called the Introspectives, who wanted as many paintings as I could deliver.

"Please don't worry, dearheart," I told her before rushing out the door yet again. "I'm fine."

And to my surprise, I was. Why not join the great ebb and flow of New York City, why not have friends like Djuna Barnes? I was haunted by the openness of her face and her reckless willingness to walk through the world unguarded. She was a regular contributor to *The Brooklyn Daily Eagle*, and even her most routine articles were so unusual as to be provocative. But of our brief meeting, I remembered the directness of her gaze, and I found myself hoping she would take up Jerome's suggestion and want to talk with me.

A week later came a brief knock on my studio door, and before I could respond, Djuna Barnes pushed it open.

"May I come in?"

"Please do," I said. Flustered, I rose and set my brushes down, reflexively wiping my hands on my smock. She seemed larger than I remembered, filling my studio with a psychic force.

"Don't get up," she said. "I want to observe you at work. In the act, so to speak."

She noticed the confusion on my face and laughed.

"Let's see what today yields, and if I decide to write about you, I'll let you know. All right?"

I agreed, struck once again by her youth. She shed the rather handsome if mannish fitted jacket she was wearing, dropped it on my extra chair, and without another word began inspecting the unfinished canvases stacked up against the wall.

"Works in progress?" she said.

"One hopes," I said.

She looked quizzical.

"For progress," I said. At that she allowed a flicker of a smile but said nothing. Unnerved, I offered her tea. Filling my small kettle involved turning my back to her which, unreasonably, I did not want to do. I had the sense that keeping my eyes fixed on her would somehow control her movements—and her opinions. I placed the kettle on my gas ring and struck a match to light it, and my guest strolled about the studio as if it were a gallery.

"Tell me about these pictures. Heavily influenced by Blakelock and Ryder, it would seem."

Her condescension curled out delicately, but the insult felt sharp. I drew a slow, deep breath.

"We share a sensibility," I said, "but I am not aware of being influenced by either of those gentlemen."

A smile flitted across her face, and I saw that I had been baited. Helpless to stop my face from blushing, I turned back to the kettle, which had finally come to a boil, spooned two measures of tea into the pot, poured the water, and set out a pair of cups.

"I believe you call your style 'Imaginative,' is that right?"

"That is right."

"Ah, yes," she said. "There are quite a few of you who paint in this manner, are there not?"

"You are thinking, perhaps, of the Introspectives," I said as evenly as I could, pouring out the tea. "I'm afraid I have no milk."

"Oh, no matter. Yes, it's the Introspectives I am thinking about."

"They have kindly invited me to join them for a gallery show-ing in the spring."

"Given the state of the world—the war in Europe, the impov-erished conditions just across town." She paused, apparently for effect. "What attracts you to such fanciful subject matter? 'Other worlds, beautiful worlds, universes of the spirit'? I am quoting from the statement you wrote to accompany one of your showings."

She glanced at her notepad, and I realized for the first time that she had come prepared with questions and, doubtless, an agenda. I had been responding to her as if to a casual acquaintance. So, this is how she puts people off guard, I thought; this is how she bores her way into their private thoughts and gets them to say all manner of things. I fought a rising panic, trying to read her intentions and avoid saying anything that could be misconstrued.

"I like images to stand for something, to inspire," I replied. Evenly, I hoped.

"I see." She reached for *River Maidens*. "And what are these figures intended to mean?"

"They are spiritual conveyances," I tried. "They intend to show that we all carry within ourselves the potential to walk in light."

"I see," she said. She seemed faintly amused, bordering on scornful. I had seen that expression on others, on the political rad-icals, for instance, who insisted that reality consisted entirely of the grime and poverty they saw around them.

I think I just babbled then like someone possessed. I could not stop myself from talking, and I tossed out phrases I had heard from one of the founding members of the Introspectives, who cited their interest in "suggestion as the depth beyond the depth." When at last I began to wind down, empty of words but feeling strangely comfortable, as though the two of us had just affirmed a creative connection, she turned abruptly from the paintings and faced me directly.

"You and Mrs. Thursby, do you have a special friendship?"

A shock went through me, and I willed myself to hold her gaze.

"Mrs. Thursby has been generous and encouraging to me, and I would not have come this far without her help. So, yes, it is a special friendship."

Barnes smiled, and the dizzy excitement I had felt since meeting her turned to cold, hard fear. I tried returning the conversation, such as it was, to the topics of Kandinsky and his theories, feeling all the while like an inexperienced skater moving too fast across an icy surface, trying not to fall. By the time she capped her pen, closed her notebook, and returned them to the carpet bag she carried, we were both subdued.

"Thank you, Miss Pelton," she murmured as she rose to depart. "I'll be in touch."

The door closed. I sank into my chair and stared at the works in progress, all of which now appeared wan and lifeless. Had Djuna Barnes perceived them that way? What would she write? Would she accuse Alice and me of unnatural behavior?

Her note reached me the next day at the studio, confirming that her profile would be printed in the next week or so. Each day as I traveled to and from the studio, I kept a wary eye on the newsstands, all of which blared news of the war in Europe and its destruction. I worried about Rome and Florence, and France, where trenches were now despoiling the countryside.

And then there it was, just days later, in *The Brooklyn Daily*

Eagle: Djuna Barnes's byline and her heading: "Local Artist Is Granddaughter of Beecher Paramour."

So, my grandmother was right: it would never end. We—now just Maman and me—would carry this history forward and enact it until our damaged lives were over. The Reverend Beecher had kept his church, kept his money, kept his place in the community. My grandparents had lost everything, including each other. I could hear my grandmother, her resignation complete, say, "Powerful men do not like being disrupted, Agnes, and their belief that who they are is more important than any one individual life, more important than such things as marital vows, is unshakable. We can do naught but accept our complicity and pay the price."

My hand shook as I proffered my nickel and hurried away with a single copy. I had told Maman nothing of Djuna Barnes or the interview, and my first thought was to go to every newsstand and buy every copy until the entire Borough of Brooklyn had been swept clean. That, of course, was absurd.

At home I made an excuse to go straight to my room, where I sank into my chair, and trembling, read Barnes's piece. I had a certain respect for her in that she had not insinuated anything about my friendship with Alice. Perhaps we had forged the connection I had intuited after all. Perhaps she felt that the Beecher scandal—a story that had dominated the tabloids for months while it played out—was fair game. After I had reread the piece several times, I was able to see it simply as an interesting bit of local history. I found myself admiring her even-handed tone. But when she finally got around to discussing my art and the work I was planning to show, her praise was muted, which was a great disappointment.

Seeing my family's history in bold black and white in the local newspaper, I grasped the depth of my grandmother's pain as never before. The scandal was not my story, nor had I participated in it, and still I was suffused in shame. It seemed to billow out of my past, like a great cloud or a sandstorm in the desert, and I could do nothing but let it overtake me. I had no intention of retreating as Grandmama had, but I didn't know what to do next. Someone gave Maman the article and, weeping, she asked why I had talked about these things with a stranger. I was never sure she believed me when I told her that of course I had not, that Djuna Barnes had access to the daily archives and could find out anything she wanted to.

And so, the heady days came to an end. Like a high-wire walker who could no longer rely on her own balance or even the wire itself, I avoided venturing out. The Introspectives' show opened, received a flurry of complimentary attention from my artist friends, and closed. Some critics praised it, while most wrote off the paintings as "charming trifles" that lacked substance.

I knew that I myself did not lack substance, but it was clear that I had been carried by the kindness of friends and mentors—Dow, Field, then my darling Alice who, I believe to this day, had no idea that she was providing so much beyond the material support she had offered so generously. I was an empty vessel who needed a muse to be inspired.

And then the Great War, which had been devouring Europe for three blood-soaked years, finally pulled America into its unspeakable carnage. While the Village radicals raised a furor and tried to stem the hysteria that pushed us into battle "Over There," I found myself in a spiritual wasteland.

Maman and I closed the house on Pacific Street and removed ourselves to my aunt's farm in Connecticut for the duration of the war. We said that it was a cost-saving measure, but really it was about wanting the comfort of family. There, working in the garden, growing our own food and living a life of simplicity, I marveled at the replenishing powers of nature—how life insisted on surging forth.

I had brought *River Maidens* with me from New York, intending to finish it, but measured against the verdancy all around me, I saw that the picture's flaws were fatal. It had a tenuous beauty but seemed to exist merely for effect. How much better the honesty of our well-ordered household than insincere art.

In my sketchbook I returned to basic contour drawing, where one studies an object or a figure or, in my case, a plant. Using cuttings from the geraniums in our flower boxes, I set my pencil to follow the outside edge of each stem, carefully rendering its curve and the small, protruding knobs where a leaf might have popped out but did not, or where another shoot could have developed had not this small branch been taken. I saw how these possibilities had been interrupted (if not thwarted) and how the branch had continued on regardless, thrusting itself in another direction.

BROOKLYN, NEW YORK

1919

WITH THE ARMISTICE, MY MOTHER and I came back home. Early in the spring of 1919, Alice also returned to New York and appeared at Pacific Street, unannounced.

"Am I unbearably rude?"

"Of course not," I replied, my certainty belied by obvious fluster. "What a lovely surprise."

"I thought I'd take a risk."

She had spent the war in London, and since the day I had watched her ship sail, I had held part of myself in suspended anticipation of our reunion.

I tried to hide my shock at how much she had aged. The fiery "New Woman" who made Sargent's portrait so remarkable was still in evidence, but a web of lines had formed around her eyes, and her once taut cheeks had begun to sag.

"Do come in," I said.

My mother, who had been expecting a new student, emerged to see who had rung the doorbell and saved me by greeting Alice warmly. Then she shooed us out to the garden and announced she'd bring tea shortly.

It was still early in the spring and therefore cool, but the sun shone, and the newly thawed earth released a delicate fragrance of minerals. Maman had planted bulbs years earlier, and they had multiplied and aggregated so that daffodils splayed out all over, nodding their trumpet blooms and dotting the garden with yellow. Maman brought out the tray, set it down, and left, insisting she had much to do and couldn't join us. Alice and I sat stiffly on the wrought iron chairs, cups of tea in hand, the plate of cookies untouched, and struggled through a series of vapid pleasantries. It was shocking how remote our shared past seemed, how it had receded into the distant country of another life.

"Look at you," she said. "You haven't changed a bit."

I laughed. "Dear Alice, I've changed a great deal."

She smiled. "Yes, I can see that now. I imagine the war affected you very deeply."

"It did, as I'm sure it did you." A sense of calm settled over us both then, and we lapsed into silence.

"I do miss it all," said Alice finally. "What we did before all that. Such exciting times."

"They were," I agreed.

"Did I tell you I saw John Quinn?"

"You did, in your letter." She had written exactly one that I knew of, but I thought there might have been others that had not reached me because of the U-boats.

"Oh yes. It was all so hopeful," she continued. "I talked about you and he seemed so interested—again—and I made him promise that after we all got back to New York, he would buy a painting."

"Yes, you said in your letter."

"Perhaps he's not come back yet. I gave him my address and told him to come and see the pictures I have."

"I imagine he's busy, if he's even in New York."

"He did promise," she repeated. "I'm absolutely certain of that. But he has not as yet followed through."

"It's all right," I said. "Really, it's all right." And, oddly, it was. I had accepted defeat and become comfortable with it.

"But I assured you that it would happen, and I failed you in that regard."

Her voice wavered.

"Dear Alice," I said quietly. "It is I who have failed you."

"Not ever," she said.

I struggled for what I might say. I could not slip back into our old dynamic, with Alice taking charge of my life—where I worked, whom I met, even, truth be told, what I painted. I had lived that life.

"But look at you," Alice said, abruptly setting down her teacup. "Now you must tell me everything."

"There's very little to tell," I said. I set my cup down as well and plucked a bit at my skirt.

"Come now," Alice said. "Don't be shy."

It was not shyness; my difficulty involved shame at not having carried on painting through the war—at having felt helpless in the face of that great conflict and needing inspiration that seemed gone from me forever—at having remained at a loss about how to proceed with an abstract style that was truly my own.

"What have you got to show me?"

"Nothing," I stammered. "Only drawings."

"Only drawings?"

"Yes," I went on. "I needed to go back inside"—I tapped my chest lightly—"back to where I might find the spark."

"And did you?"

"To a degree. Not so that I could paint, though. You know my mother and I were away? At my aunt's farm in Connecticut? We were so close to nature in the country. I found some grace in recording what I was seeing there."

"Well, then," she said after a moment. "The drawings are not 'nothing.' They are very important."

"You are kind," I said. In spite of myself I felt better. It was childish, I knew, but Alice's approval still meant something. I hauled out the stack of drawings, and she nodded and murmured over each one. I hadn't looked at them since leaving the farm, and I was surprised at how much pleasure they also gave me.

"Goodness," she said, when we were finished. "I nearly forgot." She pulled an envelope from her bag. "It's from Mabel. She wants us both to come and see the wonders of New Mexico."

"What? She says that?"

"There, right there." Alice unfolded a wad of pages filled with Mabel's exuberant handwriting and stabbed the place with her finger. She laughed. "Mabel must be mad. 'Gone native,' they say. I think we *should* visit her."

I had heard that, as with me and Maman, New York's rampant war fever had driven Mabel from the city, first for a farm upstate with her then-husband, the painter Maurice Sterne, and then to Santa Fe, where Sterne had gone to paint. She hadn't lingered there long, opting instead for the wilds of Taos, but I had found her exodus from Fifth Avenue disorienting. In my mind's eye she was still presiding over the White Salon, robed and turbaned like a Hindu swami.

"Listen to this," Alice said. She read me a lively passage from Mabel's letter, full of enthusiasm for the Indians and their drumming and singing. Alice had leaned forward slightly, as if to be sure I took in every word. She fairly vibrated with her old energy. Then her face softened and she looked up and smiled at me—"Pay attention, now"—and read on as Mabel described the landscape and its extraordinary variety of colors, even in winter, ending with the intriguing, "I've never seen the like, not even in Italy."

Alice sighed, folded the letter carefully, and tucked it back into its envelope. "I think we should go. What do you say?"

I waved her off, but Alice was in earnest. She tucked the letter back into her bag.

"We really must go see Mabel," she said, as though Mabel were just around the corner. "I'll be in touch."

She rose, and without waiting for me to lead the way, marched through the sunroom to the hallway and out the front door. I shut it behind her and watched from the window as her car pulled away.

I heard the clatter of pots in the kitchen and went to see about helping my mother. She, too, was happy to be back home. Most of her students had returned, and our bank account was healthy once more. She asked after Alice, how long she had been back in New York and how she was faring.

"She didn't say, but I think not long," I said. "She seems well; very much herself." To amuse her, I related Alice's plan about the two of us going West.

"Oh my," she exclaimed. "Wouldn't that be wonderful?"

My mother constantly surprised me—especially at those times when I had resolved to accept a life without art. Here she was, pushing me again. "You need new vistas," she said.

Vistas. Her use of that word carried the force of a lightning flash. I said I wouldn't think of leaving her on her own. She thought for a moment.

"I'll ask my sister to come stay with me."

I knew she had loved our time with my aunt on the farm and that she missed the pleasantries of sharing daily life. She met my gaze so forthrightly that I had to conclude that she was indeed sincere.

"All right," I said. "If Aunt Alice will come, I will go."

By then, my cousin Laura and her husband, who were both sculptors, had moved to the farm for its fresh air and space for their work, and as my aunt wanted to allow them their privacy, she did agree to come.

"We'll each be with our own Alice," Maman said, which startled me, but her open face showed she meant nothing by it.

EN ROUTE TO NEW MEXICO

1919

ALICE AND I, EACH CARRYING an overnight case while our luggage was checked through to Santa Fe, boarded the train to Chicago. We had never spent so much continuous time together, nor had we been confined to such close quarters. She chattered, I assumed, out of nervousness. I reacted by trying to read a book, which silenced her, but when I raised my head to look out the window, she resumed—first across New Jersey, then Pennsylvania, then Ohio. She remarked on people we had in common and people I knew only by name, and she had little good to say about any of them. I had not expected my friend to be so exhausting, and I pondered the idea of begging ill health and needing to return to New York. But once I realized she didn't need me to reply, I could sit back and relax, and eventually she relaxed as well.

In Chicago we changed trains and turned south across seemingly endless prairies. At the Texas panhandle, we saw cowboys moving their cattle north, and the bluebells were starting to bloom. The West was coming to life in front of us. I watched as the sky widened, its bottomless marine color saturating everything. I let it absorb me as well, and from that slight remove found I could recover affection for my friend while reveling in the joy of this new light.

As we neared New Mexico, we both marveled at the dramatic change in the landscape: how red rock had replaced tawny scrub and was thrusting all around us.

"Oh, look," Alice said. "Table land."

Neither of us had seen a mesa before, and we laughed, thinking of how another Alice, a giant Alice in Wonderland, might seat herself daintily at such a table and sip her tea with her little finger crooked just so. We fell into silence, awed by the land and the sky and the palpable spiritual presence that resides there. Alice reached over and took my hand, and I squeezed hers affectionately.

In Santa Fe we rested for a few days, adjusting to the altitude of the high desert and enjoying the sense of life all around. Alice was acquainted with Maurice Sterne, and we visited him in his studio. He was happy, he said, and intended to remain in Santa Fe.

"Mabel's on a new adventure," he added cryptically.

The following morning found Alice and me strolling arm in arm around the town square, where women from the Santa Fe Pueblo sat on the ground and set their wares out for sale: pottery, glazed and not; brilliantly colored woolen blankets decorated with circles, star-like symbols, and geometric birds; huge chunks of turquoise set like robins' eggs in beaten silver; and beads—thousands of beads, strung into necklaces and headdresses, all of which looked like something an Egyptian queen would have worn. The faces of these women fascinated me: at once impassive and strong, gentle and receptive. Close by, their children played as children do everywhere.

"She's left him, I think," Alice said. "Maybe for good."

I had heard about how Mabel and Maurice had spent their marriage locked into what seemed more of a battle than a love affair, using words like claws to rake at each other's most tender feelings.

"Maybe it *is* for good," I said. We were both silent then, lost in the brilliant orange sunset.

"Maybe," Alice said after a moment. "Yes, I'm sure you're right."

In the morning we left for Taos, our bags crammed into the capacious trunk of an old car. On the way, we encountered a freakish spring snowstorm. Just imagine, traveling from lilacs and spring flowers in Santa Fe to direst winter. Our driver, a burly man named Fred, inched the car forward along the steep and narrow road. In the back seat, we each clutched whatever we could to stabilize ourselves, aware that at any moment we could tumble over a precipice, or bog down in one of the snowdrifts forming faster than our car could maneuver.

When at last we entered the village, Fred turned toward the only large house in view. Alice and I consulted Mabel's directions, and then there she was, having watched for us. She dashed out wrapped in a colorful blanket, helped us take our things off the luggage rack, and herded us to shelter. Her unabashed delight was as warming as the fire crackling in the huge stone fireplace.

"You've cut your hair!" Alice was agape.

"I have, yes," Mabel said mischievously. The twin buns around her ears had been displaced by a bob that shaped her face and made her look younger, as did her unbridled happiness. I paused to look around and marvel. The white salon of New York had been overtaken by color, from bright paintings on the walls to the red, yellow, and blue Indian blankets draped over the rustic furniture. Ah, I thought, Mabel has found a new palette. Perhaps I will find one of my own.

TAOS, NEW MEXICO

1919

THE NEXT DAY BROUGHT DAZZLING sun, and by noon the snow on the road had melted. The rest of it receded nearly as quickly, and as I walked out into air so sharp it seemed to pierce my soul, I felt lightheaded and giddy. Mabel herself, who could not wait another moment to show us around, compounded my delight. I had forgotten how seductive she could be, how she could draw one close with her confidences and her lingering touch.

"You feel it too, don't you," she murmured to me as she walked us around the Pueblo. "The power in this place."

I did—so strongly I could do no more than nod my head.

Alice had walked on ahead, her hand protecting her eyes. The high desert clarity was nearly blinding, which Alice didn't care for at all. She turned back, then, and told us that she was having trouble breathing.

"That's the altitude," Mabel said. "You'll get used to it."

"No doubt," Alice said. "But for now, I think I'll go back to the house. Agnes, are you feeling all right? Do you want to go back too?"

"No," I said, almost too quickly. "But if you need me . . ." I let my voice trail off.

"No," Alice said. "I'm all right." She stepped carefully back along the rocky path.

I had thought the altitude would bother me as well, but here I was, only a bit short of breath. I simply could not bear the idea of going inside and away from the shimmer of light.

Mabel and I continued up a hill toward a cluster of adobe houses, stopping at the largest. This, I gathered, was the house of a tribal elder, maybe even the chief. I had expected an old man or woman to answer Mabel's knock, but instead, when the door opened, a tall man with long braided hair stood before us.

"You came," he said simply, to Mabel.

"I did," she said. Her happiness broke through like the sun from behind a mountain. I had to stop myself from staring at her.

"I brought a friend from New York," she said. "Her name is Agnes."

To me she said, "This is Tony."

I had thought that New Mexico's magical landscape was what held Mabel in thrall, but now I saw that it was inextricably connected to Tony Lujan. I studied his face without embarrassment; he studied mine in return.

"Friend," he said, finally. He bowed his head slightly.

I nodded to reciprocate, and Mabel and I continued through the Pueblo, our progress observed by dozens of bright black eyes peering out from the adobe structures, women and children mostly. Two or three brave little ones ran out to grab Mabel's arms, and she reached into her bag and handed out candies.

I looked back where Tony had been standing only seconds before.

"He has beautiful eyes," I said.

"Yes, he does." Mabel beamed, and I knew that her days as Mrs. Maurice Sterne were over.

———————————

Winter was retreating, although in a fashion more graceful than I had ever seen. The charcoal dawn became ultramarine the instant the sun cracked the sky over the mountains. I was struck over and over by the light-dark of land against sky—the *notan*—and how the deep hues of the Sangre de Cristo Mountains were rich with browns, reds, purples. This was earth-dark, not death-dark, and I felt part of it, cushioned and supported. As spring approached, birds appeared overhead, their beaks crammed with bits of dry grasses, and I watched as the quickly warming sun turned dull adobe into golden ochre. I covered sheet after sheet of thick paper in pastel hues, so inspiring was the depth of that blue carapace.

Now that I had a mailing address, Maman and I had settled into a pattern of writing every other day, and this had produced a pleasant stream of mutually newsy notes, even with the inevitable gaps in deliveries because of weather and who-knew-what, as Mabel put it. Our hostess delighted in the haphazard ways of what was for all intents and purposes still frontier, and when I fretted about unusual pauses in the arrival of letters, she waved away my worries like so many houseflies.

"We are in a different world," she was fond of saying—a truth I had also embraced—"and we cannot expect things to run as we are accustomed to." But when ten days went by with no sign of Maman's familiar hand on an envelope, I knew something was amiss.

Mabel told me to be patient even as she turned her attention to the construction of her new house. Her ambitions for it were characteristically grand—she had decided to re-create the vaulted dining room I remembered from the villa near Florence and was grappling with how to achieve its high ceiling. Eventually it became clear that the ground beneath the room would have to be dug, the room itself lowered. With the spring thaw, she had begun to enact this plan, and every day was accompanied by the thump and scrape of men digging. One could only reach the kitchen by going outside and around or by traversing a wooden plank over the pit.

Alice removed herself to Santa Fe to get away from the noise and dust, which was a small relief. I no longer had the worry that she might be unhappy. Instead I spent entire days out of doors. It seemed the longer I remained in Taos, the more I was finding to draw. I was intoxicated with the pale, yellow light, purple tones in the shadows, the occasional dustings of snow and its juddering effects on adobe. Each day after breakfast, I left with sketch books, pastels, and a pad of textured paper packed in a large canvas bag, along with a lunch kindly supplied by Mabel's cook. I kept track of time by the movement of sun across sky, and only returned to the house when the light began to seep away.

Mabel always set the day's mail in a basket inside the front door. Returning tired but full of the joys of another fruitful outing, I glanced through it and, finding nothing from Maman, I became more and more aware of how far from home I was. My Valhalla, my splendid new Eden, fell under a shadow, and I fought a rising sense of panic. At night the presence of my grandmother, like a figure I'd tried to paint over, worked its way into my dreams: "No one knows you here; you are alone."

Mabel could see my face darken and constrict with each letterless homecoming, and she did her best to reassure me.

"They would send a telegram," she said. In spite of my grim flights of fancy, Taos was not a netherworld. Someone—most likely my aunt—would have wired if anything were seriously amiss. I continued to wait. Finally, a letter appeared, and I studied the envelope before ripping it open. My mother's handwriting seemed tremulous, and I steeled myself. She was sorry for not writing sooner, she said. She had come through a "bad spell," about which she did not elaborate, but now she was perfectly fine.

"There, you see?" Mabel said when I reported to her. "All is well."

———————

Whether or not all was well in Brooklyn, I was happy. I felt cossetted and pampered, inspired and appreciated, and even now I wonder what path my art and my life might have taken had I stayed. I teased Mabel that she should name her new endeavor the Blue Salon for the glorious canopy that seemed to cast a benevolent eye on each of our efforts.

Mabel had established herself in Taos. She was flourishing in her husband's absence—Sterne had remained in Santa Fe in what might have been stubbornness but was more likely surrender—and Tony Lujan had become a constant presence. He would appear at the house almost magically—no sign of him approaching, until suddenly he was at the door. I thought of him as a mystic who had taken a vow of silence and whose connection to the land was ushering us Easterners to new and rarified ground.

Mabel's beauty seemed to grow each day, and in direct proportion to the amount of time she spent with Tony. Once the dining room was ready for its new floor, she asked the Indians who were part of the work crew to construct a tepee for her, which they did, setting it back on one side of the house. Tony's face betrayed nothing, but he took to staying longer each day, and he and Mabel would spend hours in the tepee, where she told me she was learning how to live. My face must have reflected my concern, for she was quick to add, "We are very chaste."

Even as Tony became a regular visitor to Mabel's house, I spent more and more time at the Pueblo, installing myself in the main trading area and making dozens of drawings of the fortress-like stack of houses, the limpid sky, the smoke that rose in tendrils from holes in roofs, the thick adobe, textured with bristles of straw. The Indians, already accustomed to the other Taos artists, took no notice as I made quick gestural sketches of them. A few of them even posed, and their bright-eyed children watched with delight as their parents' faces appeared on my paper.

I had also begun to make studies of Tony Lujan with the idea of painting a formal portrait. Having set aside my efforts toward abstraction, my time in Taos had assured me that I could satisfy my soul with more traditional genres. I could return to landscape art or, I thought, perhaps paint portraits. I knew I was no John Singer Sargent or Robert Henri, but the pastels I'd done in the Pueblo indicated I had a gift for likenesses. With nothing but an awareness of needing to be able to care for my mother who had always cared so lovingly for me, I mentioned my idea to Mabel, who beamed.

"Of course you should paint Tony. He's the perfect person to start on."

Mabel conveyed my request, and handsome, silent, majestic Tony allowed me to follow him about the Pueblo as he made his daily rounds—taking care of what I was never sure. That I wanted to paint him was something everyone understood, but for me there was an additional component—seeking to grasp the connection between Tony and Mabel, how the spiritual had taken root in Mabel and how it might also take root in me.

For the formal pose, I set up a chair in Mabel's living room next to the conical adobe fireplace, draping the chair with an Indian blanket. He settled himself, and then, no more than five minutes later—perhaps annoyed by the noise of construction in the adjacent room—arose and without a word walked out the door. I stared after him, my sketch barely begun, the project abandoned of necessity. It seemed entirely hopeless until months later, when he sat for a formal photograph and Mabel sent me a print. That image became the basis for my portrait of him, painted after I returned to New York. I always felt the picture was a little flat, but it successfully demonstrated to prospective clients my ability to render a likeness and led to many commissions.

––––––––––

My mother's "bad spell" hovered in my consciousness like a lurking storm, and I knew with increasing urgency that it was time to return home. Before I could make travel plans, Mabel—who truly did know everyone—told me she had written to the director of the Museum of New Mexico in Santa Fe, who replied that they would be pleased to show my work. (I reported to Maman that, from the preliminary announcement of the exhibit, I was now "Miss Agnes Pelton of New York and Connecticut"—an appellation sure to bring a smile to her face.) To my satisfaction and pleasure, there were some seventy pastels and about half a dozen paintings to bundle up and put on the wagon, which was ferried across the Rio Grande at the gorge north of Taos and the pictures put on the train for Santa Fe.

Mabel began to talk of more shows of my work, and I felt honor bound to tell her of my intention to return to Brooklyn.

"Oh, dear," she said, leaning close and clasping my hands in both of hers. "I'm sorry your mother is unwell. You must go to her, but then you must come back. I have plans for you."

I hesitated before returning her gentle squeeze.

"You will come back, will you not?"

"Dear Mabel, I cannot be sure."

"Ah," she said, releasing my hands abruptly. "'Miss Agnes Pelton of New York and Connecticut' is planning to abandon us."

And just like that, I saw the glint of change in her eyes, the beginning of distance between us. Suddenly I was on one side of a divide and Mabel was on the other, and as she withdrew almost imperceptibly, I felt a familiar wrench of sadness. Separation and an abiding sense of loss seemed a matter of destiny.

―――――――

In Santa Fe, Mabel and I together supervised a long day of placing and moving pictures in the museum's gallery. When we were finished, Mabel took my hand and walked me through the exhibit.

"Here you are." She paused in front of a pastel of Indians working with clay. "Here is your heart."

She tugged me forward and, pointing to a trio of paintings of the red rock landscape, said, "Here is your soul, your beauty, your strength, your integrity."

She turned to face me and took both my hands in hers: "You belong here. I want you to come back as soon as you are able."

The air between us fairly shimmered, and I felt myself drawn to her as though by a powerful magnet. I drew a deep breath, squeezed her hands gently, and, somewhat dizzy, promised to consider the idea. Mabel, knowing herself to be irresistible, beamed, and I knew in that instant I would never live in Taos. I would hold to my own path, wherever that turned out to lead.

The exhibition opened and was warmly received by the local press. Mabel declared that there was every reason to be optimistic about sales, especially given that the show would stay up through the tourist season. Thus encouraged, I returned to Taos to pack up, and two weeks later boarded the train in Santa Fe. Alice and Mabel had both accompanied me to the depot, and, in air that felt charged, we three wept at our goodbyes. My sadness at leaving Alice was especially poignant, understanding as I did that my romantic fantasy was over. As for Mabel and Alice, both women would eventually return to New York, Alice first—astoundingly taking Tony with her to exhibit him to her friends, and when that didn't go well, returning him forthwith—and then Mabel as an occasional visitor. We would maintain affectionate friendships through letters, but the days of enchantment were at an end.

I climbed aboard the magnificent Palace Pullman car that Alice had insisted on treating me to and found my seat. In just minutes the whistle shrieked, the engine chuffed, and the train, a lumbering beast, edged forward. Mabel and Alice were still on the platform waving white handkerchiefs, and I waved back through the thick window without any idea if they could see me. Inches became feet, feet became yards, and soon there were miles between me and Mabel and Alice, and between me and Taos. I was in a confusion of emotions then, feeling myself torn away from the yellow ochre and cadmium red landscape, but the desolation passed. As the train rocked its way forward, I had an extraordinary feeling of being grounded and in balance with myself, and I let the West recede into the past.

BROOKLYN, NEW YORK

NOVEMBER 1919

MY AUNT HAD WIRED THAT my mother had suffered a mild heart attack but that she would be ready to leave the hospital by the time I returned. When I arrived at Pacific Street, I did little more than throw my bags into the back room before the two of us went to get Maman. The doctor took me into the hall to explain her condition, which he called angina.

"She must slow down," he instructed me sternly. "And she must not use the stairs unless she has to, and when she does go up or down, but especially up, she must take it one step at a time and rest on the landings."

He looked at me to see if I was taking it in. "Do you want to write this down?"

"No, I'll remember."

"She must slow down," he repeated. "Oh, and she is not to have salt."

At that I raised my eyebrows, knowing how much she enjoyed her food. He seemed to relish my dismay—"No salt," he said again—and strode off.

Maman was sitting in the chair, her hat and coat on, her handbag in her lap. My aunt said, "Did you hear that, Florence? You are to have no salt."

"Nonsense," she said, pulling herself up. "What is the point of eating if everything is tasteless?" An orderly appeared with a wheelchair, and our little procession made its way to the exit door and to a taxi and finally to Pacific Street. My cousin and her husband came from Connecticut the next day to fetch my aunt, and Maman and I tried to return to normal.

What was normal, you might ask. I thought I knew, but I was wrong. Taos had changed me, and a heart attack had changed Maman. In the hospital she had seemed her undaunted self, and perhaps for that moment she was. But at home, as I settled her into her bed, thinking its familiarity would be comforting, she became uncertain and then timid.

"Agnes, I'm so afraid," she whispered, and I felt my own heart lurch.

"Are you in pain? Should I call the doctor?"

"No," she said. "Just stay here with me, will you?"

"Of course," I said, squeezing next to her and gathering her into my arms. We stayed like that for a long time. Maman's frantic breathing slowed, which was a relief, but I was caught in my own tangle of fears. There was, of course, the terror of losing my mother, but right alongside it came grief over losing the buoyant spirit I'd found in Taos and which I had believed was mine to carry home and keep. Like a tumbleweed pushed away by the wind, joy seemed to desert me, to be replaced by a familiar demon: doubt in my ability to make art.

Maman stayed in bed her first days at home, and I brought her breakfast and then lunch on a tray. Her hands, always so strong and sure, now shook with a tremor that also played through her voice.

"How about if I read to you?" I asked.

"That would be nice."

I picked out one of her favorites, *Uncle Tom's Cabin*, and began, but soon she interrupted with domestic worries that she would have waved away not so long ago: "Do you think we should have the plumber in to fix the drip in the faucet? I am worried about that tear in the hall rug. One of us could trip over it and fall. Has Nellie O'Rourke been by to do the washing?"

I forced a smile and promised to take care of everything, even as I worried about our diminishing savings. At her bedside, I placed the small crystal bell she had always given me as a child when I was sick.

"Try to rest now," I said and lowered the window shade and tiptoed out of her room. Almost immediately, once I was downstairs, I heard the bell. I ran back up, fearing the worst, only to have her ask, "What shall we do about supper? Should we make up a shopping list now?"

"I am pleased that you are interested in supper," I tried teasing her gently. "Especially at ten o'clock in the morning," I added, and to my great relief she smiled.

"We should get you up." I said, and she agreed. I ran a bath for her, and we got her dressed. An hour later we took the stairs slowly, Maman clutching the banister and me keeping a firm grip on her free arm, and little by little we made our way downstairs. Sunlight streamed in through the small transom window over the front door and caused her white hair to shine.

"You have a halo," I said. She smiled, and her cheeks took on a pinkish cast. I knew she was happy that I was home, happy to have my attention, but by the time I settled her into her chair, I was exhausted. I tried not to worry about when I might be painting again.

———————————

The inspiration that had nourished me in Taos vanished into the heat and humidity of early summer. Brooklyn's light was heavy, tinged with gray-yellow, thick with moisture and slightly metallic, and I could see no blue in its undertones.

I heard about a studio on 13th Street in the Village but could not see a way to use it, so I moved my supplies into the back sunroom and attempted to set it up. I could not paint there, though—the fumes from my oils and turpentine bothered Maman. Instead, keenly aware that I needed to practice portraiture, I started inviting neighborhood children in and sketched them with pastels. These small efforts recalled to me the Pueblo, and the hours rolled past pleasantly.

Maman and I had settled into an uneasy routine. I was two people—the dutiful daughter trying to care for her ailing mother, running to her side whenever needed, trying to be that paragon who never lost patience or entertained the slightest resentment—and the artist, once again struggling to keep working.

It was autumn when Hamilton Field belatedly learned that I was back in Brooklyn and invited me to an exhibit of his friend Robert Laurent. I went gladly but almost immediately regretted it. Field was his usual expansive self, generous and always encouraging, and Laurent seemed happy to see me, which touched me. But just as we three were beginning to trade pleasantries about Mabel and Taos, another artist whom I didn't know thrust himself into our group. Field and Laurent clearly knew him and also seemed reluctant to make room for him.

"Taos?" he said. "I would give anything to be able to go out there." He was tall and heavy in every sense of the word, and I instinctively shrank back. "I'm sure I would never come back," he added.

"My mother has been ill," I said, wanting to offer an explanation he could understand. His eyebrows rose.

"You don't mean you came back for that? Artists must put our work ahead of anyone or anything."

I must have worn an expression of utter amazement because Field laughed, and Laurent tried to explain.

"Agnes is not like any artist you have met," he said, and steered him toward a newly arrived group. When Laurent returned, we all tried to shake off the exchange. But, I wondered, what had Laurent meant by that? No artist, I thought, is truly like any other artist. And then I immediately thought, how naïve. How many times had

I looked at work (including my own) that was clearly derived from someone else's vision?

Returning to Pacific Street, I paused in the foyer, closed my eyes, and summoned the sacred face of Taos Mountain, hoping its image would sustain me even as I stifled regret at having left it. Having *chosen* to leave it. Coming home, not entirely because Maman needed me, but because I needed her.

That day's mail included a long-delayed letter from the exhibition curator in Santa Fe. They had enjoyed having the show, but he was sorry to report that although many people had admired the pastels, not one piece had been sold. "It is a matter of dealing with tourists," he explained. "They must pack these pictures up to carry them long distances, and that has not seemed feasible to any of them. I am very sorry." He closed with apologies at the necessity of shipping them all back to me—COD—admiring them as greatly as he did. It took me awhile to wonder why he did not purchase one or two for himself or for the museum.

Maman continued to recover some of her strength, which I took as a sign that we might settle into our old life. To that end, I rented the still-available 13th Street studio in the Village and began porting my supplies there via the subway.

"Should you be doing that?" Maman asked. "Isn't Mrs. Thursby driving you?"

"Alice is still in Taos."

I had told her that already, but Maman couldn't seem to detach me and my professional life from my friend. For my part, I did not want to explain that our friendship had changed, and I had not consulted Alice.

"Imagine that," Maman said. "Imagine her leaving you high and dry like that."

"Alice has not been well," I said, ready to elaborate on the increasing fragility of my friend's nerves, a condition that had not diminished even in the bright open air of New Mexico.

Maman nodded, apparently content with that explanation. This was new; she had never, to my recollection, neglected to express concern for someone else's troubles. I observed her shoulders tilt forward as if she were collapsing in on herself, her own worries being too heavy.

In the morning I settled her in the parlor with a book and her note paper and promised to be back by suppertime. I set out cheese and bread on the sideboard for her lunch, wrapped some to carry for myself, and left for the studio.

The simple act of walking away from the house brought about release, immediately complicated by guilt at leaving Maman on her own. Still, I was grateful to find the place in my heart from which to paint, and I let that suffice, keeping the studio itself spare and unadorned. On the walls I tacked pastel portraits from the Pueblo to help me recall its sights, sounds, and complicated aromas; in the room's center, Tony's portrait in progress dominated.

Rendering someone's likeness is an intimacy and a privilege of the highest order; making a portrait means seeking to grasp the fullness of the subject. In painting Tony, that experience became richly transformative. I continued from memory until Mabel sent his photograph and I could check details. Tony was, for me, Taos mountain itself, all stability and strength. His presence in Mabel's life revealed more about her than I had ever suspected. I had always admired her, but until Tony, she seemed an actress playing out the role of liberated woman. Observing them in Taos, I could see their spiritual connection for myself and understand its rightness for both of them.

BROOKLYN, NEW YORK

NOVEMBER 1920

AS AUTUMN DEEPENED, MAMAN became increasingly frail. I stopped going to the studio, as more and more she needed help to get around. And it was a shock one day, as we made our cautious way down the stairs, that she expressed a desire to repent her sins.

"My goodness," I said, putting off a real response until we were safely on the first floor. Making our way into the parlor, I said, "Dearest Maman, I can't imagine that you have any sins."

I put an arm around her shoulders, but she would not allow me to comfort or reassure her. Instead, she halted and drew from her pocket a folded-up newspaper clipping and, carefully opening Djuna Barnes's article about our family scandal, began to cry. I recoiled abruptly, very angry then at Barnes, and distraught at my own vanity and naiveté in agreeing to be interviewed in the first place.

"Please, Maman, you must not worry about all that." I tried to take it from her. "It's all past, it's over."

"It is not over," she whispered, quickly moving it away from me. "And it was worse even than what she says here."

"What can you mean?"

"I should have stopped it." I watched as her face lost its color.

"Stopped what?" I was terrified. I kept one hand firmly on her arm and with the other reached for a nearby chair. "Sit here, Maman. Let me have that paper so I can burn it." She held the clipping out of my reach and shook her head vehemently.

"You don't understand."

"Sit down," I repeated, my hands on her shoulders, and she obeyed, sinking slowly into the chair. I crouched down in front of her and took her two hands in mine. They were twisted with arthritis like knotty twigs.

"Tell me," I said, finally. "What is it?"

"Oh, Agnes, I'm so ashamed." Her eyes flooded with tears and I waited.

"He struck her," she managed.

"Who? Reverend Beecher? Did Reverend Beecher strike her?"

"No," she whispered. "My father. Father struck Mother."

I froze and she continued.

"First, he slapped her face, hard, so that she lost her balance, and then he punched her where the new baby was just beginning to show. 'There,' he said, as if he had put a stop to something. And, oh, dear God, he had, because later that night I heard her cry out in pain. The doctor came, and in the morning the baby was gone." She stopped and I tried to hold her, but she shook me off and continued.

"A few days later, when Mother had recovered her strength and Father was out, she sent Bessie, our Irish maid, to pack a small valise for each of us—there were four of us children then—and we left that house, never to return. I was twelve." She buried her face and wept.

"Oh, Maman, I am so sorry."

"I could have interposed myself."

"No, you could not, of course you could not. You were a child."

"Yes, I could." She raised her head. Her expression was quizzical, as though she were puzzling out a problem in arithmetic. "I have thought about it for a long time now, and I am sure that I could have. Please call Mr. Winter."

When she had said this, she seemed calm if terribly tired. The shock of hearing the name of the Brethren Elder robbed me of words, so I merely helped her to bed. I was too upset to do anything, including sleep, while in my head a tangle of confusion about secrets, my own along with hers and my grandmother's before her, whirled. Eventually, night folded itself around us, and as Pacific Street fell into its own slumber, I reluctantly wrote to Mr. Winter, who had moved his family to New Jersey. Two days later he replied that he would come and that he would bring his wife and daughter and son-in-law "to fulfill the teaching that 'Where two or three are gathered together in my name, I will be in the midst of them.'"

_____

In my mind's eye, I conjured Mr. Winter from the dark recesses of childhood memory: tall and thin like a pine tree, remote eyes burning out of deep facial crevices, a beard as rough as bark—a biblical patriarch—and I shuddered to think of him examining my mother's supposed sins. I folded his letter, carefully returned it to its envelope, and placed it on the desk. I paced about the room, uncertain of what to do or think. So much—*so much*—of our lives had gone unspoken. I felt it was all about to burst forth as if from floodgates and thought it possible we would drown in it.

I stepped outside. The morning was still early, and I crossed the street and stared at our house. The sun slanted from the right and washed the front door and windows, and I imagined it as a great spotlight, striking the center stage of my life. Nothing that Maman had so painfully described had occurred in this place, and yet she had carried the tragedy within herself, whole and intact. Far from shrinking with time, the years had added weight. What might her life have been had she simply been able to lay this burden down?

I tried to envision it, but my imagination failed me. I was left with the unsatisfying conclusion that much would have remained the same: She would have fled to Europe to escape the scandal. She would have studied music, married my father, and given birth to me. Because of my sickly babyhood, she would have been forced back to Brooklyn, which she would have accepted with the same steady resolve I had known growing up. She would have suffered my father's absences and his sudden death. When her own mother died, she would have allowed the Brethren to enfold and comfort her. She would have given me the protected life I had taken for granted as my right, and, I was sure, she would have encouraged my art. None of the facts of her life could be erased or even altered, but absent the guilt I had never even suspected she was carrying, she might have been happier.

It was a blustery day when I opened the door to Mr. and Mrs. Winter, their daughter Phoebe, and her husband Edward Canon, all of whom had driven in a large touring car that was now parked in front. I had befriended Phoebe during the year she spent in New York before she was married and before my year in Italy. After her marriage and while I was beginning to have a career, I had enjoyed talking to her and to Edward, who was himself sensitive and especially enthusiastic about my work.

I had feared that they would take us to task for not keeping up with the Brethren, but Phoebe's immediate embrace dispelled those fears. Maman had insisted on getting up and dressing and was waiting for them in the parlor. I was shocked at how frail Mr. Winter actually was, albeit elegant with his well-trimmed white goatee and brown fedora. Instead of launching into a thunderous sermon, he simply gave me his hat. In his other hand he held a small prayer book, and after nodding a greeting, he entered the parlor and pulled up a chair next to Maman on the divan. Phoebe's arm remained about my shoulders and seemed to hold me back from following. In the foyer Edward studied the pastels I'd made in Italy, which still hung on the walls.

"Now, Florence," Mr. Winter said, "what seems to be the trouble?" He inclined his head as she tearfully began to whisper to him. Phoebe suggested we make tea, and she and Edward followed me to the kitchen, where I put the kettle on to boil.

"I didn't think to make a tea bread," I said.

"We don't need one," Phoebe said. "What can I do to help?"

"Why, nothing. It's just a pot of tea."

"No," she said, "I meant what can I do to help *you?*" She placed her hands on my shoulders and turned me so that we were facing one another. Her expression was kind and her eyes sorrowful, and to my embarrassment I fell to weeping, covering my face with my hands. She encircled my shoulders with her arm and murmured, "There, there," which only opened a deeper grief. I had not permitted myself to know all that I was feeling, instead distracting myself with plans for painting portraits.

"My mother," I struggled with the words, but when I finally uttered them, they rolled out in great waves. "My mother, my mother, my mother, my mother."

Phoebe said, "You are not alone, Agnes."

We stood like that for a long time, Phoebe holding me as I cried. She seemed willing to stay there forever, and I felt the seed of peace taking hold in my deepest center.

Maman died that night. It was the 29th of November. I had needed Edward to help me get her back upstairs, a long, slow climb with one of us on each side, practically lifting her step by step. After the Winters and the Canons were gone, I got her back to bed. She fell into sleep at once, and I pulled a chair up next to her, intending to stay awake all night in case she needed me, but I also fell asleep.

It was still dark when something startled me awake, and I sat up as though I'd been summoned. I took her hand. She opened her eyes, looked directly into mine, and said, "Be good." She fell back into sleep, and her breathing became labored. She seemed to struggle, which made me cry. I thought it unfair that this woman who had worked so hard all her life should now have to expend great effort to leave that life. I stroked her forehead to soothe her, and after about an hour, her breathing slowed and then simply stopped. Outside the sky was lightening, and I could hear the milkman exchanging our empty bottles on the back stoop for new ones. I watched as Maman's face relaxed and grew vacant. She was truly gone. I was still shaken by what I'd learned about her—my mother, the one person who knew me through and through, whom I had not truly known at all.

I don't know how much later it was when I kissed her forehead, rose from the chair, and made my way downstairs to the telephone. Phoebe answered after only two rings, which relieved me of the worry of disturbing them too early. All I said was, "This is Agnes," and she said, "We'll be right there."

Of course, I knew that "right there" included travel time from New Jersey, but I didn't mind. I needed them to come, and they were coming, and that is what I clung to.

I could not think what to do. When my grandmother died, my mother was in charge and made the necessary calls and arrangements, including to the Brethren, who came and kept a vigil night and day. I was sixteen then and comforted by their presence, even though I kept them at a deliberate distance. Now I was nearly forty and was apparently someone who kept everyone at a deliberate distance. Except Maman. It was a shock to grasp that I had never expected to lose her. I had always thought my own frequent illnesses would take me instead, and here I was burying her.

Years later, I painted *Mother of Silence* out of this yearning. At last I could embrace grief and weep my way through it, and put all the pain of it, brushstroke by brushstroke, into the picture. I included a blue line that breaks the aura on one side only: an imperfection to open a way for spirit, and I sense a presence every time I meditate on that picture. Every time I bring it a heartache or a question. This, I believe, is how iconographers work. Is it an icon of my mother? Yes, but not just my mother.

She was sixty-four years old. I am now seventy-nine and do not expect to see my eightieth birthday. I need to write down what to do with these pictures, like *Mother of Silence*, the pictures that I have kept. Instead, I have a longing for the paintings that have left home, the ones I sold for bread. What a horror. These pictures were my children; they were created through inspiration of the spirit and not intended to provide material support. I pine for them now. If only I had money, I would buy them back—redeem them, so to speak, set them free.

BROOKLYN, NEW YORK

DECEMBER 1920

CLOUDS ROILED ACROSS THE SKY the day we buried Maman in Greenwood Cemetery, in the plot next to Grandmama. I had called my aunt Alice, of course, and she and my cousins came, and also their spouses. Mr. Winter walked us through the rites, guiding my passage as well as my mother's.

"And will you stay in Brooklyn?" Phoebe asked afterward. We both had our eyes on the sky, feeling rain might come at any moment.

"I don't know," I faltered. "Perhaps."

"You have a lovely home," she added.

"I have a lovely cage," I countered. She looked shocked, and I felt a tremor of my own, hearing myself say it out loud. It is always strange, articulating something you've allowed to remain hidden even from yourself. I wondered if Maman had felt this way, when she poured out her confession to me.

After a moment, Phoebe said, "Cages have doors that can be opened." She grew even quieter and said, "You have a resource, Agnes. You have this house. A house may be sold."

Here was a revelation. Until that moment it had not occurred to me that with Maman's passing, the house on Pacific Street was mine.

"Yes," I said slowly, "a house may be sold." The idea grew, and I could feel Pacific Street falling away from me, and me from it, which caused an instant of vertigo. Phoebe must have seen this in my face. She said, "You don't have to decide anything right now."

––––––––

I finished the portrait of Tony Lujan and next to it displayed the photograph that had made completing it possible, this to show prospective customers how close a likeness I could achieve. The Canons came by my studio to see it, and Edward immediately commissioned his own portrait. A few days later, he brought me a Daguerreotype image of his parents, both long deceased, and also commissioned their portrait. He then remarked, almost casually, "There is a lot of money in Southampton. You might think about spending the summer there. I could introduce you to several families."

They owned a house on nearby Shelter Island—Maman and I had visited them there during one of our own Long Island respites—and I saw that I could remove myself from the city, at least for the summer, and earn money at the same time. Suddenly it was obvious that I needed to leave New York. I had found over and over—beginning with my year in Italy, summers in Ogunquit at Field's school, spending the Great War in rural Connecticut, and, finally, to this recent essential trip to Taos—that what nourished and energized me was to immerse myself in the natural world. Which I could do once again in eastern Long Island, a place I knew and loved, if I would but take the leap.

A plan was forming, one that sparked a frisson of boldness, which I did not discuss with the Canons or anyone else. Instead I quietly packed up my studio and closed it. I would go to Long Island, and if I found the right setting, I would stay. I would put the house on Pacific Street, with its angry ghosts and hollow griefs behind me, and I would seek a new home, a place where solitude could open the way to what I'd glimpsed within the sacred light of Taos. I felt calm, then, as though my destiny was no longer mine to decide.

SOUTHAMPTON, LONG ISLAND

1921

HOW DO WE KNOW IF we're running away from something or running toward it? Those, I have learned, are important spiritual distinctions, and to this day I am not sure of the answer. It seems that so much of my life could be characterized by flight. And yet if one is to break through the barriers that keep one from one's true art, sometimes it is essential to find another vantage point from which to look.

It was in the Culver Hill section of Southampton where I found a studio and installed myself just ahead of the summer crush, away at last from New York and its artists and galleries and taste-makers and critics. For the first time I had no plans to return—no home, no mother waiting for me. That summer I turned forty, finally closing my childhood chapter. "It took you awhile," one might well say. It takes as long as it takes, is my only defense and reply.

Eastern Long Island—with its soft salty air and sandy hills, its tangled pine trees that bent and twisted away from the wind—was the very place where I had spent the summers after art school learning to paint plein-air landscapes. This made it a kind of homecoming to me, a return to inspiration and refreshment of soul, and I found there again an immediate sense of peace.

I also found that my friend Edward was right: here was an immediate source of income. Southampton has always been a magnet for New York society, and I was lucky to be taken up by its denizens immediately. It all felt so familiar: women like Alice with taste and money, euphoric over finally getting the vote and eager to see a woman artist succeed, trooped to my studio. The Canons, who made frequent visits to the Southampton antique shops, stopped in at my studio too, often bringing with them influential friends, including Samuel Parrish, one of Southampton's leading lights. Mr. Parrish had opened a small art museum in the 1890s and expanded it twice by 1921. Over the next years he would commission from me portraits of himself and his family. Many of his friends, eager to be in on the latest trend, followed suit.

I missed Maman but was full of optimism, as though on an extended holiday. Something about the brightness of the Culver Hill studio, the straight lines of its whitewashed wooden interior and its lack of furnishings, gave me buoyancy, as did the anticipation of meaningful income. The studio had a Dutch door, which I could leave open at the top, enjoying the flow of passersby, while shutting out curious neighborhood dogs. It recalled to me the Taos Pueblo days, the sense of being accepted by the people while not being of them.

Children naturally gravitate to an artist at work, and early in the summer I was pleased when three small faces popped up over the half-door top.

"Would you like to come in?" I called to them. The two little ones squealed and ran, but the oldest was a boy whose name I knew—Jacob, from three houses down the lane—and he nodded seriously and stepped through the door. The others quickly returned and scampered in behind him. I showed him where to sit—I had hung a drape behind a chair as a generic setting—and when he perched himself there, I quickly sketched his face in pastels. Then I drew each of the other two children, handed them their likenesses, and said, "Maybe your mothers would like to have these."

The exercise was repeated a number of times over those June days, and before long the parents of many of these children came by to inquire about formal portraits. Though I had fled from the bustle of New York, I had never been so busy; there was little time to do anything but immerse myself in the formal demands of portraiture. But rather than finding the task burdensome, I became deeply interested in the challenges of individualizing each subject and setting her or him in their best light.

So many things must happen in a portrait: the viewer must understand the picture's setting, which creates a context for the subject and illustrates as quickly as possible who this person is in the world. For example, I had painted Edward, with his courtliness, his respect for heritage and interest in history, against a cloud-darkened sky (to signify his troubles: like me, he had always suffered poor health) wearing a high starched collar and morning coat, adding a red poppy (for remembrance) in his buttonhole. He sat in a plain wooden armchair clutching one of his beloved rare books as though interrupted in reading. Phoebe I decided to seat against a dark background of lush greenery next to a large ceramic vase overflowing with lilacs, which carry the symbolism of love's first bloom.

Word about the new artist in Southampton was getting out, and I heard from people I'd not been in touch with for years, including Emma Newton, who had been one of my mother's prize pupils. Maman had believed Emma talented enough for a concert career, and with great fanfare she had gone off to pursue one. And yet here she was in Southampton, accompanied by her new husband—a portly man who exuded prosperity and seemed to fit Edward's description of my ideal client: "Someone who has more money than he knows what to do with."

Emma and I used to sit in the kitchen on Pacific Street sipping tea after her lessons (Maman always saved the best pupils for last, feeling that they refreshed her from the lesser ones), and we had frequently vowed to one another that we would never marry, that a life devoted to one's art was vastly preferable to the servitude of matrimony. Neither of us had fathers who were living, so neither of us had any idea of what we were talking about, which of course did not inhibit our judgments. But seeing her framed in my doorway, her arm tucked snugly through her husband's, her face alight with, what—joy? More relief, I thought—I had to respect the mysterious forces in life that shunt us all from one path to another.

"Why, Emma!" I managed. "I thought you were in Europe."

"I came back," she said simply. "I have so much to tell you." She presented Harold Stern, her husband, who doffed his straw boater and offered a hand. Meaty, I thought, and wanted to recoil a bit, but then I realized that for Emma meaty was probably exactly right—she needed someone who could provide solid support. Introductions duly accomplished, he excused himself on what was probably a prearranged pretext and promised to return shortly. I pulled up my only two chairs, and Emma briefly recounted her story.

Because of Maman's encouragement, she had indeed moved to Europe, to Stuttgart as it happened, where so many musicians gravitated to launch careers. I had an immediate picture of her under Stuttgart skies.

"It was marvelous at first," she said. "There were a number of other girls, singers mostly, trying for the opera. They kept calling me 'brave' for going up against the men in the concert world. Imagine me brave, Agnes!" She laughed, and the lines in her face disappeared, and we were two girls ourselves again, trembling on the brink of adulthood and wildly optimistic.

"You were brave."

"And of course I thought of your dear mother, whose passing I was so sorry to hear about." Tears came into her eyes and mine, but sadness for me was infused with relief and joy in being with someone whose connection to Maman was through music and who knew that part of her as well as I did.

"I'm so sorry I didn't write to you, Agnes. What you must think of me."

"No need. You're here now. Tell me about Stuttgart."

"Well," she shrugged. "It will sound so foolish, so naïve, but it was all so hard. I had thought I was prepared for that, but I wasn't. To be taken seriously, I needed to be a European, or male, or both. I was left in reception rooms over and over while younger men were ushered in to audition. At the office of one impresario in particular, I could hear their playing, and Agnes, I promise you, I was better than any of them. But I was not given a chance."

I nodded with real sympathy.

"Enter Harold," she said, wiping her eyes and laughing a bit ruefully. He was an American businessman with dealings elsewhere in Germany who had come to Stuttgart to enjoy the concerts.

"What you will think of me I can only imagine, but I was starving, Agnes. Harold insisted that I move into his apartments, and it felt like a temporary reprieve to be cared for so well. And then the war came," she said. Her face grew grim and determined, and I saw the pain of her choice to marry as clearly as if it had been made right there before me.

"I came back to America with him," she said, "but held off marrying until the war's end. It went on so much longer than anyone expected, you see. I had said I intended to go back to Stuttgart and 'resume my career'—that's what I said, and bless him, he didn't laugh at me. He's a good man," she said, daubing at her nose and eyes.

"I'm sure he is."

"He loves me," she whispered, her eyes dropping to her lap, where her left hand boasted a large diamond ring and heavy gold band. I reached over and squeezed them gently, and she looked up, suddenly radiant, and held up her rings to catch the light.

"Marriage is quite an adventure," she laughed. "Especially at our age!"

"I admire you for undertaking it," I said.

"It is so good to see you doing so well," she said.

If she had intended to urge me to find a husband as well, she changed her mind, and I was relieved. I had no wish to defend what I now thought of as my spinsterhood, which in spite of the word did not seem in the least burdensome to me. Indeed, I felt newly liberated by my status, on my own and proud to be. We poured out the rest of the tea, and she talked about her wedding in the registry office in Manhattan, a train trip to Niagara Falls for a honeymoon, and then home to a new house in Westchester. I concentrated on keeping my smile bright as I took it all in, all the while thinking, Not for me, not for me.

When Harold reappeared at the Dutch door, Emma jumped up and fussed over him, and he glowed. He took the time to admire the work displayed on the studio walls and insisted on writing out a check for a portrait of his wife, to be done as soon as it could be arranged.

That evening, reflecting on all Emma's news, I decided on her portrait's theme: affluence and security finally achieved in what could be termed the autumn of life. To that end I had her wear a matronly hat, a coat trimmed in fur, and fine suede gloves. I was thinking of Vermeer, and his Dutch housewives, prosperous and content. I set her in a Dutch-like landscape in which the trees had lost their leaves but the ground had not yet frozen: I hoped the viewer could sense and smell the moisture of the earth—the feeling of earth as still alive—and would notice the admittedly muted golds and greens of the landscape. I was also keen on reminding both Emma and myself that time was passing, the tenderness of youth was long gone, and that we should find satisfaction in what we had each made of our lives.

That night I dreamt of Alice. In my dream we were on our way to Taos, only instead of being on the train, we were in a hotel sharing the only bed available. The room was dark, its papered walls splashed here and there with moonlight, and knowing I was having a dream, I allowed myself to enjoy the feeling of being cocooned there with Alice. She was talking about our early times in New York before the Armory Show, our visit to Mabel's White Salon, the tea parties we had held in her home to sell my work to her wealthy friends. "Oh, Agnes," she murmured, "what fun we had." Her voice was soft and suffused with longing and caused my breath to catch. I felt bathed in her warmth and was about to tell her how happy I was to be with her again, when she said, "It's you I love, Aggie."

Her words shocked me awake. I lay in my narrow bed and opened my eyes to my Southampton studio, gathering the fragmenting dream before it melted away. The emotion so transported me that all day I thought about Alice, wondering where she was and how she was. I had an impulse to write her and even sat down with paper and pen, but I could not think what to say to her. That I missed her? That I wished I could somehow go back and find a way to tell her that I loved her? In my imagination she tossed her head and burst into laughter: "Heavens, Agnes, what a thing to say!" I shook myself free of regrets and put my paper away.

Southampton bustled all summer, and I continued to work hard, overjoyed at seeing old friends and grateful for the money coming in that kept my savings intact. It was an intoxicating time, and I observed my own elation with caution. Sure enough, as summer faded, I found myself longing for solitude. I considered returning to Taos, but to reenter Mabel's world was to risk the very access to myself I was just beginning to find. Instead I began asking around Southampton about taking a place for the winter. Almost as a joke, someone told me that the old Hayground gristmill on tiny Mecox Bay had closed its operations and was for rent. I received this information on my birthday at the end of August, which heightened the significance, and I asked Emma and Harold to drive me there to see it.

It was getting toward evening when we rounded the bend and I caught sight of it, on top of a small hillock and reaching its huge arms in the four directions as late-day sun poured gold directly onto it. I stepped out of the car and approached, and standing in the mill's shadow caught an immediate sense of its spiritual power.

"Well?" Emma called out.

"Yes."

The next day, feeling suspended in a nameless grace, I contacted the mill's owner and arranged to lease it. One month later, I watched as men from the Brooklyn storage facility unloaded my few possessions from their truck and maneuvered them into the mill. I realized that I had left my things this long in Brooklyn to create a kind of anchor; their presence here was now a sobering reminder that for the first time in my life I had no home to return to other than the one before me. A breeze gusted up the treeless hill and made me shiver and wonder what I was doing. To stay out of the movers' way, I opened my sketchbook to a new page. I drew the faded grasses as they bent in the wind, the thickets of cedar and bayberry, and the few locust trees that hugged the downward slope. Looking southward past the highway below, the slope was hugged by bayberry and beach plum, and I could see all the way to the ocean. To the north, a short walk from my front door, a cluster of pine trees surrounded Mecox Bay. The silence was made of ocean and wind, and I began to feel an enormous sense of relief at the prospect of being alone in it.

The movers emerged and waited in a cluster while their boss approached me with a list of what they had transported, which I signed. He wished me good luck—shaking his head a bit at the idea anyone would choose to live here—and joined his men in the van. I felt a frisson of triumph as the visibly lightened truck backed down the mill's dirt track, creaking and tipping as it found the potholes. The driver waved as he swung out onto the road, turned west, and drove away toward New York.

With autumnal light at my back, I entered my new home. The mill's works had been removed, but the center post and crossbeams remained. I could easily reach up and touch the one nearest my head, and I did so, feeling sheltered and protected by its weight and heft. On a thick hook that had once lifted bags of grain I had hung a kerosene lantern, and I struck a match now to light it. Immediately Maman's piano, angled against the segmented wall, took on a glow. I pulled out the bench, sat down, and played a few exploratory chords. The windmill's tall, hollow space expanded the sound. "What splendid acoustics," I could hear her marvel. This brought a sense of her companionship in this enterprise. A sudden surge of emotion caught me by surprise, and the familiar rumblings of self-doubt began to gather: my glory days, such as they were, had flashed and faded; my friends in New York—Hamilton Field, in particular—didn't know what to do with me; others, like Mabel and Alice, had scattered and our relationships had changed.

Now in a panic and suffused with grief—Maman impaired and frail was still Maman—I asked myself what she would say: "Open your music," was the clear reply. My study books were under the lid of the piano bench, and on top I found Bach's *Well-Tempered Clavier*.

It had been a long time since I had played, but these pieces seemed created for moments exactly like this one. Each one shapes out a fugal theme—drawing its contours, if you will—which allows the out-of-practice hand to find its way into the melodic line so perfectly that one seems to be creating it. To enter this music was to feel, in a sense, forgiven for my lapses. In my mind I could hear Maman's voice counting out the tempo and even felt the sensation of her hands lifting mine as she had done so often to remind me about forming the correct arch for my fingers. I leaned into the music and its precision and grace and allowed it to order the storm of thoughts crowding my mind that first night: the youthful romantic attachment that became a destructive obsession but was also the first freedom of heart I'd known; the sense of holiness that I experienced in Italy; my abiding love for Alice, who had liberated so much of my soul. I felt I could wait, then, and see what might be revealed. This, after all, was what I had come to the windmill to find.

TOWNSHIP OF WATERMILL, LONG ISLAND

NOVEMBER 1921

I CAN CONJURE A DAY THAT first autumn when winter pressed close, clouds scudding across a metal sky, heavy gusts pummeling the hill. Me, just outside the windmill's wooden door, wrapped in one of my mother's shawls and shivering, alone and loving all of it, from the ecstasy of solitude to the sharp anticipation of a season alone.

I walked to the village, which was a few miles to the west, for supplies. Mostly I wanted to speak to my landlord, Mr. Harriman, who presided over the general store. The few nights I'd slept in the mill had revealed what a drafty place it was, and I hoped he would give me some caulk to plug the places I had located.

Watermill was nearly empty. Just a few potato farmers in the store talking about weather and the storm that seemed to be on the way. Mr. Harriman, broad as a haystack, loomed in his green grocer's apron over the counter, talking to a man in carpenter's overalls. He seemed annoyed when I explained what I needed.

"I told you, Miss Pelton, it's not the Ritz you moved into." He chuckled for the man at the counter, who swung around and stared.

I gave them what I hoped was a resolute smile and tried not to shrink back. After a pause, Mr. Harriman gruffly introduced Harvey Conrad.

"You're the artist at the mill," he said, and I understood that my residency had been a town-wide topic for discussion. Rudely pulled from my fantasies of solitude, I nodded. What were you thinking? Grandmama intruded to ask, her voice raspy with fear. I had no answer for her. I was a woman alone in a town whose character was now the opposite from the lively place I'd spent the summer.

"Well, then." Mr. Conrad gave the counter a light tap and pulled his eyes away from my face, which I imagine reflected the shock of my new understanding. "Good day." He gave a brief salute and took his leave.

Mr. Harriman retreated to his supply room and returned with a large can of caulking material, which was heavier than I'd expected.

"No charge," he said and grinned as he watched me heft it into my bag along with the few groceries I'd also bought. I offered a prim smile and bade him good day, wondering how I would accomplish the three-mile return trip. I managed to get clear of the village before setting down my bag to rest, and suddenly there was Mr. Conrad in his truck, pulling over. He jumped out and in two quick strides opened the passenger door.

"Let me give you a lift."

"Oh, no," I tried. "I'm fine, thank you." Another car passed going toward the village, and I caught a glimpse of a man whose name I didn't know but whose face was familiar taking in the sight of the artist—*living alone*—at the windmill and Harvey Conrad, married man.

"Please, Miss Pelton—"

In an instant I decided that he meant me no harm. And that I truly needed help with my burden.

Mr. Conrad was quiet the entire ride, but at the windmill, he insisted on mixing up the caulk and plugging the places I pointed out, plus a few more he noticed for himself. He finished in short order and I thanked him. I allowed a prissiness to color my voice, intending to preserve a formal reserve between us. I wasn't especially worried about the town gossips, but I was intent on guarding my solitude.

"It's no trouble," he said gruffly, climbing into the truck. "I used to paint the occasional landscape," he added.

"Oh! A fellow artist."

"Naw, I was never an artist. But I liked the quiet, and being by myself, painting. There are some around here who think art is for the lazy rich, but I did enough of it to know that it's hard work and can be lonely."

I was alarmed the next day when his truck once again swung up the mill's dirt track. I stepped outside with no intention of asking him in and saw that he was carefully lifting a cardboard box from the truck bed. With a smile, he placed it on the ground next to me before returning to his truck and driving away. The box rocked slightly, and when I opened the lid, I saw a pair of kittens, tabbies both, which I adjudged to be about four months old. One shrank back—the female, I regret to say—and the other immediately stood on his brown tabby legs and waited for me to pick him up.

"Henry," I decided. I had no idea where the name came from, but he seemed pleased, so it stayed.

"Matilda," I whispered to the striped gray ball mashing herself into the corner. "Tillie. I know how you feel." I allowed the lid to fall and close the box loosely, giving her a safe, solitary space.

The nights grew cold, and Henry and Tillie took to jumping onto my small bed where we three bundled together. As winter closed in, I resorted to holding or carrying one of them to stay warm.

Mr. Conrad—I always addressed him thus—became a friend who took it upon himself to drive me to the village every week or so. While waiting for him to complete his own errands, I dropped by the library. One week, among the books on the "Recent Acquisitions" shelf, my attention was drawn to a new edition of Madame Blavatsky's *The Secret Doctrine*. Years before, H.P. Blavatsky and her new religion called Theosophy had piqued the interest of the salon crowd in New York, but when I had mentioned to Maman that I thought it sounded interesting, she had reacted with surprising fury.

"Madame Blavatsky and her Russian superstitions are not to be offered a refuge in this house," she said. "She is of the devil," she added, as though that should settle the matter once and for all. I had shrugged it off as not worth fighting about, but now I picked up the forbidden volume and opened it to the author's preface, which garnered my immediate sympathy, with its apology for the delay in the work's appearance, "occasioned by ill-health and the magnitude of the undertaking." We were fellow travelers, and I checked the book out at once.

That evening, after lighting the lamps, I began the journey I felt I had waited for my entire life. Theosophy was a universe unto itself, with its infinite worlds of creators and creation, an enormous canopy that held under its protection Hinduism, Buddhism, and the Judeo-Christian beliefs. I would have been apprehensive, expecting Grandmama's wrath at every turn, except for the kindly grace of the author, whose words were suffused with gentle concern for her readers. I read eagerly and felt the possibility of finding the spiritual understanding I had sought all my life.

I settled in at the windmill, alone except for my kittens and the occasional visits from town friends. That first year there, my work did not end with the summer. I had begun as many portraits as I could while their sitters were still available. As the days shortened and darkened, I luxuriated in the odd sense that time was expanding: alone, in the studio, I could think through each portrait and add the elements that would turn it into a work of art and not just a faithful rendering of a recognizable subject. Nothing in a painting is ever incidental. Everything in it must come together to convey each painting's message.

My self-imposed solitude had also opened the inner door, allowing memories and emotions to swirl about me as they pleased. Through the long winter nights, I dreamt a great deal and often awakened with the sense of being expected elsewhere—a feeling that was dispelled as the sun rose and scattered my dream characters back to their hiding places.

I spent the days working on portraits, or, if I was too tired, reclining on the daybed with a book, both cats keeping me company. Lying in bed at night with a window above me, I marveled at the stars, so dense as to appear clotted, one pulsing light snagged upon another—more than I'd ever encountered, even in New Mexico. Or maybe it was that my eyes had finally opened: I felt pulled up and into the heavens and lucky if I awakened in time to see Sirius, the true morning star, or Venus, the shimmering pearl that also preceded the sun. The gentle luminosity of the latter brought a sense of Maman, and I found it comforting to send her greetings with the dawn.

———

The winter passed in a series of lovely snowfalls; heavy, dark rains; brilliant blue winter skies; and rapid sunsets. I did not stop working, but I let myself slow down. I heard from my New York friends less often, and what had seemed a perpetual buzz from the art world, like angry bees in a hive, receded into silence. There had been yet another flap over—what else—who should be exhibited and who should not, and my old friend and mentor Hamilton Easter Field had loudly resigned from one group to establish another.

Field was a tireless democrat for equality among artists, insisting, for example, to give me, a mere woman, a solo exhibition back in 1913. I knew what I owed him, and yet I was relieved to be away from it all, even if a bit ashamed at not being available to furnish him with moral support. Truth be told, I had deliberately distanced myself from him along with the others who had been my champions, Walt Kuhn and Jerome Myers included.

So, when in April of 1922 I received news of Field's untimely death at age forty-nine, I was shaken to the core. Forty-nine! I myself was forty, and my health had never been as robust as Field's. To think of such a life being ended, long before its time, was to be swamped by grief and again to doubt my own prospects for achieving even the semblance of a uniquely personal vision.

"Dear Agnes," began Kitty Myers's letter, into which she had folded *The Brooklyn Daily Eagle*'s obituary. "My apologies for not having written sooner, but so much has happened so fast, and I'm afraid many essential tasks have been left undone. You will have noted from the enclosed that our dear friend and advocate has been taken from us so swiftly and cruelly as to leave us all destitute. Pneumonia, they say. Extreme overwork, I say."

I reached for a chair. I had not realized how much I had cherished Field and expected him always to be around and available should I ever wish to repair my relationship with him. I clutched Kitty's letter and tried to sort out a tangle of emotions: grief, to be sure, but also panic because I was so far away from it all. My satisfaction at having removed myself so completely gave way to desolation that I had cut myself off entirely and would never again find the fellowship we all seem to need to make our creative way forward.

I reminded myself that I had chosen this solitude for a reason, even if the reason changed and wasn't always clear. I stepped outside the windmill where the wintry landscape with its graceful arc of bare-branched trees helped steady me. There is a plan for me, I repeated over and over to myself; I have but to find it. Immediately a gentle warmth filled my chest and I felt surrounded by a luminous entity. You must go inside, I heard my inner voice say. I shivered and followed that instruction, threw more wood into the stove, and then laughed out loud: not indoors, the voice was saying, but inside yourself. It was my own guide—not Grandmama, not Maman. The fear departed, and I passed the rest of the winter reading and studying.

TOWNSHIP OF WATERMILL,
LONG ISLAND

NOVEMBER 1923

ANOTHER WINTER AND ITS DARKNESS, both of which pressed on me and drove my spirits down, and then here came the familiar thoughts: "You have failed. You are a failure." Back in New York City, where I had no desire to be, my painter friends were thriving. When I took the train in to see what they were showing, I had the sense that all of them—including people I didn't actually know—were finding their voice, so to speak. Jerome Myers, for instance, and Walt Kuhn were painting with vigor and authority—intentionality, I called it—and you could feel their energy pulsing through every canvas. I fled back to my windmill and sank lower.

But here also came an unexpected invitation, from my cousins in Hawaii, the Richards, whom I had never met. This was Grand-mama's side of the family, scorned and ignored by my grandfather Tilton as too hide-bound, too provincial, too conservative. My mother and I had shuddered at what they might have thought about the subsequent scandal, and us as its heirs. But a kind note at Maman's passing opened a cautious correspondence between us.

They wondered about me, and I certainly wondered about them. Many years earlier my cousin Theodore (called Ted, and yes, named for my grandfather before the scandal) had answered a call to be a missionary in Honolulu. Now his wife Mary wrote to say how much they wanted to meet me, and would I consider spending the winter with them? Why, thank you very much, I would indeed.

Mr. Conrad built a carrying case for my beloved cats, and I tucked them into it and sent them home with him, where he would care for them until my return. I packed paints, pastels, blank sketchpads, canvas, stretchers, and brushes and sent them for shipping to Honolulu, and my rising excitement prompted hope—that just as it had in the past, travel would open me, release me, change me as a painter.

In Los Angeles I boarded the steamship for Honolulu. Such a happy journey. No grim North Atlantic storm clouds, no disapproving tablemates at meals. Everyone was looking forward to paradise. It struck me that this was the first long journey I'd undertaken that was not in response to some specific trauma, either debilitating illness or the effects of war. Sometimes it is a matter of pure grace, and coming to Oahu was like that: even now the memory of it opens like a flower—velvety mountains the color of jade, flowers tumbling everywhere like joy, their exotic names pure music—pua kala, ma'o hau hele, 'ohi'a lehua—spiky palm trees waving welcome, welcome!

The stewards rang gongs on every deck to let us know we were near, and I joined a host of fellow passengers at the rail. Smudges of deep green in the distance became mountains, thrusting out of the sea and ringed in mist. As we approached, the ocean shimmered and broke into bands of color—the red, blue, green, and violet of the reef below, and then the white sandy ring around Oahu. Beneath the water's azure surface, large green sea turtles swam alongside the ship. Outriggers pushed off from the shore, and radiant people paddled in unison, gliding forward to welcome us. The ship's crew tossed lines over the side. The canoes emptied, and god-like apparitions

climbed effortlessly and spilled onto the deck, carrying flower necklaces, which they gently placed around our necks, men and women
alike. Then the ship was at the pier, which was also packed with
people. Here were our hosts, laden with more flowers, whose subtle
fragrance filled the air.

A sudden shyness—maybe it was all too beautiful—and a worry
about my cousins thrust itself to the surface. Ted was still an active
missionary, deeply involved with the schools that had been educating
Hawaiian boys for one hundred years. His wife Mary had been born
in Honolulu, while his own narrative had long been the stuff of family
legend: he had been on his way to law school in New York when he
happened upon a lecture about bringing Christianity to the islands.
Immediately he felt a calling and dropping his plans for study, marched
up to the speaker, and volunteered to go. I wondered what he had
known of our grandparents' history and what part it had played in his
action? I feared that my own refusal to embrace either my grandmother's
religion (or my cousin's) would make me a target for missionary work.
My own short prayer, which I directed more out of hope than belief, was
that I would remain myself as I had come to understand myself—open
to the new and desirous of connection with the spirit.

As the gangway was lowered, I heard someone call out my name.

"Cousin Agnes!" A tall and slender man with thinning gray hair
and trim mustache waved enthusiastically from the crowd. I felt a
sudden burst of recognition and waved back as though we were lifelong friends. Next to him was a woman I correctly assumed was his wife
Mary, and behind them was their youngest daughter Polly, then fifteen.

"Cousin Theodore!" I called out. Soon we were face-to-face.
I reached out to greet him with a kiss, and, smiling, he thrust his
hand out for me to shake. This caused an awkward hitch, but Mary
soon rescued us.

"Oh, Ted, really," she said, embracing me with one arm while
decorating me with another lei. "Welcome, Cousin Agnes!" She
pulled Polly forward and introduced her, and Polly, likewise, kissed

me on both cheeks and added an additional lei. Mary shot a glance at my cousin, who looked abashed. Quickly Mary picked up my light travel case from where I had set it, hooked her arm through mine, and said, "Now tell us all about your voyage!"

I tried to describe the sea and its endless variety of blues, the thrill of glimpsing the islands in the distance. They seemed pleased at my enthusiasm and guided me to an open-air touring car where my bags were strapped onto the rear. I was offered the front passenger seat, and while Mary and Polly talked about plans for dinner that evening, I took in the softness of the trade winds and the delicate fragrances that played all about. Mary proudly pointed out the places that had loomed so large in their lives—in particular, the manicured campus of the Kamehameha Schools, where Ted had initially taught and then served as principal. We also rode past the monument commemorating Hawaii's annexation by the United States.

"I remember that day so clearly," Mary said. She had leaned forward a bit as if to confide. "While all the fireworks were exploding around us and everyone was pledging allegiance to the new flag, I had to wipe away tears. Oh, don't misunderstand," she hastily added. "I was grateful to become an American, but I was born the subject of a proud kingdom, and it was hard to see that end."

"I do understand," I assured Mary, thinking back to Taos Pueblo. It occurred to me that if Taos had been as rich an agricultural resource as Hawaii, it would never have been left unmolested. Instead its "missionaries" had come from the art world—Mabel and a few others who had found their way into the valley, all of whom were interested in learning from the Indians and not converting them.

"Cousin Agnes," Polly called from the back seat, "what do you think of the hula dance?" Ted immediately stopped the car and turned to face his youngest daughter.

"I think, Polly, if you are determined to be disruptive, we can take you right home and not permit you to accompany Cousin Agnes on her sightseeing trips."

I caught sight of her soft, round face, which for an instant registered satisfaction along with defiance before settling into an expression of careful contrition. Here was the very world I had been apprehensive about, and here, too, I sensed, was an unexpected ally. "I'm sorry, Papa," Polly said, her eyes properly downcast.

"And apologize to Cousin Agnes."

"There's no need," I said.

"There is need."

"I'm sorry, Cousin Agnes," she said, raising her eyes to meet mine. Her face was open, and her eyes sparkled in spite of the situation.

———————

I settled in, unpacking my crates. I'd brought framed pastels to show possible portrait clients, and when Polly saw them, she asked if I would make one of her.

"As soon as I hear from your parents that they don't mind," I said. To which Polly darted out of my room, quickly returning to poke her head in.

"I mean, excuse me, please, Cousin Agnes."

"Of course," I replied, rather primly, I'm afraid, already feeling the weight of this pious household.

"Polly!" I called her, and she returned immediately.

"You don't need to ask to be excused."

"Oh, but I do, Cousin Agnes, but thank you." She flashed a radiant smile and disappeared again. Minutes later she was back with Mary in tow.

"How kind of you to offer to draw Polly," she said.

"I never feel settled in a place until I've begun to draw it, so you can see how helpful she has been." Mary looked relieved and smiled, and I knew then that she and I were friends.

I began at home, so to speak, making pastels of Polly and several other neighbor children. These so impressed Ted that he began to invite his important friends, and soon I was drawing their children.

When I had time to myself, I drew the flowers and the sea and landscape. The Richards's garden was a place of quiet, where one could focus completely on one flower or group of flowers at a time. I loved the sharp, brilliant bird-of-paradise, with its slash of orange against stiff green. We could also walk to the beach, and I spent hours perched by the shore, making pastels of the changing blue sea water and the bright pale sky, clouds reflecting on the water's surface. One day I saw jellyfish, moving past the shore like graceful umbrellas, opening and closing, transparency upon transparency.

_____

Polly and I were becoming fast friends, and that year I became Polly's mentor. She wanted to be an artist, and I was happy to allow her to voice her dreams.

"Cousin Agnes," she would say, "have you always been so *talented?*" And the way she said that word, her voice thrumming with admiration, made me laugh. Not at her, never at her, but for the joy of meeting a fellow traveler, even one who was not yet fifteen years old.

One afternoon she brought me her private sketchbook and asked if I would mind looking at it. She had hidden it inside her smock and darted out into the garden where I was reading. She pulled it out a bit furtively and said, "I don't let anyone see this. Except for Mother, but sometimes not even Mother. Do you mind?"

"Of course not. I am honored."

"Oh good," she said. "Mother said I wasn't to bother you with it, but I do so want to show you."

I took it with proper reverence, and slowly turned the pages. The drawings were clearly by a child, but there was a confidence in the quality of the line that was evident immediately. Also, she had a natural sense of composition. Instead of trying to fit a full-sized figure onto the page, she had the good sense to draw only part of it, the head and shoulders of a woman, and she had added a flower almost as an abstract balance next to the face.

"These sketches are very good," I said, and was rewarded immediately with a full, toothy grin.

"I think they're good too, but Father said not to brag."

"I don't think it's bragging. You are correctly adjudging your own work, which is very difficult to do. I especially like this one. Is it your mother?"

"Why, yes," she said, her face flushing with pleasure.

"It's very good," I repeated. I remembered how loath Grandmama had been to praise my art when I was Polly's age, and how Maman would take me aside and only tell me she liked it when Grandmama was out of earshot. I remember wondering whose opinion was the right one. It took years before I could begin to adjudge my own work: to see something as skillfully rendered and as what I intended, no matter what anyone might say about it.

"Are you using these sketches as studies for paintings?" I inquired of Polly.

"Oh, no," she said. "Mother says no oil paint until I'm older."

"Well, then, have you worked in pastels? You could use mine. It's like painting, only you're using your hand instead of a brush. We could work together, side by side."

Polly was worried that her parents might think she had imposed herself on me, so I did the asking. When they understood that I welcomed Polly's companionship, they were happy to grant permission. We carried a table outdoors into the garden and set out a pair of chairs, one on each end of the table. I put my box of pastel colors in the center, and we began with the garden flowers.

Once Polly was fully engaged in her drawing, I began a sketch of her at work. I was quite pleased with the outcome and asked her if she'd like to sit for a formal portrait. She would, and hers was the first of the family I painted. After hers, I painted Ted's and then Mary's. It was a small way to thank them for their unceasing generosity.

KILAUEA, HAWAII

1924

THE INNER URGENCY BEGAN LIKE a branch, tapping at the window of the serenity I was enjoying merely by being in Hawaii, reminding me that it was not enough to travel thousands of miles and simply be here. To expand myself artistically, something had to happen. And something did: Mary suggested an outing, and she and Polly and I packed overnight cases, waved goodbye to Ted, who had pressing business in Honolulu, and boarded a ferry to the big island of Hawaii and Kilauea, its magnificent volcano. We had heard that eruptions had created a lake of fire next to the crater, with lava seething and spewing in regular intervals and in all directions.

Without my cousin's schoolmasterly demeanor and his daily routine of early prayers (to which we were all summoned by a brass ship's bell), we three relaxed and became playful with one another— singing silly song-rounds, playing "I spy" and "twenty questions." Play is often the beginning of inspiration, opening the artist as vessel, making her ready to receive that which the universe is eager to supply. Such was my experience traveling to Kilauea.

We arrived at the Big Island in just a few hours, and Mary drove us to Volcano House, the closest lodgings one could get. It was a lovely old hotel, built from the old woods of the surrounding tropical forest. We three took two rooms, Mary and Polly sharing one and me in another. I protested at having the only private room, and Mary laughed: "I wouldn't know what to do in a room of my own."

Our rooms were paneled in midnight-dark mahogany, rich in color and smooth as ivory. I sat on my single bed, feeling embraced by the forest itself, and opened the shuttered windows to the joyous cacophony of the birds.

The plan was to rise early the next morning and see the volcano first in the dark. After an early dinner and early to bed, we were aroused at about four o'clock to join a tour organized by the hotel. It was raining very hard. In the lobby we joined others as sleepy-eyed as we, and the hotel handed us all oiled rain slickers, which we donned.

I felt more like a Gloucester fisherman than a tourist off to see a volcano and said so, making us all laugh a bit at how we looked. We climbed onto a bus, its engine rattled to life, and we started toward the crater. The volcano was just entering another period of activity, said the guide at the front of the bus, "so we are all fortunate about that."

Mary had first been to Kilauea some fifteen years prior, during another period of activity—"activity" being an understatement, as it would turn out. The guide launched into a sort of lecture. We learned that Kilauea was the youngest of the Big Island's volcanoes and perhaps the most active in the world. It went through active periods and dormant ones, in which the lava created the shield-like crust for which it is known, with vent holes through which steam poured.

The bus lurched and rumbled through the blackness. By the time we arrived at our apparent destination, the rain had ceased but darkness was all consuming. The bus halted without pulling over, and with the help of the guide's flashlight—he told us that the interior bus lights would ruin the effect for us—we made our way down the aisle and stepped into primal blackness. As we stood there, trying to get our bearings, the clouds, which had been charcoal smudges against the black sky, gave way and parted. The half-disk of moon appeared, its white light creating a halo against thick clusters of stars that stretched out and back and all the way to eternity. Even Polly was subdued.

We inched our way forward, stumbling a bit in the dark, and then we were at the rim of a burning lake of lava. Whoever had first described hell as a lake of fire must surely have seen such a sight. To come upon it, crusted and seething, was to feel the extreme fragility of one's physical being.

I reached into my bag and took out my small sketchbook and soft pencil. Quickly I outlined the scene, its size and shapes and parameters, roughly sketching in the fire, roaring and pulsing with power. As the dawn revealed more and more, Polly called out for us to look.

I followed her pointing finger and was astonished to see a clump of trees growing right out of the lava.

"That's the lahua tree," Mary murmured. "The natives consider it sacred, belonging to Pele, the goddess of the volcano, and to Laka, goddess of hula. I know it's wrong, Ted gets very upset with me, but I see how one could believe in Pele and Laka and in Our Lord at the same time. I don't think it's sacrilegious."

"No," I said, grateful for her thoughts. And for her trust, that I would not judge her nor mention it to my cousin. I flipped to a clean page and sketched the trees and their brilliant red and yellow blossoms, which looked like spiky flames bursting from the branches.

With the sun fully arisen, our tour group began clamoring for breakfast, and the guide called us back toward the bus. Reluctantly, I closed my sketchbook and backed away, keeping Kilauea and its crimson lake in sight as long as possible. Utterly indifferent to our presence, the molten lava continued to overwhelm the hillside like a great passion, creating new pathways and destroying others. Shaping and desolating, burning and cleaning, leaving rough black rock in its wake. Its flow could neither be controlled nor prohibited, a reminder that sometimes one's only recourse is to accede to power and its terrible beauty and work out what that can mean. Because it is not enough, is it, to command the facts of one's life; what is needed is to make sense of them and thus to perceive the design.

When I joined the others on the bus, Polly patted the seat next to hers.

"I saved it for you," she said. I put my arms around her and hugged her long and hard.

"I would have stayed out there with you, but Mother said to leave you be," Polly said.

We returned to the Richards' home the next day. As soon as I could, I made a painting of the crater with its shield-like hump and the firepit beneath it, as I had seen them in the predawn darkness. I wanted an indelible reminder that the fire of creation may slumber for years but is still there, waiting to appear. That it can neither be rushed nor extinguished. I made a solemn vow never to lose connection with that fire and the change I had come to because of seeing it. It was undeniable that other artists were barging ahead and making their own personal statements while I had somehow been held back and moved to seek a life of solitude. By whom or what I could not at that time say. But Kilauea bestowed on me true acceptance of this and gave me the patience to wait upon the Visioner.

WATERMILL, LONG ISLAND

1926

AT LAST THE SPIRITUAL SEEDS I'd been sowing began to bear fruit. I had already begun my lifelong practice of ending the day in meditation and quiet and had just reclined on my daybed—the same one I'd had in my first studio. Suddenly I had a rush of joy and gratitude, thinking of Alice and that beautiful space on 59th Street in Manhattan, long lost to the wrecking ball but still alive and present to me. Into my mind came a vision, the first of its sort: an orb or egg-shaped light was rising and spinning above a rocky and dark ground, emerging from a thick gray fog. I was so surprised and the vision was so real that my eyes flew open and it disappeared. Quickly I closed my eyes again and it reappeared. I studied it as closely as I could, and then into my mind came words: **Within the whirl of time/ The shred of yesterdays/ Holds strong the mound of earth/ Living green above/ And fire within.**

I lurched upright to grab my sketchbook and opened it to a blank page. Quickly drawing a crude frame, I scribbled the rough ground and then the swirling egg mass, lifting toward the picture's top. Next to it I wrote the lines I'd heard, which then continued:

Strongly thrusting upward through the crust/ The will to be
takes shape/ Revolving, spiraling the Blue—/ The mystery
at the heart of its unfoldment/ Still unrevealed.

When a title came, I wrote it under the sketch: *Kilauea*. Then
I crossed that out and wrote *Being* and sat back in calm amazement.
Mystery indeed, I remember thinking. But what a mystery. Why is it,
I wondered then and now, that the right answer takes so long to get
here and then presents itself full and complete, easy and effortless? I
knew that something was being born inside me, and without having
to think about it, I knew what colors I would use—a range of blues,
violets, and yellows. I knew that the shape on my paper was like an
egg but was bearing a different sort of burden. It was spiritual birth,
and I knew I would have to let it appear in its own way and time.

The next days were spent in joyous painting, so intense that
I had to discipline myself to pause and eat and rest, else I feared
I would simply be consumed by my own fire. But the visions continued, and soon after receiving *Being*, I received and painted *The
Fountains* along with another poem. The poems continued along
with the images. Why? I inquired about this in meditation, and the
answer came that the words would help viewers who were unaccustomed to imagery of this sort. So, I displayed the poems alongside the
pictures when they were exhibited, and so many people expressed
their appreciation that I found it easy to abandon what was really a
kind of artistic snobbishness, insisting that viewers be left to puzzle
the thing out for themselves. "In service to others," I could hear my
mother murmur, as she often did when doing some task that she
didn't much care for.

SOUTH PASADENA, CALIFORNIA

1928

THAT FALL, WITH MY INCOME in steep decline, I faced a quandary: accept more portrait commissions from a few remaining Long Island patrons—which now felt like a prison sentence to me—or find a way to continue my pursuit of the abstract.

Since coming to the windmill I had luxuriated in solitary winters of study and reflection, but now a viable "career" path threatened to sidetrack my true passion. I thought with resentment of the exhibition my cousins had arranged in Hawaii, and the newspaper article that gushed over my finding my true vocation with portraits. And I had a viable option right in front of me: my friend Emma, who had moved west, had written to invite me for an extended visit.

Emma's letter was full of excitement about William Levington Comfort and his commune known as the Glass Hive, in South Pasadena. "I feel I might be able to pick up my music again," she wrote. She and Harold lived nearby, and she could hardly wait to take me there. The commune's primary publication was also called *The Glass Hive*, a copy of which Emma had enclosed. Reading it was electric; so many of the ideas I'd been studying on my own were discussed lucidly and with great insight. So, I traveled west once again, planning to stay for about a month.

The community was sprawled over a hilltop, nicknamed the Knob, and was a steep climb from the lush South Pasadena neighborhood where Emma and her husband Harold had settled in a lovely Crafts-man-style cottage. I hadn't been aware of harboring a conscious image of the place, and yet when I caught my first glimpse, I was disappointed. The Glass Hive, it turned out, was a series of rather ramshackle bungalows clinging to the top of the hill.

"Just you wait," Emma said, responding, no doubt, to the dismay I was already trying to hide. She pulled into a parking area and turned off the engine. On foot now, we started up a curving grassy path, discovering at each turn a small jewel of a garden. Each featured flowers of a single color—red, blue, yellow, violet—the effect was of walking through a rainbow.

At the top of the hill a group of artists painted, each with an easel pointed in a different direction. The scene seemed arranged, like a tableau. I halted, feeling we were intruding. What was this place? My grandmother loomed in my mind, and I ticked off a mental list of what concerned me. No trees, for one thing. Emma crooked her arm through mine and squeezed my hand. I dismissed the eerie feeling and smiled to reassure her. Just then the door opened, and a young woman who seemed spun of gold dashed out, a handsome man in close pursuit.

"That's Will's daughter, Jane," Emma whispered. "And her husband, Steve. They eloped when she was sixteen and shocked everyone."

"She looks sixteen now," I murmured. I recalled myself at sixteen. Leaving home was something that had not once crossed my mind until Alice embarked on her campaign to get me out of Brooklyn. Even then, much older than Jane had been, I could not bring myself to leave 1403 Pacific Street. I had no reason, I told myself: there was no older man begging me to marry him, there was only my mother.

Jane now struck the big brass Chinese gong hanging outside the door, and people emerged from wherever they'd been. The plein-air painters covered their canvases, and everyone made their way indoors.

The room we entered was large and wood-paneled and filled with tokens of life in the West. I noticed several gorgeous pieces of Indian pottery, carefully grouped in relation to a Navajo rug, itself surrounded by a loose circle of plush armchairs. It all glowed warmly in the late afternoon light, and I beamed at Emma. She propelled us to the leather sofa. Those who arrived after the chairs had been taken simply sat where they could find a spot on the floor or stood, like attendees had at Mabel's salons in New York, and I began to feel excited. Was this the next great cycle of learning? I decided it was.

Will Comfort entered. He was tall and a bit overweight with thinning hair, but he commanded the room. I was impressed, which clearly pleased Emma. He carried a book that he flipped open. I recognized Madame Blavatsky's *Secret Doctrine* as Will began to read. The passage was one of my favorites, a poetic description of the universe as a web connected on one end to the spirit and on the opposite end to earthly matter. His face opened as he savored the words, catching the golden light; he stood like a prophet, his confidence complete. I felt the charge of recognition, a sense of returning to a truth I'd encountered eons ago which was still vital and fresh.

To center myself, I scanned the room. Among the crowd I noticed a beautiful woman, blonde and thin as a ribbon, cheekbones insisting themselves out, sending perfect shadows into the hollows of her face. She stood next to an equally beautiful man, also tall, and as soft and dark as she was angular and fair. They were Dane Rudhyar in his prime and my friend Christina. They seemed to complement one another perfectly, so it shocked me when Christina reached for a woman on her other side whom I'd barely registered at all—she had apparently tried to make herself invisible. She was shorter, older, and heavier in a shapeless dress, and she wore a dark cloche hat pulled low over her face, incongruous in the sun-washed room. This was Billie.

We are all old now, but in 1928 we were full of irrational optimism—the best kind—and all searching. The images of these three remain: Rudhyar the panther, dark and lithe, black hair a deluge over his eyes, the curve of his cheek and jaw line; Christina, the lioness, perfectly composed and serene, everything about her light and transparent; Billie, the bear, who before long would discard those dresses for pants, shirt, vest, and tie.

———

That first afternoon Will read on for a bit and stopped, lowered the book, and then his head. No one moved, and the silence was powerful.

"Jane," he finally said. His daughter stepped forward and took the book from his hands. He seemed helpless then, on another plane altogether, and unable to return to us here on earth. I wondered if he was putting it on.

Jane, still standing next to her father, smiled at us all. "Refreshments?" Voices rose, and Emma and I followed the crowd.

When Jane crossed the room to speak to us, I was struck by the forthright way she simply marched over, and her bravery—not about talking to us: good heavens, a pair of middle-aged women was hardly daunting to someone who had defied her father to marry the man she loved. No, Jane was an old soul, and soon I forgot her chronological age.

"Hello, Emma," she said. Turning to me, she thrust her hand out. "You are Agnes, and you live in a windmill."

I turned to Emma, the question in my eyes.

"Everyone was so interested to hear of your work," she said serenely.

"And that windmill," Jane said. "I should think those huge arms could lift one up to heaven."

———

Jane and I began taking daily walks during which she talked of her mother and the shock of her death, and of her father and her love for him and devotion to his vision. I talked too, which I'd not really done with anyone. I talked of my own family, of my mother and her lost concert career, of my father and his love of beauty, our sudden and irreparable loss when he took his own life. Of my grandparents, their deeply held beliefs in the equality of all people, their tragedy.

These long perambulations always took place at the end of the workday, when paintbrushes were cleaned and put away, when Emma had closed the lid on the piano, and when Jane had finished her writing. As hard as I was working, I never felt weary. I was completely caught up in the wave of energy on the Knob and in the flowering of our soul friendship, so it was a shock one day to look around for Emma's car and not see her waiting for me. This irked me more than it should have—I was terribly full of myself—and had to ask Jane's brother, Tyrone, for a ride.

I found Emma collapsed and weeping, with Harold patting her back while consulting his pocket watch. He saw me in the doorway and rose gratefully.

"Thank heavens you're here," he said. "The cook is quite upset, having tried to serve dinner over an hour ago."

I rushed to Emma's side. "Dear heart, what is wrong?"

"Oh, Agnes, I feel so useless," she sobbed.

"She had her music critique today," Harold whispered. My heart lurched.

"Oh, no," I said, "I completely forgot. I'm so sorry. Was it rough?"

Emma nodded, unable to speak. She gathered herself and managed, "I don't paint and I don't write. I wanted to return to music, but when I played today—"

She stopped to stifle a sob, while I felt shame filter into every muscle, every cell. How could I have forgotten her critique?

"When I played today," she continued, "they were silent. Rudhyar tried to come up with something, anything, and I just ran. No one stopped me."

"Oh, Emma," I started.

"If I can no longer play, what should I be doing? What is mine?"

Appalled at my own self-centeredness, the best I could offer were platitudes: listen to your heart, I advised gravely. Which she did, no thanks to me. She grew quiet and rose, blotted her tears, and excused herself. She returned a few minutes later, having combed her hair and powdered her face, went straight to Harold, and took his arm. He looked into her eyes and his own filled, which surprised me. It struck me that I didn't think of men of his type as actually having feelings. She turned toward me, anger flashing briefly in her eyes.

"Shall we?" she said. Feeling like an intruder, I followed them into the dining room. Before seating his wife, Harold gently kissed the top of her head. Suddenly I was bone weary.

The door to the kitchen swung open, and the cook, looking grim, came through the swinging door with our first course.

"I'm so sorry, Ruby," Emma said. The cook's expression took on a haughty resentment, and I felt myself shrink even more.

"It's my fault," I said. She did not reply, but the dishes came down onto the table with special force. No one reassured me that all was well, which felt strangely right. I swallowed my punishment with some dry chicken and resolved to be a better friend to Emma.

Inevitably, though, we drifted apart. I was sorry about this but aware of the passing of time and more impatient than ever for what the Glass Hive promised—and what it was delivering. My mind sizzled with energy, and instead of returning to the East at the end of the month as planned, I rented a bungalow on South Pasadena's Hanscom Drive. Emma and I hugged as Harold loaded up their car with my luggage.

1824 HANSCOM DRIVE
SOUTH PASADENA, CA

1928

I RENTED A BUNGALOW NEAR the Hive and let a rising elation take hold. I read Kandinsky into the night and being convinced that he was right—he posited that power to uplift provided by a work of art always comes via color—I set out on some color studies of my own.

My new living room faced north and became my studio. I re-created the Spartan décor of my early New York studios, using borrowed furniture: a wooden farmhouse table; what my mother would call a kitchen chair—simple wood, no upholstery; two easels; and a standing lamp for dark days, of which there were few. I also acquired a simple cot for a daybed, wanting a place where I could rest and keep the work in view.

I ordered heavy textured paper, a roll of canvas from a local supplier, additional oil paints, and new pastels. (What a joy it is to buy colors! I still feel as giddy as a child in a toy store when picking them out.) Then I started with studies on paper by laying down one color with the pastels. I am always drawn to blues, and these were the first I tried—French ultramarine, Prussian blue, and a warm cerulean blue. The texture of the pastels made me feel I was part of them, and pushing the soft chalk firmly onto the paper meant I was quickly covered in blue dust. After that I took more care; pastel dust is not something one should be breathing in or ingesting.

But worries over health did not inhibit me: I seemed to enter the color and inhabit it. That first day in my silent and light-washed house, I tacked the thickly pigmented sheet to the bare wall and stood back to look at it. In short order the layers of blue seemed to vibrate, suggesting an image that came to me whole. I grabbed my sketchbook and scribbled it down, along with the poetic explication that had also come through. Built of soft yellow threaded through with blue and soft gray, I saw a leggy flower uncurling into bloom. I titled it *Ecstasy*. At the base was a black-brown hook, threatening to pull the flower back into darkness, but the creative force, that burst of yellow, affirmed its dominance. I had to catch my breath then and fell to sudden weeping, as if the picture and I were being birthed at the same time.

———————

On salon days the Glass Hive artists showed works in progress for others' comments. I'd not done anything of this kind since an awkward "critique" I'd requested from Mabel's then lover, the painter Maurice Sterne back in New York. (His assessment: "timid," "vague," "girlish.") Now I was deeply resistant, feeling I may have come to an impasse with the group. But a session discussing one of Mabel Alvarez's works showed me how it might work. This tribe of artists, writers, and musicians, so serious and sincere, were making a spiritual practice of helping each other, and when I was invited to participate, I agreed.

From Long Island I had brought with me *Meadowlark's Song*, an abstract in progress I had planned to finish in South Pasadena. In truth, the painting was practically done—by which I mean that it already had a life of its own—so even if the group's reaction was not good, I believed I could still finish it. Its palette consisted largely of blues, and in the ovoid center a clump of yellow feathers was suspended. I wanted to suggest the spinning motion I associate with bird song. The image had come to me on a gloomy winter's day recalling the summer sunrise over the meadow in front of the windmill.

As I carried it from Emma's car—she had wanted to be there and had picked me up—I experienced a sudden jolt of nerves. Straight ahead of us the salon room was nearly full. I recognized some of the other painters, but most of the Glass Hive collective were still strangers. Someone inside caught sight of us and started to applaud, and I stopped in my tracks. Emma was smiling broadly, and Jane came out and beckoned us in: "We are all so eager to see what you're up to."

"Make room, everyone," Will's voice boomed, and the sea parted in front of me. "Today we are delighted to welcome Miss Agnes Pelton, whose many artistic accomplishments include exhibiting in the modern art show at the New York City armory some years ago, and a recent career as a portraitist with an impressive list of clients." He turned and, pointing to a nail in the wall, motioned to me. "Here," he said. I forced myself forward and placed the unframed canvas over it. The room fell silent.

"Well," I said, "it is very kind of you to include me." To stem my rising panic, I started talking—portraiture, abstracts, Hawaii, the volcano—and my interest in developing a personal abstract style.

"This," I continued, "is the second in what I hope will be a series. It is called *Meadowlark's Song*." I stopped talking and stepped aside, and the crowd pressed forward. Reflexively I reached toward the canvas to shield it and in so doing nearly knocked it from the wall.

"Careful there." The lightly accented voice was right next to me, and I recognized the beautiful man whom I'd seen with two women. "I'm Rudhyar." He leaned on a cane I'd not seen before. "I saw your work in the Introspectives' show in New York.

Unforgettable. Stimulating. Exciting. Evocative. But this—" He glanced at my painting. "This takes the entire project much farther. You have inspired me, and I am profoundly grateful."

He rested his cane carefully against his leg and seized both my hands in both of his. Leaning in close, he gently kissed my cheek and said, "You and I will be great friends."

With that he turned and made his careful way out of the room. Before I could recover even slightly, someone else took his place—it felt like a reception line—and glowingly admired the way the blues brought perfect order while the yellows encouraged abandon.

That afternoon, as the sun was beginning its rapid skid to the horizon and I was ready to go back to my bungalow, I met Rudhyar again. I was in the driveway just outside the big room where the salon had been held, waiting for my ride and laden like a packhorse. As was the custom at the Hive, once a critique was over, a work was removed—to make way for the new, Will said. So I stood now with *Meadowlark's Song* under one arm while the other looped into a pair of bags that held paints, brushes, drawing materials, a large sketchbook, and a sweater I'd worn that morning. The salon door opened and Rudhyar emerged. He had been composing, he said.

"You graced us with your work this morning, and it is my hope to return the favor." I followed him back into the empty room where he took my bags, put them down by the door, and pulled up a chair for me opposite the piano. I perched myself there, letting the painting rest against my knee. When he saw that I was settled, he flashed a smile and seated himself on the bench. He prepared himself to play, closing his eyes and seeming to find the music within himself—a habit I had often observed in my mother. Holding his long fingers above the keyboard, he let them drop, finding the melody and playing with a sensitivity I'd not experienced in years. I was struck by how long it had been since I myself had played—how keenly I had missed the rich sound. The piece was unfamiliar, and gradually I realized it was his own composition, written that very day and inspired by my painting. When he finished, I asked to hear it again and, clearly pleased, he obliged me. He had captured not only the meadowlark but also the sound of the colors I'd used to portray its song.

"I'm amazed," I said.

"I told you that you'd inspired me," he said.

"You got it all," I marveled. "The lark, and the colors, everything."

Outside I caught sight of Will's son Tyrone pulling up in the Hive's car and smoking while he waited for me.

"Oh, no," I said. "I mustn't keep him waiting."

Rudhyar closed the piano lid and we both went outside. Tyrone was scowling. Rudhyar opened the car's back seat door and helped me lay my painting across it for the trip home. Then he smiled at Tyrone, who didn't smile in return.

"Oh, dear, I've been terribly rude," I said to Tyrone, "and I'm sorry to have kept you."

Impulsively I reached out and hugged Rudhyar.

"Thank you," I said.

"Don't worry about Tyrone," he muttered close to my ear. "The Comforts have their own family troubles."

———

Rudhyar took to driving to my bungalow in the late afternoon and knocking at my door. Tired and a bit disheveled from a day of painting, I would call out to him—the door was never locked—and in he'd come, eager to see what I had been working on. As quickly as our friendship had developed, so had the visions for abstract paintings, and I was racing to capture all the images I'd received. On the walls of my living room studio I placed these sketches, which became the beginnings of paintings, six or more at once.

It was into this spiritual stew that Rudhyar would appear—a fragile time in the life of a painting, to be sure. But he had a particular way of refraining from comment, finding instead beauty in the shape of a line or the arrangement of colors. After he had considered my day's efforts, I would go with him to the Glass Hive for whatever meal had been pulled together—a happy reminder of summers in Ogunquit. The farmhouse table in the dining area off the kitchen was always full: along with Rudhyar and me were Will, Jane, Steve, Tyrone, and Maria, who was Will's lovely young secretary. Sometimes Billie and Christina would be present, and then we would all squeeze tightly together, "like orphans out of *Oliver Twist*," someone remarked. I loved it.

There was usually a large jug of wine, which made us all merrier than was probably good for us, but we all partook nonetheless. Then I began to notice the way Jane watched her father as he emptied glass after glass. One evening I was alarmed to see that while the rest of us used short tumblers, Will's had become a tall highball glass filled to the brim. I raised this gently with Jane one day on an afternoon walk.

"I know," she said after an awkward pause. "Ty and I have both tried talking to him about it, but he insists that he's fine, and then he says that it's none of our business."

"Maybe he'd listen to Steve."

"Steve agrees that it's none of our business."

"Oh well, then," I said.

"Oh well, then." She shrugged and immediately asked how my work was going. Relieved to be so easily dissuaded, I told her about the paints I had bought in Pasadena. They had been prepared in Paris and cost more than my usual oils. But the richness of their colors, I went on, was such that I had gotten dizzy staring into them.

"The red, in particular."

"They're having their way with you," she laughed.

"So it would seem. I have to be careful not to go off my head entirely."

Immediately we were back in the Hive's creative cocoon even as Will's increasing dependence on alcohol affected and changed our evenings as a group. My bungalow was close enough to the

compound that at the first sign of slurring in his words, I could quietly depart and walk home. The decision to do this was not taken
lightly but came after an unpleasant confrontation in which I'd
refused more wine when he was pouring it out for everyone.

"Oh, the high and mighty Miss Pelton says no," he said.

"No, *thank* you." I tried to inject a note of levity. Billie arose
and made a swift exit, but I had thought that even though he was
clearly in his cups, I would be able to restore his goodwill.

"Miss Agnes Pelton of Southampton," he snarled. "New York,"
he continued, exaggerating the harsh sound of the "k."

"Please excuse me," I said, rising from my chair. He thrust
himself to his feet, knocking his own chair over and stood swaying.

"What, you think you're better than me? By God, you do,
don't you?"

Jane got up and grabbed his hand.

"Please, Daddy, calm down."

He looked at her, confused, and then suddenly aware of what
he was doing. His eyes welled up. Tyrone righted his chair and
helped him sit back down.

"I'm sorry, Jane," he said. He turned to me and in a dull, practiced
voice said, "Agnes, I'm very sorry. Too much of the vino, I guess."

"That's all right, Will," I said, trembling a little. "I need to go
home anyway. I'm a little tired tonight."

"I'll drive you." Rudhyar jumped up and hustled me to his car.
"Don't think badly of Will. He can't help it."

"I see that," I said. "I'm sad for him."

I sensed a shift in our communal life—a humming tension, like
electricity in a wire, seemed ever present now. Jane banned alcohol
from the premises, which calmed our dinners and allowed us all to
quiet down at the end of a workday. Will, newly meek, allowed
Jane to monitor his diet and undertook brisk daily walks with her.

I hoped that would mean I'd see more of Rudhyar, but—
inspired by my efforts, he said—he had begun to paint. Will gave

him a room at the Hive, where he shut himself off every day and into the night. He would not, he said, task me with helping him. I pretended to be relieved about that, and later I was. But not seeing much of him gave me an odd sense of imbalance, similar to stepping off a moving vehicle and feeling the motion continue even as you know it has stopped. I had grown attached and worried that too much of my heart had been displayed, that too much and not enough had been said between us. My remedy was to remain in my bungalow for the next few days and eat a simple supper alone and try to regain my contentment.

Into this chafing solitude came Billie and Christina. Billie had an old Model A Ford that she had painted mint green, and three or four days after Will's outburst, she rolled it onto the wispy bit of lawn in front of my bungalow. The car clattered as if about to fall into a heap. It also had a large bulbous horn that Billie gloried in squeezing over and over. Not wanting to disturb the neighbors, I rushed out.

"Hullo, Agnes!" Christina squinted from under a floppy straw hat. She waved an arm lazily in my direction.

"Let's go painting," Billie called out. The car's open rumble seat bristled with easels, stretched canvases, and paint boxes.

"I can't," I said. "I'm working."

"You're missing the fresh air! Don't be such a hermit. I'll bet you don't mind when Rudhyar comes calling." And just to emphasize her point, she tooted the horn once more. I had to laugh at the absurdity of it all. This is what you get for being part of a commune, I reminded myself. Next door, my neighbor peered from behind a curtain.

"Another time," I said. "I really am working."

Billie revved her car engine, raising a noxious cloud, then let it sputter softly. "Agnes," she said. "I wanted to say that I'm sorry for what happened, for Will attacking you like that, and for not speaking up on your behalf."

I was touched and also a bit embarrassed. "You have nothing to apologize for," I said.

"Yes, I do." She fell silent while the jalopy continued to rattle. "He puts us all into a kind of trance," she said finally. "We treat him like a god. I've never seen anything like it. But he's not, is he?"

"No," I said. I had underestimated Billie. Suddenly I was grateful for her presence, even in that smoking car, with her well-tanned arm slung over the driver's side door. She seemed solid and honest and real, more so than the rest of us.

"I can't leave what I'm doing today," I said. "But I will come with you another time." That seemed to satisfy her, and with a wide, generous grin, she shifted the car into gear and out into the street and down the hill.

A few days later I ventured back to the Hive. Rudhyar was still closeted with his painting, but everyone else welcomed me warmly. I was disappointed, though, when Billie and Christina did not appear in the dining room. Jane said they had gone to the desert, to Palm Springs, and had told her they intended to return in a day or two. They did not, but a couple of weeks later I received a picture post-card of palm trees against mountains with a scribbled note, "This just might be heaven." It was unsigned, but I knew it was from Billie.

––––––––––––

In such a small community, the absence of two people creates a large gap. I felt myself at sixes and sevens and thought about returning to the East. Having made good starts on more than a dozen paintings, and with all the enthusiasm I'd received from the Glass Hivers, it occurred to me that the time might be right for another New York showing. Vanity, Grandmama whispered, but her heart seemed not to be in it. She's in retreat, I thought, but felt deflated anyway. I was relieved when Rudhyar resumed his visits, appearing at the end of one long day with a sheepish look on his face and a canvas in his hand.

"Well," he said, holding his painting with its back to me, "it's not so much that I need help, so don't worry about that. It's that—well, I need someone—I need *you* to look at it and tell me if it has an effect."

"Come in," I said.

"Oh my," he said, looking at my own paintings in progress. "Maybe I shouldn't . . ."

"Of course you should. I can now do for you what you've so generously done for me." I reached for his canvas and gently took it from him, placing it against the wall. Then I took his hand and pulled him back a bit so that we could look at it together.

"There's no more piano at the house, you see," he said. "Will gave it away, I do not know why. I'm not sure he does either, but he would not talk about it. So while I am not yet skilled enough to call myself a painter, I have fallen in love with color."

"It shows," I said. He had based his composition on a set of geometric figures—shapes, he said, that he could manage—and filled these with thick, water-based paint.

"I only had tempura," he said.

"It's lovely." I felt so protective of him, wanting him to feel safe and encouraged. I *was* responding to the canvas, although how much of my response was sheer delight in his presence and how much honest reaction to what he had painted, I could not tell. I decided that I didn't care. What mattered was that I not interfere with the creative flow coming through him. And once I saw that he did indeed have such a flow, and that he had translated it visually, I relaxed.

"You have created something powerful," I told him. "It is very moving to me to see it."

"You're the first," he said lightly. We stood in silence then, still hand in hand, and studied his work until I felt the tension slacken from his grip.

"I'm happy that you are moved," he said. He dropped my hand and put his arm around me, then drew me close and encircled me. I let my free arm reach around to hold him, let my head rest under his chin. He lightly kissed the top of my head, as though I were a child. No, not a child. I pulled my head away and looked up at him. Courage and words failed then; later I wished I had at least asked him if it might be possible that we were more than friends. The inviting silence had been there, I'm sure of that, the space to insert the question, but I waited too long. He loosened his arm, as though he had gotten what he needed and was ready to close the conversation. It was apparent that he was now elsewhere in his thoughts. What he said next seemed to confirm my impression: "We don't want to miss dinner."

"No," I barely whispered.

"I'm so happy," he said. He picked up his canvas, and I grabbed my light evening wrap and followed him out the door.

Rudhyar continued to paint. He also took up the study of astrology with his characteristic intensity and, armed with the specifics of my time and place of birth, began to create my chart.

"It looks as though the heavens are aligning for you," he said. It was morning, and he had appeared at my front door, which I had opened to court the breeze. He waved a notebook.

"I am interrupting your work, I know that and I'm sorry, but I couldn't wait."

I put down my palette and brush and waved him in. He grabbed a chair and plunked himself down.

"Agnes, I know I'm new at this, but I believe you are entering a period of expanded good fortune."

I couldn't help but agree with him, the light in his face bringing a smile to mine.

"May I see?" I held out my hand to break the exquisite tension.

"Not yet," he said. "I've really only just started. I should not even be talking about what I've seen so far, but I can't resist. You are, as we know, immensely gifted. More importantly, perhaps, to both of us, it is clear here that your gifts are of a specifically spiritual nature."

He held up the chart, which he had titled Harmonoscope.

"Astrology does not belong in the same category as for-tune-telling, nor am I some carnival gypsy. I'm expanding the field, changing it from 'fore-ordained in the stars' to a spiritual glimpse at one's whole life." His face grew somber.

"What?" I asked.

"There's difficulty here. The picture is clear, but I'm not yet sure how to interpret it. Most likely it's past-life karma, but I see many secrets and much to resolve. Please don't be alarmed."

I had snapped to, alert and wary once again.

"I should have said, much has been hidden, including from you. There's been some misuse of spiritual power. I have written out some questions, if you don't mind."

He handed me a sheet of paper. I wanted badly to know what he had seen so that I could prepare myself to discuss it. Was it about Alice and me? Was it my parents? My grandparents?

"Are you offended?" he asked anxiously.

"Certainly not." I forced a laugh that sounded harsher than I'd intended. "I thought you'd be able to see all, know all. I guess not. I see that I have some work to do."

I set the paper aside, and Rudhyar took his leave, promising to come back and pick me up for dinner as usual. I waited until his car had dropped out of sight before looking at his list of questions. He wanted to know what had happened to me at age seven, and again at age ten, and also wanted to know about possible "moral crises" after I became an adult. Seven was easy, of course—moving from Europe to Brooklyn—but losing my father at age ten was still painful, and the question of a supposed moral crisis caused a wave of dizziness. I folded the list and tucked it into the back of my journal. Here I was again, fending off a past that always reared up just as fulfillment seemed within easy reach. Rudhyar had tried to explain: "Our pasts," he said, "and the people associated with them—our families, our friends—are an integral part of the web of who we are. We must accept all that, let it be part of us. There is never any question of escaping." He then smiled as if that was supposed to reassure me.

While I puzzled over all this, a gallery in Los Angeles offered me a show of the new abstracts. This, both Rudhyar and Jane said, indicated a confluence of positive energy with nothing to impede my progress. They encouraged me to remain in Pasadena, to make it my new home. I agreed and even purchased a building lot near the Hive where I could put a house and studio. Yes, I would settle there, near these good friends and companions.

Jane was thrilled. She had been coming around more, calling me her spiritual anchor. She would appear at my bungalow, and while I painted, she would meditate, focusing on her father and how to best care for him. Then one day she told me that divine messages of encouragement for *me* were crowding out anything else. She asked me for paper and pen, and I grabbed a sheet of stationery and handed it to her. She scribbled in a halting manner, writing and then closing her eyes to listen, writing again and finally raising her head.

"All will be well, Agnes, that is what I'm getting. You are to continue to plan for house and home here, and all will be well."

Both of us excited, we rode together to the Hive where I would announce my desire to become a permanent member. This was a formality I had wanted to sidestep.

"It has never felt right to me," I said nervously. "Joining things," I added.

"The Hive is completely different," Jane said.

"Oh, I know, I know," I murmured.

"You are just telling the group you consider yourself one of us. That's not really 'joining' at all."

"No," I agreed. We were silent as Jane turned the car up the entrance road and parked it.

Rudhyar was nowhere to be seen. Suddenly I wanted—needed—to tell him of this plan. It would all fit now: Rudhyar and I would be together. Our friendship, already so close, would bloom into love. For the first time in my life I could see myself marrying and was stunned at the ease of it all, at the rightness of it. Darling Rudhyar, how happy he made me and how happy I wanted to make him.

Jane and I mingled with the others, milling about outside the dining room, while I looked around for Rudhyar. The doors opened, and I followed the group. I had just taken a seat at the table when he entered from the kitchen with Maria, Will's secretary. Their hands were clasped, and they were both radiant with happiness. I can still feel the shock and the attendant need to recover quickly. I forced a smile and glanced at Jane, whose mouth was agape.

"My friends," Rudhyar began, "a brief announcement: Maria and I would like you all to know that you are hereby invited—summoned, in fact—to our nuptials, exact date and place to be announced."

The room erupted in cheers. Rudhyar produced a bottle of wine, which he splashed into glasses and passed all around. Jane looked unhappy when Will took one. Her husband Steve raised his in a toast: "Congratulations, you two! What a surprise! I'm sure I speak for everyone in wishing you every happiness."

I was immediately grateful that I had not made a fool of myself by confessing my own feelings for him—not to Jane, not to Rudhyar himself. Later that night I could retreat to the solitude of my bungalow and let my grief—for that is what it was—wash through me and find its exit. It was familiar, recalling for me Alice's departure from New York after the Armory Show, and how I could scarcely breathe for grief at losing her. But it passed, and after the first world war, when we met again and traveled to Taos, I could barely locate its traces.

Rudhyar's announcement had caused an emotional tempest, a tender bruise at the center of my being. I had put it there, I reminded myself; Rudhyar had done nothing untoward. He had wanted to be my friend, my true friend, not a social-circle friend, and if I imagined more, the burden was mine. He seemed happily oblivious to my state, and even as he helped me hang the show in Los Angeles, he talked about New York.

"They need to see this work, Agnes. You are far ahead of anything I've ever encountered, either there or here. Everyone in the East accuses us in California of being provincial. That's laughable. You have redefined the terms of engagement."

"I hope you realize that galleries in New York charge artists for solo shows."

"It is well worth the risk," he replied.

It's not your risk, I wanted to say.

"You have tapped into true inspiration, which we only get to keep as long as we share it."

If his glibness annoyed me, I ignored it. The fantasy had shattered, which I told myself was a good thing indeed. Push on, I told myself: push past the edge. I took snapshots of a dozen paintings and mailed them off to both the Montross and Argent galleries in Manhattan. The replies were prompt and affirmative, sealing my return to the East. I wrote to Mabel that I was going to try New York again. She replied quickly with warmest congratulations. She had not given up her Fifth Avenue apartment, and she offered it now for me to stay in for as long as the shows were up. Her kindness touched me deeply even as I shivered a bit at memories of the White Salon, the ghost of my younger self, and the forbidding John Quinn. But how much had changed: no more paintings of frightened girls in thick woodlands, no more stone people weighed down by oppression. Instead I'd found a way to the truly luminous, and I thought it not a stretch that the Montross show might bring real success.

NEW YORK CITY

OCTOBER 22, 1929

THE TRAIN HEAVED A HUGE sigh, and steam rose all around. I stepped out, the morning chill palpable under the high glass ceiling of the station. I hefted my overnight bag and paused against the jostle on the platform. My trunk had been sent ahead to Long Island, and the paintings for exhibition had already been shipped to the gallery. I would spend a couple of days in the city and thence to the windmill for a week before returning to Manhattan to hang the show. Out on the street, I hailed a taxi and gave the driver Mabel's address. She had alerted her building staff about my arrival, and sure enough, the doorman ushered me through the lobby and upstairs to the apartment.

Most of what I recalled about the place had been closed off—Mabel visited infrequently and didn't want to keep a staff. I followed the doorman, his nameplate identifying him as Frank, past the ballroom where the salons had been held, and through the door to the family quarters, where he showed me to one of the smaller bedrooms, which had already been made up. He offered to open a window, but I said no, finding the room's musty smell oddly comforting. Once he was gone, I let my memories range freely—of the cacophony of Mabel's White Salon, the endless promise of it all; of Alice's nearby townhouse, sold years ago; of retreating to 1403 Pacific Street and Brooklyn and Maman—in short, all the excitement and terror of my early life as an artist.

––––––––––

It seemed I could do nothing to calm the febrile energy that pulsed through my body. I couldn't tell if it was excitement or fear, but I was glad when two days later it was time to decamp to Long Island as I'd arranged with Mr. Conrad. I tossed a few things into my bag and closed Mabel's front door behind me. I had to wait for the elevator, and when it came, George, the operator I still remembered, seemed distracted even as he greeted me cordially. Then he added, "Bad day, Miss."

"It is?"

He sighed. "Stock market," he mumbled.

Downstairs the lobby was strangely empty, the staff nowhere in sight. I stepped outside to hail a taxi, but the city seemed to have gone berserk. Cars clogged the street, horns blaring, newsboys weaving in and out of the traffic selling papers and hollering, "Wall Street crashes!" I might have been in a movie.

Finally, I found a cab and we made our precarious way to the station. The driver had tears running down his cheeks.

"Are you all right?" I asked.

"No, ma'am. I put everything into it, and now it's gone. And downtown? I hope I never see anything like it again in my life."

At a red light, he turned and faced me. "I saw a guy standing on a window ledge, and then he jumped."

I gasped, and we both were weeping. By the time he pulled into the station, I was shaking. What's to become of us, I thought.

––––––––––

The Long Island train bumped out of the city and swayed its way east. I had had to run to catch it, and I was panting. The train was crowded, and all of us seemed in the same frightened state, which I found oddly calming. Misery did indeed love company, as my grandmother might say. My plan had been simply to check on things at the windmill and take two days there to relax before the Montross show. The very idea should have made me laugh, but slowly I allowed the train's gentle rhythm to soothe me. I was not an investor, so my modest savings were unaffected, but I had many friends I now worried about: Mabel, Alice, my New Jersey friends, the Canons. And not coincidentally, my splashy and expensive New York gallery show.

When the train halted at Southampton, I was relieved to see Mr. Conrad standing by his truck.

"Have you heard the news?"

He nodded.

I glanced at my quickly dispersing fellow passengers, and all of them seemed composed. The sky was equally placid, streaked with high clouds, the air cool and autumnal. Mr. Conrad took my bag, and I followed him to the baggage car where we waited for my trunk. At its appearance, he hefted it into the truck bed, and we set off.

"Are you all right?" I finally asked him.

"I am," he replied. "I don't have investments." A quick smile crinkled his eyes. "Just a few more aches than when you left. And you?"

"Yes. I don't have investments either."

We drove on in companionable silence. And then in the distance, the windmill appeared like a presence on its bluff high above the road.

"Home," I said as we turned onto the sand track and jounced our way toward its solid frame and expansive arms. I could have wept with relief.

"Home," Mr. Conrad agreed. "Although there is talk in the village . . ."

"Talk?"

"I hear your landlord is wanting to sell."

Hadn't I always known I would have to leave the mill someday? Of course, but nearly ten years of sheltering there—years of healing from Maman's death, the joy of finding my way into painting abstractly—had created an illusion of permanence. I took a deep and shaky breath.

NEW YORK CITY

NOVEMBER 7, 1929

MR. MONTROSS, FAMOUS FOR HIS ability to generate excitement around an artist's work, had moved his gallery to East 56th Street near Madison Avenue, and I joined him there to hang the show. He was patient with my need to allow the colors and their relationships one to the other to dictate how the work should appear. Neither of us mentioned the stock market. It took us two days—hanging, then moving the pictures, then rehanging, then moving them again, but when we finished, I was satisfied. Mr. Montross returned to his office for paper and a pen to diagram what we had done. Alone, I stood amid my work and slowly studied each painting, taking them all in one by one. Silently I thanked each of them for the gift of their presence.

Mabel had supplied a list of People With Money, and Mr. Montross had sent them all invitations. She had written me just days ago, joking about her former status as a trendsetter and hoping the people on her list had not opted for the simple life as she had. "But I do worry about the impact of the stock market crash," she added.

It had been two weeks since the four-day rout that came to a devastating halt on Black Thursday, and no one yet knew what its impact would be. Should we have cancelled? And to what purpose?

Life—and art—must be allowed to go on, in spite of war, in spite of economic turmoil. That, I still believe.

Mr. Montross had reminded me to come early to the opening gala: "You will sell many more pictures if you are in attendance, I can assure you." So, on the evening of the ninth, I stood in front of Mabel's full-sized mirror, dusting my face with powder, adding a bit of rouge for luck, and pinning a satin rose onto my dress before hailing a cab to go uptown.

East 56th Street was quiet. The taxi pulled up in front of the gallery, where a few people were hesitating by the door, and then I saw Walt Kuhn. He called out immediately, "Here's Agnes!" Kitty Myers materialized from behind him, and Jerome was behind her. I saw Alice holding herself with a cane, and Mr. Montross came out of his small office.

"Welcome, welcome," he said. He fidgeted with the buttons on his jacket. "I thought we'd do better by these beautiful paintings." He gestured and shrugged. "The crash, I think."

Standing in the half-empty gallery, I saw few of my other wealthy acquaintances. The question of what this would mean for my situation gnawed its way into my thoughts. As I fought a rising panic, Alice made her way toward me.

She walked with a limp now, so her progress was halting and slow. I tried to remember how old she was now. Late sixties, I thought, but Alice had always been so vivacious; it was shocking to see her as frail. Her hair was a wiry gray and her skin papery, but her eyes had lost nothing of their fire, and her own smile was warm and genuine. For years her mere presence had meant that all would be well.

"This is a triumph," she said simply.

"I'm so glad you came," I said, grasping both her hands in both of mine. This sent her cane clattering to the floor, and we both laughed as I picked it up and handed it back to her.

"I've grown old, I'm afraid," she said.

"So have I." I was just two years away from fifty.

"Nonsense," she answered. "I must talk to Mr. Montross about *Ecstasy*. It is probably more than I should spend, but it expresses our time together and will keep me close to you."

"I would love you to have it," I said. "I will ask him to make sure it doesn't go to anyone else." At this, tears welled in her eyes, which prompted the same from my own.

"Why on earth are we crying?" Alice pulled out a lace handkerchief and dabbed at her face. "This is what we worked for. It's just that our timing was a bit off."

"They say timing is everything," I agreed.

"But I see your genius. I see it very clearly on these walls, and genius will always win out."

I nodded, more out of hope than any real conviction. I had felt genius burning in me when I'd painted those pictures, and it had come to me then that genius was not a lengthy visitor, at least for me.

No, not for you, an inner voice repeated. I recognized Maman in it and wished it gone. It was odd, but I didn't think my grandmother would have said it or thought it. Those voices never leave, not really. They have on occasion hounded me and stopped me from painting for long periods. That evening in 1929, I knew my only chance to shake them was to exercise deliberate gratitude, and I took the opportunity to say some overdue things to Alice. About all that she had given me, materially and emotionally.

"I would not have gotten to these paintings without you," I said.

"Preposterous," she said, but I could tell from the tint of pink in her cheeks that she was pleased. Or was that anger? Her eyes flashed suddenly.

"You would have come to this on your own," she purred. "You obviously had no need to bother with an old lady."

I felt my face redden. I had not wanted to engage with Alice since our trip to Taos. I thought I had grown beyond her, and recalling that arrogance caused me shame; this easy dismissal had allowed me to forget how important she had been to my arriving here, the very

evening when my career as an abstract artist was to have been established in the Holy of Holies, the Montross Gallery of New York City.

"Mrs. Thursby!" Montross stood beaming before us. "How may
I help you? Shall we admire Agnes's work together?" He took her
elbow and steered her away gently.

I needed a breath of air and headed for the door just as Edward
and Phoebe Canon came through it. They saw my rushing toward
them as eagerness, and I allowed them their perception.

"How kind of you to come!" I embraced Phoebe, brushing
my cheek against hers, breathing in her scent of violets and lilac. I
had been right to paint her surrounded by hues of lavender. I took
Edward's hands in mine. He smiled as he made a small bow.

"Mostly," he said, "I don't care for what Montross chooses to
exhibit. But how could we not come and see what you have wrought?"

"Stop your teasing." Phoebe tapped his arm in a mock slap.
"We wanted to see you as well as your new works." She looked
around the room. "My, my, what an interesting group of pictures!"

I knew what that meant, but it was so good to see old friends
I laughed it off. "Not to your taste, I expect," I said. "But do see if
anything surprises you."

They strolled off toward *The Ray Serene*, and I ducked outside. The breeze had turned chilly, and I walked quickly toward the
corner, wishing I had a fox collar like Phoebe's to block it. That was
the thing about money, I thought: when you have it, you believe
your worries are over. You live your life, and travel, and take enjoy-
ment where you find it. But when you need money, you can think
of little else. You start dividing people into those who can buy—the
Canons, Alice—and those who cannot.

At the end of the block I turned around. Cars were still pulling up to the gallery, and more attendees continued to arrive on
foot. I thought about Hamilton Field—missed him—and his energy
and passion for art, and how if he were still living, he would be
here, inside, listening to viewers and engaging them in persuasive

conversation—making the sale, he would say. I knew that my passion for art, while expressed more quietly, was a match for his, so couldn't I follow his example? Was this, I wondered, what separates men and women in the world of commerce? Just a willingness to engage and persuade? I marched myself back to the open door and the thick yellow light spilling out onto the sidewalk and decided to try.

Edward and Phoebe were on the verge of leaving, and I stopped them.

"So soon?"

"Ah, Agnes, there you are." Edward looked slightly wan.

"He's a little tired." Phoebe hooked her arm through his. "I need to get him home."

"Oh, dear, I am sorry!"

"We were looking for you," he said. "Because I have had a thought. Listen, Agnes, you realize, I am sure, that nothing you are showing here would fit our house, so I am sorry about that."

I nodded.

"We have our portraits," he continued, "and those are the most valuable paintings we own for many reasons—the record of a family, the skill and sympathy with which they were created. And now you have written us to say that you are being compelled to leave the windmill—a great shame but also an opportunity."

He paused then to catch his breath, and Phoebe looked concerned. "The doctor has told him not to overdo," she murmured to me, as if he wouldn't hear her. "It's his heart."

"Oh, let me finish, would you?" he snapped. She shut her mouth and pressed her lips together tightly, raising her eyes to mine. Edward continued, stopping between words to breathe.

"I was thinking—we would love—another portrait—a portrait of the windmill itself. I want to—commission such a—work."

I touched his arm. "Dear friend, what a wonderful idea. I gladly accept."

Journal entry, 1931

It is not necessary to go to N.Y.
Another way will be found—
The way of Peace and Quietness—
Light shining through
The Higher Light / dispelling darkness

PALM SPRINGS, CALIFORNIA

JANUARY 1932

I WAS FIFTY WHEN I fled the east and the cold and the critics and the art scene and boarded the trains that brought me to the desert. From Los Angeles I proceeded to Palm Springs, which I had imagined as an empty oasis with a cluster of swaying palm trees. Of course, the train had been packed. It was, I thought wryly, a lot like Southampton. Stepping down, I was jostled by beautiful people with tennis rackets, overnight cases, and ukuleles. I paused and shaded my eyes.

"Toot toot, Agnes, here I am!" The desert brilliance was blinding, and I had to search to locate my friend. Finally, I spotted her, standing up in that old, open-top jalopy from South Pasadena, holding the steering wheel for balance, and waving. Here was Billie, whom I'd not seen since she and Christina had slipped away from the Glass Hive nearly three years earlier. Staring right at her, the only way I could recognize her was by the slump of her bulky body. She had discarded her dark cloche hat and shapeless dress, cut off her hair and slicked it back, and was wearing a man's shirt and string tie. Next to her was Christina—lovely as ever—who sported a sundress, a wide-brimmed picture hat, and was waving her arm. Billie laughed at my obvious surprise as I made my way over.

She jumped from the car and threw her arms around me. "Welcome!" She grabbed my bags and hefted them onto the back seat. Up front Christina moved over and splayed her slender arms across the top of the seat. I slid in next to her, and she gave my shoulders a squeeze as the train shrieked and puffed and pulled away—headed where, I did not know.

"We're off," Billie said. The car rattled and smoked as she maneuvered out of the gritty parking lot and onto the straight, smooth highway.

"Did you see any Hollywood stars on the train?" Christina asked. I shook my head.

"Well, you just might before we're done today," Billie said with a grin. "Keep your eyes peeled."

We joined the flow of sleek sedans inching along on Palm Canyon Drive, passing a quaint General Store before turning east, swerving to avoid a handsome young man weaving in and out of traffic on a bicycle.

"This is the Movie Colony," Billie said. The wide boulevard could have been in Beverly Hills, except that here the trees were short and pruned like shrubs. Instead of mansions, the houses were generous bungalows, each surrounded by a very green lawn, which was punctuated here and there by shaggy palms, but care had been taken to leave the sense of openness. And of course, the ring of mountains with their solid benevolence. We passed the El Mirador Hotel with its mission-style tower, where many of the cars turned in. Soon the traffic had vanished, and we were back on the highway and alone.

"That's where the snooties live," Christina said. "Now we'll show you where the artists are." What I loved about these two women was their good humor and optimism—an ease with simply being, which I took in like a slow, deep breath. Why not try that, I thought. All around us an oceanic desert invited me to stillness.

At that time the newly incorporated Cathedral City announced itself with a pair of towers, obelisks like Cleopatra's Needles, one on each side of the highway and visible from afar in the dry desert air. As we drew near, I asked Billie to pull over. I climbed out and stepped into the wild desert. Recent rains had caused clumps of grass and flowers to shoot up, giving the landscape a sense of joyous disorder and appealing wistfulness. I realized I felt at home, which caused a sudden surge of spirit, and a powerful presence burned within me. I glanced back toward the road and listened to the silence. A truck clattered by, raising dust. And then silence again. I looked past the slope of desert to the rock-strewn foothills, my eyes coming to rest on the mountains.

The mountains. The silence. The serenity. I felt I could stand there all day and stare for as long as I wished, and no one would ask what I was working on and why I wasn't doing more.

"Agnes, look this way," Christina called. I turned, and she was aiming a camera in my direction.

"Good," she said. Dazed, I climbed back into the car and Billie shifted into gear. Farther down the street we passed a cluster of somewhat dilapidated storefronts and a building Christina said had been the Indian trading post.

"It's going to be Cleo Cree's gallery," Billie added. "Remember her from the Hive?" I recalled an ambitious art lover who had indeed wanted to open a gallery and had pledged to show my work. "Cleo's a friend," Billie went on. "Hell, everyone here's a friend." A pair of tall palms flanking the dark wooden door nodded lazily in the breeze.

"Well," Christina drawled, "that's the commercial district. Oh, meant to tell you that we met a guy who's bought a whole tract to build an artist colony. Right here."

We drove on, and I marveled again at the ring of mountains and the brilliant light warming the valley. Billie turned onto Cathedral Canyon Drive and stopped in front of an imposing stucco house, arcaded in the front.

"My house," she said, pausing while I took it in along with the earthmoving equipment parked next to it. "Still under construction."

"So, you're here for the long haul," I said.

"I am," she said. Her face was composed and serene, and I envied her. I had believed I was in my windmill for the long haul.

"I love starting over," I said, shaking off the sadness. "The windmill was sold, and now I'm a visitor everywhere, which gives me great freedom."

"I'm done with that sort of freedom," Billie said. "You can have it. You're welcome to bunk here with me—it's a little rustic at the moment—or, if you prefer, Christina has a room for you."

"Agnes wants a room." Christina gave my shoulders another squeeze. It made me feel conspiratorial and wicked in a good way. I did indeed want a room.

Billie crossed the highway and pulled into a stone-strewn drive where a small sign announced SvenSka, in honor of Christina's Swedish heritage. Identical cottages for rent ringed the house, which resembled a chalet. In the center was a thready tree with ghostly pale green limbs—my first smoke tree—flanked by a pair of exuberantly spikey barrel cacti.

"Here we are." The car stopped. Billie grabbed my bag and we followed Christina inside, where I was shown to a back room that could double as a sunroom in the winter—and an oven in the summer.

"Stay as long as you like," Christina said.

The year I arrived, the Cove was a rumpled stretch of desert sloping upward to the Santa Rosa mountains and thence to Mt. San Jacinto. The Indians had named this patch Hand of God, because it reminded them of an open palm from which the mountains extended like fingers.

The "village" consisted of little more than staked-out building lots on a small grid of dirt roads labeled—temporarily, I thought—A,

B, C, D, and so forth up to J. Our main street, which was just an extension of Palm Canyon Drive in Palm Springs, had been renamed Broadway by the optimistic developers. Slicing north perpendicular to Broadway was—still is—Cathedral Canyon Drive.

———————

Without planning it, I began to settle here. I had a decidedly odd lack of ambition, having apparently once again failed to catch the critics' eyes, and being well past my youth, found I simply didn't care anymore. I no longer felt the need to impress. I had brought with me the usual supplies—paper, canvas, tubes of colors, etc.—and found that I woke each day eager to paint. That is what giving up can do for an artist; it can restore the joyous sense of play and adventure. You could say that I fell in love, or, rather, that I felt bathed in love. I kept exclaiming to anyone who happened to be nearby about the openness of the place and the clarity of the light, which seemed to have stripped away every obstacle to seeing. I'd thought all deserts looked like the Sahara, smooth and white, a beach without an ocean. I was fascinated by the roughness all around me, the sharp heaps of fallen rocks, the umbers and the soft pastels of the hills—a world away from Palm Springs.

I noticed an empty cabin across Broadway and up the slope, complete with a lean-to made of palm fronds and broad views of the mountains to the rear, the desert floor out front. Someone put me in touch with its absent owner, who agreed to Celotex it—that is, install some insulation—and rent it to me for a nominal sum. It was painted green, and I moved my few belongings into it. Christina had a bed, linens, chair, and table I could use, and I felt like a pioneer. Many days I was happy to stay put, pulling the chair outside under the thatch and drawing the view. I began to sketch Mt. San Jacinto, which I already felt was my own. One day while staring at it, I was visited by an image, and I painted it quickly: the mountain, cool and low on the horizon, thick clouds burgeoning above it, an oval of light splitting those clouds as if being born. I do not know where that picture is. I do know it was sold.

———————

I was shedding my past, slipping off my East Coast ways and the intense focus of the Hive. Everything here was fresh and new, including Cathedral City itself—which would not exist had they not found the deep spring beneath us. Then the railroad that owned the land sold it to a group of Los Angeles businessmen who gridded out our town on the upward slope and sold acre and half-acre lots for a fraction of what they would cost in Palm Springs.

"It's exactly the same desert!" Billie pointed out.

We laughed at the foolishness of our neighbors to the west cultivating lawns. "Idiotic," Christina said. "Why would you create an English garden amid all this beauty?"

———————

Coming to the desert seemed to bring my life full circle, which I suppose is an odd thing for someone born in Europe and raised in Brooklyn to say. I think it was the sense of openness—the curve of the horizon, the feeling of being nestled against my beautiful mountains—which seemed to halt my sense of forward motion and the "what's next, next, next" of my life. Time ceased to march. Instead it flowed and became almost tidal, in and out, high and low, establishing a sense of the eternal present.

The other newcomers were thrilled to have discovered this little jewel in the desert and excited to be part of a new town. Most of us were artists and writers who felt we had landed in an open-air cathedral. Many of us were women, and we went out of our way to be helpful to each other. This created a sort of civic buoyancy that kept us all giddy. I wrote to Rudhyar, inviting him to join us. He had mentioned in a cryptic way that his marriage to Will Comfort's secretary might be in trouble, which had turned out to be the case.

"Come and see what's possible in the desert," I wrote, wanting to cheer him up.

———————

Christina was never fond of the early morning, but Billie was. She liked to appear at my door (none of us had telephones for years), which she could drive right up to and honk that bulbous car horn. I would rush out to stop her from disturbing the peace, and she would laugh at the look on my face.

"Take your time," she grinned, happy to have provoked me once again. I'd fill a ceramic bottle with water, cork it, grab my easel and paints, and we'd drive a few miles out for a morning of painting. Sometimes the road just ended, which amused both of us. I saw quickly that I could probably generate income from my fascination with this landscape. While we painted, Billie talked.

Whereas at the Hive she had seemed secretive, almost furtive, out here she was open and emboldened. I knew that she had married for respectability and that her husband had died early in the marriage.

"What happened to him?" I asked.

"Pneumonia."

I had some discomfort around the ethics of such a marriage. "Did you always know it wouldn't work out?"

Billie looked gruff and a trifle embarrassed. "Of course. I didn't kill him, if that's what you're worried about."

"Of course not, but how could you?" I asked. It wasn't meant as an accusation; I really wanted to know how anyone made such an arrangement, how they went through with it.

"It's just the way the world is, Agnes, you know that. A man affords an independent woman like myself a certain amount of protection." She told me of her youth in White Plains, north of New York City, and how her square shoulders and mannish ways attracted attention.

"There was a bar on the other side of the tracks where those of us who were different could go. Everybody knew about it, but mostly we were left alone. You'd see men dancing with men, women with women. Scandalous." She laughed.

On the days we painted together, Billie would return me to my cabin by noon, as she found the rising heat uncomfortable. I did not. I relished it. I kept thinking of how winter was bearing down on Southampton while we were enjoying crystalline days that reached 80 degrees. After an improvised lunch, I continued working under the palm thatch outside my green cabin. I could hardly call it work, though. It was more that I entered the somatic experience of painting, a whole and complete state of being. Instead of making pictures that were individual objects, separate and apart from myself—things one might scribble into being as routinely as a shopping list—I had a sense of time slowing. I could see details and feel I was missing nothing, so during the day, that meant painting desert scenes with Billie. Later, while resting, it meant recording the visions that now began to appear.

––––––––––––

Rudhyar wrote from Santa Fe that he would come. He arrived by train, and Billie and Christina drove me to the station to collect him. He descended to the platform like a dark prophet, wearing a black fedora, a black cashmere coat draped around his shoulders, and holding a black valise—this in stark contrast to the other passengers rushing past and around him, all of them in the lightest pastels and linens. I rushed, laughing, to embrace him.

"Good heavens, Rudhyar, you will frighten us all."

He set down his suitcase and grasped my shoulders, holding me at arms' length and taking me in from head to toe until I thought I would blush.

"You look radiant," he said finally. "I can hardly wait to see the new work. Clearly, the climate agrees with you."

Across the parking lot, Billie squeezed her car's horn and made everyone laugh. Rudhyar clicked his heels and proffered his arm, and I hooked mine through it. Without the slightest gesture of hurrying, he picked up his bag and we strolled to Billie's car. Dear Rudhyar, how happy I was to have him there! How delighted I was by his exotic manner and intense focus, all trained directly, I felt, on me.

Christina threw me a glance, one eyebrow raised, and hopped out to take his bag, strapping it to the back of the car. I clambered into the wide back seat while Rudhyar strolled in his feline way over to Billie and leaned over to kiss both her cheeks. Christina was in the front passenger seat and turned to stare at me directly. I detected a certain admiration, which I could not help basking in. Her head took a languid tilt as she reached into her bag, pulled out a cigarette, and held it poised for lighting. I recalled this mannerism from South Pasadena: Christina always waited, and someone always obliged. Billie did not approve of smoking and ignored her, but the ever-gallant Rudhyar complied before climbing in beside me, and we were off. I saw Billie's sharp glance at Christina and wondered if we were in for one of their battles—Billie's jealousy vs. Christina's penchant for flirting—but we rode the rest of the way in silence.

We had already arranged for Rudhyar to stay in one of Christina's cabins, and once he had tossed his bag inside it, he and I walked in a long diagonal across Broadway. No cars were visible in either direction, and he paused in the middle.

"Remarkable," he said, throwing his arms wide and listening to the silence. At my green cabin he admired the thatched lean-to with plywood floor that was my makeshift studio. He ducked under its canopy to look at the four paintings I had set out to show him. Suddenly the palm roof shook and rattled, and wind swept the loose grit of the desert floor upward and into our faces.

"Watch out." He grinned, pulling his hat down over his eyes. "The sand devils will get us."

As if provoked, the gusts increased, and we each grabbed two paintings and ducked into the cabin, where I shut the small windows. I pointed Rudhyar to my one chair and lit the little kerosene stove and made us tea. The sounds of filling the kettle and taking dishes from a shelf were barely audible against the wind, and neither of us tried to talk until I was perched on the cot with each of us balancing a teacup and so close our knees nearly touched.

After a few minutes of self-conscious chatter, Rudhyar gazed into his teacup, the tea itself forgotten.

"Well, that's out of the way." He smiled. "I've needed to talk to you," he said, and then fell silent.

"How's your painting?" I asked after a moment.

"Oh, it's fine." He smiled suddenly. "It's wonderful. I've met someone remarkable in Santa Fe, Raymond Jonson. You will meet him. His ideas are entirely compatible with your own. And mine. Painting has helped me work through the marriage, which I quickly realized was a mistake. It's hard to talk about. There we all were at the Knob, and I was trying to paint, and it wasn't coming quickly enough, and while I managed to produce a couple of pieces, I was floundering."

"I had no idea."

"That's—that's my fault. Some kind of pride, I guess."

He stopped and I waited. "I was closed off from myself, Agnes," he said softly. "I didn't want to distract you, as you were doing so brilliantly, but I was unable to bring forth either music or image."

This would have been well after his initial excitement about taking up painting, which he had shared eagerly. How sweetly boyish he'd been, exclaiming over his great good fortune in having met me and talked with me and having grasped what I was working to accomplish. His own desire to not just create spiritual images, but to make pictures that could be conduits for others' spiritual progression. He had been an excellent student, and while inspiration was flowing, it had been possible for him to create a series of remarkable abstracts. Now he told me how, when the images stopped—as I had warned they would—he had felt himself at a complete loss and had retreated into romantic love.

"I lost my mind, is what happened. I had never before experienced anything like it and thought that everything had changed and would for all time be different. You'll laugh, but I didn't even consult the stars to see if I should proceed or hold back for a more favorable time."

His voice trailed off and he shook his head. I studied the rough flooring and left the silence alone. I recalled the scene in Pasadena: Rudhyar, hand in hand with Maria, he florid and grinning, she bashful and pale—the shock of it, the pain of it.

I didn't feel a need to avert my face; the dim recesses of the tiny cabin offered the mercy of privacy. The memories of our time together in Pasadena flooded my mind, and I tried to sort through them to keep it all in perspective. I saw that in all our talk of art and the spirit and our hopes for our work—and my surprise at being able to confide in a man—I had mistaken the nature of his interest. I had also lost sight of our fourteen-year age difference. I saw myself at the Hive's dining table, just another foolish woman poised to tumble into humiliation and ruin, like my grandmother before me. *We will never be rid of this.*

Even now my mind railed with questions—why Maria? what about me?

Of course, I thought, she was young, she was beautiful; I was older, and I was not beautiful. I was suddenly fatigued, ready for him to leave, but outside the wind continued to pummel the cabin.

"It was during our honeymoon that I woke up," Rudhyar said. "I found myself in a place I did not recognize and should never have ventured into. Maria and I were not compatible, which I should have seen from the outset."

Yes, I thought, you should. I bit back the words, surprised by my own anger. I wanted to say, What about our compatibility? What about the very words you used?

"You and she were not 'soul mates'," I said.

"No," he agreed. He looked up and his eyes were filled with recognition and remorse. "Oh, my dear," he said. "I am sorry."

For an instant I felt triumphant, and then I, too, was sorry and wished I had never said a word.

"No, there's no need," I said. "This sent you back to astrology?"

"Yes," he said, relief evident in his voice. "It was the sense of being swept away, of being controlled by larger forces. How could I have ignored what I knew?"

Outside the wind seemed to die down. Inside, my cabin was coated with fine grit that had entered through the poorly sealed windows. I could taste it in my mouth as well, but light was breaking through, signaling that the storm was over. We both arose and I opened the door. Stray particles flew into our faces, and I quickly closed it. Almost at once there came a pounding on the door, and I heard Christina.

"Agnes? Are you in there?" The muffled sound of her voice was explained when I opened it again and saw her, wrapped about the face by swathes of muslin and looking like a Bedouin. "Oh, hello, Rudhyar," she said, peering past me. "Are you both all right?"

"We're fine," I said. I stepped aside to let her in, but she stayed where she was, her eyes glinting mischief.

"Well," she said. "There you have it, Agnes. Your first sand-storm. Rudhyar, I think you should come along now. Didn't anyone ever tell you that it's not proper for a gentleman to visit a lady in her bedroom?"

I shot Christina a look of what I hoped was indignant outrage, and Rudhyar's cheeks tinted red. Christina laughed and turned to go. "See you later," she said.

"She certainly hasn't changed," Rudhyar said. I agreed, even though I didn't really know. In Pasadena I hadn't been part of the flirtatious banter that occurred after dinner, when everyone was flushed and disarrayed with wine.

"Well!" Rudhyar said. "I'd best get my things unpacked and leave you in peace."

I watched him depart down the hill toward SvenSka. His back was straight, and he walked with firm confidence. He is still young, I thought.

Deflated and suddenly discouraged, I railed at myself: What was I playing at with Billie and Christina, and now Rudhyar? What was I doing here in this barren desert? Trying to invent a youth I'd never had? Trying at the age of fifty to be twenty? Clinging to an impossible romantic ideal?

Enough, I thought, and started cleaning up what the sandstorm had done. First I took a soft cloth and gently wiped the four paintings I'd brought out to show Rudhyar. I looked into each of them and was comforted: *Fire Sounds*, radiant in its joy; *Incarnation*, my tribute to my dear friend Jane; *Star Gazer*, created out of the wonder of the western sky; *The Voice*, which I had obeyed to come here.

———————

The four of us had intended to return to Palm Springs that evening to dine, but the sandstorm disrupted our plans. Billie's car, for instance, would need its engine cleaned before she would try to start it again. Instead, Christina announced that she would cook. Her house was much better sealed than my cabin, and I borrowed a broom from her. Rudhyar and I returned to my place, and together we dispatched the grit, as Rudhyar said, "putting it back where it belonged."

There is healing in the simple restoration of order, and by the time we were finished, I had resolved to simply do my work, to paint what was given to me to paint, and to let the spirit take care of the rest. I recognized it as surrender, which came as a relief.

The sun was just setting when we made our way back to Christina's. Rudhyar carried the broom bristles up, using it like a walking stick, and took my hand.

"I have missed you," he said. "Thank you for today. You're a very good listener." I squeezed his hand briefly. From behind Christina's we could see tendrils of rising smoke.

"Goodness," I said. "We'd better hurry."

To our relief and amusement, we found Christina dragging leggy branches of mesquite into a pile next to the beginnings of a bonfire. She had ringed it with rocks and already had a good blaze. Her hair was pinned to the top of her head, but it was off-center and seemed ready to tumble, and the flickering firelight revealed a streak of dirt on her cheek.

"Isn't she lovely," Rudhyar murmured. I could only nod, and we both paused in humble homage.

Christina looked up with a cheerful grin. "We can't let the weather gods keep us down," she said.

The back door was open, and I could see Billie in the kitchen, wearing an apron and scowling at something in a large pot. Coming around from the front yard, an attractive man pulled a pair of chairs to the fire ring, and Christina introduced us: "Agnes, Rudhyar, meet Dewalt Arner. He's promised to start an art colony here, isn't that right, Walt?"

The man beamed at Christina. "It is," he said. Behind him an overdressed (and very young) woman tottered into view, also dragging chairs but with obvious difficulty. She stopped when she saw us.

"Hey!" she called out to him. "You gonna help me?"

"Sure," he replied, but he seemed spellbound by Christina. After an awkward moment, Rudhyar stepped toward her.

"Allow me," he said. She yanked the chairs out of his reach, and he stopped. There she stood in her frills, clearly having prepared for a formal dinner in Palm Springs, not a campfire and post-sand-storm evening in Cathedral City. She let go of the two chairs and yelled in Arner's direction.

"Is *this* the party you said we could go to? Because I don't see no movie stars. Except her, maybe." She nodded in Christina's direction. I didn't blame her. Even wearing army surplus denims and no makeup, Christina had a look of languid amusement that was full-on "movie star."

At the ruckus, Billie, still in her apron, stepped outside. "Nope," she said, "no movie stars here."

The unfortunate ingenue burst into tears, which made Billie sigh and glare at Arner. "Maybe she needs a ride somewhere," she said gruffly.

Arner hurried over to his companion, took her elbow, and tried to guide her toward the street. "Don't you touch me, you lying son of a bitch," she shrieked, her slender heels sinking into the grit as she marched toward his car.

"I'll be back," he called to us, squeezing Christina's arm as he passed her. Billie saw this and immediately stomped back into the house.

"Oh dear," Christina sighed. "There's spaghetti on the stove. Please come and help yourselves before you fade away from hunger." She disappeared after Billie.

"I guess there's nothing for it but to do as she says," Rudhyar said, offering me his arm.

Later, we sat with empty plates on our laps and watched the fire die down. A couple whose name I didn't catch arrived, and finally Billie and Christina emerged, arms wound tightly around each other, and joined us at the fire ring.

"It's not Christina's fault," Billie said to no one in particular. "She's very beautiful." Having settled that, she relaxed and tossed more mesquite on the fire. It was fully dark by now. Rudhyar grabbed the jug of red wine and topped off our glasses. Then, as if by secret summons, additional people drifted over and joined us, tossing blankets and rugs onto the ground and making themselves comfortable. The fire crackled and hissed, the wood tumbling into coals as it burned. I thought I had never seen anything as lovely as its pulsing, liquid orange.

CATHEDRAL CITY, CALIFORNIA

MAY 1932

OUR TOWN HAD BEEN LAID out in hopes of quick real estate development, but sales at first were slow and hesitant. Now the so-called drought was over. Every day, beginning with the streaky dawn, builders bustled all about us. An architect who was spotted measuring an empty piece of desert would be followed almost immediately by a bulldozer gouging out a foundation for yet another house. And more "progress" was afoot: Cathedral City was to change its name to East Palm Springs.

"Think of the cachet we'll acquire." Christina laughed. "My property will double in value without me doing anything at all!"

I worried silently that the place would be quickly overrun. It was almost spooky, then, when we heard that Palm Springs had forbidden the change; Cathedral City would remain Cathedral City.

Spring stretched out, and as the days grew longer and the heat more intense, the sun-seeking winter visitors began to depart for more temperate climes.

"Come with us," Billie said. "We're leaving next week for Azusa."

"Yes," Christina said. "Oh, do come."

I considered the idea. Billie had told me about her house in the hill town about an hour's drive away, but I declined. With all the talk of heat and the impossibility of staying, I briefly considered returning to Pasadena. I also had been in touch with cousins living in Santa Barbara and been enthusiastically invited. (In later years their home would indeed become a summer refuge.) It took about four years for me to decide to settle here and build my own house. But that first year, 1932, when anyone asked why I remained for the infernal months of summer, I would answer thus: that my preference was always to observe a landscape through the full cycle of a year; that the ring of mountains made me feel embraced; that the silence when the merrymakers departed and construction halted because of the heat brought me to a state of bliss.

I left my green cabin and strolled idly, as one must in terrific heat, toward SvenSka. My friends had planned to leave that morning, but I was two houses away when I heard Billie, her voice full of terror.

"What do you mean, you won't go with me?" I shrank back and hid behind the only shelter available, a spindly acacia tree.

"Where are you going now?" Billie's plea was almost a wail. I wanted to turn and run, but the heat does slow one's thinking, and before I could safely scurry away, Christina opened her own front door and tossed a suitcase outside. It bounced and fell over and was quickly followed by a second bag. She emerged, perfectly groomed and dressed for travel in a linen sheath, light jacket, and hat. I watched in amazement as she righted the first suitcase, sat on it, and in the most leisurely fashion possible pulled on a pair of white cotton gloves. Billie filled the doorway with both hands on the doorframe as if she were in a jail cell.

"Wait!" she screamed. "I'm sorry!"

She seemed to have no thought for the intruding eyes that by now must have been watching from all around. I felt a little thrill, which I was immediately ashamed of. I forced my eyes away, and then stepped out and started toward them. These were my friends, and there was no justification for hiding.

"Ignoring me?" Billie screamed. She disappeared for an instant and then came back and began to hurl intimate items of clothing out the door.

"You forgot something!" she hollered and tossed more objects without the slightest acknowledgment from Christina.

"Hey!" Billie yelled again. "You're leaving your own house? Are you that stupid?"

Christina drew out a cigarette and lit it with the gold lighter that I knew Billie had given her. She remained balanced lightly on the suitcase and peered down the road.

"Christina? Are you all right?" I asked as I approached, my voice low as if all this could remain private.

"Hullo, Agnes," she said with a smile. "How are you?"

"I'm fine," I stammered.

"Oh, good," she said, looking past me. "Ah. Here comes Wilbur."

And sure enough, a touring car nearly as large as Billie's approached, raising dust behind it. The man who sat each day in the real estate office pulled up, and Christina climbed in while he tossed her bags into the back.

"Hey there, Agnes." He doffed his sweat-ringed hat. "Hot enough for you?"

"Hello, Wilbur. Christina, where are you going?" I asked.

"San Francisco." She climbed into the front seat and the car pulled away. At the door, Billie had crumpled and slid to the floor, and remained there, her back against the doorframe. I approached carefully, wondering what I could possibly say to her. She relieved me of my burden at once: "Agnes, please go away." Then she closed the door gently, and I didn't see her for two days, when she waved from her car and departed for cooler climes.

Billie returned in the fall with a new friend, a former Army nurse who was suffering from tuberculosis. Shan, as she was called, was often bedridden, which curtailed Billie's painting expeditions. I was sorry to lose her company even as I admired the faithful way she tended her friend. Christina returned as well to tend to SvenSka but kept herself at a haughty remove, which I decided to accept.

Shan died that winter and wanted her ashes scattered out over the Cove. Accompanied by members of The Dunes nightclub orchestra, Billie led a group of us up the rocky hill. Rain threatened all around as we waited for Billie to achieve the summit, for which she needed a cane. She took it slowly and made it to the top. When she opened the urn and tipped it, the wind took hold of Shan's ashes and carried them toward the mountains while the band played taps in tribute to Shan's army service. It was especially moving, I think, because we saw that we were a real community, that we could care for one another.

Then, as the last notes echoed and faded, we made our way back down. Billie stopped and glanced back for one last look and exclaimed. We all turned and followed her point to where a rainbow crested San Jacinto. When we were all safely down, most of the small crowd followed the band into the club, which had opened early for what became a raucous wake. None of us really knew Shan, but everyone knew and loved Billie. All of that is gone now.

That first summer, when the town's "desert rats," as they called themselves, asked me why on earth I was still there, I just smiled. As much as I enjoyed the community being created here, the relationship I wanted to build was with the land, the sky, and the mountains. I would follow the spirit I heard here and paint what it showed me.

It would be from the high desert east of us—Santa Fe—where new hope for my art would come. Rudhyar's promised introduction to his friend Raymond Jonson was accomplished via letter since my travel was curtailed by financial and health concerns, but Raymond and Vera, his wife, became as close friends as is possible. Raymond,

with Emil Bisttram, was creating what became the Transcendental Painting Group, and Rudhyar arranged for me to send three
characteristic abstracts to show them. Not only did they invite me
to be part of it, I will indulge in a small boast: they elected me its
honorary president.

Cathedral City, California
July 27, 1933

Dear Raymond Jonson,

What a cordial and delightful letter you sent me! And
thank you so much for the little plan of the museum
alcove. Coming in the midst of a Desert summer, the
intense heat and absolute quiet, the thought of this
little exhibition that you and Rudhyar have so kindly
arranged for me, is just about the nicest thing I could
think of to happen!

Also, I shall be so glad to be represented in your
Fiesta Exhibition and am sure that the pictures can
reach you by August 21st if not before. Some of them
could go before, if there was any advantage in that,
as I would have to use more than one box. They have
been sent out from Budworth at various times, so I
have several boxes of various shapes. One picture that
Rudhyar has asked for is square 26X30—or nearly—and
I am at work now on a new one that I would very
much like to send you if it is done in time. It is always
such a pleasure and stimulus to work on a new picture
for a special showing of my pictures . . ..

I will let you know before long how the new picture
progresses—and would not of course keep you waiting

for it should it work out too slowly. It is indeed kind
of you to take charge of my "works" in your studio. I
appreciate it greatly.

I hope this letter is clear and legible! At present
the heat is very great, also the humidity, so letters
are something of a trick. No one need be sorry for me
however, as I declined a good offer of a house at the
Beach as I preferred to stay here in the quiet and work.

With cordial regards
Sincerely,
Agnes Pelton

Santa Fe, New Mexico
December 11, 1933

My Dear Agnes Pelton,

Your fine letter of the fifth with the snap shots has arrived and been properly appreciated. Please do not be concerned about the difficulty in reading your letters— for I have had little. Having had one long hand letter from me you know that I too have messy penmanship! But I believe that is generally true of good painters!!!

I am sorry that several of your works were not acquired here. It is too bad that the glorification of the mediocre seems to be the programme these days. Make something cheaply and badly and then bally-hoo it and success will follow. Make something richly and well— of course no bally-hoo follows, for that is entirely foreign to genuineness and real honesty—and starvation is the result. We must of course choose the latter for that is the honorable and the only possible path. We have in this country a few intelligent of feeling people, but the country is so large and the few so few that we must realize the great problem of bringing to the front the sum total of this small group . . . And so our work is to do our work.

But Wells of Jade will hang on my wall and many will see it and, I hope, come to recognize its depth.

The photo of your "shack" looks very intriguing. I hope someday we can make the trip and pitch our tent along side and have some visits and discussions on painting!!

Cordially yours,
Raymond Jonson

Cathedral City
December 30, '36

Dear Friend,

Last year about this time I was expecting you and
Vera for that very happy little visit. How good it is
to remember—and how lovely it would be if you were
coming again now!

I have been thinking of you for several days and
especially yesterday at intervals all day—

The mountains are gloriously covered with snow
after several days of rain. Several rains in fact. I have
never seen the desert so sodden—but the verbena is well
on its way to a record year!

Sometime do let me have your news. I have very
little to tell. Much building going on all around me.
Too much. But this isn't a letter—just to wish you
both all the happiest possible things for New Year!

Agnes

677 E STREET

CATHEDRAL CITY, CALIFORNIA

1936

I PURCHASED MY LOT THAT SPRING—a half-acre of raw and joyously unruly desert dotted with cactus, yucca, and clumps of wiry trees, their still-bare branches waving out in all directions like tendrils. A large smoke tree was ready to bloom, which I took as a clear sign that this was where I belonged. When my house was finished, it was set into the landscape so beautifully that it seemed part of the very earth. I was fifty-five years old, and it was the first home I'd ever owned; it was all mine, and I loved it. The builder became a friend. Every afternoon during construction, as the light shifted toward the west, I'd come by to see his progress and we'd talk. We shared an abiding love for this little town and a profound reverence for the desert around it, still so open then and uncluttered. I told him of the vision I'd had for the house: a gentle upward slope, the studio door wide open and welcoming, people approaching from every direction. I'd seen them walking up a curved path to enter. The next day he was back with his bulldozer, and he cut my driveway from the desert, arced like a crescent. What happy years those were.

Before poor health and age put a stop to it, and before the town started spreading in every direction, I'd rise early. Loaded like a pack mule—easel and folding stool slung over my shoulder, paint box in one hand, stretched canvas under the other arm—I'd walk straight out my back door, up the slope, and into the desert. There I'd set up and paint for as long as the light was favorable or until the heat drove me back inside. I was a sort of cottage industry, turning out landscape after landscape of Mt. San Jacinto, Mt. San Gorgonio, the sage brush, the desert floor, the yucca in bloom, the pink of spring flowers, the soft haze of the smoke tree. These I could sell; Harriet was always happy to have a new batch. Then, once the "cash crop" was in, I could engage my own spirit, meditate and receive the images that became my abstracts, the real work of my heart and soul.

CATHEDRAL CITY, CALIFORNIA

1941

I CAN TELL YOU EXACTLY where I was and what I was thinking on the morning of December 7. It had been raining, pouring really—a kind of pummeling I think I have only experienced here, maybe because heavy rain is such a rarity in the desert. We, meaning my neighbor Harriet and our good friends the Sussmans—Corrine and Irving—had been enjoying an early dinner, when the noise of the rain on my roof caused us all to stop and wonder if it would hold. It did hold. I was congratulated on having hired such an outstanding builder as Alvah Hicks, we sipped our coffee, and then they ran out. The storm passed, and when I woke the morning of the 7th, I marveled at the clarity of the dawn, the beauty of it, the clouds looking like high feathers brushing at the sky. Later one of the boys, Mr. Hillery's son Bob I think, rode by on his bicycle and yelled that I should turn on the radio, and there came the news of the attack.

All of us in the village had been keenly aware of the bombing blitz in Britain, and Hitler's apparently unstoppable takeover of Europe. Before we knew of concentration camps and gas chambers, evil seemed to undergird all aspects of life, even in Santa Fe's high desert where the Transcendental Painting Group was headquartered and in our unglamorous piece of southern California desert.

And then, with the Japanese attack on Pearl Harbor, it all began to collapse. Raymond wrote that he had sent letters of inquiry to 120 museums and art associations and had received only four replies. This, after the warm appreciation for our group in the 1939 Golden Gate International Exposition in San Francisco. The excitement about us was genuine, but interest in our work was quickly swamped by the rising war hysteria. Fear hummed through everything like a wire, even as we pumped ourselves up with patriotism and determination. No one but us in the TPG thought that art should be concerned with spiritual matters during a time of war. "Can there be a better time?" I groused rhetorically to Raymond.

Individually we all carried on. (What else can one do?) I had met Buell and Harriet Hammett on an earlier visit to my cousins in Santa Barbara, and in '37 the Hammetts had acquired five—five!—of my abstracts, which they said would form the core of a new collection for the art museum they intended to establish there. The beautiful Santa Barbara Museum of Art, which had opened in the fall of '41.

The next summer, thanks to the Hammetts' large purchase, I was able to buy my tiny lot in Thomas Mountain, several thousand feet above the valley, and have my cabin built. I spent my sixtieth birthday there among the tall firs. I had carried a sketchbook with me as usual and, sitting on a rock, I made pastel drawings of the trees. It struck me, as I worked, that the images were different in character from my desert landscapes. The height, thickness, and solidity of the trees, for instance, as opposed to the desert flora, which often seems composed of tendrils going outward in every direction and which of necessity remains close to the ground. I pushed my pastels heavily into the paper, wanting to grasp the difference: the dark umber of the tree bark with its flares of yellow ochre, the thickness of it and the flatness of its layers; the sturdy green of the needles; the height of the canopy and its denseness.

With the long-resisted war upon us at last, even eccentric little Cathedral City was mobilized. The official word was that in the case of invasion or more attacks from Japan, refugees would overwhelm the desert, and all of us here would be responsible for housing and maintaining them. Our local population organized itself into an ad hoc police force and began distributing instructions about what we were to do. It was quite appalling, really, to have our easygoing friends suddenly puffed up with their own idea of authority. This was quickly dispelled when the army arrived and set up a "headquarters" in the post office. Later we would learn of the horrific internment of Japanese Americans farther inland.

I built a storage box under my studio ramada for the dozen or so abstracts I was holding and tucked them quietly away. I needn't have worried; they were not considered worth much by the locals and certainly not by the military. Fortunately, the emergency never came to pass. The army left, and the village quieted down.

But because of the war and the immediate difficulty of obtaining supplies for such frivolous efforts as oil paintings, Raymond formally dissolved the TPG in 1945. Poor Emil Bisttram had started an art school in Los Angeles, but returning soldiers, who now could attend college on government grants, kept asking him how painters actually lived and supported families? Emil put a brave face on it, but he and his wife were barely surviving financially, and their obvious struggle put off many prospective students. They soon closed the school and returned to New Mexico.

677 E STREET

CATHEDRAL CITY, CA

1948

LIGHT CENTER, I MEAN THE first iteration, was the only abstract I finished that year. My practice was always to keep works in progress in my sight, keep them on the horizon, so to speak. It was not unusual for me to reach a halt on a picture with no idea at all how to proceed. Instead of giving up—that is key—I'd move the whole works, picture and easel, to one side. Every now and then I would see where a new color might reveal something to me. I would immediately stop what else I was doing—that year especially it would most often be a desert landscape—and daub the color on lightly, here maybe, there maybe, and step back. If I saw where I could add more, I would cautiously do so, but I made sure never to make marks that might destroy the picture as it was trying to emerge. Never to force the vision. Instead, make a gentle effort to coax inspiration into revisiting; sometimes it worked.

Light Center had arrived whole and complete—a vital vision that blazed into my mind's eye and quickly had me laying out the picture in detail with the colors I expected to use. Always, at the start, a great rush of joy and energy, and gratitude that the Spirit had once again returned with a priceless gift, which was my responsibility to effect, to birth into being.

The painting itself went quickly. The vision was grounded by mountains—a red, purple, and lavender range in circular disks on the bottom of the canvas—and crowned, in this case, by ephemeral clouds gathering at the top. Dominating the center, a glowing white oval was flanked on either side by a shaft of ultramarine. I was thrilled by it and looked forward to tending it, listening to it, watching for what it needed—keeping it with me for a year or so, as was also my practice. My abstracts are my children, they are my issue, and I have kept them with me until I felt that they were complete.

A few weeks later, with the paint barely dry, my friend Edwin, a supposedly retired dealer, happened by. I was still aquiver with the excitement of a new work, that tender sense of new love, which makes me eager, yes, and more vulnerable than usual. That day I also had realistic desert scenes on three out of five easels. I was supremely tired of making them and was trying to hasten their finishing. I had decided to use a freer brush stroke to make it all go faster and, I thought, make them more expressionistic (i.e., salable). I did not like the result on the first one, but to change it at that point would have meant redoing the entire canvas; it was a large piece and so I was simply soldiering on. Edwin took his usual tour of the studio, hands clasped lightly behind his back, chin thrust out as he leaned into each picture. I had kept several as necessary to my own spiritual practice, and he reviewed these. *Light Center* was next, and I recoiled a bit, fighting the urge to cover it and protect it from his gaze. He stopped next by the desert scenes.

"Why are you wasting your time on these?"

"I thought I might like to eat this year."

"Good God, Agnes," he said. "You have a gold mine here!" He waved his arms at the works on the walls: *Mother of Silence, Transcendental Being, White Fire, Star Icon I, Orbits, Challenge.*

"I agree," I said a bit dryly. "But it seems that I am the one who values them, and therefore here they will stay."

"Excuse me for saying so, but that's a bit selfish, don't you think? These paintings need to be seen by a lot of people!"

He faced me directly, and I saw the idea flash across his face. "I'll get them seen," he said. "Let me have them. Including the new one. It's stunning. What are you calling it?"

"*Light Center*," I answered abruptly, suddenly frightened for it. He took no notice.

"Let me take them right now," he said. "I can leave tomorrow. Lord knows I'm not doing much of anything here. Look, I'll crate them and load them into my station wagon, and off I'll go, to Chicago and then New York. I know a lot of people. I can get you good prices. I might visit a few museums. Big ones. What do you say?"

His calling me out as selfish had shocked me. I struggled to either refute that characterization or simply admit it but could only manage to say I could not do as he asked. He sat down on the divan and motioned me to sit by him; I complied. He took my hand and seemed to be studying it. I wanted to pull it away, to hide the dark spots and wrinkles, and the veins rising under the transparent skin. At length he returned it to my lap.

"Agnes," he said softly. "You are a great artist. I want the world to know that. Please. I can do this. Let me do this."

I waited for the right response. Surely this was too much, surely the Spirit would say no to it, but that did not happen. Instead the Spirit said, They are not your private property. Immediately I was awash in what I call the what-ifs. What if it works? What if a museum buys one, and then another museum, and then a fancy gallery decides to get in on the action? What if they *sell*? What if I could put aside these tiresome desert scenes and only engage in the abstracts?

"All right, Edwin," I said finally. I wondered how Rudhyar would respond when I told him of this. I would also tell him of my fear, that sending them out would invite ridicule and rejection. That no one would want them but me. "Never mind," I could hear him say. "If they are meant to go out into the world, then it will be God's will. If not, they will come back to you, and that, too, will be God's will." Then I realized Rudhyar didn't talk about God's will; that was more in the character of my mother and grandmother. I relaxed then, feeling all would be as it was intended.

That evening I felt the most tremendous excitement. The what-ifs had become fresh hope. And not just for myself and my puny sense of fulfillment. Perhaps the world actually did need them, perhaps these paintings could supply what was needed, perhaps the world was ready for them. I couldn't sleep, so I went outside and did something I'd not done for a long time. I unfurled an Indian blanket, laid down on my back, and allowed myself to gaze at the stars, to fall upward and be absorbed by them.

In the morning, Edwin returned in his big, wood-paneled station wagon. His suitcases were tied to a luggage rack on the car's roof, and he had removed the rear seat to accommodate the paintings. We packed up the pictures together, wrapping *Light Center* last. As we worked, my excitement began to fade. I tried to push away fear and not to show how bereft I already was, and I suspected that he was trying not to regret his own braggadocio. Neither of us talked, and his leave-taking was solemn. When he drove away, I hurried back inside and wept—at my own vanity for letting him flatter me, at the empty walls where the pictures had been, and the stark hole their absence had already made in my heart. Then I sent a prayer that my beloveds would be safe and, if possible, come home to me again.

Some months after he drove off with my pictures to sell, Edwin returned with nearly all of them. I cried because I was so happy to have them back. He misunderstood and kept apologizing, and finally I said, "Please don't, I'm very relieved. These were never meant to be sold."

"It's just as well then," he said.

"You took a lot of trouble. I should be apologizing to you."

"I didn't mind, Agnes. I came to the desert to retire, and now I truly am retired."

He carried each of the paintings inside and helped me rehang them.

"Where is *Light Center?*"

"Didn't I tell you? I meant to write. I was in Chicago, at one of the galleries, and the owner was much kinder about telling me no. When he saw *Light Center,* he looked at it very carefully. Then he left his office and returned with another man, a patron who happened to be there. The second man pulled out a checkbook and bought it on the spot."

He fumbled a bit for his wallet and found the folded check. "I added a bit to the price you set." I was surprised to find myself holding five hundred dollars.

"Well," I said. "I owe you something for this and for your efforts."

"No," he said. "It was a privilege. Let's call it square." He smiled then and waved goodbye.

ART 21—ART APPRECIATION,
14th wk. January 5, 1949

Instructor: Raymond Jonson
Student: Sarah Rainey

(Agnes, last week I "taught" you. Miss Rainey took down the talk in shorthand—some of it is not too exact.)

Agnes Pelton: THE ESOTERIC AND SPIRITUAL IN PAINTING

After the usual Christmas or New Year's spirit, it seems appropriate to present works that lie in the direction of the mystical, the occult, the metaphysical, and there may be one or two other terms that could also define the approach. Also, due to the fact that we have used only members of the male species, I thought it would be only fair and just to present the female of the species, so today we have with us Agnes Pelton.

In order to relieve you of any perplexity, I might give you the titles right off. The first on the left is called *The Voice*, the center one *Wells of Jade*, the third one *Star Icon*.

Miss Pelton is in her sixties, has lived in Cathedral City, California, which is a small village-like settlement—at least it was in 1935 when I was there—six miles from Palm Springs, almost in the heart of desert country, with a certain fascinating vegetation, particularly a tree called the smoke-tree, and certain cacti.

Miss Pelton is about the only painter I know, or know of, who has a decidedly and definitely dual esthetic personality. There are two opposite compartments as regards her emotional make-up. For the last fifteen or twenty years, one has worked primarily with smoke-trees, and the other in the direction of what we are calling the mystical, or the esoteric, or the occult, or metaphysical, or all of them, if you like . . .

Wells of Jade I have had in my possession for a number of years . . . [I]t is a different kind of painting . . . It is absolutely mysterious; it is magnificent. The touch is like the finest note on a violin. It has . . . everything in it that pertains to mystery.

677 E STREET

CATHEDRAL CITY

FEBRUARY 8, 1953

THE UNEXPECTED THING ABOUT SETTLING myself in one place, particularly our odd little village, is that time leveled out. I painted in a different way, taking the images I was given and working them through in a settled way—no more forays into ecstasy, which were at once stimulating and then almost immediately exhausting. None of this was planned or intentional; it simply happened. It seemed to be a complete level of comfort and acceptance of where I was and who I was. With the sun out nearly every day, there was little to remind me that time itself was passing—sort of like watching a train get underway, staring at the wheels as it picks up speed until suddenly, they seem to be reversing, spinning in the opposite direction. Or walking and walking out in the desert, feeling you are floating and making no progress at all until abruptly you have arrived at where you were going.

February 8—how can I be sure of this date? Because I had written to several people that day and was very conscious of scribbling the date over and over, pleased with myself for taking care of all the backlogged correspondence. Everything was as usual, including my dragging my feet about finishing the latest realistic desert landscape, which I had promised to the dentist who had bought Billie's house for his office. I was so tired of these paintings. I had made hundreds of them by then, and I just wanted to stop, but of course I needed the money. I noticed that the sky was filling with bulbous, burgeoning clouds, an enormous treat, and I went outside to watch for rain. The air carried the rare scent of water, which I inhaled hungrily. I do so love the winter rains. Whatever storm that was brewing, however, passed us by, and reluctantly I went back to work.

That night brought an array of indistinct and troubling dreams, and when I awoke the morning of the ninth, I knew something was wrong. All day I moved about the studio, waiting to come upon what the matter was. I thought it was with the work, with the abstracts in progress—the usual four or five unfinished pieces that kept me company. I thought perhaps I had missed a signal and was interpreting a vision incorrectly. But it was very like the child's game of "hot-cold": I would approach a picture thinking I was "hot," only to have the impulse fade. After circling the studio like that two or three times, I had the sensation of being watched. What sort of presence was it? Malevolent or benign? Gentle or destructive? I didn't know and couldn't tell, which disturbed me even more. I grew afraid of staying in the studio at all.

Outside in the long shadows of afternoon, I tried sitting quietly in the garden. I focused on the mountains, breathing deeply and slowly and inviting the presence to reveal itself. As the early winter darkness covered the desert, I felt calmer. I reminded myself that long ago I had made a friend of the Spirit and that nothing in its realm would do me harm. Gradually that feeling expanded, and it struck me that perhaps it was the entity itself, if it was an entity, that was frightened. I set about reassuring it: "I don't know who or what you are," I said out loud, "but I only want what is best for you." I waited then. Nothing came to reveal itself, but even though the air was chilly and a fog was rising, I felt better and went inside to get some supper.

A few days later, when the letter arrived from Mabel, I learned what had happened and who had troubled my sleep. I'd not been in touch with Mabel for years, so I opened it immediately: "Our friend Alice has died, in her sleep, in New York," Mabel wrote. "I wonder if you were alerted to her passing as I feel I was. It was well after midnight here, in the darkest hours, and I awoke suddenly and looked for who had called me. I brushed it off as an odd dream, but when my telephone rang in the morning and I learned of her death, I knew it had been Alice. It was as though she had dropped in to say goodbye."

So close to Mabel's was my experience that I immediately sat down to reply. The grief that was storming through me was countered by an elation of the sort that arises when a distant someone has shared an experience you had thought entirely private. Something that had puzzled you, even frightened you, and has explained it, which has pulled you into full alertness, and now you can see it for what it truly was: reunion, reconnection, at-one-ment—with Mabel and, yes, with Alice.

I told Mabel that I, too, had been "dropped in on," and that her letter had confirmed this. I thanked her for letting me know and told Mabel that I loved her, which indeed I did—and do—and that I loved Alice. I felt rash, and free, and reckless. "Why," I wrote, "do people say, 'I loved her,' or 'I loved him,' past tense, when speaking of the dead? Does the love disappear when the life ends? Certainly not," I wrote. "Certainly not." I set the letter aside and wandered outside.

In my garden a few new shoots were poking their way up, and my large prickly pear cactus was getting ready to bloom. I settled down next to it and tried to work out what it meant that Alice was now gone—so many years of pushing her away, and why had I done that? After our awkward excursion to Taos, I told myself that I had simply outgrown her. Not that I wasn't grateful for all she had done for me, I hastened to remind myself. The paintings she had bought. The studios she had rented for me. The telephone she had installed in my first studio. The persistent effort to convince the lawyer and tastemaker John Quinn to buy my work. Which would bring on the buyers and lead to acquisitions by museums. "Everyone will want one then," Alice said. I remember her face, ablaze with triumph. It was 1913, and we were having lunch at Delmonico's to celebrate the conclusion of the Armory Show and What Was To Be. It was inevitable, Alice said, dabbing the corners of her mouth gently with the heavy linen napkin.

"Your place in the pantheon of modern artists is secure," she said.

I remember the electric shock of ecstasy at that and struggling against a powerful wave of joy. I clasped my own napkin and rather primly replied that the Armory was just one show, that there was so much work to be done.

"To be sure," Alice replied. Then she reminded me that one of my pictures was going to Chicago with the Armory's travelling exhibition. "One of just a few American artists. It is just a matter of time."

––––––––––

I stuffed my reply to Mabel into an envelope and carried it to the post office, dropping it in the mailbox before I could change my mind, pull the letter back, and throw it away. Because there's more to the story, which Mabel surely recalled:

The year Alice and I visited Taos, 1919, I confided in Mabel that I had once had feelings for Alice. It was our tender habit, Mabel's and mine, to take long, slow, leisurely walks through the Pueblo. The high desert air being soft with spring, the grasses tender and green, we inhaled their fragrance and inclined our heads toward one another, clasping hands, ready to share our secrets—or rather, Mabel was. I was ready to listen. She talked, and always her talk was about Tony and her happiness and her visceral connection to him and his people. Then she stopped and turned to face me.

"And what about you, Agnes. Have you ever felt owned by another?"

I was shocked by the question, and my first impulse had been to hide, to deny, to give a vague answer, knowing that Mabel was happiest when talking about herself, that she'd accept whatever I said. But then I was seized by an inexplicable desire—to be able to say yes, your spinster friend has felt the same longing and passion as you—wanting to add, even if none of it was played out for everyone to see.

Before I could change my mind, I answered Mabel honestly.

"Yes," I said, "I have."

She had grinned with delight. "Why, Agnes, talk about still waters running deep. Who is he? Do tell!"

Would Mabel laugh, tease me, make fun of an unnatural attachment? My heart was skipping and thudding, and stinging tears spilled onto my cheeks because I knew I would tell her and that once told, it could never be retracted.

"Why, you're shaking," Mabel had said. "My goodness, dear, it's nothing terrible." She tried a laugh. "I am completely unshockable."

I finally spoke.

"It's—it was Alice."

"Oh!" Immediately Mabel's demeanor changed. She became all compassion and concern, which caused my words to tumble out—they were like water rushing over rock, unstoppable and uncatchable. Her eyes had widened when I described coming to her White Salon on Fifth Avenue, how at the end of that very long evening, I had collapsed from nervous exhaustion. How gentle and kind Alice had been, scooping me up and driving me home to Brooklyn, holding me against her all the way. How I had wished time could stop right there.

"I thought I had never been so happy, which astonished me—how easy it was to be happy—and then it came to me that I loved her," I had said. "I had no illusions about it—I knew it was one-sided—but I told myself it was enough. And then she sailed off to Europe."

I had covered my face while Mabel steered me to where I could sit down—a trailside boulder as I recall.

"Poor lamb," she had said. "Alice is not capable, dear heart. Just not capable. You need to find someone else."

We had headed back to Mabel's house under that huge blue sky, her arm around me. I tried to regret my candor, thought I should want to gather my words back and un-say them, but instead there had been enormous relief.

"I am trying not to envy you, Agnes," Mabel had continued. "Your life seems very clean to me, very clear. I have had many heart connections as you know, all of them dramatic, all of them difficult. Yes, even this one with Tony. Actually, this one with Tony will likely turn out to be the hardest because my quest for true love is over. I have found it—I will never leave Tony—and that means giving up the search, which is another sort of heartbreak."

Years later she would tell me how Tony had inadvertently infected her with syphilis. "The poor darling didn't know," she said, adding, "This is how the great love story ends."

———

I walked home and sat back down at my desk, this time to write to Alice. I recommend it: there is great liberty in writing to someone who absolutely will not receive what you say. "I know you were with me on the night of your passing," I scribbled. "I hadn't realized it was you until Mabel told me that you were gone, but I felt your presence keenly. I feel it now, warming me like white fire." And then I poured out my thanks for the way she had supported my early years as a painter. I added my regrets at not having made the splash she had counted on.

"I am old now myself," I continued. "I keep working, and some days I wonder why. I can hear you laugh at that: 'What else is there to do?' you would say. Well, you would be right, but at the moment I can't for the life of me understand why that is. Artists start off so full of promise and hope, and if we're very lucky we are given friends like you, who are there to believe in us and support us and tell us that what we are doing matters."

In a fit of self-pity—I was weeping loudly now, missing Alice, missing *us* and the long-ago days gone by—I wondered why it had all been so hard. I knew the pattern: a burst of light, a vision, a clear sense of image coming forth. The quick jotting in the sketch book, the notation of colors to be used, the joyful energy that accompanies purpose. The mapping out on canvas, the under-drawing, the first colors applied thinly for quicker drying—the rush of joy at the beauty of the color—the thrill of seeing the image for a second time, now coming by my hand. And then the fog. Where does the clarity go? Why does it depart before I am finished? Why does it sometimes take years—years—to finish a piece? Mere self-indulgence? Is this why I've not been more successful?

"Goodness, Agnes," I could hear Alice's voice, "you cannot expect to isolate yourself in some backwater"—there's that word again—"and reach the heights of fame and fortune."

I found myself laughing. Was I demented, having conversations with people who were not present, entering arguments that I could easily win because they were between me and me?

"You're right, dear friend," I said out loud. I had taken myself right out of all the action, as Alice would have put it, and twice, first to Long Island and then to this desert, with its endless shimmering light.

522 ½ B STREET

CATHEDRAL CITY, CALIFORNIA

FEBRUARY 10, 1961

IF I COULD, I WOULD DRAW this room. Not because it's beautiful—it isn't—but for practice, as an exercise in seeing, a way to find my center and accept new surroundings and the consequent disorientation. I would start with four quick strokes to outline the window, intentionally bare of curtains or covering, where Mt. San Jacinto is just catching the first light. To the right of the window, the easel and the painting that waits to be finished. On the left, against the wall, a work table with my paint box, palette, brushes, turpentine. Above, the ceiling with its web of tiny cracks radiating from the overhead light. Wall smudges where the paint was applied in haste. The plywood floor. The circular rug. A chair for visitors. Making such a drawing would help me, I know, to be present in the here and now and not to be pulled, again and again—over and over and over—into the past. I want to spell that "passed." I wonder why we don't.

I thought it would be easy, selling my house and moving here. I tossed off the decision lightly—arrogantly, I now see. My friends greeted the news with horror: "Agnes! You can't do that!"—and I felt the first tremor of fear. Even so, I refused to back down. What kept me so resolved? My mother, my grandmother, what would they say to this? I could hear them separately, each of them approving, whispering, "Never let yourself depend on others for the basics. Never be without your own resources."

What happened: It was last fall when I knew I was very ill. I had gone to the doctor in Palm Springs, who had run some tests, and a week later I returned to his office. I gazed out his window at a clump of swaying palms while he studied a clipboard, cleared his throat, and told me in detail the reasons for my relentless pain and fatigue. It should not have surprised me, but it did. Shock was followed immediately by panic—a terrible acid anxiety about money. I would need more of it than I had, and I could not, would not, ask family or friends to help. These were the people who had already been supporting me all these years, buying my desert scenes, keeping me in groceries.

I thanked the doctor and left, climbing into the car where Wilbur's son Bob waited to drive me home.

"What'd he say?" Bob asked.

"Oh, nothing." We lapsed into silence. That was the excellent thing about Bob Hillery: he could bear silence.

"I have cancer," I said. "The doctor said I have cancer." Bless him, Bob Hillery just nodded.

The idea of selling had come then, out of the blue, as they say, or directly from Spirit as I saw it, in a flash of memory of all those years ago in Brooklyn, and my dear friend Phoebe suggesting I could turn Grandmama's house into cash and move. Here in our village, a new builder had been eyeing my property—a large lot, fronting on two streets, from E to F. Once back home, I telephoned him to ask if he was interested—he was. I then asked if he could construct a cottage—this cottage—where I could live out what was to come.

"It needn't be large," I told him. "All I need is one room for painting."

He agreed, and the deal was done.

I had envisioned this room, large and nearly empty, full of simplicity and light and silence, and I had seen a single painting on one easel. This, I recognized, was my long-lost *Light Center*, its image returning to me that very afternoon, when I trembled with illness and fear and despair: pillars of French ultramarine, one on each side of violet-blue mountains, and in the center, surrounded by a soft cerulean sky, an orb of pulsing white light. Miraculously I found the snapshot photo I'd taken of the original and was able, once I'd stretched the large canvas, to lay the picture out again in charcoal, noting the colors I intended to use and applying the first layer. I laughed out loud, feeling the vision had waited until I really needed it, that it must have been hovering nearby all the time.

I worked on it steadily until the cabin was finished and it was time to move. I crated it up to work on as soon as I was settled. But moves are messy and exhausting, and I was barely able to leave my bed for several days. Finally, somewhat adjusted to the clutter and the mess, I resolved to set up the easel and uncrate the picture as a good first step. But before I could make even the slightest dent, there was a knock at the door. That will be Billie, I thought. Go away, I thought. But the tapping persisted, so I flung open the door to say exactly that, except it wasn't Billie.

I stood in the doorway and stared. The stranger was young but not that young. Thirties? Maybe older. She had blue eyes, high cheekbones, and long fair hair that was beginning to show threads of white and gray. A bashful smile and an aura, a glow that radiated. She seemed so familiar that I kept trying to place her, and it took a moment for me to realize that we had never met. Who does she remind me of? And then I thought, ah, of course: Alice. But Alice's hair had been a thick dark chestnut. No, it was her carriage and the attitude of her expression, her warmth that was so like Alice's.

She was an artist, she said, and new to the desert. She had been to the gallery in town with her portfolio, and the gallery's owner—who else but my former neighbor Harriet—had recognized a quality in the work reminiscent of my abstract pictures.

"She told me you and I were on the same wavelength."

"Oh?" I said as dryly as I could. The same wavelength, indeed. This from Harriet, who had repeatedly refused to show my abstract work on the grounds that no one would buy it: "The tourists want your desert scenes, Agnes."

The stranger's glance dropped. "Miss Pelton," she said, "I would be so honored if you would look at my work and tell me what you think."

The nerve of that Harriet, I thought, and nearly shut the door right then.

"I see," I said. "I'm terribly sorry, but I can't."

She looked chagrinned, like a rebuked teenager, which was satisfying for an instant and then made me ashamed of myself.

"I shouldn't have just shown up like this," she said, and turned to flee. "I hope you will excuse me." She started to walk away, her face resigned but her back straight and firm. I called to her.

"I can't right now because I'm working, you see. A new picture."

"Oh?" She turned.

"How wonderful," she said, suddenly radiant. More than anything, I think, it was that generosity of spirit that changed my mind.

"If you'd like to come back tomorrow," I said, "I'll be able to see you then."

————

Somehow her arrival provided a lift, an unexpected gift of energy, and I was able to assert some order over the cottage's chaos. A few days later she returned with her portfolio. We put my two chairs together and slowly turned the pages of her drawings. Her name was Sarah and she was from New Mexico—a former student of Raymond's—but even so, I was surprised at the quality of the work.

"You have a true gift," I said.

Her face opened into joy and touched me deeply.

"I wish I could be of some help to you," I said. "But I am so far removed from the business of art . . ." I held my hands open in an empty shrug.

"That's all right," she said softly. "You like it."

She began to stop by at the end of the day to show me what she'd been working on. I think what she needed was not so much a critique—which I am entirely inadequate to supply and said so—but a viewer: someone to look at what she had done and to receive it; someone to bear witness. I have always been a good witness.

—————

As the winter passed, pain made it harder to get up mornings. Many days I just lay in my bed and listened for Sarah's step, ignoring the remaining boxes in the corner and *Light Center* on the easel, its charcoal under-markings taunting me. I regretted my practice of sketching out a picture in charcoal, and then layering over the markings carefully—even though in the past this technique had yielded an aura of radiance, which I valued greatly. Old friends came by, but once they spotted Sarah, they'd smile and withdraw, as though they were interrupting something. I let them go, sent them all away, wanting—needing—the peace and serenity I seemed to find around Sarah alone. In an astonishing act of grace and without my having to ask, she put aside her own work. Every day she came, her hair tied back in a kerchief, her steady optimism buoying me up. When I felt strong enough, we folded linens together and made tea. I took frequent rests on a chaise we'd set up outside, comforted by my stolid mountains, and it was hard to feel terribly glum.

Finally, on a rainy day when we were trapped inside, she pointed to the boxes.

"What's in those?" she asked.

"My past," I said.

The top one, labeled "Journals" in my handwriting—made me recoil. She dampened a rag and carefully began to remove many years of dust, while I sank into a chair, overcome with a bone-deep fatigue.

"Shall I?" she asked gently. I nodded. She grabbed a knife and cut the string on the first one. Flaps open, we saw sketchbooks of all sizes, fit together like bricks. Some of them were dated, some not. Sarah pulled out the one labeled "Ogunquit 1911." She handed it to me, and I opened it. Here were drawings of fishermen mending nets, of boats hauled ashore, the beautiful curves of dories leaning against the sand, waiting for the tide. I could smell the salty air and the tang of the Maine mudflats at low tide.

"Okay," I said, a bit dizzy. "That's one box." I passed the sketchbook back to her and she carefully turned the pages. "These are stunning," she said.

"Next box," I said, reaching to close the flaps. She tucked the Ogunquit book back into its slot and pulled over a wooden box, which I recognized immediately. I had packed it up all those years ago in Brooklyn and not looked in it since. Sarah waited for me to nod before untying the twine I'd wrapped around it and lifting the lid. Yellowed newspapers protected half a dozen old framed photographs, and she unwrapped each one and handed it to me. Here were my young mother and father, probably on their wedding day, even though my mother was not in a white gown. She held a small bunch of posies in her right hand while my father circled her shoulders with his left arm. He looked triumphant, as did she. Then we unwrapped my grandmother in her best black crepe, wearing a black lace cap over her softly curling white hair, and my heart started pounding. "Are you all right?" Sarah asked, breaking the spell.

"Yes," I replied, "let's continue." My aunt Alice was next, and then I'd had all I could take. "This box should go to my cousins."

"Can we see the rest?"

"Yes, all right," and she continued the unwrapping. There was my grandfather, and then, there I was—a studio portrait of a frail-looking, dreamy girl who knew pain but not life. It had been made by the then-famous photographer Alice Boughton, and I remembered it well. Miss Boughton had told me I was beautiful while my mother frowned. I removed it and set it aside. Behind it was a familiar scrapbook. "And that," I said. "Let me have that." Sarah pulled it out. On the cover my mother's handwriting, "Agnes Lawrence Pelton," and inside, "Works and Achievements." I closed it and hugged it to myself.

522 ½ B STREET

CATHEDRAL CITY, CALIFORNIA

FEBRUARY 26, 1961

TIME IS AN IDLE CLOUD, wafting along, changing its shape, shrinking, growing, getting snagged on the mountains—and not in my control. Pain has receded but not fatigue, and I'm able, just, to get about and feed myself and wait for Sarah, who arrives in the afternoon. It is she who shapes my days now, opening the door with the key I gave her and favoring me with her smile when she sees I'm awake.

This morning I drifted into what I expected would be a pleasant sleep, thinking of how beautiful the spring is this year, how the recent rains have doused the sky and turned it into the most extraordinary blue. And then I was outside, and it was day's end, my favorite time. Sarah had told me how splendid the wildflowers are this year and I wanted to see them, and suddenly there I was, and there they were, in gorgeous arrays of the warmest yellows and pinks, coursing down the wash. What a joy, I thought, and decided to paint it. Hurrying home, then, up the hill to my circular drive— marveling at the streaky sky, the mountains, the palm tree I planted when I bought my lot, now very tall indeed, with its happy tangle of small birds flitting about—when I noticed the front door ajar. That's odd, I thought, but isn't that exactly as I intended? The door open to welcome visitors to my studio and my art. But why was the door open? No one locks doors around here, even as crowded as we've become, so is someone visiting? Or could I have left it that way?

I took off at a sort of trot as panic rose—Don't fall! Be careful!—panting my way to the open door and nearly tumbling into the relative darkness inside. Only to find—Oh, no! Oh, no!—the air thick with dust, the studio in a shambles. The door, I could see then, was not open; it had been torn from the lintel, which itself was splintered. Dust rose about me as if a bomb had been set off. There was a taste of plaster in the air and the sting of it in my eyes. And then, as it settled, I saw the paintings. My paintings! The ones on the walls slashed—*White Fire, Mother of Silence, Star Icon, Transcendental Being*—gaping holes in them, while the ones in progress, including the new version of *Light Center*, ripped into shreds, their stretchers splintered, as though broken over some giant, angry knee. I heard a scream and looked about, but it was coming from me. My children, my issue, the fruit of my heart, all destroyed, all gone. I sank to my knees, my head in my hands. So, this is death, I thought, and wept with bitter disappointment. What, no kindly light? I called out to my wounded *Transcendental Being*, the personal icon I could have sold many times over: "Could you not protect us?"

Drowning in grief and a loneliness more acute than I've ever known, nearly consumed by the darkness, I wrenched myself from a sleep as deep as an abyss. A dream, I said, forcing my eyes open; just a dream. But so vivid as to have me still sobbing, my face wet with tears. Cautiously, tentatively, I climbed out of bed. It was just coming dawn as I made my way down the hall and into the studio, forcing myself to look.

All was peaceful. My beloveds were safe on the walls, the paintings in progress still leaning against the walls where I had left them, *Light Center* still on its easel.

In the kitchen I lit the stove, put some coffee on, and talked to myself as if I were a frightened animal, quivering in the corner: It's all right, you're all right, do you see? Everything's all right, you're safe.

Calmer then, relieved to be in my home, I steadied my shaking hands and took my breakfast plate from the shelf—the one with the blue pear in the center—and placed it on the counter. Carefully I cut a slice of bread for toasting. Plugged in the electric toaster, inserted the bread. Took my cup and saucer from the shelf. Sat where I had laid silverware for breakfast and gentled myself. Ah, yes: it's because moving day will soon be here, and off I will go to the one-room cabin. My one room for painting.

Outside, the sky was purple with green streaks. What? And then I understood that I was still dreaming—a dream within a dream, something I knew to be powerful. I looked about to see what I might do with this moment, and there were the cartons. I opened the first box, which was full to the top with loose sheets of paper, curled and brown at the edges like autumn leaves. I reached in and tried to pick up the top one to see what it was, but it crumbled before I could read anything. All gone, I thought, and shut the box. And with that I truly woke up to find myself here, in this shack on B Street, the sun coming in. See? I thought. You're all right. Except I wasn't.

I had never expected to be afraid.

––––––––––––

I looked about this room and thought again that I should draw it. It would help me. But I can barely move. I am down to bones. My skin is draped over my skeleton like worn muslin. I am a mass of tiny lines, a web of them. Sarah will be here soon, I thought. Making us lunch, the comforting clink of dishes, the two of us together. After my mother's death, I did not think there would be another who would see me in all weathers, flesh exposed and weakened by illness, soul pinned open.

I stared at *Light Center* on its easel, still waiting to be finished—the white, egg-shaped orb, which is the promise of light, the what is to come, pure and unquenchable. At the picture's base, struck by a ray of light, are mountain shapes of violet—the end of the spectrum. Apotheosis: the enlightenment.

And finally, between sleeping and dreaming and thinking and communing with the painting, I have come to a solution.

"Pull a chair up for me," I said to Sarah when she arrived.

"A chair?"

"Yes, in front of the easel."

"What are you going to do?"

"Don't worry, I'll be fine."

She stared at me for a moment until she was satisfied that I meant it. Then she picked up one of my two chairs and carried it to the easel, setting it down to face *Light Center*. I started to climb out of bed.

"Wait!" she said, rushing to my side. "Let me help you. Let's get your legs over the side first."

We accomplished this with some difficulty; these days my legs don't want to do much moving on their own, and she was reluctant to move them for me.

"I'm afraid I'll hurt you," she said.

Unwilling to waste precious energy explaining, I shot her a sharp look. Finally, she pulled them over the side. I took hold of her arm to keep myself upright, and together we waited while I balanced on the edge of the bed.

"Are you dizzy?" she asked.

"A little," I admitted.

"Want to get back into bed?"

"No."

We waited, and the vertigo passed. Then she stood in front of me, my hands grasping her forearms, and she carefully—and oh so kindly—pulled me upright. We stood like that for a minute, and then she helped me walk—a strange dance, a shuffle—to the chair in front of the easel.

"Can you lower it, please?" She fumbled a minute and then found the right nuts and bolts for adjustment. The painting was now directly in front of me.

"Give me a pencil," I said.

"A what?"

"A pencil," I repeated. "The big one." I waited while she located my flat carpenter's pencil. She looked even more shocked when I grabbed it and began to sketch a rough box around the orb on the canvas.

"Agnes!" I took a breath.

"I want to crop it," I managed. I cannot finish it, but the heart of it is done, the heart of it is right—the center—my kindly light—*is all that is needed*. The center is where I am pulled, where I am going.

I deepened the lines across the top, both sides down the rim of the orb, across the bottom. Then my hand jerked, and an arc of graphite broke the line to the right. A mistake. Never mind. The imperfection necessary for a true icon. I reached up again and added emphatic arrows outside the box pointing at these lines to indicate that, yes, I mean to cut the canvas *here*.

And I was exhausted.

"Back to bed?" She was practically encircling me, the nervous parent of a toddler.

A brief nod. She moved the easel back and stood in front of me and reached her arms around me to pull me up out of the chair. I laughed a little, she did as well, and we caught a glimpse of this strange embrace in the mirror. Triumphant now, I dropped a quick kiss on her shoulder, and together we shuffled toward the bed. She lowered me gently and I sat. She quickly plumped up my pillows and lifted my legs as I leaned back, then pulled the covers over me and told me to get some rest.

When I wake, I will tell her this:

Find out what you can do, and then do it with all your might. Forgive yourself for what you cannot do. Find out who you are and forgive yourself for that. Try to put these two things together. Avoid the "if onlys." Try very hard not to think of what a picture *should* be and instead study it hard to discern what it *is*. Avoid regret, which stops the flow of creative energy, acts as a wall of concrete, prevents the successful development of an idea. "Regret" could be another word for "regress."

I am committed to the present. I am grateful for the present, including its pain and the tremulous unreliability of my legs, my arms, my hands. I am grateful for the knowledge I carry. Which is, "Never finished."

CREDITS

The alternate font on pages 108, 228-229, 261, 283-287, 298-299 indicates a direct quotation from Agnes Pelton's journals and papers as housed in the Smithsonian Archive of American Art, Washington, DC, and the Raymond Jonson Archive at the University of New Mexico, Albuquerque. Cover image by Alice Boughton, used courtesy of Nyna Dolby.

SELECTED REFERENCES

Applegate, Debby. *The Most Famous Man in America: The Biography of Henry Ward Beecher.* New York: Doubleday, 2006.

Barnes, Djuna. *Interviews.* Washington, D.C.: Sun and Moon Press, 1985.

Brown, Milton W. *The Story of the Armory Show.* New York: Abbeville Press, 1988.

Burke, Flannery. *From Greenwich Village to Taos: Primitivism and Place at Mabel Dodge Luhan's.* Lawrence: University Press of Kansas, 2008.

Dow, Arthur Wesley. *Composition: A Series of Exercises in Art Structure for the Use of Students and Teachers.* Berkeley: University of California Press, Thirteenth Edition, with a new introduction by Joseph Masheck, 1997.

Gale, Zona. *When I Was a Little Girl.* New York: The Macmillan Company, 1913.

Hillery, Robert A. *Cathedral City: The Early Years, 1925–1981.* Cathedral City: Outskirts Press, 2015.

Kandinsky, Wassily. *Concerning the Spiritual in Art.* New York: Dover publications, Inc., 1977.

Moss, Karen, ed. *Illumination: The Paintings of Georgia O'Keeffe, Agnes Pelton, Agnes Martin, and Florence Miller Pierce.* Newport Beach: Orange County Museum of Art, 2009.

Phoenix Art Museum, Gilbert Vicario, Chief Curator. *Agnes Pelton: Desert Transcendentalist.* Chicago: Hirmer, 2019.

Reid, B.L. *The Man from New York: John Quinn and His Friends.* New York: Oxford University Press, 1968.

Rudnick, Lois Palken, ed. *Intimate Memories: The Autobiography of Mabel Dodge Luhan.* Albuquerque: University of New Mexico Press, 1999.

Shaplen, Robert. *Free Love and Heavenly Sinners: The Great Henry Ward Beecher Scandal.* New York: Alfred A. Knopf, 1954.

Trenton, Patricia, ed. *Independent Spirits: Women Painters of the American West, 1890-1945.* Berkeley: University of California Press, 1995.

Waller, Altina L. *Reverend Beecher and Mrs. Tilton: Sex and Class in Victorian America.* Amherst: The University of Massachusetts Press, 1982.

Zakian, Michael. *Agnes Pelton: Poet of Nature.* Palm Springs: Palm Springs Desert Museum, 1995.

ACKNOWLEDGMENTS

My thanks to the many who helped bring this book into being:

Brooke Warner, Cait Levin, Shannon Green, Pam Nordberg, Tabitha Lahr, and Julie Metz of She Writes Press, for your professionalism and expert guidance; Ellen Bryant Voight, for your genius in creating the Warren Wilson MFA Program for Writers; my WW teachers Margot Livesey, Kevin McIlvoy, Jim Shepard, Joan Silber, and Karen Brennan; the vast community of writers that is Warren Wilson. One of these is Peg Alford Pursell, who created the Why There Are Words reading series (and Press), and who with her husband Cass Pursell each month hosted the wonderful group dubbed Marin Co. Writers. Repeated thanks to those generous writers: Peg and Cass again, Olga Zilberbourg, Kate Milliken, Scott Landers, Judy French, Genanne Walsh, and Charles Smith.

Michael Zakian, curator extraordinaire, the first to present Agnes Pelton and her mystical paintings in a retrospective exhibition, which introduced me to her modernist calling. Nancy Strow Sheley, who kindly shared her dissertation, "Agnes Pelton: Bringing Light to Life."

Ann Japenga, lover of California desert art, whose brilliant sleuthing located Agnes Pelton's Cathedral City home at the very moment when Peter Palladino and Simeon Den were moving into it.

Peter and Simeon, for their friendship and generosity to me, and for falling in love with Agnes Pelton and sharing their home—and her studio—with other devotees. Marilyn Cooper and the Cathedral City Arts Council, for filling the City Hall with Pelton's paintings and inviting me to read among them. Jane Glover of the DeYoung Museum in San Francisco, who patiently and repeatedly threaded microfilm of the actual Pelton Papers for me to read.

The gift of time at these residencies, which is truly how enough words made it onto paper: I-Park, Ragdale, and, three times, Hypatia-in-the-Woods. And at Hypatia, the support and friendship of Carolyn Maddox, Colleen Keoski, and Allan Roth.

Margot Livesey, for her friendship and support; my cousin Kathy Stricker for invaluable time in Taos; Diane Olivier, brilliant drawing teacher; Kim Rosenblum, who helped me bring a website into being; Agnes Pelton's cousin Nyna Dolby for use of the cover photograph.

Most fervent thanks to Helen Fremont, truly without whom there would be no book, and to Gloria Galindo, my lawfully wedded wife, who never flagged in her support and enthusiasm for this years-long project.

ABOUT THE AUTHOR

MARI COATES lives in San Francisco, where she was an arts writer and theater critic before becoming a senior editor at the University of California Press. She graduated from Connecticut College and holds an MFA from the Warren Wilson Program for Writers. Her stories have been published in the literary journals *HLLQ* and *Eclipse*. She is grateful for residencies at I-Park, Ragdale, and Hypatia-in-the-Woods, which allowed her to develop and complete *The Pelton Papers*.

Author photo © Lynn Shepodd

SELECTED TITLES FROM SHE WRITES PRESS

She Writes Press is an independent publishing company founded to serve women writers everywhere. Visit us at www.shewritespress.com.

The Velveteen Daughter by Laurel Davis Huber. $16.95, 978-1-63152-192-8. The first book to reveal the true story of the woman who wrote *The Velveteen Rabbit* and her daughter, a world-famous child prodigy artist, *The Velveteen Daughter* explores the consequences of early fame and the inability of a mother to save her daughter from herself.

Hysterical: Anna Freud's Story by Rebecca Coffey. $18.95, 978-1-938314-42-1. An irreverent, fictionalized exploration of the seemingly contradictory life of Anna Freud—told from her point of view.

The Black Velvet Coat by Jill G. Hall. $16.95, 978-1-63152-009-9. When the current owner of a black velvet coat—a San Francisco artist in search of inspiration—and the original owner, a 1960s heiress who fled her affluent life fifty years earlier, cross paths, their lives are forever changed . . . for the better.

The Geometry of Love by Jessica Levine. $16.95, 978-1-938314-62-9. Torn between her need for stability and her desire for independence, an aspiring poet grapples with questions of artistic inspiration, erotic love, and infidelity.

Anchor Out by Barbara Sapienza. $16.95, 978-1631521652. Quirky Frances Pia was a feminist Catholic nun, artist, and beloved sister and mother until she fell from grace—but now, done nursing her aching mood swings offshore in a thirty-foot sailboat, she is ready to paint her way toward forgiveness.

Eden by Jeanne Blasberg. $16.95, 978-1-63152-188-1. As her children and grandchildren assemble for Fourth of July weekend at Eden, the Meister family's grand summer cottage on the Rhode Island shore, Becca decides it's time to introduce the daughter she gave up for adoption fifty years ago.